DAN SUGRALINOV

BLOOD OF FATE

*May every new day
in your life
become a Level Up day!*

Dan Sugralinov

WORLD 99 BOOK 1

MAGIC DOME BOOKS

Blood of Fate
World 99< Book One
Copyright © Dan Sugralinov 2019
Cover Art © Vladimir Manyukhin 2019
English Translation Copyright © Alix Merlin Williamson 2019
Published by Magic Dome Books, 2019
All Rights Reserved
ISBN: 978-80-7619-084-9

TABLE OF CONTENTS:

CHAPTER 1

LAST DAY IN THE LIFE OF LUCA DEZISIMU

L UCA'S DAY was turning out average. They'd caught his sister at the market again, trying to steal a couple of soused apples from a merchant. The fruit cost a copper a basket, but to pay the girl's bail, her mother would have to wash other people's clothes non-stop for a week. At least an old friend of hers, another washerwoman, had gotten sick and passed her clients on.

That was why it had been two days since Luca last ate when his mother, herself barely staying upright, fed him some hastily cooked broth of potato skins. Nemania Kovachar, the owner of the only inn in the entire district, sold potato skins and similar leavings on the side.

To help his mother collect the bail money, Luca climbed into his wheelchair with her help and slowly rolled out of the hovel they lived in, heading toward the temple. The porch there was always full of professional beggars, but if he made as if he was just rolling by, he might get a few coins.

His mother didn't even want to discuss allowing him to join the beggars' guild. She had been and always remained the proud wife of a gladiator. They might live in a hovel on the edge of town now, since his father's death, but there had been a time when they had a good house almost in the center of the capital, and apart from babysitters, Luca had had a nanny that taught him his letters and various sciences.

His father had been called Severus. He fell in the Arena three years prior. Only his earnings as a professional gladiator had allowed them to buy a wheelchair for Luca in those better times.

Ignatius the Furious had killed Severus, becoming a six-time Arena champion. It was whispered that not all had been clean in that battle, but Luca did not have the power to bring back his father, no matter what people said. Severus's bones now decayed in a tomb, and Ignatius, rumor had it, headed up the capital's criminal underworld.

Slowly, slower than a swamp turtle, Luca wheeled himself across the small plot in front of his home and onto the street. It took him almost ten minutes to go just fifteen feet. Luca had been paralyzed from birth, or maybe even while still in his mother's womb. Those muscles he had allowed him to move his hands; not good enough to hold anything heavy, but enough to roll the wheelchair. His legs had never moved as far as Luca could remember.

"Look, it's the cripple again!" shouted one of a group of guys whose appearance made Luca turn around at once to run.

Although the words 'at once' and 'run' had nothing to do with it. Usually they quickly caught him and then bullied him for some time, taking advantage of his helplessness. Karim, the son of the innkeeper Nemania, was particularly cruel in his abuse.

Luca span his wheels as fast as he could, retreating homewards. He even managed to get a few feet from the yard... But he wasn't fast enough.

Splash! A cobblestone landed in a fetid puddle nearby, throwing up a fountain of dirty water. It soaked Luca through. The boy clenched his teeth and tried to move faster. The worst of it was his mother's wasted labor. She always tried to give him clean clothes before he went out.

He pushed the wheelchair onward. Karim and his gang stayed at a distance, kept having fun throwing stones. The same huge deep puddle blocked their path, spreading from sidewalk to sidewalk. Days of showers had flooded the roads, and people walked at the edge of the sidewalks, where it was shallow enough to keep the water below the knees.

The stones flew one after the other, throwing up dirty water and mud, breaking spokes in the wheelchair and generously peppering Luca in cuts and bruises. The boys hollered and cackled, shouted abuse at him and got even more excited, congratulating each other on particularly good hits or insults.

One of the stones hit Luca in the shoulder. The flash of pain stopped his retreat: it was as if his right arm was dead. His eyes began to sting, but not from pain; from resentment. How he hated how helpless he was! How he dreamed of standing! Even crawling! He would have crawled up to each of them and bitten them!

Luca aimed his fury at the gods, if they existed, at the injustice of the world, at his parents... His father had spent so much money trying to make his son stand, but no matter how many wise women he saw, or rare shamans specially brought in from the planes, or professional physicians from the healers' guild, none could do anything to fix his ailment.

One fortune teller said that the sins of the parents had fallen on the son. She was probably making it up, but for some reason Luca remembered her in particular. Most likely because it was easiest to blame his parents for it all. They were close by...

They had been close by. His father was gone, his mother faded with each passing year, and his sister Kora would end her journey in a brothel. Luca was sure of that. She was light-footed, curvaceous for her fifteen years, carefree and entirely without moral principles. Her knees were always cut-up, too.

BLOOD OF FATE

Kora took everything that wasn't nailed down, and wasn't afraid to get into a fight with much older boys, and as for where and how she got certain expensive luxuries like makeup, jewelry, new dresses... Luca didn't even want to know. He loved his sister and she loved him, and that was enough.

"Hey, cripple!"

Luca turned around unwillingly. In the last second of his life, he saw a huge cobblestone flying toward him, blotting out the sun.

CHAPTER 2

INTERDIMENSIONAL UNIVERSAL TRAVELER

ESK'ONEGUT, AN INTERDIMENSIONAL universal traveler, ended his life on Earth in the twenty-first century in the body of a Russian student whose name sounded far more exotic than his nickname — Craster. Ilya Pashutin, a student in his final year of a journalism course, had little interest in journalism and studied at the university only at his parents' insistence. More specifically at his father's, a former soldier who had given his son an ultimatum: army or university. Ilya chose the second one, along with... games.

Esk'Onegut found the world of computer games so gripping that he'd spent almost all his waking hours from the age of ten sitting at a computer. For Esk, this was his ninety eighth reincarnation, and, like every traveler, he got stronger from life to life as he earned Tsoui, which meant, in a long-dead language, 'balance of deeds', something that determined one's influence on the harmony of the universe. Tsoui points could be spent to turn the Wheel.

You could spend Tsoui points to turn the Wheel as many times as you liked, as long as you paid. Millions of sectors were marked on it. Many were empty or unfavorable, but there were also very powerful ones that gave the current body supernatural abilities: incredible strength, ludicrous speed, deadly combat skills, magical or creative abilities...

The talents spread across the Wheel were split into four levels: from common to peerless, the best in all the worlds. Esk vaguely remembered winning the skill of becoming invisible on the Wheel in a previous life. That had been a good one! That world probably still had legends about the thief whose body he'd inhabited for almost six years.

On Earth, the concept that Esk had found closest to Tsoui was karma. Only he was certain that karma was a blasphemous fiction, because it took into account actions measured by the scales of individuals themselves and those around them. In Tsoui, the traveler's deeds were weighed by their influence on universal harmony. After all, every action, every word, caused ripples in the past and the future of the entire universe.

Esk had ended up in Ilya's body when the latter reached the age of four. While his mother wasn't watching him, the young boy fell under a rapidly moving metal seesaw in the small park outside his house. His innocent spirit was moved to the universal archive to await its next revival, if it had one. And Esk'Onegut set up shop in little Ilya's body. It just so happened that at that very moment, he'd died in the last one.

In his life before Earth, he had reigned as emperor on a peripheral planet in the Galaxy, enjoying total power and his very own cult of personality. The finest women, the best intoxicants and narcotics, delicious meals, the fulfilment of all his whims, from the simple pleasures to the most perverted...

In truth, he had become the worst emperor in the history of that planet, whose name he could not recall due to the effect of the Waning. It was no wonder he'd been poisoned.

The Waning was the curse of every traveler. The effect wiped memories from previous lives, but the knowledge of their existence remained, along with the memories of the last minutes before death. And the shorter the time between lives, the more Esk remembered. Before his imperial reign, he had been a great musician and singer who wrote his own songs. He knew that, but, lightning strike him down, he could not remember a single line of what he had written.

His memory of his years as an emperor, his ninety eighth life, remained with Esk in Ilya's body. He was so sick of power and authority that on twenty-first century Earth, he wanted nothing to do with it. With the taste of all those accessible and inaccessible joys of life still fresh in his memory, Esk discovered the world of computer games on Earth. Realizing that virtual worlds were basically the same as what he did, only on a smaller scale and with the ability to switch between worlds and virtual bodies at any moment, Esk fell headlong into them.

By the end of his earthly journey in the body of twenty-year-old Ilya Pashutin, Esk had earned minus Tsoui thanks to his idleness and indifference to the world around him. Not only had he spent his entire life on Earth without using the Wheel, Esk's luck also seemed to have turned negative.

And when Fortune turns her back on you, it's pointless to make stupid jokes. Esk'Onegut, or Ilya Pashutin to everyone else, died before his time, hit by a car while rushing to a lecture after a sleepless night at his computer.

God, anything but that! Esk thought, with an entirely earthly god in mind; he still considered himself an earthly student. *There's a guild raid tomorrow! I'm going to miss it... Vanka will be pissed.*

In the next moment, he moved to another world and another body. Here it was — his ninety ninth rebirth. His ninety ninth world.

Twenty five again! He sighed inwardly. He'd have to learn a new body, study a new world... He was sick of it.

Esk opened his eyes and tried to move his

limbs. His legs weren't listening. That sometimes happened when the new body functioned differently from the previous one, but the genome was clearly identical — human. It seemed there was something wrong with the body.

Deciding to deal with it later, Esk immersed himself in the input data.

Esk'Onegut, life ninety nine.
Influence level: 9.
Tsoui points: -971 (negative value).
Orion Arm, Milky Way, Solar System, Planet Earth.
Universe variation: #ES-252210-0273-4707.

So he was still on Earth, but in a parallel universe. That was good, he wouldn't have to relearn too much. Not like when he'd revived in the body of an eight-armed reptile. But the fact that his Tsoui points were in the red — that was very, very bad. Why were they so far in the negative? He hadn't done anything bad, he'd just played computer games!

Reincarnation unavailable. Tsoui point balance must be above zero.
Right to reincarnation with negative balance: exhausted.
One-time Wheel spin privilege: available.

Esk swore internally, mentioning all the gods

he'd known from previous lives. As an emperor, he had gone into minus points for the first time in all his incarnations, but he was sure he would earn the Tsoui back in Ilya's body. He'd decided to simply not do anything that could negatively affect his balance. As it turned out, doing nothing carried a harsher Tsoui penalty than all the deadly sins performed in the emperor's body...

After landing in the body of the future Russian student Ilya, Esk had used his one-time spin of the Wheel, but an empty sector came up. Good that it wasn't negative, at least. He could have gotten some curse like an incurable illness or limited mental abilities. He didn't have enough Tsoui points for more, he'd wasted too much as emperor. Wasted and lost.

Having decided that since he had no right to reincarnate again, then he had to start living as soon as possible, he returned to the real world and realized that he was lying in a deep, stinking puddle. The smell was nightmarish. Esk grimaced and tried to stand, but couldn't.

The water covered his face, went into his eyes, nose, mouth and one ear. It was extremely unpleasant.

Making an effort, Esk's mighty spirit absorbed the personality of this new body, including all its skills and memories, and corrected the body's damage and defects on the cellular level.

Then, stumbling, he lurched to his feet and looked at the new world around him.

Some grimy youths stood at the edge of the puddle, their mouths wide open in amazement. One of them — Esk-Luca realized that it was Karim — shouted, wide-eyed.

"What the hell, cripple, you can walk now?!"

The memory of Luca Dezisimu, crippled seventeen-year-old son of the dead gladiator Severus, finally settled and structured itself in Esk'Onegut's mind. The cripple's personality boiled with such fury that Esk recoiled, as it were, retreating before the primal anger of the helpless pariah. He felt uncomfortable.

Damn! He was tired of living. Life wasn't just pleasure, but also sadness, grief, pain, hunger, the loss of loved ones, the need to strive and achieve... Centuries, no, millennia of ceaseless living had wearied the universal traveler.

The traveler mentally whispered: *Damn it, live then. I'll watch.* And then he handed to the former cripple the reins over the body, the Tsoui system and the mind.

Luca, incredulously clapping himself on the sides, on his arms and legs, realized that he was absolutely healthy.

He raised his head and cast a baleful gaze on Karim.

CHAPTER 8

MAGICAL HEALING

"**K**ARIM HEALED the cripple!" Fat Pete shouted suddenly. "With a magic stone!" The joke didn't land. After the last hit, Luca fell from the wheelchair and lay for quite some time in the puddle. They'd decided that he might have died and were about to run away before a guard appeared. Unlikely as that was. But the cripple rose!

Unable to believe their eyes, the boys continued to gawk at Luca. He himself wasted no time. Whether his recovery was real or not, he had no idea when it might end. The boy wiped his face with his sleeve, climbed out of the puddle, chose a couple of likely stones nearby and, waving his arm inexpertly, threw one.

The stone flew three feet and splashed straight into the puddle. The hooligans were shocked, then broke into laughter.

Without delay, Luca threw the second, and it fell into the mud nearby. Angry with himself, Luca kept picking up and throwing stones at the boys, who continued to mock him even now that he had control over his body, but he couldn't throw a stone even to the middle of the puddle. The ruffians stood on the opposite side, dying of laughter.

Karim even started choking, grabbing at his stomach, and the other boys laughed with him. Fat Pete, Karim's right-hand man, laughed louder than anyone. He supported his leader with subservience in all his endeavors; the innkeeper's son generously shared any uneaten leftovers from customers' plates with him and the other boys, and in this district of the capital, food was the most valuable resource.

Luca had dreamed so many times of being able to pick up and return a stone thrown at him! And here he finally was... But he'd spent his whole life bedridden, he'd never learned to throw stones. If only his father were here... Or at least Kora, she could have taught him easily! But his sister was somewhere in a city watch jail cell while his mother saved up for her bail.

Luca looked around, but there were no more stones nearby.

"Hey, cripple!" Catch!" Fat Pete shouted, throwing another stone at him.

Out of habit, Luca watched motionlessly as the stone flew. But then he suddenly heard thoughts in his head. As if his own, but also... not. *Move! Sorry, but I can't just sit here and watch!* Then his body began to move by itself, turned and leaned, dodging. The stone flew past him, nearly hitting him.

"Wow! Come on guys, let's make him dance!"

The target was moving now, and that provoked the bullies. They got to work grabbing whatever was to hand and throwing it at Luca. But the boy even found a certain pleasure in not letting them hit him. Moving only as much as he needed to, he easily dodged all that came his way.

I'm bored, Luca-Esk thought. *It's my turn now.* With confident, accurate throws, he put Natus out of action, the son of a fish merchant, then Jamal, a grubby halfwit without a single glimmer of intellect. Then it was Fat Pete's turn — the stone hit him right in his jelly-like belly, knocking all the air out of his lungs. Pete doubled over and fell face-first into the puddle.

Luca tossed another stone in his hand, considering which part of Karim's body to throw it at. Karim hesitated, not knowing whether to run or to help his friends. In the end, he hid behind Fat Pete, pulling him out of the water like a hippo out of a swamp.

Luca aimed. Karim's shoulder stuck out from behind Fat Pete's back, so Luca aimed at it. The stone was small, around the size of a quail egg, but that just made the throw even more accurate. The cocky and bold-faced seventeen-year-old innkeeper's son wailed like a girl. His crew groaned at the sight, exchanged glances and... ran off!

"Wait for me!" Karim wailed before staggering after the others.

He turned as he fled and shouted in faltering tones:

"You're dead, cripple! You're dead!"

Luca watched as he went. He felt an unfamiliar feeling in his chest. It was satisfaction. He liked how well his body responded, how quickly the blood flowed through his veins, liked the crackle of his pent-up anger finally bursting forth. Before, he could only cry himself to sleep in silence so as not to wake his mother and sister, or grind his teeth and roll his eyes. He never allowed himself to express it, not wanting to appear weaker than he was, so his anger built and built, long since reaching the point of no return.

Now he'd let his feelings loose, and a quiet, peaceful satisfaction replaced his all-encompassing anger. The incident amused Esk, but he also felt the same as Luca.

They shared the same body, after all.

A body which now began to hurt terribly. Its atrophied muscles had apparently gone into shock from such excessive use. Luca's legs bent, but he managed not to fall. Staggering, the boy reached his wheelchair, stood it upright and fought through the pain to pull it out of the puddle. No sooner had he done this than he fell into the seat, got into a comfortable position and rolled toward the house.

He walked into the hovel on his own two feet. His mother didn't notice him coming in and kept scrubbing some laundry on her washboard. Sweat fell off her in streams, but she kept furiously scrubbing the clothes as if her children's lives depended on it. And they did.

Horvac take me, where am I? Esk thought, and the same thought appeared in Luca's mind. The boy looked at the place where he'd lived for the last few years with fresh eyes. And from a new height, to put it plainly — his height.

One room for everyone. One half of the poorly lit room housed all the beds, a small dining table, a chest full of old junk. The other half was the laundry area, strewn with clothes and sheets, with an ironing board and an old black iron sheltering by the wall. His mother scrubbed in the corner opposite. The washing water in the basin and buckets was already black from dirt, and soon his mother would have to venture across the neighborhood to the local well. There were no lakes, rivers or other natural bodies of water in the capital, and for the residents of the slums, the only source of clean water was the community well.

She squeezed the water out of the sheet she was scrubbing, put away the basin and stood up. Luca began to hobble toward her.

"Mom..."

Prisca raised her head, saw her son standing before her and fainted, started to fall, but Luca rushed toward her and held her up.

No strength at all, Esk noticed as he failed to hold his mother up and fell to the wet floor.

Gently holding the woman, he sat down and stroked her head. Prisca had been very beautiful when she married his father, but recent years had been far from kind to her. Her face had become lean, bags swelled under her eyes, her hair had thinned, her breasts had hung low since Kora's birth. But she was still attractive, even if it was hard to notice right away.

"Mom, mom..." Luca whispered quietly. "Mom, wake up!"

He touched his lips to her forehead. Prisca opened her eyes. Luca stood himself up and helped his mother stand.

"It's not a dream! It's not a dream!" His mother's eyes filled with tears. "Luca! My son!"

"Yes, mom..."

"But how?!" the woman cried.

Luca told her everything, leaving out only the fact that he'd thrown stones back. In his version of the events, the hooligans ran off as soon as he stood up.

"It's a miracle! A miracle!" Prisca kept repeating, kissing and hugging her son.

Tears fell from her eyes, she was wet from the washing and sweat, and Luca had only just climbed out of a puddle. They stood in embrace for a long time. Luca held his mother to his chest and looked down on her from above for the first time. Now he saw how many grey hairs she had.

"Mom, I'm going to go get water. Rest in the meantime."

"Are you sure you can?" Prisca looked her son up and down sceptically.

"I'll try. I'll carry just one bucket at a time, don't worry. Rest, mom."

Luca led her to the bed and sat her down, then grabbed a full bucket. Gritting his teeth and taking tiny steps, he carried it out of the house to pour the dirty water into the gutter and bring back clean water.

Watching this, Esk thought the boy would break in half from the strain.

Time to spin the Wheel.

CHAPTER 4

ONE-TIME WHEEL SPIN

LUCA STOPPED by the fence and set the bucket on the ground. His fingers burned, his shoulder felt leaden. Swapping hands would help, but a bell rang insistently in his head, demanding attention.

The hidden Esk smirked inwardly. *Come on, dude, get on with it!*

Luca wiped his eyes, grimaced and shrank back from a block of text that suddenly appeared in the very air in front of him. The boy stretched an arm toward the letters, but felt nothing. They hung before his eyes and moved as his eyes moved. The text stayed at the center of Luca's vision!

What a dope! Esk sighed, but let Luca stay at the helm. The balance of two minds sharing a single body was incredibly fragile. The boy didn't have enough spirit to recognize the impossible and preserve his mind if Esk intervened directly.

Pressed into the back of his consciousness, his personality would rot quicker than Esk could say "Horvac take you!" Horvac'Onegut was an old friend of his, and had managed to become a divinity in a world where Esk had trudged along as a priest of the local Veridic until he changed his faith. In that war, sacred for half the planet's population, Horvac had been cast down, but he and Esk encountered each other again in other worlds and remained friends. And tales of Horvac remained.

While Esk reminisced, Luca had gotten a grip on himself and read the text several times, unwillingly whispering it aloud.

"Luca Dezisimu, of the essence Esk'Onegut... Tsoui points: minus nine hundred and seventy one... Activated privilege for one-time Wheel spin. Use? Yes... No..."

Luca's mother poked her head out of their little window.

"What happened, son? Are you feeling alright?"

"Everything's fine, mom. I stopped for a breather, my arms hurt."

"Let me take it..." Prisca began, but the son interrupted her.

"No, mom. I can do it!"

Spoken with surety and confidence. The mother shook her head, but a flash of a smile told the true story; she was not only happy, she was proud! Her head disappeared from the window, and Luca returned to the strange text.

Thinking for a couple of seconds, he jabbed his finger at "Yes."

The world around him froze and fell silent. The text disappeared, and a gigantic wheel took up his entire view. It looked entirely real, but was as much a mirage as the text before it. The surface of the wheel spread to either side of Luca, blotting out his surroundings. In height it stretched far into the sky, so that Luca could only see one segment of it, the one facing him. That segment was green, and on it was writ in huge letters: *Start!*

Esk planted some knowledge in the boy's mind, and Luca realized that the divisions of the wheels were in different colors.

There was only one green sector, the starting sector. If it appeared again after the spin, he'd be able to make three more spins for free.

The red sectors gave the player illnesses, injuries, reduced stats or negative talents. For example, the talent of smelling like a cesspit. There weren't many such talents, but each red segment was several times larger than the others.

The empty white spaces gave nothing to the player, just wasted the spin. They amounted to over three fourths of the total number.

The blue ones were very rare. They awarded useful talents, and the deeper the color — from pale blue to ultramarine — the higher the gift level. The ultramarine sector gave the player a highly demanded talent in their local community and turned them into an unparalleled master of the field, the best in the entire history of the world.

But the most desirable, and Luca felt it intensely, sensing the payoff, was the gold sector. The golden section of superpowers, gleaming as it reflected the sun's golden rays. Each of those powers could violate the laws of physics and magic and act in opposition to all. Full invulnerability with no magic shields or armor, teleportation to any point on the planet, perfect invisibility, incredible strength and power that could bring down mountains with a single touch...

The chance of getting a sector like that was close to zero no matter how many times you span the Wheel. Every traveler lucky enough to get that coveted sector reached incredible heights in the world where they got it.

There was also a purple sector, the only one on the entire Wheel. At least, so said the rumors among the travelers. Esk had never seen it, though he'd tried his luck many times.

Glimmer by glimmer, idea by idea, step by step; that was how Esk slowly revealed the truth of the world to the boy, let him come to realize what had happened to come, so that sooner or later, they could achieve a full meld and live as a single individual.

Luca took a deep breath and touched the Start button.

Slowly, almost screeching into motion, the

Wheel started to build up speed. The starting sector rolled past Luca, after which came a run of white sectors, then the flash of a gold sector, another group of whites, then red, white, white, more red, white, white, white, blueish...

The Wheel span faster and faster, building up to such a speed that the colors of the sectors merged into a single rainbow blur before Luca. He saw nothing, and both Luca and Esk lost control over their body. As the Wheel span, time stopped across the entire Universe, and only the consciousness of the player spinning it remained active, so that they might see the outcome with their own eyes.

Luca lost track of time when the mottled blur finally became clearer, then even clearer, finally reforming into the colors of sectors as they raced past.

A row of white... blue... white...

The Wheel slowed its pace...

CHAPTER 5

THE BIRTH OF A NEW TRAVELER

LUCA WATCHED with disappointment as the Wheel slowed its pace. The speed slowed down so much that a broad red sector took up his entire field of view for several seconds.

Both the boy and Esk'Onegut, the traveler in his head, prayed to the Wheel to move beyond the cursed red zone. Luca no longer even thought of superpowers or talents. He wanted just one thing: to remain healthy. With any other segment, he had a chance of over ninety seven percent to remain as he was. But the red segment could bring him something worse than paralysis.

The traveler himself grinned with irony; this was how Tsoui worked. If the carrier's body was cursed, then the recent healing would turn into

25

something similar — red. The sector was too wide. Any other would have already passed by.

The edge of the sector hove into view somewhere at the edge of vision. *Come on, come on,* Luca begged. *Please! Curse you in the name of all the gods!* Esk growled inwardly, furious at the possibility of spending his final reincarnation in the body of a twice cursed boy. How could it be otherwise, if he was born a cripple and would become one again now?

The border between the sectors almost stopped in front of Luca's face. The next sector after the red one was purple, and this was the first time the traveler had seen that color in all his ninety nine lives.

"Impossible! Seriously? Are you serious, gods?" The irony of the situation drove Esk, and Luca with him, to hysterics. The results hadn't yet been declared, which meant the Wheel was still turning.

Esk began to personally address every god with whom he'd aligned himself in his previous lives.

"Cruel Horvac, Timeless Akatosh, Faceless Veridic, Almighty God, K'Tun the Defiler..."

He had time to address them all and start from the beginning again before the Wheel stopped. It seemed to Luca as if the line between the sectors was precisely between his eyes, but Esk'Onegut exulted. The difference must have been in microns, but the Wheel had stopped in the purple sector!

BLOOD OF FATE

One-time Wheel spin token used.
Spin outcome: purple sector.
Rewards: Reminiscent title.

Esk'Onegut is freed from the effect of the Waning, and shall keep all the accumulated experience of his mortal years, beginning with the current reincarnation;

Esk'Onegut shall keep all positive talents, superpowers and effects, beginning with the current reincarnation;

if the purple sector falls again, Esk'Onegut gains the right to choose one lost superpower from a previous reincarnation.

The noise of the street descended on Luca. He was back in control of his body, and the world came alive.

The boy frowned, reading the strange text again and again.

The traveler burst into laughter through his mouth. The Wheel had settled on the purple sector — the mythical purple sector! — at the very time when none of its rewards could have any effect on him. Even the weakest talent would have been better, even the skill of playing any musical instrument! At least he could have made a living in the inns that way.

Esk'Onegut found himself in the position of a billionaire whose entire fortune was being kept safe and sound away from him right up until the day the final nail was hammered into his coffin. What was

27

the point of removing his Waning if this was his last life? Among other things, it was impossible to earn back his almost a thousand minus Tsoui points in the body of a beggar boy. In his best reincarnations, Esk had managed to earn several hundred, but never more than five hundred.

That meant there was no point in even thinking about any new talents that might stay with him in future lives if he got the purple sector again. Because he would have no future lives, and he had no Tsoui points with which to spin the Wheel again. All he needed was ten measly points — the cost of a single spin — and he didn't have them!

While Esk was busy going insane, Luca enjoyed scratching the back of his head — not out of habit, but because his dirty hair was greasy — then picked up the bucket, tightened his grip on it and carried it to a nearby drain. Although really, the entire road had turned into a drain. It flowed not only with the recent floods and spring rains, but also the day-to-day refuse of the people of their entire destitute district.

The boy added the dirty water to the flow, then took his bearings and wandered toward the local well.

In the meantime, Esk thought over his options, calculated probabilities, decided what to do. Nothing he came up with gave him even the smallest chance. The weight of his sins in the life before his last pulled him down into a chasm. In that life he had burned everything he had and gone into minus points, and in the one following, his idleness only sent his balance deeper into the red.

He was doomed to eke out an existence in an unfriendly and underdeveloped world, and with no talents or abilities to speak of. At the end of that woeful journey of life, the traveler's existence would end once and for all. His would. But what about Luca?

Understanding began to dawn in his consciousness, burning stronger and stronger, giving Esk — no, not hope, but a sense of the right path. The already unfortunate boy wasn't guilty of his — Esk'Onegut's! — past sins. And that meant...

He had to decide now, before it got too scary! And then a particle of his soul would go on to live many, he hoped, new lives. As long as the boy lived up to his expectations and didn't let him down.

Esk sighed deeply and reflexively closed his eyes. Through the beating of his heart, he activated the Exodus.

Esk'Onegut, life ninety nine.
Reminiscent (immune to effect of the Waning).
Influence level: 9.
Tsoui points: -971 (negative value).

Excarnation selected with subsequent merging with individual Luca Dezisimu (life one), resident of zone Orion Arm, Milky Way, Solar System, Planet Earth. Universe variation: #ES-252210-0273-4707.

Luca Dezisimu will receive Esk'Onegut's positive legacy.

The eyes that Esk had closed led to Luca tripping, losing his balance and falling. He tried to pick himself up, but fell again into the mud. A sharp pain pierced his head, then immediately disappeared, only to reappear in another part of his skull. The flashes of pain bounced around his head for several minutes, and just when Luca finally thought he'd rather die than continue the hellish punishment, it all stopped.

The boy's hands dropped from his head. He cringed in anticipation of more pain, but none came. He sat down haltingly and saw a block of text before him. The text repeated in his head in his own clear thoughts, the whisper of his own voice.

Luca Dezisimu, from this day forth, you are a traveler.

Live a life worthy of Tsoui, observe the balance and harmony of life, and after death you will revive in another world of the infinite universe.

Luca'Onegut, life one.

Reminiscent (immune to effect of the Waning). Successor to Esk'Onegut.

Influence level: 0.

Tsoui points: 0.

Orion Arm, Milky Way, Solar System, Planet Earth.

Universe variation: #ES-252210-0273-4707.

Reincarnation: available.

One-time Wheel spin privilege: available.

BLOOD OF FATE

The inheritance from Esk, including the rewards of the purple sector, became Luca's personal experience and knowledge, so this time he didn't need to reread the text to understand it.

Luca smiled. Now he would bring his mother water, then get Kora out of jail, and then...

Then he would spin the Wheel again.

CHAPTER 6

NEMANIA KOVACHAR'S OFFER

WHISTLING SOMETHING playful and melodic that floated up from Esk's memory, Luca returned home with a full bucket of clean water. Nobody had been at the well. Apparently, many still had stocks of rainwater collected during the recent downpours.

The boy swapped the full bucket of water in his hands more than once as he walked home, but didn't stop to rest. He took pleasure even in the painful sensations in the muscles of his tired arms, back, and everywhere else; the pain meant that he could feel. He was alive!

With his inherited knowledge as a traveler, Luca realized that Karim had killed him, had split his skull with a large rock with sharp edges. Esk'Onegut's inhabitation of his body had allowed him to survive, and the traveler's boredom, laziness and self-pity had allowed him to keep his individuality. The initial restoration as the traveler had settled into his body had instantly healed all his cuts and bruises. It was a good thing that Luca had thought to wash the blood off his body with water from the barrel in the yard before he went in to see his mother. That water was no good for laundry, but it was fine for day-to-day needs.

He stopped by the door. He heard a hushed conversation from within. Since his healing, Luca's hearing had become perfect. He could pick out every word.

"Admit it, Prisca, you don't have a chance of paying the wergild," said an oily male voice in even tones. "Do you want your son sent to the mines?"

"You speak nonsense, Nemania," his mother spoke in tired and quiet tones. "Everyone knows Luca has been a cripple since birth. How could he have maimed your son?"

"You mean to say that Karim is lying to me, woman? My son is no liar! That monster of yours broke his collar bone! You'll pay for the treatment and compensate for his suffering."

"How much?"

Luca heard the resignation in his mother's voice. She still hadn't collected the seventy five silver she needed for Kora...

"Seven gold. Without delay. Pay today, right now..!" Nemania fell silent, chuckled and added: "Or come see me after midnight. Pay it off that way!"

Luca's mother fell silent, and Karim's father took on a comforting tone, still just as oily.

"Prisca, listen to me... If you are diligent and obedient, perhaps I will reduce your debt. What do you say?"

Luca didn't hear whether his mother said anything in response, but he knew for certain why the innkeeper had invited her over. He was old enough. He himself had only dreamed of such things in restless and sweaty dreams. But his mother and Nemania in the same bed? It was a shame his father wasn't here to...

But *he* was here! Angry with himself, he rushed into the house just as Prisca was about to agree to the innkeeper's terms. Nemania's hand was already snaking its way under her skirt.

Luca's eyes widened in fury. Breathing heavily and clenching his fists, he shouted.

"Get away from my mom, creature! Get your filthy hands off her!"

"Feisty boy." The innkeeper chuckled, but removed his hands. "But what does she herself have to say? What do you say, Prisca?"

"She says: get out of our house! Mom won't come to you, don't even think about it! Your son and his friends threw stones at me and nearly killed me! They split my skull!"

"Wow," Nemania breathed in shock. "It's true, he walks. I thought that brat of mine was lying, making it all up. But here it is... Well, where are your bruises? Got anything to back up your words?"

Luca reached for his temple to move his hair aside and show his wound, but then froze, remembering that it had disappeared.

"They... healed," he said falteringly. "I'm telling the truth..."

"I thought as much." Nemania's gaze switched to Prisca. "What have you decided?"

Prisca cast a sidelong glance at her son, and her tired indifference to the whims of fate, the submissiveness with which she had been ready to accept her impending degradation, her shame at that willingness — it all disappeared, replaced with pride.

For the first time in her long years, she saw her son's resemblance to her husband, Severus Dezisimu, saw the same bravery and nobility that he had poured into his sword to achieve standing in society and to capture her heart.

"My son has answered for me. No!"

"Well, no means no," Nemania agreed readily.

Roughly elbowing his way past the boy, he walked to the door, but then stopped, thought for a moment and turned back.

"But still... this..." The innkeeper frowned, looked Luca up and down. "How? You just up and started walking? No temples, no healers, just you? All it took to heal a cripple was a good knock on the head? Really? I should patent that idea!" He laughed. "Alright, boy. Live your life. For now. Prisca, if you don't bring me the money by the evening, I'll send your bastard to the mines. You know that the word of a Kovachar is stronger than oak!"

He slammed the door hard as he left.

At that moment, a line appeared before Luca:

Tsoui points: +1. Current balance: 1.

Connecting this information with what had happened up to now, Luca realized that the two events were interlinked. Nodding to himself, he approached his mother and put down the bucket of clean water he'd been holding all this time. He wiped the tears from her cheeks with the back of his hand and hugged her. He held her close, realizing that they were the same height His mother sobbed as she spoke.

"What's going to happen, son? What now?"

"Nobody will believe him, mom. Look at my arms; they're thinner than canes. How could I break his collar bone? Sir Judge is a sensible man, he won't believe their tales."

"Yes, of course, he's fair..." she agreed with some doubt in her voice.

Prisca calmed down completely once Luca reminded her about her unfinished laundry and Kora, who was still languishing in jail. She had no fear of ending up in the mines, but if they didn't pay her bail in time, the girl risked being sent to an orphanage. The deadline was the next day. Stumbling, Prisca rushed to the basin.

"Mom, let me help you. I'll hang the laundry."

"I can do it, son. We need to boil the pot, bring clean water..."

The day passed in these labors. Luca carried water back and forth, brought wood from the yard, hung and took down laundry, gave it to his mother to iron, helped to fold it. His muscles burned as if bathed in acid, but the boy bore the pain, remembering that his mother had done all this on her own.

At dusk, they put the newly clean laundry into baskets, each of which belonged to a separate house for which his mother worked.

Prisca never tired of praising all the gods for her son, and when Luca got ready to go with her to deliver the laundry, she took it as a given. There was a man of the house again!

And so she felt her anguish even more harshly when the watchmen forced their way into the hovel, led by a small and angry constable distracted from his dinner.

"Luca Dezisimu! You are accused of attempting to murder Karim Kovachar! Take him, boys!"

CHAPTER 7

POLLUTED GENE POOL

THE GUARD GAVE HIM a last kick in the behind. Luca fell over the threshold of the cell and slid on his belly along the slimy floor. The guard closed the door, snapped the lock shut and hurried back to finish off his cold dinner.

"What're you in for, sonny?" a low and hoarse voice said from the darkness.

Luca strained his eyes, trying to make out his surroundings, but he saw nothing. The moonlight shining through the tiny barred window lit up only a small section of the floor.

The boy considered it best not to ignore the man that called him sonny, and answered.

"I threw a stone at an innkeeper's son and broke his collar bone. Or so they say."

"What really happened?"

"I was throwing stones in self-defense. He ran off. I don't know if I really broke anything. But I hope I did. He's a scumbag."

His unseen interlocutor laughed. His laugh was deep and guttural. It seemed as if the bars of the cell shook from the sound alone. The prisoner calmed down and moved into the light. He lifted Luca's chin with a finger and looked him in the face. The whites of his eyes shined in the darkness. He spoke softly.

"What's your name, little one?"

"Luca Dezisimu. Yours?"

"Terant was what they called me in my homeland. Here I have no name, but that's another story. How old are you, ten?"

"I'm seventeen."

"What? Two-horns take me... Seventeen! Incredible. Gods, how polluted is the gene pool in the Empire?"

"Mom says it's bad to curse," Luca answered simply, to continue a conversation barely above water. "Mentioning the gods in vain is bad. Mentioning Two-horns..."

"Is bad! I know, boy. But I swear on the perfect genes of the shining Taira, I've never seen such an emaciated teenager in all my life! You look weaker than my daughter, and she's just seven!"

"You have a daughter?"

"Have... Had... It doesn't matter! How do your legs hold you up, Luca Dezisimu? I can see all your bones!"

"My father said that you have to always stand up, even if your legs are cut off. And I have legs," the boy answered and collapsed to the floor.

He could withstand hunger for as long as he wanted, but everyone needed to refuel at least sometimes.

When Luca came to, it turned out he was lying on some kind of cot, and there was something soft under his head. His cell mate held the back of his head with his large and meaty hand.

"Hungry?"

Luca blinked in response, without the strength to even open his mouth.

"Then hold on."

The whites of Terant's eyes darkened.

He placed the palm of his free hand on Luca's forehead. Then he squeezed the boy's head as if trying to crack it like a nut.

The boy tried to cry out, but not a single sound emerged from his throat. Terant also was silent. Luca tried to escape, but his body wouldn't listen.

A strong heat came off Terant's palms in waves. It pulsed, spread into his head and from there throughout his entire body.

External influence detected!
Forced energy supplementation recorded. Transformed for further use: 64%... 66%... 68%...

At eighty percent, Terant fell back and breathed heavily, hoarsely.

A few heartbeats later, Luca also started

gasping greedily for air. He thrilled in every breath of the stuffy, moist gloom of the dungeon.

Opening his eyes, the boy wondered at how clearly and brightly he now saw things. He actually felt overwhelmed with strength, lots of strength. He wanted to run, jump, do something. And the sensation of hunger was gone. Completely gone.

Terant lay a few feet away. His skin looked completely black as if absorbing light, but the gleams from the droplets of sweat covering it made the man visible. A similar image appeared in Luca's head along with the word 'ke-har'... His father had fought people like Terant in the Arena. Apparently this was a ke-har.

"Terant?"

"Yes, boy. Feeling better?"

"I've never felt so good in my life! How did you do that?"

"Oh... Let me catch my breath..." Terant sat up and wiped his brow. It seemed to Luca as if the man was thinner. "What do you know about the world, sonny?"

"Um... I didn't go to school, but I know that we live in the capital of the Empire. Emperor Ma Ju Ro the Fourth rules the land."

"Hmm... Alright, let's say that. Do you know who rules the world? Who the racants, khhars and olaks are?

"I don't know those words..." Luca thought a moment. "Wait, khhar, that's it! Are you a khhar? My father fought a khhar, and he was like you!"

"And do you know what lies beyond the Empire's borders?"

"Nothing. Just water, and beyond that is the edge of the world and the great nothing, where the streams of the world ocean cascade down. That's what nana taught me."

"Son, the world is far larger than that. Do you know what percentages are?"

"Parts of a whole. One percent means one part of a whole split into a hundred parts."

"Within your Empire lives less than one percent of all the people of the world."

"Horseshit!" Luca burst out. "Everyone knows that the Great Empire spans the entire world!"

"The Great Empire, son, is a reservation," Terant pronounced a word Luca didn't know, but still understood. "Listen."

The kkhar coughed, cleared his throat and raising his forefinger, began to speak.

"The first family was the Ra'Ta'Cant family. I'll explain genetics to you later, but for now, remember: the First Family had perfect genes. Flawless. The benchmark for the human race. One-hundred percent perfect!"

"They're ideal?"

"Oh yes, son! They're ideal. Those that do not quite reach perfection, but strive toward it at all costs — they are the racants. There are very few of them, but they own everything. The racant families rule the entire world, but each has their own part. Each family is responsible to the First Family for its territory. They also divide segments of the economy between them..."

"The economy?" This time Luca understood the word, but had time to ask before the understanding came.

"Remember all the words you don't understand, I'll explain them later. There's more to hear. Most people are olaks. Those are ordinary citizens, specialists in their fields: scientists, lawyers, craftspeople, merchants, servants... They are all united by the imperfection of their genes. They are at least ten percent away from the benchmark."

"And who are you? A khhar?"

"Yes. Our species was created artificially. The army, combat and security organizations, guards and warriors, athletes and bodyguards — that's us."

"Our guards don't look like you at all."

"Your guards aren't khhars. They, you and all the people of the Empire are syahrs."

"Syahrs?"

"Forgive me, boy. That which I am about to say... it is not my words. I am merely quoting what has been repeated thousands of times." Terant coughed again and spoke harshly, enunciating every word. "In all the world, you are the genetic pollutants. Outcasts. Pariahs. The recants maintain that all human life is sacred, but they do not allow the syahrs rights to any of the planet's natural resources or the achievements if modern civilization. To avoid polluting humanity's gene pool, the only place available to the syahrs is the so-called Empire."

"Why doesn't the Empire just attack these racants of yours? Its strength and power..."

"Son, all your strength and power are sticks and stones made out of shit. You have nothing. And you live on an island two thousand miles from the nearest civilization, across a treacherous ocean. You are condemned."

Luca fell silent for a long time, breaking down the old foundation of his world view and erecting a new one. He believed Terant unconditionally, intuitively, and the intuition he had inherited from Esk was sublime. He had only one question left to ask.

"So how did you get here, Terant?"

"Oh, did I not say? Criminals have no place in the glorious and blessed land of the racants."

CHAPTER 8

PRIZES OF THE WHEEL

THE MEASURED BREATH of sleep had been emanating from Terant's cot for a while, but Luca couldn't sleep. Esk'Onegut's legacy — the traveler's knowledge and experience — hid in the dark alleyways of his consciousness and came to the fore only when he needed them, and only in tiny doses. Like with those new words the boy had heard from the khhar.

That was why what Terant had told him had stunned Luca, and he'd been trying for quite some time to imagine a world without hungry and sick people. Self-moving carts, the gleaming skin of the racants of whom the khhar had described in vivid detail. All this seemed far less incredible than the absence of hunger and disease.

"You syahrs live in a cesspool of humanity," Terant had said. "And all the good things that the powerful and noble people have — it's all just contraband garbage smuggled in from our trash heaps."

What a long day! Luca thought. *And so much happened! This morning I was a paralyzed cripple dreaming of bread crusts. Then I died, resurrected and started walking! And now I'm in a cage with an alien khhar and I've learned more about the world than I ever knew! And in the morning I'm going to be tried for breaking Karim's collar bone! Amazing!*

He didn't bother worrying about what would happen after the trial. Whatever happened to him from then on, it couldn't be worse than what he'd been through already.

He tried to fall asleep again, tossing and turning, enjoying every movement of his newly healthy body. He felt a joyous amazement just at the ability to scratch himself by merely stretching out a hand.

The young blood and energy transferred from Terant bubbled within him. Luca stood up and started pacing back and forth in the cell. He'd missed something, but what?

The Wheel!

As soon as he remembered the Wheel, some text appeared before him again and he heard it read out in his own voice in his head.

Luca'Onegut, life one.
Reminiscent. Successor to Esk'Onegut.
Influence level: 0.
Tsoui points: 1.

BLOOD OF FATE

One-time Wheel spin privilege activated.
Use?

Luca froze, reading it again and again. Then he confidently pressed 'Yes.'

This time, the Wheel looked different: maybe because he was in a dark prison cell, or maybe because it was the first time he'd spun it as a traveler. The huge wheel with its thousands upon thousands of sectors stretching into the starry sky had disappeared, replaced by a small one about the size of a tray.

It appeared to hover in the air a few feet from the boy, and each of its segments was lit from within. Most of the Wheel was lit in pure lily-white, but there were also narrow multicolored segments. Luca couldn't see a purple one among them, nor any red or gold segments. It was pure white almost everywhere, with hints of blue melding with the dominant color.

He gained some understanding from Esk's trove of knowledge: the Wheel's leveled up with every use, increasing its abilities to change the traveler. At first this saddened Luca, but then he calmed down. At least there were no red sectors! In one of his lives, Esk had gotten an incurable disease. He'd become patient zero of a pandemic that had destroyed a civilization. The infected became extremely aggressive, and could only be killed by destroying their brains, which was quite difficult in a world without ranged weapons. Such as were in Esk's penultimate life, for example.

Luca looked over his shoulder. Terant continued to sleep, his breath still as sedate as before. In spite of the Wheel's light, the cell remained dark. The light existed only in the boy's head. When he realized that, he calmed down, took a deep breath, and set the spin in motion.

The starting green sector was replaced by a series of white, then a flash of pale blue, then it got too fast to tell them apart. The Wheel built up speed.

Not exactly convenient, he thought. *I can't make anything out. If only I could make it bigger...*

The Wheel reacted sensitively, and its size multiplied by ten. Now Luca could make out colors other than white in the blur of sectors. Was that a flash of gold?

The boy grew bored as he watched the monotony of melding sectors and heard only the thrum of the Wheel, as if a bumblebee had gotten into the cell and was beating against the walls in search of freedom, but just as it seemed that both the bee and Luca himself would languish together forever in the dark of the cell, the spinning began to slow.

Passing over a range of white sectors, one deep blue sector and a couple of blueish ones — all talents of various power — the indicator stopped.

Luca stared at the thin sector gleaming in gold. He couldn't believe his eyes. Text appeared in front of his eyes and made him believe, but it was far from what he was expecting.

One-time Wheel spin token used.
Spin result: gold sector.
Reward:
Luca'Onegut receives the superpower (applied to current body and world of existence): Metamorphosis.

Metamorphosis? Luca Dezisimu had hoped that he'd get a talent for some rare profession, some skill that could help him pay his way in the Empire, but this?

At the same time, Luca'Onegut rubbed his hands in glee. He remembered some kind of association from his earthly life — a piano? A music box? It didn't matter.

Esk had never managed to get this superpower, but he'd seen it in action. The ability to control all the processes in his body with the power of thought; just like beauty, this was a terrifying power! He'd known one clawed traveler that had covered his skeleton, all his bones, in a rare alloy...

Metamorphosis
Ability level one.
This ability allows you to control your body on a basic level: temperature, energy expenditure, immune system, metabolic activity, rapid healing, tissue and organ regeneration, sharpened senses.

Impulsively, Luca closed his hand into a fist and struck the stone cell wall. Inwardly recoiling in expectation of the coming pain, he willed his fist to become stronger than stone. Iron was stronger than stone!

Transformation impossible. Not enough iron in body!

The dull thud of the little fist on the stone turned into an agonizing wail, which woke up Terant.

CHAPTER 9

THE JUSTICE OF JUDGE CANNON

HIS BROKEN and bleeding fist healed before the night was over. Luca didn't know when exactly it happened. Terant, now awake, was just like the boy's father; fierce in the Arena and gentle in the home. He stroked Luca's head.

"I can't promise that everything will be fine, but I know one thing for certain: even after the darkest night, dawn always comes. Sleep, little one, and think not of what tomorrow will bring. Sleep."

The khhar knew nothing of the Wheel, of travelers or the reward that the boy was trying to test out. With his own interpretation of events, he just tried to console the boy.

Luca lay down and fell to sleep at once. Then, when he woke up, he tried to pull together all the fragments and multitude recollections from the previous day.

"How are you, little one? I'd wish you a good morning, but... I don't think they do breakfast here," Terant said. "And rightfully so, I guess. Why feed those that will belong to a new master before the day's end?"

Luca rubbed his eyes, yawned, stretched and shrugged his shoulders. He'd been happy to eat even just once a day. And nobody was obliged to feed him. But why not dream? Any moment now, he'd hear the footsteps of a guard approaching the cell door, and he'd throw some stale bread crusts through the bars! That would be a great start to the new day!

"Two-horns!" Terant exclaimed. "Just look at that! I almost pulled it taught without noticing!"

Only now did the boy see that one of the khhar's legs was bound not to a chain, but to a very fine, thin thread, a colorless line. It was hard to see it, but once he saw it, he couldn't tear his eyes away. It flashed with reflected light in the most bewitching way. As if the line was catching beams of sunlight and absorbing them.

"Do you know what this is?" the khhar asked.

Luca shook his head.

"It's a tether. Tethers like this are one of the few things that the racants agree to share with your emperor. They are stronger than an iron chain and lighter than a washing line! They are a creation of Two-horns made flesh. They bind themselves to the prisoner's nervous system. Anyone insane enough to try to pull it out loses their entire nervous system with it. Death comes before they can even scream."

They heard a guard's footsteps and the clatter of keys. Luca perked up: maybe they were bringing food?

"Luca Dezisimu, approach the cell door! Now!"

The boy turned to Terant in confusion.

"Be strong," the khhar nodded farewell to him. "Remember what your father said."

As the guard spurred him on, Luca walked back along the same path he'd walked the previous night, when he'd been brought in, but when they came to the stairs, the guard took him down another corridor, not to the prison exit. All the cells they saw on the way were packed full of people. People lame, crooked of limb, monstrous, covered in wounds and scabs. The prisoners fit in perfectly with Terant's story of the Empire's genetic pollution. Luca looked at the guard's face and noticed that even he had such defects; a low forehead, a cataract on one eye...

"What're you starin' at?" the guard barked and clouted the boy around the head. "Come on, scum, move it!"

His crooked blackened teeth, which had always seemed an ordinary and normal occurrence in Luca's world, suddenly no longer looked normal. Esk's legacy was making itself known again, from an unexpected direction.

What a monster! the boy thought, but tried to start a conversation all the same.

"What will happen to him?" he asked.

"Who?"

"The khhar I was with."

"The black boy? He'll be punished or bought to fight in the Arena."

"Who will buy him?"

"Enough chatter, boy! Forget your loverboy!"

The guard gave him a swift kick and Luca increased his pace to stay upright, rubbing his fresh bruise. Some text appeared in front of him telling him he'd taken damage and that his soft tissue was regenerating. A heartbeat later, the pain disappeared.

They finally reached the other wing and climbed some stairs to a street. The broad closed yard of the prison was full of spectators, gawpers and relatives of those awaiting judgment.

Judge Cannon — a gnarled old man barely holding off the desire to fall asleep right at the table — mumbled something. The aide standing next to him made a loud declaration.

"In the name of the emperor! The life of Rakhim Darishta is declared the property of the Empire from now until the end of his days. The slave Darishta has been sentenced to stone for his numerous sins against the people of the Empire in the Oltonius Mines!"

The convict, with tethers at his arms and legs, cried out.

"That judge is a sell-out rat! Suck my-"

A dogpile instantly formed where Darishta

had stood objecting to his sentence. The guards enthusiastically beat the dissident until he stopped making any sounds at all. Then two of the largest guards grabbed the body by the legs and carried it out of the yard.

The judge looked at his notes and either whispered something again or just yawned. Either way, the aide stood up straight and gave a signal. Luca's escort kicked him in the back, shoving him into the center of the yard. Luca opened his mouth to say something in his defense, but nobody even bothered to ask him — Cannon had already decided the matter.

"The boy Luca Dezisimu, who stands accused of causing bodily injury to one Karim Kovachar, is sentenced to pay a fine of fifteen gold pieces! Seven of them will go directly to Mister Kovachar, seven to the Empire, while the last gold piece will pay for legal fees!" the aide's voice rang out. "Accused! Are you or any of your family capable of paying this fine here, now and in full?"

"Luca!" his mother's voice rang out, followed by the clear and clean voice of Kora.

"Brother! He's standing on his own! It's a miracle!"

"Mom! Kora!" Luca shouted in joy. He started to run toward his family, but tripped over the leg of a guard with a good sense of timing. The crowd laughed.

The judge looked toward Luca's family with displeasure and gave a signal with his hand. His mother and Kora were dragged before the nebulous gaze of the high judge.

Kora was still smiling happily at the sight of her brother healthy, and not helpless as he had been all his life.

"Name!"

"Prisca Dezisimu, Sir Judge!" the mother answered in tears. "Luca isn't guilty! My boy couldn't even lift his arms until yesterday..."

Cannon made the slightest gesture with his forefinger and the aide shouted deafeningly, interrupting Prisca.

"Answer only what you are asked! Woman, are you capable of paying this bastard's fine?"

"I don't have that kind of money," Prisca whispered.

"I'll find it! I'll get it! Give me a day!" Kora rushed toward the judge and he flinched.

The guards grabbed the girl, but she kept trying to wrestle herself away.

"Take them away!" the aide commanded, and the guards carried the women off, ignoring their cries and wails. "Who among those present wishes to purchase seventeen-year-old Luca Dezisimu as full property for a period of five years?"

The crowd murmured, discussing the boy's characteristics. The aide looked over the crowd in frustration, leaned down to the judge, listened to him and changed the conditions.

"Fifteen years! Who among those present wishes to purchase the seventeen-year-old Luca

Dezisimu as full property for a period of fifteen years?"

The people stayed silent, exchanging glances. Someone coughed and a hand went up.

"I guess I'll take him. For twenty five years, if Sir Judge would allow it..."

Judge Cannon nodded his blessing, and Luca saw his future master — a lean swarthy man with a huge beak of a nose. Luca pegged him at forty at first glance, but then looked closer at his pockmarked face and the liver spots on his hands and added another twenty years to his estimate.

The buyer counted out some coins and, without rising from his seat, proffered them to the aide. The aide appeared by his side in an instant, took the money and cried out triumphantly.

"In the name of the emperor! The life of Luca Dezisimu is declared the property of Mister Yadugara for twenty five years henceforth."

"Heh-heh..." the judge chuckled. "A wonderful purchase, Mister Yadugara! Fresh blood! Hah-hah-hah! Fresh blood!"

CHAPTER 10

SENIOR APPRENTICE PENANT

RIGHT AFTER THE COURT, once they'd left the prison, Luca's master condescended to say a few words.

"My name is Nestor Yadugara, slave. That's Master Yadugara to you. This," he nodded toward the boy next to him, "is my senior apprentice, Penant."

Not knowing how to answer, Luca just nodded. The senior student looked like a normal boy around eighteen years old, if it weren't for a certain strangeness. A certain slouch, somewhat dry skin, a slight shortness of breath. Although they'd only walked a couple of hundred paces, all this together created the impression that Penant was getting old before his time.

"Your collar, slave... If you go more than a

hundred paces from me without permission, you die," Master Yadugara continued dryly. "If you do anything I don't ask you to, you die. If you touch me without my permission, you die. Got it?"

Luca unwillingly touched the power collar, nodded and then immediately felt a cane crack across his head. His vision blurred and the pain brought him to tears.

"When master asks you a question, you answer!" Penant hissed cruelly.

"Careful now, Penant! Are you going to carry him if you knock him out?" Yadugara asked spitefully.

"Sorry, master, next time I will match the strength of my strike to the severity of the slave's misstep."

"And I'm sure next time will come very soon. This idiot doesn't seem like someone who gets the point the first time. Speak, slave! Eh?"

"Yes, master."

"'Yes' what?"

"I don't seem like someone who gets the point the first time. I understand."

Penant's next strike made it obvious that he was lying about matching the punishment to the sin. The senior apprentice laughed, and his master couldn't hold back a crooked grimace at the sight. After his laughter subsided, Penant explained:

"Say 'master' when you speak to the master, worm!"

"Yes, Master Senior Apprentice Penant! Your

wish is my command, Master Yadugara!"

Luca continued muttering everything they wanted to hear, at the same time reading a message before his eyes: something about the need to strengthen the bones of the skull...

"Look at the master when you answer, you..."

"Enough, Penant," the old man said as his senior apprentice raised his arm again. "Give me that cane back and take him to the baths. Make sure they scrub him clean and shave him. I don't want him to stink and spread lice all over the house.

"It shall be done, master!" Penant nodded, returned the cane and, squeamishly urging him on and shoving him, shepherded Luca away.

Yadugara climbed into the waiting carriage with practiced ease and said something to the driver. "Clear the road!" he shouted, driving right into the crowd.

Since the senior apprentice had forbidden him to turn his head — *Look straight ahead, oaf!* — Luca looked at the world sidelong. This was the part of the capital where people of means lived. It hadn't changed much since he'd strolled through here when his father was still alive. Or rather, his nanny had strolled through with little Luca in a pushchair. The memories had faded, blurred, but he recognized some things.

For example, the public baths that Severus had loved to visit. Luca even remembered that he'd been here as a small child with his father, but maybe he was just imagining it.

BLOOD OF FATE

A cruel hit in the back swept away the wave of nostalgia.

"Move it, slave!" Penant commanded him.

Luca picked up his pace, examining the senior apprentice sidelong. Then he decided to risk a question.

"What does our master do?"

Penant was so surprised at Luca's insolence that he answered without thinking.

"Master Yadugara is a great healer. Even the palace uses his services!"

Angry at himself for answering and at the slave for daring to open his mouth unasked, he clouted Luca around the ear. The strike was so strong that Luca stumbled over a step, flew a dozen feet and hung there, holding the staircase's metal bannister.

Lifting himself to his feet, he tried to let go of the bannister, but couldn't pull his hand away. It was as if stuck to the warm wrought-iron railing.

Fearing another blow from Penant, he used his other hand to force his fingers to unclench themselves and tear the hand away from the bannister.

He managed just in time. The senior apprentice had just reached him and stopped by the door to the baths. Luca looked at his traitorous hand and stared dumbfounded as the barely noticeable gleaming specks of metal from the banister seemed to be absorbed into his very skin. A couple of seconds later, his palm was clean again.

***Transformation interrupted! Not enough
iron in body!***

*Luca'Onegut, based on an analysis of
aggressive environmental influences and damage
taken, an increase in the survival capability of your
body has been initiated:*

— *skull bones strengthened by 0.001%*

— *right hand bones strengthened by 0.002%*

— *right hand skin enhanced by 0.0013%*

— *posterior skin enhanced by 0.00001%*

*It is recommended that you immediately
strengthen your entire skeleton and enhance your
entire skin!*

Luca didn't bother following the
recommendations. Instead he cleared all the text
covering up his view just by wishing it away, then
rushed to open the door.

Penant entered and headed across the hall to
the bath attendants without a backward glance.
After coming to an agreement with them, he looked
around in search of Luca and saw him frozen at the
entrance.

The senior apprentice narrowed his eyes. He
couldn't understand what was happening to the
slave, who was hanging off the door handle and
squirming instead of just coming in.

"Slave! Luca!" he shouted, using his name for
the first time. "Here, now!"

The boy didn't respond at all. Except that his
face twisted even further.

"Damn you, you little brat!" Penant exploded. "Just wait, I'm about to..."

The slave managed to tear himself away from the door and fell onto the floor while Penant was still a few steps away. Master Yadugara's senior apprentice didn't stand on ceremony. He set about teaching the boy the only way he knew how. He furiously rained down strikes on the boy's prostrate body, and only a sudden fear of the prospect of destroying his master's property stopped him before he killed the slave.

"You alive? Huh?" he shook the boy's shoulder. "Luca Dezisimu!"

The boy opened his eyes, spat out some blood and nodded.

"Yes, Master Senior Apprentice Penant. I'm alive."

Overcoming his disgust, Penant helped him rise and walk inside.

Master Yadugara's senior apprentice was frightened and angry, so he didn't even notice that of the large bronze door handle shaped like a bird's head, nothing now remained.

CHAPTER 11

BAD NEWS

LUCA ONLY LATER learned what had happened at the baths. The durability of the bones and skin of his head, the joints of his right arm and his buttocks had increased by more than a hundred percent, but it stopped there. After that, no matter what he touched, it didn't happen again. He couldn't figure out what had happened on his own, and Esk's spirit was silent.

All the boy managed to figure out was that the strengthened and improved parts of his body were the same spots that had been damaged when he'd punched the wall and been struck by the cane. The bruises from Penant's beating had almost gone when he sat before the barber. But that beating had brought him no more improvements.

As they walked out of the baths, he took advantage of the fact that Penant walked ahead and punched a wall hard. He didn't feel the sharp pain he'd felt in the prison, but his punch left a fist-shaped imprint in the building's facade.

The walk to the healer's home was amusing. Penant, scared that he'd almost killed or, worse, maimed his master's property, blathered at Luca all the way from the public baths to the house about the details of life with the healer.

The main thing the boy understood was that their master was strict and quick to punish, but just. Penant himself had once been like Luca, although he hadn't been sentenced for attacking someone, but for vagrancy. You could panhandle and beg all you wanted in the capital, just as long as you slept under a roof at night.

The guards caught Penant, or Pen as the ten-year-old orphan had been called on the streets, on one happy — so he said himself — night. The night before, the boy had fallen out with the head of the band of street urchins that he'd been sharing a roof with in an abandoned hut on the outskirts. They banished him to teach him a lesson, and Pen had to sleep on the street. Some bored city patrolman grabbed him there while he was sleeping and lifeless, otherwise he'd have run away.

The very next morning, intending to send him to a foster home, put his penalty up for auction.

And so in just one golden day, Pen had become the property of Master Yadugara for five years. And three years ago, when his term expired, he took the position of the healer's junior apprentice. He adored his master and was truly thankful to the heavens and all the gods in it for the night the guards had caught him. Although he darkened and said nothing when Luca asked him how much Master Yadugara had profited from all this.

The cubbyhole in the attic of the healer's house couldn't boast of even the semblance of comfort Luca had in the prison cell. At least the roof wasn't leaking there. The whole place was filthy, strewn with garbage, covered in cobwebs, and the ceiling rafters hung lower than the boy's height so that he had to constantly stoop. Years of dust glimmered in the beams of sunlight from a tiny window.

"Your place is here," Penant said. "Tidy up and await further instructions."

The senior apprentice left, and later Luca saw him drive away somewhere with Yadugara. Even later, when he wanted to take out the trash he'd collected, he found a huge brunette blocking his path down the stairs, mopping the steps. She gasped and raised her head.

"Sacred Mother! Who are you?" she cried, pointing a fat finger at Luca with a droplet of dirty water at its tip.

"Luca," he answered.

"Ah... So you must be Master Yadugara's new boy!" the woman nodded in understanding. "And the old one is... all gone..."

"Who are you?" Luca set the garbage bag at his feet. "And where did the old one go?"

Ignoring his questions, the woman wiped her hands on her apron, shook her head and asked her own.

"You hungry?"

Expecting nothing good, Luca remained silent, but unwillingly swallowed. His stomach rumbled.

"I'll say..." she said thoughtfully. "So thin! Alright! The master will be away a while. Since he took that bastard Penant with him, that means the patient is heavy. He left with his surgical case so he might even be operating. What's in the bag?" she nodded at the offending item.

"Garbage from the attic."

"Take it outside and throw it on the heap in the back yard. When you come back, follow the smell of cooking," the woman said with a laugh.

Easily lifting her bucket of water, she started walking down the stairs, then turned back.

"Call me Auntie Mo."

"Alright, Auntie Mo," Luca nodded.

Not counting the attic, the master's house was three stories high. The first floor was for the household and servants, and Master Yadugara saw patients on the second. The third floor was the living quarters, with the bedrooms of the master and the senior apprentice and an office with a library. Penant explained this to him, telling Luca where he could go and where he absolutely couldn't.

The boy carefully tipped out the trash, sneezing as he shook the dust out of the sack and threw it over his shoulder. Before he went back in, he stopped at the well to wash his hands and face.

"Hey!" he heard a voice say behind his back. "Luca?"

The boy turned around and his face lit up with joyful surprise as he saw the strained face of his sister appear above the ten-foot-high wall. He waved.

"Kora!"

"Luca! Hah! They shaved you clean! Hah-hah-hah! Baldy, baldy!"

Luca ran to the wall and a happy smile lit up his sister's face.

"I swear on Two-horns' corrupted mother, you really are walking! You can run, brother! Argh..." His sister's face disappeared from view, then reappeared. "This wall is slippery, bro, nothing to get a foothold on... Can you come out?"

The smile fell from the boy's face. The seemingly ordinary leather strip on his neck, which was actually a slave's collar — called a power collar due to the unseen power hidden within it — wouldn't let him leave his master's yard without permission. He shook his head, pointing at his neck.

"Is it enchanted?" Kora asked. "Don't worry, I'll find enough money to buy you back! The important thing is that you weren't sent to the mines! Nobody ever comes back from them..."

"Kora, don't! You and mom need the money more, and life will be easier for you now without me as I was! They've given me a room here," Luca said, bending the truth by calling that wretched attic a room. "They're feeding me! Look! They even took me to the baths and gave me clothes!"

He span in front of his sister, showing off his new outfit. The clothes almost fit. Penant had given them to him when they returned from the baths. He needed to be convincing to stop his sister from getting into any trouble or danger for his sake. Then his mother would be left all alone!

"Mom..." Kora's face turned more serious. "She's sick, Luca. She has a fever, she's burning up! I don't know what to do! Your master is a healer. Maybe he has some kind of medicine? Maybe you could convince him to visit us? Mom would be so glad to see you..."

"I'll talk to him, Kora. I'll make sure I talk to him! Today, right away, as soon as he comes back! But if..."

An wrathful roar interrupted him.

"Luca! Cursed boy! What do you think you're doing?"

"Oh, damn. It's Aunt Mo!" Luca jabbered. "Kora! I have to go! Hug mom for me! And don't you dare..."

"Luca! I'm going to beat your skinny ass! Come here, now!" the woman kept shouting as she approached. "Who's that there with you?"

Kora laughed and let go of the top of the wall. Luca heard her moan as she landed, then she cursed Two-horns' mother and shouted:

"Hold on, brother! I'll be back!"

"Don't get into any trouble, Kora! Do you hear

me?" Luca kept shouting before Aunt Mo grabbed him by the ear and dragged him back into the house,

where she did everything she'd promised. She beat his skinny, though metamorphosis-strengthened ass, which Luca endured without a wince, then fed him full of fried offal with onions and potatoes . The boy had never so much as seen so much tasty food at once, let alone eaten it.

She averted her gaze as he thanked her endlessly. It seemed to Luca as if tears appeared in her eyes, but she turned away and he couldn't tell for sure. Raising herself heavily, Aunt Mo got him another portion and rapped the bowl on the table.

"Eat!"

Looking at her drowsily, he took the spoon, belched and reddened in embarrassment.

"Aunt Mo," he asked, "what happened to the person who was here before me? You called me the master's new boy, and said the old one was gone... What does that mean? Does Master Yadugara like to share his bed with boys?"

Luca had heard of such things from Kora, though he poorly imagined how it worked. His sister didn't know the nuances either.

"Sacred Mother!" Aunt Mo ran her finger across her right cheek three times, invoking the mother of the gods. "Think before you let such filth out of your dirty mouth. The Master Healer is fond of young flesh, but only that with a hole between its legs, you foolish boy!"

"Then why..."

"Enough! Don't you ever dare ask anyone about the master again! Do you understand me, Luca? And definitely don't ask him any questions like that, or any! Otherwise you'll see your final sunset in the grave, do you understand? Back up to your room!"

Luca slid off the high chair, thanking Aunt Mo again and, barely able to move, slowly climbed up to the attic. Whatever she said, he'd have to ask the master a question today for his mother's sake.

Penant did say he was just and generous, after all.

CHAPTER 12

LET'S GET STARTED!

L UCA TIDIED UP the entire attic. He threw out all the garbage and trash, washed the floors and all the surfaces, pulled the spiderwebs from all the corners and ceiling beams. He tidied mechanically, as if he'd done it many times before, but in reality it was the first time he'd ever done it, and the magic of turning chaos and dirt into order and comfort inspired him.

In the evening he was fed again, although this time along with the other slaves. They were many: Aunt Mo he already knew, then there was the funny girl Reyna and a lean muscular man with a military bearing whose name Luca had not yet learned. The latter took his portion and went back to the gates, where he fulfilled the role of doorkeeper.

Reyna never tired of trying to extract details of Luca's personal life. She herself had ended up in the capital against her will. Her mother caught swamp fever and never got over it, and the very next day after the funeral, her stepfather sold his stepdaughter to a passing slaver whose route took him through their village. At the very first auction, Master Yadugara bought the girl, and the reason was so obvious that Luca tactfully avoided asking about it. Reyna was twenty now, and had spent almost a third of her life in this house.

After dinner, Luca retired to the attic, got bored and started thinking about his gift. He thought about it purposefully, asking himself questions about its nature, abilities, about how he'd gotten it and who he could become now — not just in this life, but in general — and his mind, digging around in Esk'Onegut's legacy, came up with answers and *knowledge.*

Luca, or rather Luca Dezisimu, was a mere vessel. But Luca'Onegut, the personality that was him, that had grown in him after combining with Esk's experiences, would continue to exist after this life, assuming he ended up with a positive Tsoui balance. Even if it was in another world and another body.

This knowledge led him to thoughts about the Wheel. There was no limit on the number of spins you could make, and the more you did, the higher the Wheel's level got, but each attempt cost ten Tsoui points. By chasing after new talents, you could drop your Tsoui level into minus points, and with a negative balance you lost your ability to reincarnate.

Luca didn't fully understand how to get more

Tsoui yet. Were points awarded for any deed that benefited universal balance and harmony? And how had the balance of the universe improved when he stood up for his mother and got his first point for it? What did the universe care for an elderly female of an intelligent species from one of infinite worlds? Especially since, as it turned out, her genetic code was defective.

However, none of this understanding changed Luca's plans at all. First and foremost, he was still a boy — son to a mother and brother to a wayward sister, — and his highest priority was to convince Master Yadugara, if not to heal his mother, then at least to allow him to visit her.

And if all was well with his mother, he would think of how to gain his freedom. He couldn't help his loved ones if he remained Yadugara's slave.

The healer and his student returned home late in the evening. Luca had gotten thoroughly bored by then. He was used to spending hours and days immobile. He'd spent his whole life that way. But his new health had brought with it a desire to move that was natural to a boy his age.

With nothing to do, he grabbed a ceiling beam and tried to pull himself up, not as a purposeful act of exercise, but more to catch up on the youth he missed, and to learn the abilities of his new body. He couldn't pull himself up, so he just hung there, swinging back and forth and waving his legs.

Moonlight trickled in through the small window, but not nearly enough to fully light up the attic.

So Luca hung in the darkness, sometimes dropping off to rest, and his metamorphosis, recognizing the requirement to strengthen the corresponding muscles, decided, somewhere in its invisible plan, to do so as soon as its body could get the required material. Ideally with some to spare, so that the ability's owner could have the required endurance to grip and pull.

When his arms finally tired, Luca gripped the beam with his legs and hung upside down. It was in this position that Penant found him when he walked in to see if his task had been completed. Narrowing his eyes, he walked around the room, seeking faults. He lit an oil lamp and looked around the room, muttered something and then started shouting.

"What are you doing, Two-horns take you?! Get down from there right now!"

Luca jumped down onto the floor and stood up straight.

"I completed the task, Master Senior Apprentice Penant!"

"I see..." he chuckled. "You will sleep here. Get a mattress from Moraine."

"From Aunt Mo?"

"I have no information about your blood relationships, slave. But yeah, from Mo. Be ready at dawn, I'll come get you. Master Yadugara wants to carry out some... research."

"Consider it done, Master Senior Apprentice Penant!"

Penant chuckled again and left the room. Luca waited for his footsteps to fade from the stairway, then he went down to Aunt Mo for the promised mattress. She was nowhere to be found, but he did run into Reyna.

The girl sat before the mirror in the lounge, putting on make-up.

"What's up?" she asked antisocially.

"I'm looking for Aunt Mo, Reyna."

"She isn't here."

"Where is she?"

"I haven't the slightest idea. Get out of here!"

"Um... Are you alright?" Luca decided to ask. The girl's behavior had changed sharply from what he'd seen before. "Reyna?"

"It's none of your business!" She sneezed, which sent a cloud of powder into the air around her. That sent the girl into a fury. "Disappear, small fry!"

"Could you at least tell me where to get a mattress? Master Senior..."

"Leave!" She jumped up, grabbed the boy by the ear and dragged him out of the room. "I don't want to see you here again! Out!"

Discouraged by this, Luca shambled upstairs. Where had the happy and friendly Reyna gone, the one that sneakily gave him an extra big portion of offal mush at dinner? Luca had grown up among women, and he'd come to realize that sharp changes in mood were to be expected from them. But Reyna's transformation into a hateful viper was too sudden.

Once he got to the attic, he collapsed on the wooden floor, rolled into a ball and fell asleep.

Luca woke up in the middle of the night, freezing. He decided to walk around and squat to get his blood flowing and warm up, then he tried to sleep again. He finally managed it when the first rays of sunlight began to shine in, which made his awakening even worse.

"Get up, slave!" Penant kicked him in the side, but Luca just mumbled something without opening his eyes. "Up!"

Angered, the senior apprentice kicked him in the ribs with all his strength. The boy couldn't ignore a strike like that and leapt up, his head spinning in confusion. He wiped his eyes and yawned unwillingly.

Penant cuffed him around the head.

"Downstairs, now! Wash your face and go to the master's office!"

Luca took a few uncertain steps to the door, staggered, and then took a heavy kick to the backside. The educational measure worked: it gave the slave a sense of urgency and he picked up his pace. Penant smirked crookedly. Even this little bit of authority filled him with a feeling of significance and an intoxicating sense of superiority.

After the terrified Luca flew down the stairs and hesitatingly knocked at the master's door, his heart was beating like a trash sparrow's wings. The realization that the hot-headed healer would be unlikely to help his mother scared him more than his hypothetical punishment for being sluggish and late.

He heard some muted voices from within the room. Luca knocked louder, then heard steps and someone unlocking the door from inside.

"The slave Luca," Penant announced after opening the door.

"Sit him down," Master Yadugara commanded, apparently focused on examining something in a vial as he held it up to the light.

The healer agitated the transparent liquid, chuckled in satisfaction and poured it into another vessel. The liquid changed color to a bright yellow, and Yadugara clicked his tongue in excitement.

"Wonderful!"

Penant had already pushed Luca onto a long and low chair. He placed Luca's arms and legs into special depressions in the chair, then restrained each limb with straps. Yadugara squeezed his cheeks painfully and forced his mouth open wide.

"Drink!" the master ordered, pouring the burning saccharine liquid into the boy's mouth.

The liquid didn't dampen his throat. On the contrary, it made it dry as a desert. A fire lit in his stomach, his eyes darkened, and heard his heartbeat like war drums in his head.

"What's that for?" Luca's throat was dry, but the master still understood him.

"Take a spit sample and cover his mouth and eyes," he said to Penant. "He hasn't had breakfast, I hope?"

BLOOD OF FATE

"No breakfast, master! I kicked him awake and sent him to wash and then straight to you."

"Good."

Luca heard the master washing his hands.

"Then let's get started!"

CHAPTER 13

AN EXTREMELY CURIOUS SPECIMEN

MASTER YADUGARA's research continued all morning, and then, after a filling lunch through which Luca lay unconscious, it started up again. By that time, the motionless teenager, deprived of all sensation, felt himself floating in a bottomless nothing, as he'd felt his entire life.

"One-hundred-percent compatibility!" "Wonderful, wonderful," Yadugara purred, letting out a loud and satisfied belch. "Let's prepare for the transfusion."

"Can I have it too, Master Teacher?" Penant asked in a voice quivering in excitement.

"You're still too young, Pen. If used correctly, the boy's body will last a couple of years. Anyway, we haven't tested him for compatibility with you."

"But I'm compatible with you, aren't I? That means I might be with him, too..."

"Don't get distracted, Pen! And don't forget that there's a long queue of influential and respected people for restoration! Their patience is not unlimited, and we have only one suitable sample! And if the Imperial Healer finds out... Two-horns save us!"

"But our customers..."

"No, Pen! They won't flap their tongues, you know that."

"Maybe I could at least try it?"

"No!"

"But, Master..."

"Later, Pen!" Yadugara waved him away in exasperation. "Get ready..."

Luca was out for a long time, and when he woke up, he smelled something rank and acidic in the air.

"Turn him over," he heard the healer say as if from afar.

The only thing telling the boy he was now on his stomach was the blood rushing to his face. His entire body had lost all sensation.

"Scalpel... Incision..." the voices were indistinct, as if his ears were full of wax. Which they were.

The boy's eyes had also been covered, but suddenly he saw some text.

The letters appeared in the darkness. Line by line, they informed him:

Detected multiple lacerations in skin tissue...
Detected multiple lacerations in muscle tissue...
Detected significant blood loss...
Activated enhancement mode!
Detected available materials: 72% iron, 9% nickel, 18% chrome, 0.07% carbon...
Absorbing...
Transforming...

"Two-horns!" Master Yadugara swore, stunned. "What the hell is happening with this instrument?"

The healer couldn't believe his eyes. Nothing remained of the scalpel but its wooden handle. The entire blade had disappeared. Penant blinked several times and rubbed his eyes before thinking about it, forgetting that his gloves were covered in the slave's blood.

"What does this mean, Master Yadugara?"

"Another scalpel, quickly! Hurry, the incision is closing!"

Luca more realized than felt Yadugara delve into his flesh again.

"Sacred Mother! What kind of monster is this Dezisimu? Scissors! Clamp!"

"Master, it won't cut! The scalpel isn't cutting him!"

"Is it blunt? Needle!"

A rustle, panting. Luca felt his sensations returning, along with an insufferable pain.

"It broke! I swear on the perfect bosom of the

Sacred Mother, the needle broke!"

"It didn't break, idiot! The needle is stuck in this Two-horn-cursed body!"

"Did you see that? Master, did you see that?!"

"Stick it in here, we'll transfuse now! Bring a vessel! The catalyzer, quickly! The tether! Ugh..."

Yadugara collapsed into a chair and closed his eyes. Life flowed into him, life young and full of strength.

Lines appeared before Luca again, which Esk's legacy defined as 'logs'. The boy didn't have time to read them, or understand what they meant.

Detected unsanctioned withdrawal of energy reserves...
Detected unsanctioned trade of...
Detected aggressive influence on cellular...
Activating countermeasure...
Redirecting flow...
Accelerating interchange processes...

Luca's hearing and mobility returned to him. He heard the sound of a falling body and Penant's scream next to him.

"Teacher! Teacher!"

Luca raised his head and looked around. He was lying on his stomach, completely naked. He didn't like that, and the boy rose, feeling tubes fall from his body.

Yadugara lay on the floor, and Senior Apprentice Penant fretted next to him. He saw that

Luca was conscious and trying to stand.

"Daler! Daler!"

"What's up with the master?" Luca asked.

"This is your fault, murderer!" The senior apprentice's eyes flashed with fury. "Whoreson of the abyss!"

Penant suddenly leapt at the boy and raised his arm. Metal gleamed in his hand. Luca raised his hand mechanically to cover himself and felt an explosion of pain. The scalpel blade stuck out of the back of his hand.

But the next moment, the senior apprentice screamed even louder: the blade dissolved, absorbed into the hand, and mere heartbeats later, the wound knit itself shut.

Luca looked at his hand in astonishment, nodded to himself, *understood*, and then looked around the healer's office, deciding what to do. Run away? But where to? Penant was twice his size. He couldn't take him in a fight, but he'd have to, because his mother was waiting for him, and if he was accused of murder...

A fist started banging on the door. Penant rushed toward it and unlocked it. The gate guard slave appeared at the threshold.

"Daler! The slave killed the master!" the senior apprentice babbled. "Bind him immediately!"

Roaring, the guard rushed toward Luca and spread his arms wide to prevent his escape. Recognizing that something irrecoverable was happening, the boy ducked under his elbow and ran to the door of the office.

Penant barred his path. The senior apprentice shouted something and threw his fist forward. Luca didn't have time to dodge, he took the blow to the face and stopped, grabbing his cheekbone. A hit from the guard rushing up from behind sent the boy to the floor.

He came round a little later, when Daler threw his body onto the cold, slimy earth of the cellar floor. He heard the clank of a lock and familiar voices from beyond the door.

"Something's definitely wrong with him!" Penant's voice dripped with spite and shock.

"Yes, you're absolutely right, senior apprentice. And thank Two-horns that he broke the tethers himself, otherwise..."

The muffled voice quietened, started whispering, then Reyna asked a question.

"What kind of beast is he, Master Yadugara?"

"Oh, Reyna, my dear, this is a very curious specimen!" The healer had a coughing fit, then triumphantly announced: "I haven't found any references to such as him in all the two centuries I have lived in this world. This is an incredible discovery! And we *are* going to find out what is wrong with him..."

CHAPTER 14

MASTER YADUGARA'S EDICTS

"SLAVE LUCA DEZISIMU, I forbid you from leaving the bounds of the room in which you now sit!" the master's words were imprinted as sure as death in Luca's mind. "I forbid you, knowingly or unknowingly, to do harm to me, your Master Yadugara, my senior apprentice Penant, or my property, slaves or servants, including Reyna, Moraine and Daler. If you break these edicts, your heart and all your brain activity will be forcibly stopped. Do we have an understanding, slave Luca Dezisimu?"

From behind the door came a rustle, a cough and the boy's strained voice.

"I understand, Master Yadugara."

"As punishment for what happened, you are deprived of all rights to warmth, food, water and conversation for seven full days. Next time you wish to interrupt my... research, remember the suffering you will endure. And be more compliant."

His speech over, the healer knocked on the metal door with his fist and started climbing the ladder from the basement. Penant, Reyna and Daler followed him. Each of them had had to sit in the basement as punishment, but never for such a long time. As a rule, the master limited himself to single days, not wishing to damage his own property.

"Will he... survive?" Penant dared to ask. "The chinils are down there! They'll suck out all his blood!"

"The collar will let me know if he is near death," the healer answered. "I won't let him die just like that. He's going to pay me back for everything a thousand times over!"

Yadugara stopped in the lounge and started giving orders.

"Pen, go to Master Judge and find out everything the court knows about Dezisimu and his family. Reyna, invite Mister Arden over. We will try taking advantage of his glassblowers' services, for it is clear that metal must be avoided when we work with Dezisimu."

Penant and Reyna nodded and rushed to carry out their orders. The master himself sat in an armchair by the fire and lost himself in thought.

Daler patiently waited for the master to address him, but the pause stretched out.

"Should I return to my post, Master?" Daler

dared to interrupt his thoughts.

"I am not afraid of enemies from outside. We have one inside now. Your task from now is to guard the basement. If you hear anything suspicious, tell me at once!"

"Understood!"

Once alone, Yadugara sat for another half an hour, digging through his two-hundred-year memory, but recalling no cases like Dezisimu's.

He grunted, rose from the chair and walked to his office. The interrupted and reversed transfusion and his old age bit hard. His mind was scrambled, his body a wreck.

In his office, he looked over the remnants of what had happened and sighed deeply. He wanted to lie down and sleep, but he had to record it all.

Once he finished his notes, he tidied up personally. He couldn't stand disorder, and he didn't want to trust Moraine — Aunt Mo — with valuable instruments. Once he'd finished, his senior apprentice returned.

Yadugara sat behind his desk and waved Pen into the chair opposite him.

"Master, I went to the judge..."

"Slow down! All in good time, senior apprentice."

Pen nodded and prepared to listen.

"So, what do we have?" Master Yadugara raised his forefinger, twirled it and pointed at Penant. "Tell me again what happened while I was unconscious. Remember carefully, senior apprentice, and try not to miss a single detail!"

Penant scratched his head, wrinkled his brow and rolled his eyes to the ceiling to create the convincing impression that he was thinking. He didn't remember anything new, but he spoke in a serious, confident tone, knowing how easily his master could detect the smallest signs of doubt.

"You fell, Master. I rushed over to you, then I heard his voice. Dezisimu asked what was wrong with you. I thought you were dead, since I couldn't feel your pulse. In desperation, I shouted for Daler and attacked the slave. Forgive me, Master I lost control, my anger clouded my mind."

"If you had ended his life, you would have had to replace it, Senior Apprentice Penant. A role you luckily retain, for now," Yadugara noted with displeasure. "I hope you understand now?"

"Forgive me, Master!" Penant turned white.

He had learned of his master's greatest secret only when he became his apprentice. Previously he had perceived the procedure of transfusing life force as a part of some sort of research. Pen feared even to think of how many years of life he had given to Yadugara in his service, but the appearance of a suitable donor gave him a chance to get back what he'd lost. They'd spent years searching for the previous donor, but he turned out to be an imperfect match for the master and died. The next was Luca.

"Tell me more," the healer chuckled.

"I swung the scalpel at him, but he blocked it

with his hand..."

"More details now."

"The blade pierced his hand, he screamed. I pulled out the scalpel to strike again, but the blade was gone. Disappeared."

Penant thought for a moment. During the fight, he had been so scared at the prospect of life without a master that he'd gone into a fury and desperately wanted only one thing: to punish the killer. The details of what had happened in that instant were hazy, they wouldn't come easily.

"Pen? What next?"

"I got scared. The wound on his hand closed up. Even the blood flowed back in, or maybe just disappeared. I rushed to the door to open it for Daler. I told him to grab the slave, but the boy slipped past him and attacked me. I kept my cool and stopped him, punched him in the face. Then the guard got to him and knocked him out from behind. We bound him... And then you woke up, Master."

"The bastard somehow put the transfusion procedure into reverse!" Master Yadugara slammed his fist down on the table. "So what is our conclusion?"

"He's a monster!" Now that Penant had reviewed recent events with his master, he was even more scared.

"The slave possesses supernatural regeneration. He can somehow absorb metals. And — although this requires testing — his capabilities activate only if physical harm is done to him."

"Sacred Mother! What a monster he is!"

"Enough wailing, Pen! You are not an illiterate bumpkin from the Empire's outskirts, you are first and foremost my apprentice! Everything in this world has an explanation. And we will find it."

"Forgive me, Master."

Yadugara frowned.

"What do we know of his family?"

"His mother and sister were present at his sentencing. Master Judge gave me their address. Shall I bring them here?"

"We must be more subtle about this, Pen. You understand that his sister is of the greatest interest to us, both for the transfusion procedure and as a carrier of the same gift of regeneration and absorption." Yadugara smiled at some hidden thought. "Do we have any other information about the girl?"

"Master Judge gave me the name of the complainant, a certain Nemania Kovachar, an innkeeper in the slums. He may know more. I could question him and his offspring, see what the neighbors have to say, learn more about the family."

"No. Let Reyna do it. It'll be easier for her to gain trust. She might even manage to make friends with Dezisimu's sister and secretly take a sample for analysis."

"Forgive me, Master, but would it not be simpler to capture the girl and put her in our basement? Who would go looking for her?"

"Unacceptable, Pen. Without a power collar,

we can't guarantee that she will be obedient. And if her mother complains to the imperial chancellery that we are breaking the law of free birth... All that we have will collapse! You know that not everything done in this house is entirely within the law."

"So first we need to organize some accusation and a trial..."

"Exactly right," Yadugara nodded.

They heard a tentative knock on the door.

"Come in, Reyna," the healer responded loudly.

The door opened and the girl's elegant figure stood outlined on the threshold. Reyna brushed a disobedient lock of hair out of her face and spoke.

"Master, I've come with Master Arden. He awaits downstairs."

"Pen, go down and entertain our guest for now. As for you, Reyna, come closer. I have a special assignment for you."

CHAPTER 15

CHINILS

ONCE THE FOOTSTEPS behind the door faded, Luca was in total darkness and silence. He feared neither, just as he did not fear Yadugara's threatened punishment. But the fact that his mother needed help, which he couldn't provide no matter how much he wanted to — that tore at his soul. He was also worried about Kora, who would probably come back tomorrow, and if she didn't see him, she might try to get into the house, which could end in her being sent to the mines.

Luca felt his way from one corner to the other in the basement. It turned out he was in a small space; five paces long and six wide. The low ceiling tickled the crown of his head as he walked, and that made the boy stoop out of fear of hitting his head on some unseen protrusion.

Luca knew exactly how long he'd sat analyzing Yadugara's (the boy's new, growing personality felt it would be cowardly and pathetic to call the man Master when alone) actions — almost six hours. Patiently waiting for things wasn't one the boy's strong suits.

He started studying the traveler interface out of boredom. A miniature sun span in his field of vision, somewhere on the very edge. It was bright, but not blinding. It disappeared when Luca didn't pay attention to it, but then reappeared and pulsated invitingly as soon as he remembered it. If he mentally stroked the little sun, text appeared before his eyes as if hanging in mid-air. As he moved, so did the text, always remaining visible without blocking his vision. The text was as if alive, growing and shrinking, or sometimes becoming completely invisible, at the boy's slightest wish.

Luca'Onegut, life one.
Reminiscent. Successor to Esk'Onegut.
Influence level: 0.
Tsoui points: 1
Orion Arm, Milky Way, Solar System, Planet Earth.
Universe variation: #ES-252210-0273-4707.
Reincarnation: available.
Wheel spin cost: 10 Tsoui points.
Right to respin Wheel: none.

Talents:
Metamorphosis. Ability level one. This ability allows you to control your body on a basic level:

temperature, energy expenditure, immune system, metabolic activity, rapid healing, tissue and organ regeneration, sharpened senses.

Luca knew from Esk's legacy that as he increased his influence level, he'd get more points for deeds worthy of Tsoui. The level showed how much the traveler's deeds affected universal harmony and how widely the traveler was known in the multiverse. In addition, the higher the level, the less it cost to spin the Wheel and the better the sectors were, which meant better abilities and talents and fewer negative and empty segments.

Hours went by. Luca felt himself falling asleep when he heard something strange. Something rustled in the far corner of the basement. The boy tensed and froze, then screamed and shook his leg, but the pain in it didn't stop. In a panic, he slapped his knee, but then pain shot through his hand too.

Chinils!

Nimble, bloodsucking centipedes about as long as a man's hand. They were the true curse of the entire Empire. They inhabited moist, dark places and were as enduring as the roaches of the Wastelands. Poison them and they wouldn't die. Set them alight and they'd scatter, able to withstand the very hottest flame for a short time. Trying to squash them was useless. Their thick, chitinous shells were far stronger than a crab's, hard to break even with a hammer. A sledgehammer wielded by a strong blacksmith could just about do it. Sharp spines like a comb down the creatures' backs quickly taught people not to try to stamp on the bloodsuckers.

Although they did have one peculiarity — chinils lived in small colonies of about a dozen individuals that strictly maintained a constant population and range. You never got more than one colony within a half a mile.

Luca jumped up, panicking even more. He'd heard that a colony of these centipedes had drank one of their neighbors dry. The man had been drinking cheap, but effective moonshine and lost consciousness. By the time he came to, it was already too late. It was very strange that Yadugara was comfortable living in that house with such a deadly colony in his basement.

While Luca tried to detach one chinil that had latched on not only with its beak, but with all its legs, another laid its eggs on him, and the rustle and whisper of numerous legs on the floor got louder.

Detected lacerations in skin tissue...
Detected lacerations in muscle tissue...
Detected blood loss...
Activated enhancement mode!
Detected available organic materials...
Absorbing...
Transforming...

With a scream at the edge of ultrasound, two centipedes, deprived of several segments of legs, fell from the boy's body. His ability continued to knit his wounds together, and once done, considered its master's needs: it transformed part of the absorbed organic matter to recover his lost blood and increase the muscle mass of his arms and core[1]. But there wasn't enough of the absorbed material to do it all, and Luca himself was too scared to comprehend the text as it rapidly flashed by and to use the bodies of the two surviving centipedes. Both of them scrabbled on their backs, losing blood from their torn-off legs, their bellies looking as if rubbed raw by sandpaper.

Luca sat until midnight, getting angrier and angrier with the cursed healer. The understanding of what Yadugara had tried to do to him didn't affect him as much as his despairing helplessness. It was all because of that damned slave collar!

He tried to tear it from his neck, but it only strangled him tighter. He couldn't get his fingers under it. His nails scratched his skin until it bled. Luca wailed and cried in his impotence, but the more he tried, the tighter the collar gripped him.

Suddenly, he felt a stabbing pain in his heart and lost sensation. Collapsing against the door, Luca opened his mouth and tried to breathe, but his lungs weren't working. The boy had lost control of his body.

Detected injection of paralyzing toxins!

---

[1] The core muscles are a set of muscles responsible for stabilizing the spine, waist and hips.

Analyzing reaction options...
Releasing neutralizing agents.

Detected impact on nervous system!
Analyzing reaction options...
Blocking nerve receptors in compromised locations.

Detected aggressive asphyxiation influence!
Analyzing reaction options...
Cannot reinforce neck skin!
Insufficient required elements in organism!

More intuitively than consciously, Luca jerked and touched the door.

Detected available materials: 97.9% iron, 2.1% carbon...
Absorbing...
Transforming...

The hand pressing against the iron panel slipped through a hole. Luca could breathe again. The collar no longer constricted his strengthened throat, although it continued to send controlling signals to the rebellious slave's body.

Effect level critical.
Analyzing reaction options...
Initiating absorption of aggressive structure...

BLOOD OF FATE

Insufficient energy reserves!

By absorbing certain chemical elements and transforming them into others, reconfiguring the structure of the boy's organs and counteracting the aggressive outside influence, his metamorphosis ability had expended all his available energy. It couldn't use fat supplies because he didn't have an ounce of spare fat on him, and it had no authority to absorb its masters flesh without his command. The command didn't come, and the ability went to sleep.

Exhausted, Luca fell into a coma, and the power collar achieved its purpose: the rebel was paralyzed and close to death, and the alarm signal had been sent to the slave's master.

Master Yadugara's theoretical plans had worked. There was no way the creature could resist the transfusion process in this state.

CHAPTER 16

AT THE BEHEST OF LENTZ

"**I** MADE FRIENDS with her!" Reyna declared at the threshold and gasped in surprise. "You did it! You look wonderful, Master!"

"Oh yes, my girl! And this evening I'll show you how young I've become."

Yadugara couldn't hold back a self-satisfied smile. He had undergone the transfusion procedure so many times, had delighted so many times in the respite it gave him, the multitude of pleasant things given only to those glowing with health and seething with the hormones of youth.

"How is the creature Dezisimu?" Reyna asked anxiously.

The healer had taught the girl from a young age to divide people into two camps: namely, people and 'creatures.' The impressionable girl's eyes had widened as she listened to her master's 'discoveries' of terrible monsters hiding inside human guises.

But by the will of the gods, who maintain the harmony of the world's design, these creatures also possess something very useful to us, Reyna, he had explained. *Their monstrous essence has something that allows us healers to create the elixir of youth. When the time comes, my girl, you will taste it. You will be eternally young, Reyna!*

She would make an excellent wife... until he grew tired of her. The term of her slavery would end soon, but Reyna would stay with Yadugara, seeing in him everything: husband, lover, patron, defender, head of the family, and most of all — the one who would gift her immortality.

"It all went perfectly! We managed to neutralize it. We didn't even need the new tools from Master Arden." The healer fell silent, then remembered something and frowned. "What about Dezisimu's sister?"

"I wandered around the district yesterday, met some locals. Karim Kovachar, the innkeeper's boy, told me all he knew. The creature was bedridden his entire life, only occasionally going out in a wheelchair. His father was a gladiator, he died three years ago. His mother, Prisca, is a washerwoman. The creature's sister is a year his younger. Her name is Kora. Three days ago, Dezisimu encountered Karim and suddenly stood up and attacked him."

"Is that so..." the healer nodded thoughtfully.

"Perhaps Dezisimu wasn't a beast until something possessed him... This will require thorough research! Two-horns! Cursed imperial healers!"

"Has something happened, Master?"

"It certainly has... I'll deal with it myself. The important thing is that we get Dezisimu's sister!"

"I made her acquaintance yesterday. I told her that her brother sent me, that he's been punished, but asked me to meet with his family to reassure them. She believed it. I promised I'd bring her to the house so she could speak to Luca."

"Warn Daler. He must take her at once, as soon as she comes in. We'll accuse her of trying to burgle me."

"As for the mother, Master..."

"Tell me the details later. For now, leave me. I must think."

"Very well, Master!"

Reyna's curvaceous hips swayed as she walked to the door. Master Yadugara's gaze swept across her strong calves clad in grey stockings and smiled. The girl turned, feeling her master's gaze.

"Master?"

"Go on, Reyna."

She nodded and left the office. Young blood may be roaring through his veins, but he had to forget about the pleasures of the flesh for now. He didn't know how, but the emperor's physicians had learned of the healer's discovery and immediately demanded the slave be taken to the palace.

Now Yadugara was waiting for Dezisimu to

come round and get fed in the kitchen, so that he could at least look presentable. Bringing a half-dead slave to the palace would mean drawing the ire of Lentz, the chief of the imperial medics, and losing his healing license because of it. In the best case.

The mere fact that he had hidden from Lentz that he had found a boy suitable for transfusion threatened Yadugara with grave danger. The yarn he'd spun for Penant about 'compatibility' could be explained by the healer's desire not to increase his apprentice's sense of his own importance. All he needed was for him to go talking and trading on his uniqueness.

In addition, this saved Pen for Yadugara himself as a last resort.

We're compatible, senior apprentice. This is a unique case! Keep this secret, otherwise my enemies will seek to do you harm! He'd said then to Pen, making him proud of his master's trust and thrilled at a sense of unity with him.

Especially for the first few procedures, before the ageing changes began to scare the youth. Later, once the slave was free, he became senior apprentice and started to get an inkling when he looked at his wrinkles. He sought explanation. Then Yadugara had promised his apprentice that as soon as they found another 'compatible' option, Pen would regain his lost years of life.

In reality, the issue was not 'compatibility', but the mere unnatural nature of the process of transfusion. Human nature itself rose up against the forced removal of its life-giving cells! Suitable donors were very rare. Two or three dozen in an entire generation in the Empire, and Yadugara had searched for them all his life, starting out like Penant, the senior apprentice of a healer whose name he had sworn to forget. It had taken him half a century, but he'd done it.

He thanked all the gods and the Sacred Mother that the imperial healers had learned of Dezisimu only this morning. By the time they'd conferred and sent a runner, midday had passed.

But he'd done all he needed to in the night. First he'd performed the procedure on Penant, fearing new surprises, but everything went peacefully and as usual. An hour and change later, the senior apprentice was two years younger, and by midday, Yadugara himself had lost fifteen years. He could have done more, but with each fresh year, the risks rose. This was something to be approached slowly, steadily, for the health both of the donor and the recipient. Rejection was a sorry affair, but it had happened in the healer's rich practice.

In the next couple of hours, he and Pen brought the slave out of his coma — before the next procedure. The boy came round incredibly fast after an intravenous injection of a glucose solution. His regeneration abilities were stunning!

Then, once Luca was able to move on his own, Yadugara sent him and Pen to Moraine to eat, while he himself stayed with Reyna.

It's time! he thought. He left his office and

carefully locked the door. Went downstairs, walked into the kitchen.

Pots and pans bubbled away happily, and the slave Dezisimu sat at the table, his head bowed over a metal bowl. Nobody would have the heart to call him a boy anymore — although his figure was still childish, it nonetheless showed the signs of the transfusion procedure. His hair was dull and grey here and there, his skin dry, covered in pigment spots, his face was covered in wrinkles, his hands shook and his body hunched.

The slave ate greedily under the sympathetic gaze of Aunt Mo.

"I don't understand how he fits so much in," the cook said, spreading her hands. "He's eaten a whole pot full, and it's still not enough."

"It's enough. Stand, slave! Follow me. We're leaving."

Luca rose, took the bowl in both hands, threw back his head and drank what was left. Yadugara looked at the donor's distended stomach and cringed with disgust.

It didn't matter. He'd gotten his. He didn't doubt that the imperial healers would drink Luca dry.

By the next morning, the slave Luca Dezisimu would be dead.

CHAPTER 17

IN THE EMPEROR'S PALACE

SEVERAL PINTS of Aunt Mo's thick aromatic stew pleasantly splashed around in Luca's stomach. Blood rushed from his brain to his digestive tract, and the boy sleepily shuffled along, losing all sense of time and space.

In the district in which he'd spent his recent years, people didn't go against the flow. Kora didn't count — his sister had always been a little strange, striving for something more with no understanding of how to achieve it.

Three nights ago, Luca had been a paralyzed cripple in a slum, grateful for leftover potato skins, and in the mind of that Luca, matters were simply running their course: he had died, been revived through some miracle, received an ability from the Wheel, whose nature he didn't entirely understand

and which he didn't strive to use. The villainous Karim and his father Nemania were bastards for accusing him as they had, it went without saying. But maybe he really had broken the innkeeper's son's collarbone when he threw stones. That would mean that Luca was guilty and serving out a punishment he earned. It was just of the judge to allow him to pay for the damage, and good that Master Yadugara had done so. Otherwise it would have been the mines for Luca. People don't come back from the mines.

So thought Luca the Cripple, the seventeen-year-old Luca the Boy, who had the knowledge of a ten year old, roughly speaking. That Luca simply surrendered himself to the currents of the turbulent river that his life had become, and his capacity to be surprised by all the strange things happening to him had withered. Surprise was an emotion, and after the transfusion procedure, the boy fell into apathy, incapable not only of surprise, but of any feeling. Even his mother's fate no longer concerned him.

But then came a moment when he, spurred on by Penant's kicks, was following Yadugara, and happened to see himself in a mirror. Something broke through the scab of indifference then. Or rather, someone. The new personality that seemed to be melding more and more with the legacy of the traveler Esk'Onegut — that mind reeled. It didn't matter how many reincarnations awaited him in the future. It would be better not to live than to live like this! The reflection showed who the boy had become, the mind recognized the culprit, and the brain began to feverishly think.

Outwardly, this showed only in Luca's slightly more confident stride. He squared his shoulders and stopped shuffling along like an old man. His awakened metamorphosis studied the changes in his body and sighed. His veins, heart and liver had taken a beating, his vision and hearing were weaker, he had kidney stones and his body's cells had aged rapidly overnight.

Luca'Onegut himself was also horrified. He and Penant climbed into a carriage and sat opposite Yadugara, and he really didn't like what he saw in the healer's eyes. He evaluated the man's body language, caught a glance quickly redirected. That glance held disgust, and... pity? Luca also noted that Yadugara was dressed differently than when he went to see patients, somehow more ceremonially. And he noticed that the old man looked far younger.

Luca moved his gaze to Penant. He too looked younger, though it wasn't as extreme with him. His wrinkles had smoothed out and he carried himself with pride. The senior apprentice's eyes held such clear superiority that Luca nearly averted his gaze out of habit.

But he resisted. He asked a question, barely holding back his fury.

"Where are we going... master?"

Showing such respect to a person who had taken away years of his life wasn't easy for Luca.

The hesitation didn't escape Yadugara's eye. The healer's hackles rose, but he considered it necessary to answer. It was no secret.

"To the Imperial Palace. His medics want to examine you. And enough questions, slave. I forbid you to ask more."

Buildings, signs and richly dressed people flashed by behind the small window. The horse slowed its pace. The path to the palace led upwards, to the cliff of Ma Ju Ro the First, the Ruler, the founder of the imperial family, but the boy knew none of this. The Imperial Palace had always been a distant concept to him. Luca knew the place existed, but he had never seen it in all his life.

He stayed silent for the rest of the trip, as his 'master' wished. He wasn't just sitting quietly, though. He was carefully studying his 'logs' (a word that came unbidden from his inherited memory again) of what had happened to him in the last few days. In prison he had wished for a fist of iron, and his ability had reacted with a message that it didn't have enough iron available.

Which meant...

Luca covered his right fist with his other hand and thought about having longer nails, and more durable — steel ones, for example. Maybe a foot long, sharp and deadly, capable of cutting... cutting off that damn slave collar!

Crack!

Something burst under the wheels of the carriage, maybe some kind of fruit, and a displeased murmur came from the driver at the front.

"Careful, you! You're driving the master!" Penant shouted, turning round.

And nothing more happened. No messages in Luca's eyes, no changes. He'd interpreted something wrongly, but what?

He immersed himself in the text once more. Ah, there it was. Yadugara had somehow initiated a transfusion of life force and run into the defenses his ability had mounted... And the best defense is a good offense, as his father had said. The metamorphosis had reversed the process, and Yadugara had almost died, not only returning everything he had taken, but giving away some of his own years.

Luca frowned. From the legacy in his mind came vague memories of certain extremely unpleasant nocturnal creatures of a certain world, who extended their own lives by drinking the blood of victims. He had to admit, Yadugara's methods were far more elegant. And apparently more effective.

As it turned out, it would have been possible to escape from the healer's basement. All he had to do was absorb those two chinils that had lost their limbs, then break down the door. He was sure he could have strengthened his fists enough to do it, though he didn't know where that confidence came from. He shouldn't have tried to tear the collar off right away. He should have gained strength and tried to absorb it or get rid of it some other way.

However, he still had time.

But first he needed to understand how to control his metamorphosis. It was clear that the ability was focused on improving its carrier's survival chances. When there was a direct threat to his health, his metamorphosis switched on and used everything it had to hand.

Right now, the leather collar, even strengthened as it was with its control circuit, wasn't a direct threat. But when the collar attacked his nervous system and injected him with paralyzing toxins, the metamorphosis fought back. It was a shame that it had exhausted his energy so fast — the consequences of a whole day without a single bite to eat — and gone to sleep.

Luca touched the collar reflexively, imagining it as an enemy with a mind and the ability to kill him.

The pseudo-intelligent collar felt the interference in its control center and anxiously tightened. Luca wheezed. Penant, recalling the slave's oddities, shied away to the edge of his seat.

Initiating absorption of aggressive structure...

Yadugara frowned suspiciously and looked him in the eyes. He hissed through his teeth.

"Whatever you're thinking of doing, slave, I order you cease at once!"

And Luca stopped, cancelling the command.

This wasn't the time or the place. This part of the city was well guarded, and he wouldn't be able to hide or escape. And if he spilled the blood of the city watch, the imperial guard or his master, he'd never be able to feel safe anywhere again. After all, if Terant had spoken the truth, then Luca was on an island. He couldn't escape from an island. He didn't even know how to swim.

Sure that Dezisimu had understood him, Yadugara turned away. Penant also averted his gaze and stuck his head out of the window, making as if he was looking out for the palace appearing on the horizon.

And so neither of them noticed the baleful gaze of Luca'Onegut, son of Severus Dezisimu.

He looked at his right hand again, at his sharpened nails that were now half an inch longer than before, with a new metallic luster. He gave the command to turn them back.

Not the time or the place.

CHAPTER 18

MA JU RO THE SOUR

EMPEROR MA JU RO the Fourth, known among the people as Ma Ju Ro the Sour, thoughtfully looked out of his panoramic window overlooking the ocean. The nearest continent was somewhere out there, over five hundred miles away. The real world was out there, but he was the only one who knew it.

The calm, but treacherous ocean waves lapped against the western shore of the isle of Syahrs. The cliff of Ma Ju Ro the First, the Ruler, once bore a different title long before the Resurrection, as did the island itself.

On the day the young Ma Ju Ro the Fourth was crowned, Fourth Advisor Cross came to him and requested an audience. It lasted all day. The advisor opened the young man's eyes to the true design of the world, and it turned out to be far more complex than the people of the Empire had believed, including Ma Ju Ro himself. Unlike what his tutors had taught him, unlike the stories of the priests and schoolteachers, the people of the Empire, as it turned out, were not the only inhabitants of this world.

Long before the Empire, the island had been home to the khhars, a dark-skinned people who were considered backward, but were genetically almost perfect. By the order of the ruling family of the Ra'Ta'Cants, represented by Queen Taira, known as the Sacred Mother, the khhars had been resettled to the mainland. The khhars found their niche in the structure of society in the greater world. They became a martial caste, strengthened by generations of genetic improvements and augmentations.

Their place on the giant island, which would be more aptly named a continent on its own, was taken by the syahrs. Some journalist had come up with the name, and it had stuck for all those who were considered carriers of defective genetic code. The syahrs were forcibly relocated.

They couldn't gather them all up. Many resisted. The relocation and purification efforts took almost a half century of civil war, but in the end, around a hundred million defectives had been confined to a reservation in the hope that they would die out on their own in total isolation, from hunger and a lack of the conveniences that civilized people were so used to.

But the syahrs didn't die. Many of the first

syahrs had relatives remaining on the continent, friends, sympathetic people who organized deliveries of humanitarian aid: food, tools, clothing and much more. These deliveries were mercilessly cut off, but the volunteers kept finding new routes.

Although, as the years passed, these humanitarian efforts dried up. Family connections were lost, mentions of the syahrs faded from mass media, and within a generation or two, the exiles were almost forgotten. Conversations about them came to be considered tasteless.

In the meantime, the syahrs, even with their defective genetic code, remained human, with all the skills of social organization that came with it. The humanitarian aid wasn't enough for everyone, and the syahrs began to unite into groups, each of which was led by whoever within it was the strongest.

A primitive war began over resources, over women, over the remnants of the khhar settlements. Groups rose and united, and by the end of the second century after the Great Exodus, several would-be countries and independent settlements had emerged.

The leader of one such settlement, which would later be called the capital of the Empire, was one Ma Ju Ro. No information of his life before his emperorship remained, but it was he, called the Ruler, who captured all the land of the island and declared himself Emperor Ma Ju Ro the First.

Toward the end of his short-reign, the palace was captured in the pre-dawn light by terrifying fifteen-foot-high iron men in black, shimmering metal helmets. Their leader was a handsome and tall blond man with glowing skin. He called himself the racant Cross. Bored and yawning, he explained to the emperor who ruled the world, and who was a mere genetic pollutant.

"The Cross family," he had said, pinning the emperor with his sharp blue eyes, "will henceforth oversee all activity on the isle of the syahrs, by order of Queen Taira Ra'Ta'Cant. All the island's resources — fish, fruit, ore, precious stones — must be systematically shipped out and handed over to the Cross family. The cult of the Sacred Mother is to be the island's main religion, and you will declare a yearly collection and transfer of resources as an offering to her. We will perform a preventive action of intimidation at midday, including visual effects and an appearance of the Goddess before the common folk."

It remains unknown how much of this Ma Ju Ro the First understood, and how much of it he refused to understand, but by the end of the year, temples to the Sacred Mother Taira had opened all across the Empire, Two-horns was declared the enemy of all humanity, and Ma Ju Ro the First, the Victor, was replaced by Kiloug, also the First, but dubbed the Defender.

The Cross family representative had since then become the fourth advisor to the emperor, humble and unnoticed. But all subsequent empires listened to his advice, and only his. For centuries, one Cross had been replaced by another, but the style of rule over the Empire remained the same: population control, keeping the society's advancement at the same — low — level, and shipping out resources to benefit the Crosses...

"My lord, all is ready," the chief imperial medic Lentz appeared behind the emperor's back. "The donor awaits."

Ma Ju Ro the Fourth nodded, relaxing.

"How much will we be able to transfuse?"

"At least fifteen years, I think. That crook Yadugara, the one who found the donor, managed to perform the procedure on himself. He took twenty years at least. Do you wish the bastard punished?"

"Give him the promised reward," Ma Ju Ro the Fourth shrugged uncertainly. "I don't know, decide for yourself."

"We shall give him the reward," Lentz nodded so fervently that his glasses almost fell off. "And then, should we punish him?"

"If we punish everyone, there won't be anyone left to find donors!" the emperor muttered, annoyed. "Reward him and let him make himself scarce."

Lentz nodded again, though not with the same enthusiasm. His disappointment flashed in the reflection of his glasses. Two-horns take Yadugara! Lentz could have used those years himself! And that rogue Yadugara had even tried to teach him how to perform the transfusion procedure correctly... Him! The chief imperial medic!

The bastard muttered something about the

donor having to be in an exhausted coma for the procedure to work, because he has extremely high resilience to it. Hah! Lentz had a time-tested anesthetic formula that he'd used on many subjects. What could Yadugara possibly teach him? That arrogant fool! If the donor was in a coma, the transfusion could kill him faster than necessary!

Lentz led his ruler to the specially prepared room that had always been used to perform the miracle of rejuvenation. Ma Ju Ro took off his armor and tunic and shivered. He was not embarrassed of his nudity, and it was warm in the room, but the prospect of rejection or failure in the transfusion process scared him every time. It got harder and harder to find a new donor each year. Either the population was dwindling (although how could it get any worse?) or bastards like Yadugara were keeping the donors for themselves.

The donor lay on the next cot, unconscious. He was clearly a *drained* boy, scrawny and ugly with age beyond his years, with narrow shoulders and a childishly fragile neck. Ma Ju Ro thought the boy moved. He looked closer. He had only imagined it, it seemed.

"Once you start it, leave and order the place locked down," Ma Ju Ro said, not wanting anyone nearby in his time of helplessness.

"As usual, my lord! I will return in precisely twelve hours/ As you know, more than that…"

"I know!" the emperor interrupted Lentz in annoyance.

BLOOD OF FATE

Wheezing, Ma Ju Ro climbed onto the cot, making it screech in complaint.

Over three hundred pounds! Lentz thought. *What a whale! He knows all about the strain on his heart! But he still eats like a pig!*

He suppressed those seditious thoughts and got to work. He injected the emperor with a sedative, and in a few minutes, Ma Ju Ro snored peacefully. Then Lentz connected the tethers to the ruler's body and initiated the transfusion.

He stood for a while to ensure that the procedure had begun, then hurried to leave. If the emperor learned that he'd stayed nearby for some reason, there would be questions.

A minute later, the door was locked from the outside, and silence reigned within.

According to the plan, the donor was meant to stay unconscious right up until he died. Instead, he opened his eyes.

The cobblestone streets blushed a warm crimson in the light of the setting sun. There wasn't a cloud in the sky, nor so much as a light breeze to refresh the face.

Somewhere on the outskirts could be heard the shouts of street criers, summoning all comers to the evening prayer, but that would be unlikely to help Kora. Last time she had attended a prayer service in honor of the Sacred Mother had been before her father had departed for the realm of Two-horns.

Back then, the service had seemed somehow magical. People dressed in beautiful clothes had come to the temple, attentively listened to the priest and praised the goddess. Now, on the other hand, Kora realized that she probably wouldn't even be allowed within the temple walls in her dirty rags, no matter how strong her faith might be. It was a mere fair of vanity, lies and sycophancy, a congregation of rich citizens, nothing more than a place to show off. Their eyes greedily darted around, assessing the others: who had a more richly sewn frock, who had larger gemstones, who had a fatter purse? Kora knew that the day would come when she would walk arm-in-arm with her chosen love. Her dress would be better than all the rest. But for now...

Using her last strength to drag a wooden bucket cracked on one side, she poured the soapy brown water into the drain. The girl's muscles cramped with fatigue, and she hurried to rub feeling back into her numb shoulder.

Her mother couldn't get out of bed at all. The neighbor women said that all her symptoms pointed to swamp fever, an illness not to be taken lightly. Her mom needed a doctor right away. It would cost three silver coins to call one out, but the family didn't even have fifty coppers to its name.

This work was so hard! The girl didn't know how her mother did it day after day. In horror, Kora imagined her future as a washerwoman and shivered from the mere possibility.

Two-horns take this poverty! She wanted to hurry and get married so she could live like a human being!

Returning to the tiny family home, the girl cast her tired gaze over the dilapidated little room and the laundry hung all over on ropes. The heat and the constant washing of laundry made the room as damp and stuffy as the public baths. That thought made her chuckle. The baths! Some people actually willingly went and sat in the sweltering heat from white-hot stones! Kora herself had never been there, but she had friends from the brothel near the market. They were only a couple of years her senior, but they'd seen more than the sinners from under Two-horns' tail...

Her mother moaned quietly in the corner. She hadn't regained consciousness since the evening of Luca's trial. The girl sat down tiredly on the edge of the bed. Sticky sweat covered the woman's pale face. Her cheeks were sunken, her eyes puffy with dark circles beneath — far darker than usual. Kora wiped her mother's brow with a damp apron that had been washed so many times it had holes in it. She stared through her mother with a glassy gaze, anxiously biting her lip.

Where was she going to get the money? Kora knew only one method available to her...

The sun finally sank beneath the sharp-pointed roofs. The first lights began to shine in the houses. The girl quickly made herself look relatively presentable and quickly walked up the street, toward the only goal she knew. If anyone who knew Kora saw her now, saw her brow knit in a frown and the fine line of her pursed lips, they would envy her decisiveness.

She was going to the inn in the hopes of making some money. There was only one person who could help her — Vindor. He was an old man permanently displeased with life. Tall, gaunt, but bowed by the hard lot of a one-legged shoemaker. He was once a gladiator at the Arena, where he'd lost his leg and the best years of his life. But his strength of spirit and skilled hands, which sometimes seemed to work all on their own without bothering to consult his alcohol-drenched brain, kept him from falling all the way to rock bottom.

In the girl, he found a grateful listener. When he span out old stories of the Arena after a glass or two, stories of past victories and glories, she listened with half an ear, but made the appearance of sincere interest. Kora was very young when she first discovered the secret of how to stay in people's good graces: all she had to do was listen to them.

In any case, the old man treated Kora well. He never hurt her, and he fed her from his scant stores. And the girl was willing to accept certain minor inconveniences in her struggle to adapt and survive. It didn't take much with Vindor, after all. She just had to listen and smile sweetly.

Of course, there were days — one or two per

week — when the old man lost control of himself. His mood turned particularly vile and his hands got a little too free. That wasn't uncommon in their district, especially at the market, so the girl took it in her stride. Anyway, Vindor always made amends with a coin or two, and the girl's agility helped a little more to disappear from his pockets unnoticed. All in all, it was worth it.

The old man didn't abuse her, and there was a certain threshold he didn't cross. Normally he limited himself to merely pressing up against her in a dark corner of the inn, breathing heavily and stinking of stale whiskey, greedily fondling her barely formed breasts and stroking her backside. By the standards of the slums, he was a true gentleman.

Kora knew that she was beautiful. She'd heard that too often from all kinds of people, but how could she hope that some prosperous member of the capital's high society would see it in her? It was silly!

With the way her life was going, sooner or later she would give in to her friends from the brothel and join them on their path. It wouldn't save her from poverty, but at least she'd always have food and shelter. So far, Kora had somehow kept herself from that fate, whether through some miracle or just disgust. It was better to steal than risk catching diseases that could make her nose fall off, like what happened to Crooked Servilia from their district...

Kora pushed the inn's heavy door open. A

heady mix of sour beer, smoke and male sweat filled her nose. But through these partly familiar spells also came the subtle, barely perceptible scent of roasted offal. Her mouth began to water treacherously, and Kora remembered that she hadn't eaten since the morning, and that had been the usual fare of sickening potato skin soup.

She quickly glanced around the inn. Sadly, the old man Vindor was nowhere to be seen. Cursing her ill-fated plans, the girl hurried to leave before Nemania saw her. When Kora went there with the limping old man, the owner of the inn's only district watched her with his flashing, predatory eyes, but kept silent. That money-grubbing crook would sell his grandmother for a copper, but he wouldn't let a regular customer go, even a not particularly wealthy one like Vindor.

But this time, danger reached her in a form other than Nemania. Irma — a thirty-three-year-old barmaid who would provide certain off-the-menu services for tips — looked worn out in spite of her far from old age. Her eternally greasy slick hair and a crooked scar on her lower lip — a gift from an ungrateful client — did nothing to improve matters.

It wasn't clear when it had happened, but she'd started to see a competitor in Kora. Each time she saw her, she tried to run her off, or sometimes to keep her from getting in at all. Like now...

"Where do you think you are, little fly?" she asked in unfriendly tones, her hands at her sides. "Grow some tits first, harlot!"

Kora didn't deign to respond, though she liked arguing for fun, sharpening her already sharp tongue. Instead, she spat disdainfully at the barmaid's feet and quickly ran outside before Irma threw something heavy at her. It had been known to happen.

Finally, a breeze! As she came outside, Kora flung her arms out wide. Where, oh Two-horns, where has that old man gone in this hour of need?! Her mom was getting worse, and in despair the girl realized that she'd need to find money for a doctor and medicine no matter what it took. Should she steal again? But she'd promised Prisca that she wouldn't...

Thoughts of money were overwhelmed by the dull ache in her back and the soreness in her knuckles from where they'd rubbed on the washboard. She'd done nothing all day but drag buckets and press sheets heavy with water, and she'd half broken herself hanging them all up.

Kora thought for a moment as she stood by the door to the inn, and failed to notice another danger: Karim's crew had appeared from around a corner. To the right of him walked Fat Peter, the fish merchant's son, cackling, with gleaming smooth cheeks. A little farther away, to the left, Jamal bared his rotten teeth. Not a single glimmer of intellect showed in his grubby face and idiotic smile. Sometimes Kora thought that Jamal could easily gut his own mother when he bared his teeth like that.

"Well, whore, is your cripple of a brother still

alive? Or did they put him out of his misery?" Karim laughed at his own joke.

Kora jerked as if slapped. Anger boiled within her. She could have just spat and run away, but she'd missed the moment and now she was cornered by three boys in a very sour mood.

The girl thought feverishly about what to do. She couldn't run, that'd just spur them on even more. They'd have fun chasing her down, grabbing her, they'd twist her arms, grope her, maybe even kick her. And she had no time to get hurt now! She had to somehow outwit them.

"Hah! He isn't a cripple anymore! He got into a good home! His new master feeds him real meat, not that disgusting gruel your dad thinks of as food! Luca has good clothes and his own room! Maybe I should even thank you. Or should I throw stones at you too? Maybe Master Yadugara will take me in then as well. I wouldn't mind hanging around all day and eating my fill!"

Karim's eyes widened and his nostrils flared. He must have painted himself an entirely different picture, one of Luca being whipped to death in the mines. But this version worked for him too. The boy roared in laughter.

"The cripple has gone to Master Yadugara? Idiot girl! Everyone knows his slaves die quickly!"

Fat Pete grunted like a pig behind him, and Jamal rumbled a low bass laugh. Kora always started fuming quickly when it came to her family. She gritted her teeth and clenched her fists. She took deep breaths like her mother had taught her, tried to steady herself. This wasn't the time for a fight, and the odds clearly weren't in her favor. Measuring all three with her baleful gaze, she tried to squeeze past the boys.

"Out of my way, Karim, I'm in a hurry."

"I'm not done with you yet!" The big guy shoved her so hard she barely stayed upright.

"Get away from that girl!" said a sonorous, authoritative voice as if from nowhere behind their backs.

The boys, not expecting such insolence, clenched their fists and turned around to teach the clever interloper a lesson.

It turned out it was a girl. Tall, full-figured and very beautiful. All three stood dumbfounded with their mouths hanging open.

"Close your mouths. You'll catch flies. Kora, come on! Hurry!"

Kora didn't need telling twice. She dodged around Fat Pete and quickly ran behind the strange girl's back.

"Who are you anyway?" Karim got enough of a grip on himself to say, but with none of the previous confidence in his voice.

"I live in Master Yadugara's house, you grubby little lout." The girl laughed deliberately, baring her fragile white teeth previously hidden by her full lips. "You just try touching me, you'll get torn to shreds!"

The girl turned around with a flourish and

walked away, with her head high, back straight and hips swaying. Karim's gang were still struck dumb, whether by the mention of a man whose dark reputation preceded him, or by a woman more beautiful than anyone in the slums had ever seen.

In the meantime, the unknown girl quickly scampered down the street, away from the inhospitable inn. Kora barely kept up with her.

"I'm Reyna," the girl said, turning. "I have some news from your brother Luca."

CHAPTER 19

ACTIVATING COUNTERMEASURE

FOR THE REST of the trip to the palace, Luca prevented his ability from spending any energy at all. Based on his traveling companions' stressed faces, he guessed the purpose of taking him there. That pity in Yadugara's eyes that the boy had seen was merely the regret of losing a slave, it wasn't sympathy.

The carriage stopped when they reached the palace walls. The guard post reported the healer's arrival and they had to stop at the side of the gates and wait to be met. Yadugara was clearly nervous the whole time, and even lost his temper with Penant, whipping him with his cane. Luca was willing to bet that he was the first choice of target, but bruises from a fresh beating on the boy's body would probably not improve the healer in the eyes of those taking the slave.

The chief imperial medic, Master Lentz, came for the boy personally. He looked strict and youthful, had a bald spot on the back of his head, and wore glasses. He greeted the newly arrived healer dryly and asked just one question.

"Where is he?"

Yadugara ordered Luca to come out, pronounced the words required to transfer the slave to the property of Master Lentz, and tried to pull the highly ranked courtier aside to add something important. Lentz tried to wave him away, but Yadugara was persistent. In the end, Lentz allowed himself to be drawn away a few paces, but Luca's traveler-enhanced hearing caught every word. The key words were about "exhausted coma". Parts of the puzzle began to make sense: the metamorphosis required energy to work and protect its carrier.

While the healers talked, with Yadugara heatedly trying to convince his colleague of something and achieving nothing but boring Lentz and making him want to leave, Luca looked around the area.

He saw the palace gardens beyond the gates, with a broad cobble path winding through them. Its tortuous path led upwards to the palace itself, and an imperial guardsman stood every twenty paces along it. It was nothing to do with tradition or romantic ritual. It was more from the numerous coup attempts, both by the aristocracy and by people's rebellions from the poorest districts.

BLOOD OF FATE

The last attempted coup was in the year Luca's father died. Many spoke about it at home, and the little Luca had been horrified. The life of the emperor seemed to him the most important life there could be in the Empire. How could someone try to kill him?

"Follow me, Luca," Lentz enticed him in using his name.

It was unexpected, but nice to hear his own name. The boy followed Lentz.

As he walked through the gates, he turned back. Yadugara pierced him with a reptilian gaze, the veins in his temples pulsing. Penant, still leaning out of the carriage window, frowned and gnawed on his fingernails. Dezisimu felt no hatred for either of them. From the rational point of view he'd inherited from Esk, they'd acted correctly. They hadn't even broken the country's laws! But nonetheless, Luca had no plans to let them go unpunished. He wouldn't go out of his way to take vengeance against them, but if they happened to cross his path again, he'd repay them a hundred times over.

"Are you hungry, boy?" Lentz asked as they walked. "You are worthy of the honor of sharing part of your health with his imperial majesty, and that means you need plenty of it. Don't worry, the procedure is absolutely safe!"

Luca cast a sidelong, distrustful glance at Lentz. Lentz merely stared ahead and spoke, not turning to the boy. Would he not even try to hide the fact that he planned to extract the boy's life? If Esk were with him, he would have laughed, but Luca just shook his head in amazement. *Worthy of the honor indeed!* Oh, if only he could say what he thought about *his majesty* and the safety of the transfusion procedure. But instead, he answered simply.

"I am hungry, Master."

Lentz stopped for a moment, looked at him, nodded, then resumed his rapid pace.

In the palace, the chief medic handed him over to his secretary with orders to wash him, disinfect him and feed him. It would have been better if the food came first, because 'wash and disinfect' took a lot more time than the boy Luca could imagine.

He was shaved again, although his hair hadn't really had a chance to grow since the baths, and covered in something that smelled so strongly that his eyes streamed tears. Then they covered him in a burning powder and forced him to suffer it while his metamorphosis screamed about the aggressive influence and toxic substances all over his skin. Luca forbade his ability from synthesizing the neutralizing compounds that it planned to release through his pores, wanting to preserve energy. *I can handle it*, he decided.

Once the burning powder was washed off, he was taken to the bath. Some fat old woman with nothing but an apron over her naked body dealt with him there, wheezing as she trimmed his nails and rubbed him with sand and a bronze scraper, raking off not only dirt — or indeed, no dirt at all, just skin. Then his metamorphosis reacted without warning, both regenerating his skin and absorbing part of the scraper.

The fat woman couldn't understand how the scraper had worn away so quickly. All she could do was mutter to herself.

"Looks like I overdid it..."

Her mouth agape, she looked the boy over for injuries, but found nothing. Luca carefully kept his eyes away from her pendulous breasts and didn't complain.

After his ablutions were finally over, he was sent to a separate room in the servants' wing. Then dinner was brought in, in two trips. Nothing too refined according to the traveler's tastes, but a divine feast for the yesterday-healed poor cripple. And more importantly, there was lots of it!

He'd never eaten such tasty food, and Koerlig — assistant and Lentz's secretary, a small nimble man with mischievous eyes and a face mottled with pox scars, — had let slip that Lentz wouldn't take him to the procedure looking so ragged, and that he'd be fed for three more days.

And so it was. The morning began with giving various samples for analysis: blood, urine, feces, spit. All this came with a mechanical examination of the body, measuring his chest size and lung volume, comparing his height and weight with the standard for his age. Lentz was trying to figure out how many years Yadugara had taken.

Then he was brought a hearty breakfast, after which Koerlig took him to the ocean and forced him to swim.

Luca overheard Lentz saying to one of his colleagues, "This will strengthen the body and increase the possible transfusion volume."

At first he joyfully floundered around within thirty feet of the shore, the water only up to his knees, but over time he got braver and started going farther and farther out, trying to stay afloat on the surface. And so he discovered the ecstatic experience of weightlessness, when, lying on his back, he felt his body floating on the waves, the salty water stroking him.

His Metamorphosis ability used the sea water in full, pulling in and absorbing salt for some goals to strengthen him that only it knew.

Then, again under Koerlig's tutelage, the boy ran along the beach, where sand had been brought from the south of the Empire. He breathed the salty, pure sea air and felt his heart beating, growing and becoming stronger and more enduring.

Unfortunately, there was no way to escape from the palace without them coming after him, so he just used this gift of idle time and relative freedom to restore his strength and study his own ability. Or rather, abilities — after all, even the most ordinary actions of which his body was capable were new to the former paralytic.

Even Lentz was astounded by how quickly

Luca gained strength, boosted by his metamorphosis. *Phenomenal!* he said. *It's a shame we don't have time to study him in detail. The emperor is in a hurry...*

Every morning, as soon as he'd woken up and before he'd even gotten out of bed, His Imperial Majesty would summon him and demand that the transfusion procedure be performed immediately. He couldn't wait any longer.

In his forty two years, Ma Ju Ro the Fourth felt like a rickety old man. Many ill-judged nights of drinking, the Tassurian weed prescribed by First Advisor Naut, and steady gluttony were killing the emperor faster than new donors could be found.

Another problem was his indiscriminate attitude to women, who could carry hidden diseases sent by Two-horns the Tempter. Sure, Lentz checked the regular courtesans almost every day, but Ma Ju Ro could point to the first lady he liked the look of at a ball and she'd be immediately dragged to the throne so that the ruler could satisfy his lust before the eyes of a public that was no longer surprised by anything...

By the end of the week, His Imperial Majesty's patience ran out. The reason for this was the embarrassment that arose in him when, despite all the efforts of three of his courtesans who were enacting a truly unthinkable fantasy with surprising success, his primary weapon failed him.

So the next evening, right after dinner, Koerlig took Luca to Lentz in the medical wing.

Then the boy was laid down and the chief medic injected him with a depressant that was guaranteed to turn any person into a limp vegetable for at least twenty-four hours.

Luca'Onegut, realizing that the important thing right now was not to screw anything up, ordered his metamorphosis not to fight the intruding substance, to let it work and neutralize it only when the previously identified transfusion procedure starts. He had been studying his abilities systematically over the last few days, and he'd practiced this a few times, initiating something when certain conditions are in effect.

Luca fell unconscious with those thoughts, and when he woke up, Lentz was gone. He himself lay in full darkness, with someone breathing heavily and loudly nearby.

Shining text before his eyes told him that the psychotropic and anesthetizing agents in his bloodstream had been neutralized, because an 'unsanctioned withdrawal of energy reserves' was detected.

Activating countermeasure...
Redirecting flow...
Accelerating interchange processes...

Luca decided to wait for as long as he needed for the procedure to end, and lay listening patiently as the breath of the man nearby steadily grew quieter.

BLOOD OF FATE

The emperor didn't have much life left in him, and by midnight, Luca had regained only part of what he had lost, gaining youth at the cost of the now late Ma Ju Ro the Fourth. Or rather, soon to be late. His numbers were all under ten percent.

Without catching the tethers, Luca sat up on his cot and thought of what to do next. He knew he had to run, but where to? His knowledge of the Empire's lands were limited to the district in the slums where he lived now, and the district of his parents' former home. What lay beyond the capital? How large was the Empire? Were there other islands nearby? Did there really exist a land of mutants somewhere beyond the mountains? That was where, rumor had it, all those infected with Two-horns' curse in the mines were exiled.

Luca either heard or imagined some sound, and immediately after it, messages filled up his vision.

Operation successful!
Absorbed: 5.27 years of life force.

Tsoui points: +21. Current balance: 22.

Metamorphosis: +1.
Ability level two reached!
Gained the capability of copying other lifeforms of the same kind.
To avoid abuse and for the sake of universal balance and harmony, this ability may be used only

once a year (in Wheel time).

In the moonlight, Luca looked over at the body lying nearby and smiled.

The morning of the new day had long since faded into noon, but Yadugara was still in his bed. No, he wasn't sick. On the contrary, adrenaline still rushed through his veins from the sleepless night he'd spent in the company of the passionate Reyna. Each new transfusion procedure overjoyed him like an exquisite and rare treat, each representing another extension of the time left to him. He savored his newly obtained youth and the vibrant health and roiling hormones that only it could provide.

But this time everything was different. His body wasn't just younger. It was as if he had soaked up all the thirst for life and passion for the novel and unknown that the country boy Dezisimu had. He seethed inside. His body demanded a new dose! More, more, more! These long-forgotten feelings were so heady and intoxicating. But it was harder to find a new donor with each passing year.

His brain released the torpid tendrils of disappointment into his veins. They stretched toward the mage's heart, entwining it and squeezing the life out of it. His prey had fallen from his grasp and gone instead to that fat bastard! Ma Ju Ro was unworthy of transfusion! Better he lay down and die, that spineless, dull pig!

Yadugara anxiously suppressed his seditious thoughts and looked around. There were whispers in the palace that the emperor's carefree mother may well have borne her son by a man other than her husband, but there was no point in thinking about that. The watching oracles — old women who survived through their wisdom — might intercept his rebellious thoughts. Of course, nobody believed them to be effective, but the healer had always prided himself on his caution. You never know.

However, thoughts of the fifteen years of life he had snatched away were an excellent remedy for his bad mood. However painful it was to lose Luca, the healer's hopes for the former slave's sister warmed his heart, encased though it was in narcissistic ice. He would drain every last drop from that creature! And this very day, no less!

Their initial analyses and tests showed positive results — it was incredible! Two full-fledged donors, rich with decades of life, had been found in such a short time! The elder Dezisimu may be lost to him, but the girl, what was her name — Kora? — was at his full disposal.

Yadugara stretched in pleasure and smiled as he thought about visiting the House of Inspiration, a high-class brothel that took pride in the fact that the emperor himself had frequented it in his teenage years. He had no time to finish the thought. Someone came rushing loudly up the stairs and rapped on the door.

The man hissed in anger, lazily swung his legs off the bed and spoke in an amiable tone.

"I'll kill you."

He stood up easily and freely, no longer feeling the sickening familiar arthritis in his knees that had plagued him for years. He smiled, tensed his muscles, crouched and jumped, almost reaching the ceiling with his outstretched arms.

The one standing outside the door listened. It seemed they'd realized what they'd done and they were now shaking in fear. In the healer's house, it was strictly forbidden to disturb the master's rest. Be there fire, flood or plague, none would dare distract the master from his affairs.

The desperate knocking at the door was replaced by a timid tapping. Truly, the consequences shouldn't be too dire. Yesterday Yadugara could have banished his underling to the basement for several hours for such an offense, regardless of his mood.

Today everything was different. Regardless of who was behind the door, Yadugara would keep the punishment to a light whipping.

He smoothed the edges of his silk pyjamas and pulled the door wide open. He saw young Reyna, her eyes red with tears.

"What's wrong, girl?"

The girl fitfully clenched her fists at her breast, trying to gather herself, but her lower lip trembled and her tongue failed to obey, frozen in fear. Yadugara sensed disaster and his heart began to pound.

"Speak, damn you!"

"Kora... She..."

His good mood jumped straight off a cliff. Frowning, Yadugara moved Reyna aside and shouted in a low voice that boomed throughout the entire house.

"Penant! Senior Apprentice! Abyss take you! Come here, now, before I come down there and pull your stupid head off!"

"He isn't here..." Reyna uttered, hiccuping and snivelling.

"Calm yourself!" Yadugara grabbed her by the shoulders and gave her a good shake.

The girl's teeth chattered a couple more times, then she swallowed and seemed to get a grip on herself. At least, her stupor passed and she managed to blurt out some words.

"I brought her lunch as you commanded, Master I swear on the Sacred Mother, I..."

"Stop!" The healer pulled his hand from the girl's clinging grasp in disgust. "Who is 'her'?"

"The girl! The creature's sister! I did everything as you wanted, sir! She's gone! She... She..."

Yadugara began to realize that his long-awaited guest had scorned her host's hospitality and left his cozy home.

"What?!" the healer roared. "She what?!"

"She... ran away."

"Idiot girl!"

Yadugara pushed his lover to the wall with such force that she hit the back of her head and fell down in a heap on the floor. Paying this no heed, he was already running down the steps two at a time, roaring and nervously plucking at his fluttering silk pyjamas as they strained to contain him.

A blood mist filled his vision. If the girl suspected something, then losing a donor wasn't even the worst of it. Lentz could find out everything! The idiot Penant had let slip at dinner that he'd taken Luca to the palace, and if the sister went to her brother, Yadugara would never see the donor again!

Morons! He'd cut them all into little pieces with his scalpel and feed them to the chinils. Nobody could be trusted! Why wasn't he woken? It was all falling apart! Where was everyone?

It was as if the home had died.

"Who let her out?!" Yadugara shouted. "Penant, you filthy rat, I'll strangle you!"

Not a sound came in answer. The man ran out onto the porch. The sunlight blinded him for a moment, and a cold gust of wind gave him a sobering slap. His veil of fury fell.

Clenching and unclenching his fists, Yadugara sighed and went back upstairs to beat the truth out of the only witness to what had happened that he had.

BLOOD OF FATE

Kora stopped. She had a stitch in her side. Her breath came out in wheezes. The toes of her bare feet were on fire from striking against the pavement.

What now? Where could she run? She couldn't go home, that would be the first place they'd look for her. Mom was there! Although she was unconscious with a fever. They'd be too squeamish to touch her.

She'd made such a fool of herself! Why had she trusted them?! The fact that she'd been fed tall tales all the previous day and then locked in a room come nightfall clearly showed that she'd gotten into the kind of trouble she'd never dreamed of before. Karim was right.

And maybe back then she would have been able to twist her way out, but not now.

Her gaze slid to the prize clutched in her small fist. Sparkling with cut facets and multicolored gemstones, the silver candlestick glimmered in the sunlight. Kora couldn't help but admire its fine filigree stand, entwined with leaves made of wire, and its crest in the shape of flowers.

Remembering herself and glancing around furtively, she sat down and covered the object in mud, so it wouldn't stand out in the dirty and fetid district. People's throats had been cut for less.

She was such an idiot! She had nowhere to go now, and this trinket was weighing her arm down.

Who would she sell it to? It was too noticeable, too expensive. She should have chosen something small.

The night before, after some so-called 'medical research,' Reyna had let Kora into a room and then instantly slammed the door behind her. She'd heard the crunch of the lock as the key turned.

The girl was lost. Luca wasn't in the house, but at first, they'd tried to convince her that her brother would be back. That self-important Penant, who strutted around like a peacock, told her that he was in the palace, but Kora noticed the flash of Yadugara's angry gaze, and the senior apprentice immediately corrected himself, saying that her brother would return soon. One day soon. All she had to do was wait.

Luca was in the palace? Did they take her for a complete fool? Kora didn't believe a single word from them after that, and the locked door in the room finally convinced her — nobody there was on her side. Her brother was probably already dead, and the same fate would have come to her if she hadn't escaped.

Estimating the thickness of the bars on the window, Kora quickly glanced around the room and then put her eye to the keyhole. At the last moment, she saw Reyna calling someone called Daler as she walked away. If they put a guard outside her room, her chances of escape would be paltry.

The girl was used to adapting quickly and taking decisions instantly. Survival at any cost was the only goal in the life of anyone who lived in their district. The skill came down through the mother's milk, and it forced the dwellers of the slums to rise each day from their sorry excuses for beds and go out to find food.

That was when Kora's gaze landed on the ill-fated candlestick. It had the fine wires of a flower ornament coiled around it. Not hesitating for a second, the girl twisted out one of the wires and broke it. Running to the door and falling to her knees, she started to fashion a lock-pick out of the wire. The old man Vindor had taught her this once.

Her thin fingers with their broken dirty nails shook and disobeyed her. She kept dropping the lock-pick on the floor. She held her breath each time, listening. Finally, the crooked end of the wire caught and pulled at the weighty lock catch. As if it was doing her a big favor, the catch lazily and slowly turned, releasing the prisoner.

She didn't remember running through the house and garden, hopping the fence, rushing barefoot through the empty alleyways. Only now, standing and trying to calm her galloping breath, did she realize that she'd stolen something. And if she'd nearly been sent to the mines for some soused apples, then for this...

She couldn't return what she'd taken even if she wanted to. It wasn't her conscience that bothered her. On the contrary. Master Yadugara had a whole cabinet of trinkets like this one. He wouldn't even notice right away that one had gone missing.

On the other hand, Kora could sell this expensive bauble and get treatment for her mom! Now that her illusions about her brother had been dispelled, she was ready for everything. She tried not to think about the fact that the city watch would probably be looking for her. She needed to solve problems as they came up, as the alcoholic former gladiator had taught her.

Getting her bearings, the girl saw the familiar crooked and discolored sign of the inn.

Vindor! That was who would help her!

Opening the heavy and screeching door slightly, Kora saw just an empty room with flies flying around near the ceiling. Of course! It was still morning! All the local drunkards would be sleeping off last night, some at home, some in a nearby ditch.

The barmaid Irma jumped out from behind the door and grabbed the girl by the arm.

"Where do you think you're going, harlot? You come in here like it's your home! I'm going to tell Nemania that you're looking around for something to steal, he'll sort you out!"

"Let me go!" Kora said quietly.

"Why are you here?"

The barmaid's cunning eyes landed on the dirt-covered candlestick. One silver flower bud stuck out from the clumps of mud.

"Two-horns' impure mother! Are you sick of living?!" Irma whispered, covering her mouth in shock. "Where did you get this, tramp?"

The gears in the barmaid's head began to turn. Her nostrils flared and her eyes turned crazy. She was already imagining the heap of shiny new coins that could be gotten for selling such a thing. She'd be able to pay off all her debts and leave that damned innkeeper!

Keeping hold of the girl's wrist, apparently afraid that she might run away, Irma quickly tore off her filthy apron and shouted to someone inside the building.

"I'm going out for a while!"

Pushing the girl out into the street, she dragged her skinny, newly appeared guardian angel into a nearby alleyway. Kora had no more strength left to fight and flee.

CHAPTER 20

METAMORPHOSIS LEVEL TWO

THE IDEA of turning into the emperor came to Luca as soon as he realized what level two metamorphosis gave him. He didn't know what he'd do with Ma Ju Ro's original body yet, or how to explain to Lentz how his own had disappeared. All he knew was that he had to escape by any means.

But after the idea came the decision. Luca realized that if he did have to explain anything to anyone, it wouldn't be to him. Rulers didn't have to explain themselves to anyone, right? But in that form, he could surely help his mother!

It was decided!

All he had to do was think it. There were no buttons, interface icons, nothing but the will of the carrier.

BLOOD OF FATE

Copying requires physical contact with the subject.

Luca slid off his lounger and sat on the neighboring one. The former emperor's fat body left him almost no room, and the boy had to push his cold arm off the couch. That was when his level two metamorphosis got the physical contact it needed.

Analyzing sample...
Species match: 100%.
Subject satisfies copying requirements.
Continue?

Luca nodded unwillingly and got a range of warnings.

The body of carrier Luca Dezisimu will be transformed into the subject Emperor Ma Ju Ro the Fourth.
Estimated copying time: 6 hours.

As soon as Luca thought again about how he might hide Ma Ju Ro's real body, and how Lentz would take the slave's disappearance, metamorphosis suggested a solution.

Do you wish for the subject Emperor Ma Ju Ro the Fourth to transform into Luca Dezisimu?

Do you wish to record the genetic code of

the body of Luca Dezisimu?

Do you wish to overwrite the carrier's memory?

Attention! The carrier's memory will be partially lost!

"Yes! Yes! No!" Luca nearly shouted, panicking out of fear that the ability might not understand him correctly.

But it worked. The ability performed his mental commands as he wanted: it left him his own memory, the essence of his self, and entered the information on his own body into the archive.

Copying process started.
Transformed: 0.000000001%...

The percentage points rose, and Luca started itching like he never had before. His entire body itched, and then tiny probes finer than a human hair started emerging from his every pore. Thousands of them kept growing and growing until they reached the emperor's body and melted into it.

The very sight of it made the boy feel sick, and the skin on his shaven scalp tightened, non-existent hairs raising on the back of his neck. Luca fell to the floor, curled up and prayed for only one thing: that all this would end quickly. He didn't just feel himself changing. He saw it. The ability grew his bones, his muscle fibers, his tendons and ligaments, actively generated fat cells, forming the same strategic supplies that Ma Ju Ro the Fourth had.

The changes didn't come in stages, but all at once all over his body: his hair grew, and everywhere, since Ma Ju Ro was very hairy. His vision turned poor, his teeth rotted, his liver cells withered and the walls of his veins thinned...

At the same time, the ability caught its carrier's wishes — Luca was going insane from the itching — and reduced his sensitivity. The itching stopped. The boy stopped feeling anything at all.

Metamorphosis created a perfect copy, two at the same time. Esk would have told him it would have been easier to swap minds, but Esk didn't exist anymore, and Luca's thoughts were too chaotic and entangled. What next? Why was he transforming into the emperor if his first conversation would give him away as an imposter? How were mom and Kora doing? What should he do with the Tsoui points he'd earned? Spin the Wheel, or save them? Why was his heel itching?

His heel itched with incredible ferocity, and his ability was too busy with the copying to fix it. Luca tried to reach down, but his body refused to obey...

By the time it all ended, the boy's mind had switched off entirely, and the first rays of sunlight shined through the shuttered window.

Copying process completed.
Transformed: 100%.

Finished with the operation, metamorphosis went to sleep, having exhausted all its reserves. The transformation had devoured everything. It hadn't touched the emperor's fat supplies, since that contradicted the command to make a perfect copy.

But Luca woke up. He intuitively felt that Lentz would appear at any moment. It would be a shame to screw up at the first stage of the plan he came up with in a moment of doubt before starting the transformation.

Through sheer strength of will alone, twisting from the ache in his stomach, almost falling over from hunger with this new, heavy and clumsy body, he carefully lifted up the puny and small body that he recognized as his own and placed it on the sofa he had been lying on. It was important not to break the tethers, which turned out to be difficult, but possible.

Then he lied down himself, on the seat the emperor had been on. Something stung in his chest, and he instinctively activated his ability to find out what it was.

Attention! Detected increased blood clotting in heart vessels and chambers!
Attention! Harmful microorganisms!
Blood clot detected!
Blood clot detected!
Blood clot detected..!

A column covered his entire vision, screaming

about the avalanche of ever new blood clots. Luca realized that he was dying, and as he was dying, he wanted more than anything to live. His desire matched the action his metamorphosis had already begun, having decided that the carrier's health was more important than the copy's accuracy.

His fat supplies provided enough energy to neutralize all the harmful microorganisms, break up all the blood clots, and then the metamorphosis seemed to take a liking to the job and started fixing his organs.

Luca was lying down with his eyes closed when he heard someone enter the room. There were two of them. He recognized one by his voice.

"Good morning, my ruler!" Lentz said with exaggerated enthusiasm and volume.

"Good morning, Your Imperial Highness!" the second added in oily tones.

The boy in the emperor's body wanted to respond to the greeting, but something told him that he shouldn't react for now. Moreover, it was best not to reveal that he could hear them at all.

"Did it work, Lentz?" the second one asked in a whisper.

"It surely must work, Naut! The injection I gave him before the procedure had a delayed effect for half a day. If I'm right, his heart has already stopped!"

"I hope you knew what you were doing!" Naut whispered hotly, the first imperial advisor, as Luca had managed to determine previously. Rezsinius will nail us to the wall if we let him down!"

"Stop worrying!" With those words, the chief imperial medic walked to Luca and touched his neck, feeling for his pulse. "Two-horns!" He's still breathing!"

"Did he hear us?" Naut asked in horror.

"I doubt it. But even if he did, what does it matter? His blood is thickening with clots as we speak. They'll kill him soon enough."

Luca heard the physician's clothes rustle as if he was shrugging his shoulders.

"What do we do now? Wait for him to die, or call the Council? We could say the emperor is ill, the transfusion procedure went wrong..."

So someone wanted him dead here too! Luca mentally went through all the curses he knew and those he'd learned from Esk, naming in vain a range of otherworldly gods. Then he sat up sharply and spoke.

"You know, Lentz, it seems the transfusion procedure really did go wrong."

First Advisor Naut screamed like a girl and fell to the floor as his legs gave way. Lentz behaved with more courage. He just whispered:

"Sacred Mother!"

A few years before, when the entire country was lousy with thieves and unemployment, some of the population fell into unprecedented poverty. But as in all times, there was another side to the coin. There were always enterprising people in society that were willing to earn off anything and everything. Nemania Kovachar, at that time trading in vegetables, was one of them. A smooth, slippery and unpleasant character who would sell his grandmother for a copper.

Easily and with a smile, Nemania cheated citizens that were already poor enough: he had his fingers on scales, he made old produce look fresh, he short-changed and swindled, and all the while was in his element.

It seemed there were so many complaints against the dishonest merchant that the Sacred Mother had listened to the aggrieved. Or perhaps he himself was guilty by cheating someone he shouldn't have. Whatever the case, his dark reputation played a cruel trick on the cunning fox. Thieves found out where he hid his ill-gotten gains and cleared him out in full.

It was like a hammer-blow to the gut, losing spoils so hard-earned through backbreaking labor that had nearly sent the merchant to his grave. But time went on, his well-fed and healthy body had no intentions of dying, so he had to keep living. Nemania had no intentions of being poor.

In his despair he decided that he didn't have much left to lose, and went to the thieves' guild to request an audience and mercy.

His trading skills, the ability to converse with

anyone, even a fellow shyster, and his endless, but measured flattery helped him to cosy up to one gang leader. A captain, as such criminal bosses called themselves.

History is silent on the subject of what Nemania promised the captain, but aside from getting back part of his lost money, he was also given a building for a small watering hole, where all the gang members could go at any time, to spend time without fear of getting caught by the guards, to discuss their illegal activities and celebrate the guild's victories.

By hiring poverty-stricken workers willing to be paid in the most meager food, Nemania continued down his path to riches at double the pace.

On one of those days, the young and naive orphan Irma came to him, wandering around in search of alms and finding the inn. Perhaps it was their similarity that drew the innkeeper's attention to the girl, or perhaps the circumstances aligned just right, but the position of barmaid became hers.

The girl had a watchful eye, a calculating mind and a strong fist. She quickly realized that cushiest spots were where coins rang. And she had been marching staunchly toward her goal for many years, searching a path upwards, to riches and prosperity. Away from the dirty, befouled tables eternally stinking of sour beer, away from the ever drunk, fetid, brawling peasants. As far away as she could get from the tortuous and stuffy nightmares of poverty that plagued her day and night. To a place where the ring of small, lonely bouncing coins grew into ringing streams, and the coppers within them, spinning, their metal edges gleaming, fell into rivers of money, which in turn merged with the magnificent ringing echo of a golden ocean.

And maybe this was it, the first small step to that dream? Irma kept hold of the girl with a death grip.

"You don't understand anything! Let me go, idiot!" the girl hissed. "Don't take me to Nemania! I just need money! Now!"

"Worried about your cripple brother, are you?" Irma chuckled. "Stop struggling and shouting, fool girl! As if I'd share with that skinflint! He'd swindle milk from babies!"

After realizing that Irma was only interested in selling the candlestick, the girl even relaxed a little at first, and walked obediently along a couple of streets, letting the girl lead her. But then she got worried again.

"You know, this is my candlestick! And I almost got killed when I got it! Let me go, you hear me?!"

Irma turned and spat in response,

"If you don't shut your mouth, little bitch, I'll finish you off myself so you don't suffer! You forgotten where we are? Look around and shut up!"

The words had no effect on the girl.

"Irma!" Kora dug in her heels and yanked Irma by the arm. "I said stop!"

Irma took a deep breath to try and calm down. She kept her eyes on the bundle in Kora's arms.

"If you don't want to come, then don't!" The barmaid dropped the girl's arm and grabbed the candlestick. She pulled it from Kora's weak grasp and shot her a spiteful glare. "Only I'll take this with me."

The girl finally lost it. Kicking out at Irma, she pulled the valuable find back. Irma just laughed, watching as the girl's eyes widened in her vain efforts. The skinny, fifteen-year-old Kora with her barely noticeable chest and the grown-up, wide-hipped, always well-fed Irma, who hadn't felt a lack of food in many years. The inn's customers appreciated the ever accommodating barmaid's services enough to feed her from their own plates. The barmaid's powerful build and healthy diet made her good at fighting for a place in this world. Sometimes she personally dragged limp drunkards out into the nearby ditches without the bouncers' help.

One more pull and the girl fell on her ass on the sidewalk. Irma chuckled victoriously, held her newly won prize close and hurried away.

The girl didn't give up. She jumped up and scurried after her. Soon Irma realized that the girl had decided to change her tactics.

"Irmy, honey," Kora began to snivel and pluck at the barmaid's skirt, "they forced themselves on me, and they wanted to take me away and leave me outside the city. I played dead and just managed to get away while they were in another room. I took that candlestick specially! There has to be at least some kind of payment..."

The words resounded in Irma's heart with something familiar and close to her. She stopped. Subconsciously, she had always envied Kora's natural beauty and she knew that in a year or two, she'd make a serious competitor. Maybe that was why she'd always given the girl the cold shoulder and chased her out of the inn? Although sometimes, usually when she'd been drinking, sympathy awoke within Irma, and then the barmaid wiped away her tears and complained of her rotten life, of how men were ungrateful pigs. All they wanted was to get off, and as soon as it came to payment, they'd start arguing. There were exceptions, of course, but they were very rare.

Kora kept talking, and Irma listened.

"My mom has swamp fever, Irma! If I can't pay for a healer, she'll die! They already killed Luca! And soon," the girl sobbed, "they'll get mom and me too. Please... I need this money..."

Irma stood holding the candlestick to her chest. She chewed on her full, wind-chapped lips and shifted in doubt. Money was all she ever dreamed of and thought of twenty four hours a day. When she'd seen the precious object, she hadn't even considered sharing with the girl. Now she hesitated. The picture she saw developing before her was far too familiar for her liking... She had had nobody to help her when she'd needed it.

Biting her lip until it turned white as if trying to decide something, the girl freed one hand and began to estimate the cost of a healer with her fingers. A couple of minutes later, Irma sighed heavily.

"Ugh, you dumb pesky chinil, fine," she muttered and smiled crookedly. "What are you staring at? Let's go! But be quick and quiet!"

The port district was not famed for its cleanliness and tidiness. Although both girls were used to that in their own district, the stink of rotten fish seeping from every inch of the place made their eyes stream.

"Ugh! Where are we going?" the girl asked nasally as she pinched her nose closed.

"Shut up and keep up. I hope he's there."

"Who?"

Irma walked decisively to one of the port's huts with Kora barely keeping up behind her. A drunken and discordant choir mixed with curses drifted from the entryway The songs extolled the virtues of the sea king, a rich life and dockside whores all at once.

"Abyss! It's the morning and they're still hammered. This is the third day since they moored up and they're still boozing. Stay here, I'll be quick," Irma said to the girl.

"Fat chance!" Kora knitted her brows decisively and stuck with the barmaid. She didn't want to let her treasure out of her sight for an instant. "I'm coming with you!"

"Hah... Sure. Come on then. Entertain the boys. Since when did you get so brave? These guys aren't like sweet old Vindor. And this district is much more dangerous!"

But the girl didn't want to hear it.

"I'm coming with you!"

"Go where you like. You don't have anything left to lose!" Irma laughed hoarsely at her own joke and ducked into the low entryway.

From that point, events developed so quickly and unexpectedly that they didn't have time to know what was happening. A man flew out of the door and nearly bowled Irma over. And that would be fine, but then another came rushing out with his fist raised, cracking the first one in the jaw. Flying to the side, that one knocked the package from Irma's arms and the brawling crowd forced her away from the hut.

More and more drunk men ran out of the house and jumped into the melee with victorious cries of "For the Sea Father!", indiscriminately beating whoever was closest. The dirty priceless object lay at the entrance, trampled into the mud. None of the men paid the slightest attention to it.

Irma saw Kora choosing her moment to slip between the brawling men, grab the candlestick and start to slowly retreat around the corner of the house. Sacred Mother forbid that they see her and take it!

But the girl didn't even have time to scream

as someone grabbed her by the scruff of the neck and dragged her into the black maw of the entrance.

The room was gloomy, and after the light of the street the darkness seemed particularly creepy. There were two tiny holes beneath the ceiling in place of windows, but they let in practically no light.

Tripping over the threshold and falling, Kora nimbly scurried on all fours away from her attacker until she banged her forehead into a wall. There the girl froze, listening, seeing nothing before her and not knowing where to go.

"Gotcha, little slut!" a sinister voice whispered.

Kora heard some sort of rustling nearby, someone unfamiliar swearing and a catty shriek from Irma. Suddenly she felt freer, nobody was holding the girl anymore. Irma stole up to her and quickly grabbed her by the leg. Kora wailed loudly.

"Don't fall behind!" Irma whispered angrily. "What's the matter with you? Follow me and stay quiet! And keep your head down..."

Kora, sighing with relief, shuffled after the barmaid. A long walled corridor of roughly hewn planks brought them to a small cubbyhole. The entrance was covered with a lop-sided sheet. Irma moved the cloth aside as if she owned the place and walked inside.

"Hello, Ramo!"

"Irma?" the ragged man sitting in the small room said in surprise. "What're you doin' here? I don't have time for this!"

"Look what I brought." Irma unfolded the package. "We need to sell this at a good price."

"What's this?" He turned the candlestick in his hands, bit it. "Where's it from, huh? And who's this piece?"

"From nowhere special," Irma cut him off. "And the girl is with me. So are you gonna help us?"

It was crowded for the three of them in the tiny room lit by the stub of a candle. The short and scrawny Ramo looked like a teenager next to the full-bodied Irma, but at that moment he held himself proudly, puffing out his meager chest. He was a new recruit to the thieves' guild and hadn't had a chance to stand out yet, but this shiny trinket could turn into a feather in his cap and a pass into the inner sanctum. If Irma understood anything, it was this world. Ramo's boss, Bakhr, was highly selective. It cost a lot to become part of his clique.

"Nobody saw?" Ramo asked, his eyes narrowing.

Irma shook her head. He nodded, pulled a rag from under the bed in a businesslike fashion and wrapped up the loot.

"That's good," the thief grinned, his teeth gleaming with metal.

CHAPTER 21

THE CLEAREST EVIDENCE

LOOKING AT THE PROSTRATE First Advisor Naut and Chief Imperial Medic Lentz, Luca the Emperor's imagination ran wild. He could change his plans with consideration for new circumstances.

It was incredible, but even without Ma Ju Ro's memory, Luca knew how to talk to these two. The copying had left its mark, and certain templates of behavior and shallow memory remained in Dezisimu from the original Ma Ju Ro the Fourth. It was worth trying to use it. In any case, he could always correct it as he went along.

"Why have I not lost weight, Lentz?" he whined. "What is this, I ask you?!"

He slapped his huge wobbling stomach to demonstrate and knitted his brows into a fearsome frown. Esk's legacy told him how to behave, and the only correct position in his situation was to demand, insult and attack. Luca decided to hold back his knowledge of their unsuccessful conspiracy and assassination attempt. It could be his trump card. Let them squirm and wonder whether he'd heard.

"Um... Forgive me, great ruler!" The chief imperial medic fell to his knees and pressed his forehead into the cold marble floor. "Something truly went wrong! I will fix this, your magnificence!"

"You have lost a little weight, my ruler!" First Advisor Naut muttered fawningly. "You know that I never lie to you, that is what you value me for, my lord, that I always tell you the truth, no matter how bad it is..."

Luca kicked him in the side in disgust. He'd have to show his cards after all, but he could put pressure on one. If they both attacked him in desperation, he'd have to kill them both, and he needed information.

"What crap are you spouting, worm? Do you think I'm so stupid that I can't tell myself whether I've lost weight?"

Naut shook even harder.

"Master of the palace guard! To me! Now!"

He couldn't help but reinforce his words with another kick, this time on the first advisor's fat backside. He overdid it. The advisor's face crashed into the floor before he could get his hands down, and he broke his nose.

"Do you wish me to summon him, o great

ruler?" Lentz offered his services. His eyes darted around. It didn't take a mind-reader to realize that he was planning to run!

"His Majesty made it clear that the assignment was for me," Naut wheezed out nasally through his bleeding nose. "I will fetch him, lord!"

He rose up heavily, his knees cracking, and staggered toward the door. There was a reason that Luca had decided to let him go, and not the cunning Lentz. It was best to clarify the conspiracy one on one.

"Stand up and sit on the couch, Lentz. Let's talk seriously without that dumbass."

Raising himself from the floor, the chief imperial medic cast an astounded glance at his ruler, something flashing in his eyes. He sat and even went so far as to look into the ruler's eyes with some scientific interest.

"Forgive me for that little demonstration, but otherwise you might not believe me and might make a fatal error for yourself, my dear healer," Luca said with a barely visible smile. "Watch closely! And don't move!"

He lifted his hand palm forward to Lentz. The healer's eyes widened and his forehead began to sweat. Something living emerged from the center of the emperor's palm, with oily whitish scales and a gleaming stinger at its tip. When it reached Lentz's forehead, the tentacle stabbed its sharp tip into him. A drop of blood fell. The healer's breath caught. He would have run as fast as he could if only he wasn't paralyzed by fear.

"You see, the procedure really did go wrong. The body of this young man," the ruler nodded toward Ma Ju Ro, now a copy of Luca, "was home to a divine entity. And in the transfusion, it became part of me. Which means that your treacherous plan to kill me has failed. Now I cannot be killed by any means. You, however, will die if you lie to me about anything."

Luca ordered the tentacle to pull back. In the main, it was entirely useless. His ability created it from surplus fat cells, adding a little iron to imitate a stinger, but the newly crowned emperor knew that if he had the desire and the building material, he could grow more than just props.

"A part of this entity is now within you. Do you feel it?"

Lentz' eyes crossed as he looked at the stinger and he nodded, covered in large droplets of sweat.

"If you do or say anything that somehow harms me, you will die. Even if I die, your loyalty from then will be measured not by me, but by the divine particle inside you. Name those party to the conspiracy against me. Who is their leader? You?"

Luca fashioned two new tentacles and jabbed them into Lentz's temples. He gulped and froze, fearing to move a muscle. Sweat covered his brow.

"Oh, well. I think Naut will be more talkative..."

"Wait, my ruler!" the healer choked out in a whisper. "Promise me that you will not sentence me to death or touch my family!"

"You're stealing time from yourself," the emperor yawned. "Naut will be back any minute with Hector, and you'll both go to the gibbet. Or the block, I haven't decided yet."

"Emperor! Ruler!" Lentz begged. "I'll tell you everything, and you decide, just listen!"

"Speak."

"The Empire is falling into the abyss, my ruler," the medic said with exaggerated vigor, then winced, awaiting a reaction. Luca nodded encouragingly and Lentz continued. "The high circles of the capital's aristocracy — and the whole country's! — is under the impression that..."

"That what?"

"That your majesty is, as it were, not very interested in ruling the country. In practice, your power extends only to the capital, while all the other territories have long been under the control of local barons. They pay no taxes, they ignore the Empire's laws, their people grow poorer and poorer. Epidemics are breaking out all across the Empire! And that's without the Wastelands, which has long been a separate country."

"What's there, in the Wastelands?" Luca asked. He knew that somewhere to the north was a giant desolate area full of mutants, entirely twisted monsters, those who had been banished from cities and villages for centuries. "Are there problems?"

"The last raid by the mutant horde reached the northern edge of the capital, ruler. This was reported to you."

"And what did I do?"

"Does my ruler not recall?" Lentz asked with interest, forgetting the tentacles and leaning forward slightly. "Is this the action of the entity?"

"Yes, it is a side effect, Lentz. You will be my memory now, if... If you remain loyal to me and alive after your tale. And I advise you for now to limit yourself to details of the conspiracy. Your time is running out."

"Your younger cousin Rezsinius, heir to the throne, has decided to overthrow you. The attempt to do this through me is just one of his plans, and not even his main one. He has managed to assemble an army in the south from a number of veterans that you tricked by promising them land and gold after they captured the throne."

"Tricked?"

"It is a long story, my ruler."

So, Rezsinius then... Luca thought for a moment. The original Ma Ju Ro rarely recalled his cousin, long ago sent to the southern province, and Luca could only bring up an image of a skinny boy with a stubborn gaze. He recalled the cousin coming to visit last year, but why?

Thinking of Rezsinius as a cousin suddenly jogged his memory. Family! Kora! Mom! He had to order them to be brought to the palace at once! He could say that he wanted to thank the family for... Himself? Yes, for the boy who gave his life for his emperor.

"Who else among the courtiers is in on the plot? The other advisors? The master of the guard?"

"No, ruler. Only Naut and I. He was promised the Oltonian Mines and to keep his position as first advisor."

"What were you promised?"

"Nothing special, your majesty. I agreed to this from idealistic motivations, as I could see the great Empire falling into hell. Rezsinius seemed to be more enterprising and... worthy, ruler. I am not worthy of forgiveness!" Lentz wailed, somewhat theatrically.

The emperor raised an eyebrow. "Is that it?"

"I was also promised a threefold increase in our biological and medical research budget, my ruler. As you know, I am the deacon of the university's medical faculty..."

Lentz bowed his head. At that moment, someone burst into the room. Luca cut off his decorative tentacles just in time. One fell, but the other remained hanging from Lentz's temple.

The ruler calmly pulled the hanging tentacle from the healer. "What's this? Something stuck to..."

Girlish laughter behind him interrupted his words. "My little piglet is awake!"

Lentz couldn't hold back a smirk. Turning around, the emperor saw Keirinia, his current favorite courtesan, a heavily rouged lady with huge thighs hidden by nothing but fishnet stockings. And oh, Two-horns, it had a part cut out! Right there!

The boy blushed and automatically turned his

eyes away, but then took a hold of himself and looked at the woman strictly.

"Emperor Ma Ju Ro the Fourth is your ruler as well, woman. Now leave this room, otherwise you'll live the rest of your life in a pigsty! Where is that damn Hector?"

Keirinia laughed.

"You're so strict today, my little piglet! So it all went well and your blood is boiling, huh? I want to check that right now!"

"I am not joking, Keirinia. Get out and close the door behind you."

Something in his tone made her believe the threats. She shot a frightened glance at Lentz who nervously twitched his shoulder. Luca didn't know what that gesture meant, but his ex-favorite bowed low, her breasts popping out of the tiny gown she'd stuffed them into, and, without hiding them, left the room.

Following her with his eyes and making sure the door was shut, Luca came closer to the healer. A broad and happy smile lit up Lentz's face.

"You truly have changed, my ruler... Carnality and the lower pleasures always clouded your gaze."

"The entity has changed me, for-now chief imperial medic Lentz. I want more than anything for the Empire to flourish and its citizens to be happy!"

Luca spoke those words earnestly, but whether it was the legacy of the creature Esk within him or his own built-in sense of justice, he didn't know. It all melded into one single 'I' for him.

Lentz slid off the couch to the floor, fell to his knees, rose his head and whispered ardently.

"I trust you unreservedly, my ruler!" He pointed at the door. "I just saw the clearest possible evidence of blessed times!"

Ramo was brought up by the streets. At fifteen, sick of boring and exhausting farm work in the baron's fields, he fled to the city.

As far back as he remembered, he'd made a living from thievery, focusing his efforts on a particularly hateful village ape whose carts he robbed. There could be anything in the bags: potatoes, cassava, hay, and he'd somehow had the bad luck of standing in a sack of manure, but he didn't complain.

Thanks to this unsophisticated, but stable source of income, Ramo more or less flourished, and when a couple of more serious jobs turned up, he was even able to save for his own little bedsit. In those days, he felt like he might as well be a baron. Daily strolls and an endless procession of women, half-witted and not very attractive, but available.

But although the life of a thief was fun, it was also short, and one day, the guards caught their band of merry men. The stars on that day smiled on Ramo. He was the only one that managed to get away. All the others were sent to pay off the damage they'd done, some going into slavery, most going to the quarries. None returned from penal servitude at the pits, plagued as they were with the curse of Two-horns, and Ramo mentally buried his partners in crime.

For almost a month, he wandered and hid in the outskirts, fearing to show his face in the peopled areas of the city. He kept thinking that his former 'friends' would all surely inform on him, and guards would be waiting at his house. Time passed. A couple of times he even ran into patrols, but they showed no interest in his pathetic figure.

Almost a year had passed since then. He was sick and tired of living in constant fear, looking over his shoulder and scraping by on stolen farmers' feed bags. Ramo knew that his destiny in this life was far loftier than stealing food from livestock. Following the rich citizens with an envious gaze, each time he imagined himself in their place.

A month ago, he'd appeared at Bakhr's threshold, a lieutenant to one of the thief captains, Otolik. You couldn't join the ranks of the 'elites' from the streets, and Otolik was considered the right hand of the criminal mastermind Ignatius the Furious. He had to prove himself, draw Bakhr's attention, otherwise he really would spend his life scratching at the bottom of feed bags. But Ramo hadn't managed to do it yet in the last month.

His hut was in the dock district, and his roommates were mostly loading hands and sailors. All in the hut held the deepest indifference for each other. The happy residents appeared separately at the threshold of their home with an enviable inconsistency and various degrees of intoxication. There were also group drinking sessions, at which the neighbors sometimes saw each other's faces for the first time. But every drunken binge ended without fail in a fistfight, and then fraternization all round.

Yesterday's job, which he'd wasted a whole week preparing for, had failed spectacularly. As was traditional, Ramo drank practically an entire bottle of firewater the night before. In the morning, having woken up with a pounding headache and the taste of cat shit in his mouth, he wasn't in the best of spirits.

He didn't have a copper to go toward anything to make him feel better, which naturally did not improve his mood.

When that persistent large-breasted Irma darkened the door of his hut, the man even spat in despair. Back in the good days, he was a regular at Nemania's inn. He'd met the highly accommodating barmaid there. Once she'd wanted to throw him out into the street for his drunken noise, but she'd felt bad for him and warmed up the poor man, at the same time robbing him for all he was worth.

And now she'd come to him personally. The wench must really be in trouble if she couldn't think of anywhere else to melt down that obviously expensive trinket. Sensing his mood, Irma got nervous. She bit her lip.

"Well? Will you take it?"

He ignored her question, feverishly thinking through the options. He knew where to sell the candlestick, but Ramo's next actions would depend on who the girl stole it from. He'd learned to use any chances he had, and now his intuition told him that the opportunity wasn't in selling the item.

"Where did you get this?" Ramo asked Kora directly.

"Nowhere special!" the girl started to get smart with him, repeating the words of her older friend and nervously shifting from foot to foot. "If you like it, give us money and we'll leave!"

"Bite your tongue, little girl, before I hit you round the head with that paperweight!" Ramo snapped.

The sounds of the fight approaching began to come from the corridor. Ramo rose rapidly.

"Two-horns' radiant dick!" he cursed. "We have to get out of here before we all get it in the neck!"

He got out of the dangerous district with Irma and the saucy girl without incident, by putting the most fearsome expression on his face that he could. He already knew what to do with the little thief.

The prestigious area that Bakhr's house was in was very nearby, strangely enough. A questionable neighborhood, of course, but a house with a view over the sea was considered a worthy achievement, and the land here grew more expensive every day.

It was incredible to watch as the dirty, garbage-ridden streets transformed magically into clear, clean pavement with each step. New expensive houses sprang up on each side, surrounded by trees and flowers, and their tall carved fences astounded the eye with their extravagant and original patterns.

The girls gazed from side to side, their heads constantly turning, the younger one with a certain amount of fear — she expected to see guards around every corner. Irma, on the other hand, had a silent adoration in her eyes. Life in a luxurious home was all she'd ever dreamed of, as she'd admitted to Ramo more than once.

He didn't notice the magnificence around them, and was too tired to worry about guards. The man deftly and confidently walked toward his sole target. His consciousness rejoiced, painting him pictures, each rosier than the last. If this worked out, and the object in his hands really was valuable, then this was a real chance to stand out!

"You'll give me half the money, got it? It's my candlestick, I stole it!" The little one seemed to be worried that he'd forget her when it came to splitting the profits. So there was nothing left for the girl to do but remind him of herself and nag him.

"You're like a troublesome fly! Girls nowadays! It's obvious you're growing like a weed and have nobody to give you a thrashing!

The girl turned crimson, but didn't back down.

"I'll be sixteen soon! And I've been feeding

myself for a long time!"

"What nonsense!" Irma laughed. "You're a beggar and a thief! Know your place, little girl, or you'll be in trouble! Not now, but later, and sooner than you think."

"You'll hear my name again more than once!" Kora spat. "One day I'll turn up in an expensive carriage, wearing silk, on a rich man's arm! And you'll both bow at my feet!"

"Alright, enough, calm down! And be quiet, I need to think of how to play this with the boss," the thief said, ending the conversation. "We're here."

The scale of Bakhr's house was impressive. Ramo couldn't even imagine why someone would need so much space.

Walking around the house via an alleyway, the company approached an unassuming solid wooden gate covered in ivy, and the thief knocked. After a long wait, a voice came from the other side.

"Who in Two-horns' name are you?"

"It's Ramo, I have a gift for Bakhr."

CHAPTER 22

SPECIAL ASSIGNMENT

FTER THE EMPEROR'S courtesan Keirinia left discouraged, another interruption to their private conversation turned up in the form of Priscilla, the second of Ma Ju Ro's favorite lovers by preference, but Luca sent her away as well, to Lentz's elated laughter, trying not to look at the alluring black triangle.

But Priscilla's nudity — she wore only an airy transparent shawl — lit a fire in Luca, just as it should. At the end of the day, he was a seventeen-year-old boy, and now in the body of the lustful and shameless emperor. Ma Ju Ro was still showing off his naked body, and the reaction of a certain rebellious part of his body was eloquent. Fortunately, Priscilla had already left before she could see the moment of her triumph. The chief imperial healer maintained a tactful silence, deciding not to draw attention to the blood-filled organ.

For some time, Lentz continued to bring Luca up to speed on events until First Advisor Naut interrupted them with the master of the guard, Hector. The first dropped to his knees just in case.

"Your command is done, my ruler! I brought Captain Hector!"

"You brought me, did you..?" the aforementioned captain frowned. "What do you need from me so early in the morning? Naut dragged me from my table as I took breakfast! My food is getting cold! If there is no good reason for it, then I swear on the Sacred Mother, you will be sorry!"

The grey-haired and powerful man with his eagle's nose and massive shoulders looked around. He was dressed in a shirt carelessly tucked into his trousers and clean high-top boots. Luca realized that this was the captain of the palace guard, and much depended on whether he could bring him on side.

The situation was familiar: Esk'Onegut's legacy in the boy's memory instantly brought him examples and templates of behavior. Judging by the fact that neither Naut nor Lentz looked surprised, this sort attitude was typical for the captain of the palace guard. But Luca-Esk was astounded by Hector's arrogance. Seriously? That's how he speaks to his emperor? It seemed the body's former owner had let his authority fall to rock bottom.

"There is a good reason, for-now captain of the palace guard. Just an assassination attempt against your ruler." Ma Ju Ro shrugged and smiled wryly. Lock the door, Hector. This is a conversation that should not be overheard. Oh, and don't let him leave!"

Hector deftly grabbed Naut, who seemed to suddenly have important matters to attend to elsewhere, and then punched him in the gut. And then, kicking his fat ass as a preventive measure, he locked the door and looked at the emperor with interest.

News of an assassination attempt was almost boring. They happened nearly every month or two. But Ma Ju Ro's reaction contrasted sharply with what he was used to seeing: there were no hysterics, stamping of feet or demands to 'stake up every last one of them'! Or had the pig just smoked too much Tassurian weed?

"I gather it was Naut who made the attempt? But how? He can't even hold a spoon for long." Hector looked at the first advisor with disgust as he moaned and writhed on the floor.

"The former first advisor Naut used his position to administer a poisonous substance during the procedure. Unfortunately, he betrayed my trust." Lentz bowed his head with shame. "The emperor is aware and has already decided my punishment."

"What?" Naut wailed, trying to stand. The captain smiled and kicked him again, pinning him to the floor under his boot. "It wasn't like that!"

"Shut him up!" the emperor ordered. "I know how it was."

Hector pulled one of the first advisor's socks off and stuffed it in his mouth. Thinking over what he had heard, he frowned even more and chewed his lips before speaking.

"Ruler..." It was clear that such respectful language came with difficulty. "As captain of the palace guard, and therefore the person bound to protect you..."

"Bound to?" Ma Ju Ro raised an eyebrow. "Oh, dear Hector, I don't want to 'bind' you to do anything! I value that you find yourself able to overcome your reluctance and... disgust? But I would rather you performed your duties willingly. Or do you wish me to sign a corresponding order? Lentz, call the second advisor. We must discuss the structure of the new government."

Turning a deep red, Hector slowly fell to one knee, thinking furiously. Something strange had happened to the emperor, but it wasn't clear what. The captain, forged in decades of covert intrigue as he was, decided to play along for now. The palace guard and the inquisitors were on his side, yes, but Hustig, the general of the army... He hated the captain so much that he would attack him at the slightest hint from the emperor without hesitation.

"Forgive me, ruler. I am an old soldier and rhetoric is not my strong suit. I merely wanted to say that Chief Imperial Medic Lentz is perhaps being... disingenuous. Allow my inquisitors to question him! They can confirm the healer's involvement in the attempt on your life! I doubt this wimp," Hector spat on the cowering Naut, "could have organized it all himself!"

"Stand up, Hector. We will discuss that later," the emperor nodded. "In the meantime, take care of Naut. Lock him in a cage and let your boys deal with him. Confiscate all his money and property into the imperial treasury and isolate his family until we've cleared things up. Make sure you keep a particularly attentive eye on anyone close to Naut, see who twitches after his arrest, who talks and what they say, who meets with who..."

The emperor continued to provide detailed and surprisingly intelligent orders, and Hector's jaw dropped. The same happened to Lentz, and even the former first advisor on the floor stopped writhing and sniveling. The healer was at least prepared, knowing the emperor's true new nature, but for the other two, his words were a complete shock.

Ma Ju Ro had never cared about details. He usually just waved a hand and said "Handle it," and the most qualified person would then handle whatever "it" was. The head of the merchant's guild was complaining of exorbitant taxes? "Handle it," the emperor grumbled without raising his head from Keirinia's ample bosom. The northern barons were asking for protection from mutant raids? General Hustig would take care of it. Only attempts on the head of state shook up Ma Ju Ro, but each bout of hysterics (which could be safely ignored) always ended in the same words: "Handle it!"

It was also worth noting that oftentimes Naut, Hustig and Hector solved such problems behind the scenes in ways that fattened their own pockets. The merchant was given a tax rebate, with a percentage fee paid directly to Naut. A legion was sent to the north, and sacks of Tuaf hops and grain added to General Hustig's personal stores. In a similar manner, Hector took control of the capital's market and seized the villa of an aristocrat who fell from grace.

The master of the palace guard was the first to collect himself.

"It will be done, my ruler! The only thing is..." He hesitated, but then plucked up his courage. "I am afraid that observation in the form your imperial majesty requires is not possible. I have requested many times that you raise the budget allotted to the inquisitors and observers, but both you and the first... the former first advisor Naut have always found reasons to refuse me!"

"Naut, you old rogue!" Lentz delighted. "How did you know that Hector's chained hounds aren't to be fed?!"

Naut bellowed something. Ma Ju Ro nodded and Hector pulled out the stocking.

"And I see you've managed to wriggle your way out of this, Lentz," Naut spat in fury. "You'll see, I'll tell them everything..."

Lentz looked at the emperor nervously, and at

the captain's listening ears.

"I know everything about Lentz's involvement in the conspiracy, and he is forgiven," the emperor said. "As for the lack of funds for observers, use those confiscated from Naut, Hector. We have lost control over the Empire and we are losing it over the city. The people are poor, and the barons, my cousin Rezsinius and the mutants are tearing the country apart. The day has come to do something about it!"

Captain Kolot Hector saluted with his fist to his chest. He wasn't wearing his breastplate, so the sound wasn't right, but the gesture impressed Lentz anyway. The captain usually only performed that salute at the military parades that Ma Ju Ro held every year. And Naut and Hustig had initiated those parades — they cost almost no money, but demanded a significant amount of the city budget.

In the meantime, Naut threw himself at Luca's feet and started begging for forgiveness. Hector wanted to stop him, but Ma Ju Ro signaled to let him speak.

"My emperor! My ruler! For years I have served you faithfully and honestly! When you were... busy with other important matters, I practically bore the weight of ruling the Empire! Taxation, the army, the economy, laws... Nobody but me is capable of grasping all the intricacies of our country's politics! Forgive me, my ruler, and I can still be useful to you! My heart bled when I saw you losing interest in matters of state! What is this physician to you? He knows nothing!"

"It is very clear to me what your 'ruling' has done to the Empire!" Luca said fiercely. "However, that is exactly why I have not ordered you beheaded right here and now. You may indeed still be useful... If you pay for what you have done. Hector, get on with it."

The captain picked Naut up and dragged him to the door. When it slammed behind him, and his agonizing wails in the corridor faded, Luca found his clothes on the floor, his armor and imperial tunic. He pulled them on with the healer's help and shrugged his shoulders. His body was still refusing to obey him. He needed time to get a handle on it, to get used to his center of gravity with all this weight.

"What do you think, Lentz, should I lose some weight?" he asked, preparing to give the order to his metamorphosis.

"Most assuredly, my ruler!" the healer answered. "But this must be approached delicately."

"How do you mean?"

"It must be done very, very carefully. Gradually," Lentz traced a flowing, just slightly sloping curve in the air. "The people see you once per year and will be very surprised if they suddenly see an athletic man in place of the well-fed emperor they know and love. Your profile is printed on all the coins, and you aren't thin there at all! Never mind the full-length portraits of your Imperial Highness! They may suspect an impersonation, my lord!"

"Very well," Ma Ju Ro agreed reluctantly, ordering his body to reduce his fat deposits by five percent over a week.

His obedient metamorphosis ability accepted the command, and it occurred to Luca that it wouldn't hurt to go for runs along the shore. It would make a good explanation for his future weight loss.

The sound of the emperor's rumbling stomach could clearly be heard in the reigning silence.

"Would his imperial highness like to have breakfast?" Lentz asked, gulping. "On my way here, the most breathtaking smells were coming from the kitchen..."

"We will break our fast together soon, Lentz. But right now, I have a delicate assignment for you. I would like to somehow thank the family of this boy," he nodded toward his former body. "Invite them here and bring them to the palace, but so that nobody finds out about it. And when you go for them, take medicine — the mother has swamp fever. Don't ask how I know, I just know."

"Fever? Then I must hurry!" Lentz nodded and automatically repeated Hector's gesture, striking his chest with his fist. "Consider it done, my ruler!"

"And something else... A week ago, a certain Terant was languishing in the city jail. Find out how he's doing."

CHAPTER 23

SURPRISE FOR THE SOVEREIGN

L UCA WAS LEFT alone. He heard voices beyond the door, but the newly rejuvenated emperor was still apprehensive. Without Lentz's support and hints, he might make a mistake, fail to remember a name and thereby raise suspicion.

He might have sat on his own for a lot longer if it weren't for a knock at the door, followed by a hoarse old voice.

"Where should I serve your breakfast, ruler?"

Who was that? A name came to the tip of his tongue, but the shallow memories from Ma Ju Ro failed him. Or maybe Ma Ju Ro just didn't know his servants' names? Fully possible. However, one piece of knowledge came to Luca clear as day: the man beyond the door was an old servant.

"Bring it all there, but not before I come out!"

Luca said as harshly as he could. "I'm busy! I'm thinking about the people!"

A surprised silence hung beyond the door, but it didn't last long. With hushed voices in the background, the old man coughed hoarsely.

"It will be done, my ruler!"

As he left, the old man whispered to one of the people in the corridor: *What a wonderful emperor we have, always thinking of the people... He's with some whore again! He could'a just let us in, pretty sure we seen it all...*

It was said with a great deal of sarcasm, and the laughter afterwards confirmed it. Luca realized he'd slipped up. By all appearances, attempts on Ma Ju Ro's life were a common affair. And if so many were eager for the real emperor to shuffle off the mortal coil, then Two-horns himself would be after the new fake one! The fact that Luca wasn't who he appeared to be would be clear from such details and oddities in his behavior. That spiteful old servant had probably known the emperor from the teat!

He had to prepare and take measures. He had no fear of poisons, his metamorphosis would handle them, especially with its endless supply of fuel in his fat cells. Physical attacks were another matter.

An axe to the neck, a knife to the heart, or they could even just cut him to pieces! Could the ability handle that? He didn't want to find out. He'd had enough of pain and suffering.

The emperor locked the door and thought for a moment. To start with, he wanted to strengthen his skin so that no treacherous knife or huge halberd could pierce him, but he imagined the consequences: he had to sometimes come into physical contact with people, to shake hands for example. Should he leave his hands as they were? No, they'd be vulnerable. And what if he were to lie with one of his courtesans? Leaving them alone entirely would stir up even more rumors than if he got slim.

Luca went red at the thought, although there was nobody with him to see it. The chance that this would happen that very day aroused him thoroughly, but he tried to drive away his fantasies. Useless things. And those girls were old and... too available. Although now everything in the Empire was available to him... That thought calmed Luca. The easily obtainable lost its attraction and couldn't possibly cause the same anguish that had come from secret dreams of a neighbor girl when he was paralyzed.

He delved back into thoughts of strengthening himself. The skin... He could leave the skin as it was, but... He felt his entire body from his ears to his heels. There was fat all over. Even his fingers were like Tuaf sausages! Remembering one of his favorite treats of childhood, when his father's paycheck let them eat well, he felt another sharp stab of hunger. But Ma Ju Ro ate less than a day ago!

Whatever, let his stomach moan, Luca was no stranger to hunger. So, the fat. A thick, blubbery layer, and if you created a fine super-strong film over it, hard enough and still elastic, then his internal organs would be protected. As for his head, he could completely strengthen his skull.

It should be metal, but which metal? The most durable in the world!

Luca began to recall the most unfamiliar names from Esk's legacy: tungsten, osmium, iridium, titanium... One after another, messages floated before him.

Carrier request accepted: strengthening subcutaneous fat layer, strengthening durability of visceral fat around vital organs, strengthening skeleton.

Request accepted.

Performing...

Transformation impossible. Not enough tungsten in body!

Transformation impossible. Not enough osmium in body!

Transformation impossible. Not enough iridium in body!

Transformation impossible. Not enough titanium in body!

The same happened for ruthenium, chrome, beryllium and rhenium. Luca went over to the medical instruments left on Lentz's table, picking up one after another in the home that at least one of them might contain some of the metal he needed.

BLOOD OF FATE

Activated enhancement mode!

Detected available materials: 73% iron, 9% nickel, 17% chrome, 0.07% carbon...

Absorbing...

Transforming...

Scalpels, scissors, forceps, retractors, needles and saws — they were all made of surgical steel. The tools, which had doubtless traveled a long path through the large country into Lentz's possession, dissolved right in the emperor's hand. The chief medic would be very upset.

His entire body got horribly itchy. Luca couldn't stand it anymore, he took off his breastplate and tunic and started frantically scratching everywhere he could. Everywhere itched, but mostly his head. His fingers moving furiously, the emperor nearly tore the skin off his skull. But it all stopped just as suddenly as it started.

Transformation complete!

Luca'Onegut, based on your request, the following has been performed:

— added 0.1 mm thick layer of fine-meshed chromium steel to internal subcutaneous and visceral fat deposits

— skull bones strengthened by 762%

— skeletal bones strengthened by 369%

— skin enhanced by 92%

It is recommended that you source material for strengthening skin and hair for increased fire-

resistance, chemical and radioactive protection!

Attention! Non-organic energy reserves exhausted!

This was the first time he'd heard of chemistry and radiation, but some examples popped up in his mind as if they'd been there all along. Popped up and astounded him. It amazed Luca that invisible lethal rays and existed in nature, and liquids that could melt even the strongest metal. Promising himself to learn as much as he could about this later, he got dressed, and just in time. Although perhaps at just the wrong time, considering what happened next.

The voices beyond the door had long since faded, but the emperor had only just noticed it. He heard the tapping of high-heels on the marble floor of the corridor, and someone tried the door handle and then rapped on the door lightly.

"Your imperial highness!" a sonorous women's voice said. "I have come to beg my lord for forgiveness! Master, please let me in and I will atone for the little misunderstanding I caused."

"Keirinia?" Luca recalled the name of his first courtesan. "I'm busy, you can atone after dusk."

"But, my lord!" she said in playful tones. "I can't wait to get started, there's a lot of atoning to be done! I'm so hot for you, my emperor! And, forgive me, but this is so unlike you!"

Another oddity in his performance. He had to

fix this, otherwise his offended lover would start flapping her tongue, and tomorrow the entire capital would be whispering that the emperor had changed. He had to let her in and let her 'atone.' Otherwise she wouldn't leave him alone.

Ma Ju Ro opened the door. Keirinia was leaning against the door frame with her hand on her alluringly curved waist. She smiled, baring her delicate and even teeth, then slowly swept her tongue along them.

"Come in, Kei," Ma Ju Ro said. The correct mode of address came to his tongue on its own, and he took a step back to let his lover enter. But she didn't hurry to do so.

"Here?" she smiled again, pressed herself against him and whispered in his ear intimately, "Piglet, let me atone for my guilt where you'll be most comfortable! Let's order them to bring your breakfast to the bedroom, drink some wine and stay in bed all day? The weather outside is awful, and you had that assassination attempt! You've been through so much already today, piglet, you need to rest from all this hassle! If you like, I can call Priscilla and Olga! You know I don't usually like that, but for your sake..." She embraced him and looked him in the eye.

Not knowing how to react to such grandiose plans, Luca frowned just in case, and Keirinia interpreted it in her own way. She fell to her knees before her lord, lifting the hem of his tunic. For the first time, he felt the touch of a woman's hand *there*.

And not just her hand! Sacred Mother!

Luca let out a moan and drew back reluctantly. Confusion flashed in his lover's greedy, lustful eyes.

"Is something wrong, my lord?"

Detected intrusion of toxic substance!
Effect level critical.
Analyzing reaction options...
Unable to release neutralizing agents —
insufficient non-organic energy reserves!
Cannot generate antidote — does not exist!

Luca felt that agonizing itch in his body again. It seemed to penetrate into his very bones. It became difficult to breathe. He felt a stabbing pain in his heart. The emperor was covered in sweat. Grabbing at his throat, he tried to say something, but all he could do was wheeze indistinctly. Then he fell in a heap at the feet of his first courtesan.

Keirinia rose lightly. She kicked the emperor's head carelessly. His wheezes got weaker, rarer. Pulling a small vial from her stocking, the courtesan poured the contents into her mouth, gargled it and spat it out.

A triumphant smile danced in her eyes.

CHAPTER 24

SPECIAL ATTENTION TO COURTESANS

RY AS SHE MIGHT, Keirinia couldn't resist the temptation, and struck her hated 'piglet' as hard as she could, at first in the stomach, then in the temple. The sharp toe of her high-heeled shoe hit the bone and broke. The courtesan gasped, swore and jumped on one leg, grimacing in pain.

Stumbling, she carefully watched the fat slob lying at her feet. He had finally fallen still and silent. Not a single sound came from his lopsided mouth, and a brown foam was drying on his lips. Gathering saliva in her mouth, the lover spat on his disgusting corpulent body with pleasure, aiming at his repulsive face.

Then she walked out, slamming the door loudly behind her.

The small room now contained two corpses:

the former emperor in the body of the used-up boy, and the former cripple boy in the dead emperor. Both their hearts were stopped. Only the first body, unlike the second, had no superpower endowed by the Wheel. Logs continued to display in the emperor's vision as if he was still there to read them.

Detected extensive damage to internal organs!
Nervous system afflicted.
Breath — absent.
Heartbeat — absent.
Detected clinical death of carrier.
Providing cells with oxygen... failed! Insufficient non-organic energy reserves!
Carrier brain death in: 00:49... 00:48... 00:47...

A conversation began to resound behind the door. The old servant had come again, but was intercepted by the courtesan.

"The emperor is resting and has ordered that he not be disturbed! He has expended much energy and... fluid, Nem," Keirinia pronounced in a singsong voice and laughed. "He needs to sleep."

"As you wish, my lady," the old man answered in his shaky voice. "If you wish, I can bring you both breakfast and serve it right here."

"So nice of you, Nem..." the courtesan purred laughingly. "Thank you, but I'd best go back to my chambers...”

The voices faded. Metamorphosis continued to review the options for counteracting the toxin, cycling over the data received at the moment the emperor was poisoned. The power continued to regenerate the body, but it was all in vain: its cells were dying too rapidly, falling like dominoes. All non-organic reserves, the energy of the Wheel that powered everything it gave to travelers, were exhausted. They were recovering, of course, but slowly.

And the pace was the same in any world, in the body of any carrier; roughly one percent of the reserves every twenty four hours and change, as time was measured in Luca's world.

Only when the carrier's condition was approaching the point of no return, with the risk of brain death and the loss of the carrier's consciousness, did the metamorphosis power update its information on its surroundings.

Detected slightly alkaline liquid on skin!
Analyzing...

Identified human saliva. DNA matched to individual 'Keirinia.'

Detected available materials: 99% water, less than 0.01% chlorine, sodium, potassium, calcium...

Detected unknown organic component!
Analyzing...

Probability that component is antidote — 99.9992%!

The lines of information fluttered past Luca's dead, drying eyes. If his metamorphosis could sing, it would have. The Wheel knew no other worlds ruled by a sentience similar to that on this planet that had toxins like those that had entered the carrier's body. But the metamorphosis didn't care. The non-existent antidote had been found.

Separating out the active substance, the superpower immediately distributed it throughout the entire body. Information on the antidote's molecular structure was saved in the Wheel's archive.

After ensuring that the poison had been neutralized, the metamorphosis ability began regenerating tissue at full speed, using every tiny percentage of Wheel energy that had been saved. It succeeded — Luca'Onegut's brain was still whole, and the emperor himself awoke a mere few instants before his final death in this body and reincarnation in his second world.

Ma Ju Ro looked around with a dim gaze and made an attempt to stand. His eyes were filled with blood, his flaccid legs disobeyed him and he nearly fell. Stopping, he stood for a long time, listening to his own heavy breathing and regaining strength.

Incredible as it was, Luca could remember very instant he spent on the tightrope between life and death. He recalled it not as an active participant, but as an observer. And in that capacity, he had managed to see every single detail of the scene, right down to the smallest wrinkles of expression in the corners of Keirinia's eyes.

And so, as he recovered, he began to walk around the room, furiously pacing and grinding his teeth. He frowned and thought about how to punish the girl after this sordid and almost successful attempt to kill him, and about how to prevent further attempts. He even began to wistfully daydream about his calm and uneventful days in his crippled body. But there was no time for nostalgia.

Luca was angry, and it was a concentrated anger at everything, focused on his favorite courtesan. He even had a feeling thought — could he now consider Keirinia his first woman, and was he himself no longer a virgin? He decided the answer was no, for many reasons. Firstly because the act wasn't completed, and secondly because of suspicions that it was all meant to go a little differently. That wasn't the right way. Yes, it was definitely not done that way. These aristocrats did everything... wrong.

The emperor's brain, now recovered from its hypoxia, feverishly generated all manner of tortures and punishments for that treacherous snake Keirinia, venomous in all senses of the word. His fantasies went all the way to taking off her skin layer by layer before bathing her in a mix of salt and chinils. Ideas tumbled chaotically in his head. Luca thrashed around and nearly called the servants to send them to Yadugara's basement to collect the bloodsuckers, but common sense won out.

His mind seethed, but the empathy and unsleeping conscience that had developed in his crippled body asked an important question: was the courtesan guilty?

The answer to the question was obvious; she was. Yet how could Luca judge her? Judging by her behavior, she hated Ma Ju Ro, and it was obvious that she had good reason. But Luca wasn't Ma Ju Ro, and the boy saw with surprise that his anger dissipated and only cool rationality remained; the situation had to be turned to his advantage. He had to either punish and banish all his lovers as an example, which would certainly make his life easier, or...

His stomach rumbled and twisted. His hunger had awoken, he had no energy left, and the emperor, still without a decision, flew out of the room and went the main hall of his chambers. He saw a head disappearing behind the doorway and shouted.

"Breakfast! Here! Now!"

A gray head appeared in the doorway to the imperial chambers.

"I am serving it as we speak, my imperial majesty!"

"Wait! Bring Hector and Keirinia here!" Ma Ju Ro added.

The captain's presence should help him make the right decision based on how the girl behaved. Or the woman? How old was she anyway?

The carved wooden doors opened wide, and a

stream of servants bearing trays began to dexterously lay dishes and jugs at a huge table that could have seated thirty. Luca gave in to his wonderment at the sight of so much food just for a single emperor. This would have fed his family for weeks!

He didn't have enough knowledge of the world to determine what all the food was. He could only say with certainty that whatever was in the pots was probably soup or stew, and he saw could see some kind of mush in a dish with more meat (again, he didn't know which kind) than vegetables. He supposed there was a better name for it than mush.

In any case, the boy was in no condition to ponder on the injustice of the world. He greedily threw himself into some hearty fish stew generously spiced with fiery Tassurian pepper, and then at the sky-burningly hot mush, or whatever it was called.

The emperor sweated profusely and his eyes were streaming, and his metamorphosis struggled to neutralize the hot peppers, seeing it as a threat, and to disintegrate the animal fats before they could add to the carrier's personal fat stores.

His ability gradually told him which of the foods would be healthiest, and the boy wolfed down eggs and seafood, recovering his nutritional deficits.

The old man Nem stood immobile nearby, hurrying his servants with whispers. Dishes disappeared as soon as Luca had dipped his spoon just a few times.

At first he watched them with longing and

confusion as they were carried away, but later, after tasting a roasted sea bass, he grabbed the dish and roared. The servant froze, looking over at Nem, unsure what to do. The old man waved at him, shooing away his overzealous underling, then broke into a smile.

"My lord... Have your tastes changed? Allow me to note that..."

"I do not allow it!" Luca snapped, enraged that the servant had pilfered a lobster on a tray from under his nose while he was distracted with the servant. He'd only gotten to the pincers! "Everybody, get out! I'm going to finish eating, then you can come back and tidy up. But first... bring me back that lobster!"

The old man fell to his knees in horror, trying to grab the ruler's hand and kiss it, and he did so. Luca pulled his fingers from the old servant's grasp. His metamorphosis instantly awoke with a declaration: "Detected human saliva: 99% water..." Nem lost his balance and fell under the table, with the tablecloth following after him. A servant rushed after his superior and dropped his tray on his imperial majesty. Which was the final straw.

"Get out!" Luca roared, but then saw that the captain and his courtesan had arrived and disappeared behind the door, taking the shout as intended for them. He had to shout again: "Hector! Keirinia! Come here!" Something floated up from the uncharted depths of Esk's legacy and he added: "Right now!"

For a moment, chaos reigned at the threshold to the imperial chambers. The servants were trying to get out, Nem crawling on his knees in tears, already fearful of his impending sentence. Keirinia tore at her dress and also wanted to fall to her knees and beg her revived ruler for mercy, but the senior servant was already taking up all the begging room... Hector watched it all in disgust.

"Your imperial majesty," he said. "Your will is done. I was on my way to report to you when I met a messenger. Has something happened?"

Luca remained silent. He nodded at his courtesan's silent pleading. The servants had already cleared out, and the girl remained in the center of the chambers, fearing to run and to approach.

The emperor pointed at the empty chairs nearby.

"Nothing has happened, captain. It occurred to me that you might have missed breakfast in the commotion of the morning. So you will share breakfast with me, Hector." He moved his gaze to the frozen girl. "You too, Keirinia. There's too much food here for one person..."

He dropped his head, biting into a well-cooked piece of marinated meat, but still had time to notice the surprise in their eyes. It was unclear to him what had caused it. The offer to share breakfast, or the remark about the amount of food? Either way, he'd done something wrong again.

Keirinia didn't touch her breakfast. Hector

didn't stand on ceremony, and for a long time, the only sound in the hall was that of men's jaws, tearing, chewing and grinding through exquisite delicacies as if it was all simple peasant food. The courtesan cringed, but then took hold of herself and put on a mask of caring tenderness, playing the role of hostess as their table. She had an enlightened conversation with herself, prattling away about something or other, but Luca didn't know what exactly. He couldn't hear it over the sound of chewing in his ears. As a result, he and Hector limited themselves to interjecting the occasional noise of approval.

Once the emperor was full, the captain of the palace guard put aside his cutlery, wiped his mouth with a napkin and, without preamble, began his report, but a belch from the emperor immediately interrupted him. Luca blushed in embarrassment, but it was taken as a sign of disapproval.

"Forgive us, your imperial majesty!" Keirinia apologized for the captain, burning him with her gaze.

"Um..." Hector didn't understand the reason for the apology. Luca considered it best to stay silent, and the captain continued. "The previous first advisor has told me all the names. Apart from the doctor, whom you have forgiven, a number of other high-ranking individuals were involved in the conspiracy..." A hand went into a pocket and he pulled out a piece of paper. "Here is a full list of those named. Lentz was merely the executor of the plan, and Naut was present in the morning at his own initiative. The cretin couldn't wait to spit on your lifeless corpse, my lord. All the conspirators have been arrested or placed under guard. We are currently seizing their properties, including country manors. The families of these traitors to the Empire have been isolated in the palace tower. We are tracking down suspects not named by Naut by means of the observers, with the involvement of some... freelance agents."

The slight hesitation in the captain's report did not escape Ma Ju Ro's attention.

"What agents?" he frowned, recognizing that merely playing with his eyebrows immediately lent power to his words.

"Apologies, my lord. There is a band of thieves in the city. I am well acquainted with their leader, Weasel..."

"Captain?" Keirinia exclaimed. "You? With a thief?"

"It so happened, my lord," Hector admitted, paying no attention to the courtesan, "that he is the son of a comrade of mine, an old friend. Since my comrade died, I have been keeping watch over the boy. In short, I hired his crew for surveillance. They are quick, clandestine and inconspicuous, and they know the city like the back of their hand."

"Very well," Luca nodded. "There's something else. I realize that the inquisitors are likely very busy, but I would like them to pay special attention to all my courtesans. I have reason to suspect that some of them may have been hired by my cousin Rezsinius."

"All of them, my lord? All as in... all?" The captain's eyes widened. "Who has counted them all?! Except for Lentz... They all see the doctor for obvious reasons..."

"No, only those who... with whom I..." Luca coughed. "The recent ones, let's say."

"It will be done, your imperial majesty!" The captain stood up quickly. "Do you have any more orders?"

"No, that's all for now. You are dismissed, Hector."

Such polite address from the emperor astounded the captain. He gulped, not knowing what to expect, then bowed and left Ma Ju Ro alone with Keirinia. Just before he reached the door, something suddenly occurred to him. He stopped, glanced at the emperor's first courtesan.

"Does your last order concern... the lady present here?"

The girl froze. The spoon in her hand began to shake, tapping against the edge of her cup.

"No, Hector. I am sure of her loyalty."

Just as the doors banged shut, Keirinia's chair clattered to the floor with a bang. All together, the morning had been too much for this one particular girl, even if she was the first favorite courtesan of Emperor Ma Ju Ro the Fourth.

CHAPTER 25

THE GREATEST
SECRET

T O KEEP AWAY from listening ears and maintain
the legend, Luca spoke with Keirinia in the
bedroom. The door was locked. The emperor
himself sat on the bed, with the girl sat in a chair
before him, frozen upright like a stake. She shifted
from foot to foot and nervously wiggled her toes.

"Keep your tongue behind your teeth," the
emperor told his courtesan. "Everything we have
agreed on must remain only between us!"

She nodded and looked him in the eye with
loyalty, although that meant nothing. The previous
owner of this body had seen that look many times.
And what had her 'loyalty' led to?

But this time, Ma Ju Ro was inclined to
believe that the girl was truthful. The former favorite
had gotten everything she wanted: freedom, the

ability to marry the man she loved, and still she kept all the privileges she'd had at court. And most importantly, she had the emperor's forgiveness. In exchange, she had to continue to play the role of an agent of Rezsinius, and moreover, to achieve complete trust from the imperial cousin and the displeased aristocrats of the capital.

Ma Ju Ro was certain that there would be more and more displeased aristocrats. Those rich gluttons would choke on his future reforms. And having an informant within their circle was more important than making an example of Keirinia. That said, Luca doubted that his decision to forgive her was purely rational. After all, she was his first... almost first real woman.

"I will not let you down, my lord," Keirinia assured him. "But how will we explain... the unsuccessful assassination attempt? They were certain the poison was deadly!"

"I had an antidote. Tell your clients that Lentz made me take a certain potion as a preventive measure in the mornings, and that it protects me from all poisons."

"And how do I explain that my head is still on my shoulders?"

"That's easy. I got sick, but due to the antidote, I didn't even realize that it was poison."

The girl's face darkened. "And how did I find out about this miraculous potion?"

"Don't worry about that. You're a good actress, Keirinia. Just act indignant that their poison didn't work even though you did everything right. And Lentz is to blame. Say he told you personally about the preventive potion. They'll have their doubts, but they'll decide to check whether you're telling the truth. And the healer will confirm it in some private conversation."

Thinking it over, Luca hoped that this mythical antidote would prevent the conspirators from trying poisons again. The logs he studied after his revival showed him that even metamorphosis wasn't all-powerful. If they used another poison unknown to the Wheel, then it could all end far worse.

"My reputation in the palace might weaken if... my lord stops spending time with me," the girl said playfully. "Now that I see how magnanimous you can be, I... my view has changed, and if my ruler desires it..."

A line scrolled past Luca's vision.

Tsoui points: +1. Current balance: 23.

Something imperceptible had changed in the universal balance of harmony. Although perhaps not entirely imperceptible.

The woman who had spat in his face with hatred a mere three hours ago now rose, climbing onto the bed, elegantly bending at the waist and sticking out her impressive backside. She crawled on all fours behind the emperor's back and snaked her hands under his tunic. Her gentle fingers played across his chest and began to make their way lower. Her hot breath and passionate whispers in his ear aroused his desire. A little more and Luca would have fully given into his passion, but they were interrupted.

There was a knock at the door, and Lentz's voice brought the emperor back to more pressing matters.

"My lord, I have important news of the boy's family. I need a decision from you."

Keirinia muttered something in aggrieved tones and raised her eyes. Luca cast a glance at her and realized for the first time in his life that a woman wanted him. The rational part of Esk's legacy told him that the reason was unlikely to be a physical attraction. It was more likely an attraction to his power that made her green eyes flash with fire.

"Stay here and rest," the emperor said. He stood up quickly, straightening his tunic. "Wait there!" he shouted to Lentz as he headed for the doors.

"Piglet..." his courtesan reached out to him. "Don't be too long, I'm on fire for you!"

"No more 'piglets,' Keirinia," Luca said automatically and narrowed his eyes jealously. "Cover yourself up. Nobody should see you undressed except me."

"Forgive me, my lord!" The girl dove under the sheets. "There's something else..."

"What?" The emperor turned back

impatiently, his hand on the door handle. Mentally he was already far away, somewhere with his mother and sister, thinking about what he'd say to them. "Hurry up!"

"We need to discuss your behavior, my lord," she spoke in a whisper so that Lentz couldn't hear her from outside the door. "You've always called me Kei, and never Keirinia. You've always had breakfast alone and made others stand as you eat. And you've never called Hector or Lentz by their names... Or anyone. You've changed. There are a few other details, but only I know about those, and they mean that..." The girl fell silent, realizing that she'd said too much.

"They mean that I'm not Ma Ju Ro?"

"I didn't say that!"

"But that's what you mean to say."

"No, my lord, it isn't like that!" She jumped off the bed and fell to her knees. "Forgive me, my ruler, I'm just a foolish woman with the brain of a pigeon, I say all sorts of..."

"Stand up, Keirinia, and get back in the bed," Luca offered her a hand and helped her rise. Impulsively, he embraced her and whispered: "Everything is fine, don't worry. There's a grain of truth to your words, but the explanation is far simpler than you think. We'll return to this subject later."

His instinctive wish to open up was immediately blown away by cold rationality. Telling *her* about his superpowers and true nature... If Esk had been there, he'd have gone mad and shown Luca hundreds of examples of women destroying men, but the traveler wasn't there, and only one thought from his experience made itself clear: this wasn't only foolish, it was also dangerous. Women were unpredictable, they often made emotional decisions, and Ma Ju Ro's greatest secret would cease to be a secret as soon as this affectionate and far from foolish girl learned the truth. He would tell her that he had some amnesia from the transfusion procedure. That should serve as a sufficiently likely explanation.

Lentz impatiently paced around the large room in which the emperor had recently broken his fast. When the latter appeared, the healer opened his mouth to talk, but stopped when Ma Ju Ro the Fourth raised his hand. He couldn't wait to find out how his family was, but there were too many listening ears here.

"I suggest we go out and take in some fresh air," Luca said, pointing toward the panoramic window. "The air should be fresh enough on the terrace."

Nodding his understanding, the chief imperial medic followed him. The terrace opened over a stunning view of the calm, green ocean, extending out from where they stood in all directions. The cries of seagulls filled the air. Amazed, Luca completely forget why he'd walked out there, and stood for a long time breathing in lungfuls of fresh, sea air. Lentz waited patiently.

Noticing the medic's presence, the emperor suddenly remembered himself. Mom! Kora!

"Give me your report, Lentz," he said dryly, trying to hide his worries.

"The woman, the boy's mother, is in the final stages of her illness," the medic reported indifferently. "Unfortunately, the time for successful healing has passed. She is living out her final hours. She is unconscious, and her hovel was robbed. Nothing was left, they took even the rags the woman wore. I found her naked, the back of her head cracked against a wall. Either the robbers went out of their way to hurt her, or she hurt herself in a fit."

"Where is she?" Luca asked, hiding the tremor in his voice.

"Still there. One of my men remained to keep watch over her in her final moments. She will be given a worthy burial, my lord."

"I must see her! And what about the boy's sister?"

"There were problems with her..." Lentz faltered.

"Speak!"

"The girl turned out to be a thief. She infiltrated the home of a respected healer and stole something. She has already been judged. The victim herself bought her, the one whose home was robbed."

"Why?" Luca asked, already knowing the answer.

"My lord, it is the same healer that found

Luca. I mentioned his name yesterday. Yadugara. They say the bastard has a predilection for teenage girls, so he buys them in bulk. But I think the true reason is something else. It may be that the boy's sister could also be a donor! Should I order that the girl be confiscated?"

"Do it at once! If a single hair on her head has been harmed... execute Yadugara!"

"I gladly would, my emperor, but his name is already in the list of those you awarded with the Order of the Empire! For special services! And what would be the reason for the execution? He has the right to do what he wishes with his slaves!"

"And?" Ma Ju Ro said in confusion. "Am I not the emperor?"

"Yes, but... My lord, the healers' guild has already arranged a celebration dedicated to Yadugara's medal. He has a good reputation, he is respected, and the enmity between him and myself is widely known... If he is executed, then I will be blamed of settling scores by your hand. This requires a more delicate approach..."

"I see," Ma Ju Ro darkened. "Then bring the girl here."

"Your will be done!" Lentz saluted with his chest to his fist, appreciating his ruler's restraint and care for his reputation. He lowered his head, saying goodbye. "My lord!"

"Wait, Lentz... How do I give orders? I'm always alone, except for Keirinia. Where are my servants?"

"You sent them all away, as is usual before a procedure," the healer answered. "And Naut gave them another day off in the morning, believing the assassination attempt to be successful. I can send my secretary Koerlig to replace your own for today. Do you remember who that is?" Lentz winced. "I advise you to replace her immediately."

"Her?" Ma Ju Ro said in surprise.

"Yes. Herdinia. A very peculiar lady... At court, she is called the Crane. She trades in positions, lobbies for the interests of those who pay her, signs documents in your name."

"I will take that into consideration. Now send Koerlig to me and go straight to get the girl, Lentz!"

"Before I send my man to you, will you tell me what you intend? I may be able to help more."

"Possibly," Luca thought, calculating how to explain it and whether it was worth it. He decided it was. If he was to trust him, then he had to completely trust him. For effect, he grew several sharp-pointed tentacles from his palm. They waved like strands of seaweed in the water, and reflected a metallic sheen. Lentz unwillingly gulped, staring at them as if spellbound. "I think I can help the dying woman. I must get to her hut."

CHAPTER 26

ALL HAIL THE EMPEROR!

K OERLIG, THE SECRETARY of the chief of
imperial medics and a weaselly and cunning
figure, kept an impassive and cool expression
on his face. This was extremely difficult. His
gelatinous imperial majesty was currently trying to
get outside by climbing through a window.

His mentor Lentz had given him a special task
— to quietly escort the emperor to a hut in the
capital's slums and find the donor boy's mother,
who was dying of swamp fever. He was told that the
ruler wanted to thank her for her son. Hah, sure!
That sounded likely!

It all looked very strange and smelled fishy,
but Koerlig was used to worse. And Lentz had
promised to explain much when all was resolved.

Getting the heavy and noticeable Ma Ju Ro

out in secret turned out to be a difficult task, but Koerlig was no stranger to complexity. There was a reason his career had progressed so quickly for his twenty and some years, and without any patronage. As the top student at the medical faculty, he had drawn Lentz's attention in his third course, and for the last, he was working as his secretary. And his administrative skills had developed as fast as his doctoring skills. The idea of having the emperor change into a healer's dress, hiding his face under an air-filtering mask, was excellent evidence of his capabilities.

Ma Ju Ro finally managed to stuff his body through the window, but he didn't fall, he landed nimbly on his feet. Looking around, he quickly walked to the carriage in which Koerlig awaited him.

"Get a move on!" he commanded.

"Take this, my lord..." Hesitating, the secretary poured a few silver coins into the emperor's palm. "You are unlikely to be recognized where we are going, so money may come in handy. You never know..."

The ruler studied his barely recognizable profile with interest, and it occurred to Koerlig that this might be the first time Ma Ju Ro had beheld the coins of the Empire.

Two carriages left the palace grounds. Lentz sat in the first, Koerlig and the emperor in the second. In the city, the carriages separated and turned in different directions.

The guards openly yawned under the burning

sun, sweating and roasting alive in their plate armor. All the courtiers were hiding in corners as they wilted in the heat, and so nobody noticed the emperor leave the palace in such a strange manner and without guards. Koerlig mentally praised himself, although anxiety soon came to replace his initial joy.

He and his imperial majesty were headed to a place he had never been, and shivers went up his spine as he considered that this could be a one-way journey. It was bad enough that he had to drive the carriage himself; they'd also gone without guards. The emperor remained calm. Lentz had also showed no concern when he gave his orders, and only that calmed Koerlig. Perhaps they did have guards, and they were just clearing them a path?

Because of these thoughts, or because the winding and monotonous grey streets could confuse Two-horns himself, Koerlig got lost. He feared to reveal this to his ruler, hoping instead to ask some passersby for directions. The only reference point his teacher had given him was a nameless inn owned by one Nemania Kovachar, but he hadn't seen anything that could be that. Low, crooked shanty houses crowded the district, with grubby children loitering in the dirt in front of the doors.

When he realized he was lost, Koerlig made a loop of the district and swore when he realized he was going round in circles. He stood up and saw a crowd of boys. That was all he needed! The children surrounded the carriage! And there were lots of them! Two-horns!

"Giddy up!" The secretary whipped the horses and the carriage jerked into motion.

The children shouted something excitedly and roadside stones started clattering against the carriage's sides. He had to whip one who let himself get too close, but that only made the boys worse; now they were aiming at Koerlig himself instead of at the carriage. The next stone hit him hard on the shoulder, and the secretary swore in pain, then looked back in fear.

"Stop the carriage," the emperor's voice rang out.

"But..."

"Right now!"

With a certain malicious joy, Koerlig did what he was told. It looked like his ruler had gone completely mad. Well, a little real life couldn't hurt! And if fate was in a good mood, maybe one of those stones would break his foolish head. Welcome to the real world, your gelatinous majesty!

Ma Ju Ro opened the door and jumped out with shocking agility for his build. The boys, who had cautiously run a short distance away, now guardedly returned to the carriage and surrounded the emperor on all sides. He took a coin out of his pocket.

"Who knows where to find the house of Prisca Dezisimu?"

The boys exchanged glances. The outsider didn't seem dangerous, but they expected nothing good to come of this. He might be a rich man, and in a carriage no less, but he was still an outsider.

"I am a doctor," the emperor explained. "She is sick. I can heal her."

He didn't wait for an answer, but Koerlig saw that the boys were surrounding them. Locals began to emerge from their huts and hovels to see what the commotion was about. They were sickly, dirty and deformed one and all. Koerlig didn't doubt that they also stank. What happened was amazing. Usually, such impudence toward his gelatinous majesty would cause far more important heads to roll, but right then, the emperor was serenity itself.

"I was sent from the palace," he said patiently. "The woman is sick with swamp fever. I can help her."

"Who're you then?" a filthy and ragged peasant said as he approached and jabbed a finger at the emperor's chest (Koerlig nearly fell off the carriage in shock). "What d'ya want?"

"I am a doctor," Ma Ju Ro answered. "I'm searching for a sick woman called Prisca Dezisimu."

"What d'ya want?" It was as if the peasant hadn't heard what the emperor had just said! "Who're you?"

Koerlig couldn't take it anymore, and climbed off to bring some order. His fist was clenched around a surgical scalpel in his pocket, and he was ready to use it. Nobody could talk to the emperor like that, even if he was in disguise!

"Show some respect, you there!" he shouted

threateningly.

"Wha'?" the peasant said in amazement. "And who're you then?"

The emperor shot a glance at the secretary, annoyance flashing in his eyes for an instant. But why?

"Get back in the carriage, Koerlig!"

The young man frozen in confusion. It was odd enough that the emperor had decided to remain alone with this aggressive rabble... He'd also called him by name! Koerlig returned to the carriage in a stupor.

Unfortunately, the ruler continued his conversation quietly. He shook (so disgusting!) the peasant by his dirty hand, and the latter checked himself, cringed and looked at the 'doctor' with respect. The coin resurfaced in the peasant's hand, then he shouted something and the crowd dispersed. All the boys ran off, apart from the eldest. He nodded to the peasant and clambered up to the reins with Koerlig. Lentz's secretary smelled an acidic stench of sweat. His uninvited new neighbor fidgeted a little and started touching everything with the same hands that had just been digging through the mud. Koerlig decided to be strong and patient. The important thing would be to properly disinfect everything later.

"The boy will show you the way," the emperor said, climbing into the carriage. "Onwards!"

The route the boy sent them on was extremely complex. It occurred to Koerlig that he would never have found the right turns on his own, hidden as they were in this warren of miserable hovels. Once again, he felt admiration for Lentz, who went out that morning alone, quickly found the right place and returned whole.

Finally, the grubby boy told them to stop.

"Can't drive further," he said with a sinister smile. "You'll get stuck. Go on foot."

The guide jumped down and was off like a shot. While Koerlig thought of whether to escort the emperor himself or stay and guard the carriage, it was all decided for him.

"Keep an eye on the carriage," the emperor ordered.

He started tramping along the muddy street without a shadow of hesitation. Up to his shins in sticky slurry, Ma Ju Ro confidently walked down the road and then disappeared into a house. A couple of minutes later, an unfamiliar man walked out and froze at the entrance like a statue.

The emperor stayed inside for a long time. Koerlig, at first attentively keeping lookout so that none of the local vagrants could come on him unawares, finally calmed down and started daydreaming. Some flies snapped him out of it when they decided to brazenly crawl on his face. He slapped one of them and accidentally poked himself in the eye. His lord still hadn't returned.

The sun had moved noticeably across the western horizon when three men approached the carriage: the emperor, the unfamiliar man and a tall woman. They held her up, one at each side.

The ruler helped her into the carriage, then climbed into the carriage on the other side. The stranger sat next to Koerlig at the reins.

"I'll drive," he said. "Keep an eye out, it isn't safe here... for people like you."

Koerlig nodded. Lentz had told him that the woman was in the final stages of swamp fever. In that condition, she should be barely breathing! But although she looked exhausted, this woman showed no symptoms of swamp fever. She was absolutely healthy, and the top student of the university medical faculty was one to know.

The carriage quickly made its way out of the slums under the control of the stranger, who explained to Koerlig that he was also Lentz's man. On the edge of hearing the secretary heard the emperor lying to the woman, telling her that her son was alive and well. She began to ask him about her daughter, Luca's sister, in a hurried stream of words. The emperor disingenuously calmed her, promising her that the girl would be found and brought to the palace.

"Everything is going to be fine from now on, Prisca," Ma Ju Ro assured her. "You have nothing to worry about. And you'll never need to do anyone else's laundry again, you will be served like an empress!"

None of my business, Koerlig thought. *Apparently everyone in this Dezisimu family is a suitable donor.* True, he didn't understand the purpose of all this mystery and the emperor's personal involvement, but he'd had plenty of time to get used to his eccentricities. However, when they again passed by the spot where they'd had stones thrown at them, Koerlig realized what it was all about. Did the emperor want to get closer to the people, gain popularity among the poor? Considering Rezsinius's growing power, the move was understandable.

"All hail the emperor!" that filthy peasant shouted as they drove by. He held a pitcher of ale, apparently bought with the emperor's kind donation. "Sacred Mother protect Emperor Ma Ju Ro the Fourth, kind and benevolent!"

To the secretary's surprise, the other street thugs supported the filthy peasant fervently, shouting the emperor's praises. Koerlig turned back in his seat and spoke before thinking.

"What did you say to them, my ruler?"

Ma Ju Ro stroke the woman's shoulder and raised his head. Koerlig sighed with relief when he saw that his eyes held no anger, only... joy? The ruler smiled.

"Nothing that you need to worry about, Koerlig."

"All the same, what..?"

"I declared that by imperial decree, from today onwards, all healing for all subjects of the empire is free. After all, what is more important than our people's health?"

The secretary opened his mouth, closed it,

opened it again. Nothing he could think to say seemed at all appropriate.

"That's right, Koerlig," the ruler nodded. "Nothing to worry about."

CHAPTER 27

CONSTANT VALUE

ALL THE WAY to the palace, Luca tried to touch his mother and even took her by the hand, but she flinched and pulled away. He could understand that. She didn't know where her son was, what had happened to Kora. She was sick with worry, and she found the fat doctor's awkward attentions inappropriate. And it was obvious that she didn't quite believe his assurances that Luca was fine. The emperor could tell. He saw it in her eyes. His mother emanated mistrust, and even the fact that he'd healed her changed nothing.

When Luca had first walked into the hut, she didn't even know what was going on, what day it was. She had no memory at all of the last few days. Events flowed together in her fever-struck mind, layering on top of each other; Kora in prison for stealing an apple, a few days on her feet scrubbing sheets, Luca's incredible recovery, the accusation that he attacked Karim, the court, Kora's disappearance and...

Tortured with fever, unable even to stand, she quenched her thirst with the water that accumulated in the corners of the shack as it leaked in from the street. In her delirium, the woman was always speaking with someone: with him, or rather, with Luca, or with her daughter, or customers, or the judge. The name of the innkeeper Nemania came up a few times too. Luca's mother was trying to convince him to have mercy on her son.

The emperor, ravaged with sympathy and pain, had intuitively embraced the burning woman and desperately wished for her to be healed. In that very moment, tendrils finer than thread grew out of him and joined the two bodies together, giving his metamorphosis power all the relevant information on the subject 'Prisca Dezisimu.' The infection had already made its way into her brain tissue and devastated all her organs. She couldn't be healed. The only option was to clear out her body, absorb all the old organs and recreate them anew. It was imperative that the subject's memory be preserved and that she be fed and provided with oxygen during the operation. Not a complex task, but one that required time and Wheel energy reserves.

The son had lain pressed to his mother for several hours, patiently waiting for her to recover. When she woke up, she found herself in the embrace of some disgusting fat man and screamed loudly. Lentz's man ran in when he heard the cry, and together they somehow managed to convince Prisca that they weren't robbers or rapists. It had been even harder to convince the woman to go with them to the palace.

"An audience with the emperor?" Prisca frowned suspiciously. "Why on earth..?"

Luca himself found the right words, saying that Kora was in trouble and only the emperor's direct involvement could save her.

He felt his mother's mistrust as they went, and Luca accepted it and locked his emotions inside. His mother was alive, well and safe. All he had to do now was save his sister, and as soon as possible. If Lentz couldn't handle it, he'd go to that bloodsucking healer's home himself and grind the man into a fine powder, along with anyone else who tried to get in his way.

The palace medical wing had its own entrance. Lentz's man dropped off the emperor and Luca's mother there. There was nobody in the reception room, and Ma Ju Ro calmly walked inside unnoticed, not counting the dozing guard. There he cleaned off the day's dirt, got changed and then set off for his quarters with his mother in tow.

"Let me introduce myself again, Prisca," he said, once they were alone. "I'm not really a doctor. My name is Ma Ju Ro the Fourth. I'm the emperor."

Luca's mother had always had a sharp tongue, and it was obvious she wanted to say something like "well then I'm the Sacred Mother," but something stopped her. The woman was undoubtedly in the palace, and the courtiers they ran into in the corridors all bowed low. And it seemed unlikely that they would address her companion as 'your majesty' if he were a simple doctor. Spellbound by her understanding of what was happening, Prisca had no words.

"Make yourself at home," the emperor said simply. "You'll be fed. Later, if you want to rest, the far bedroom is at your complete disposal. In the meantime, I have matters of state to attend to."

Koerlig rushed in, breathing heavily and barely getting out his words, to report Lentz's return. Ma Ju Ro left his mother and went to meet the healers.

The palace courtiers, newly emerged from their holes, stared with surprise as their ruler rushed so purposefully and quickly through the halls. Rumors began to float through the palace halls, each more outlandish than the last, and from there they flew out through the entire capital. Something was happening, but nobody knew exactly what yet. The emperor had time to think about this on his way to the medical wing, and made a mental note; he needed to learn about his government's communication policies, and find out who handled them. It also wouldn't hurt to find out who all these people were and what they were good for.

Once he reached Lentz's domain, the emperor burst into the chief imperial medic's office.

"Where is she?"

Lentz nodded to the emperor in a businesslike

fashion and began to report immediately.

"My ruler! We managed to take the girl right from Yadugara's operating table, fortunately before he had time to begin the transfusion procedure. She was drugged. She is currently recovering in a private chamber."

"I want to see her."

Lentz led him to Kora's chamber. Luca touched his sister and requested her status.

Subject: Kora Dezisimu. Vital signs: 38%.
Detected toxins harmful to the nervous system!
Subject is extremely malnourished!

Luca gave the mental command to heal the body. His metamorphosis reacted instantly.

Analyzing reaction options...
Releasing neutralizing agents.
Energy reserve saturation... Successful.

It suddenly occurred to him that when his sister awoke, it would be best if she saw her mother first, and not him. All it took was a thought to send Kora into a deep and restorative sleep. His power affected the brain directly, imitating the effect of the hormones responsible for sleep.

"Allow her mother to remain here, Lentz," Ma Ju Ro said. "The girl will sleep until tomorrow morning, she needs to recover her strength."

"It will be done, my ruler! I intended to

suggest that myself."

The rest of their conversation was not for listening ears. Ma Ju Ro and Lentz set off for the imperial chambers. Koerlig tagged along, but walked at a distance behind them.

It was a long way from the medical wing to the part of the palace with the emperor's chambers. They had to walk across almost the entire palace, and then go up to the third floor.

And people scurried all over the entire way there. Another public appearance by the emperor, efficiently moving about on his own two legs, sparked a furore. A man dressed like a peacock separated from one of these groups of loiterers. As he walked past, the emperor noticed that the courtier had unusually rosy cheeks.

"Remind me who that is," Ma Ju Ro asked Lentz.

"Reyk Lee Vensiro, your majesty," he whispered. "He is from a noble house, an unlanded aristocrat."

"Reyk?"

"Reyk is the title of the ancestors of the comrades of your magnificent ancestor Ma Ju Ro the first..." Lentz explained.

"Your imperial majesty!" the approaching reyk bowed deeply. "Good day to you!"

"Reyk Vensiro," the emperor nodded somberly without slowing his pace.

Lee Vensiro ran past Ma Ju Ro's large figure and placed a pleading hand on him.

"But, my ruler! Spare me a minute of your precious attention! I have wonderful news for you! Each piece better than the last!"

Ma Ju Ro stopped. Lentz crossed his arms, snorted sceptically and choked back laughter.

"Tell me, then," the emperor ordered.

"My ruler! Three beautiful flowers of the South were delivered to the capital this morning! Fresh, unspoiled and burning with desire! And each of them thirsts this very minute to..."

"Next."

"Um..." Vensiro lost his train of thought, but quickly corrected himself. "The purest Tassurian... spices, my lord! Distilled ten times, the strongest ever concentration!"

"Any other news?"

"A circus of monsters, my lord! The ringmaster has collected the most monstrous monsters from all corners of the Empire! He even has mutants! A bearded lady! A pig man! It's enchanting!" It's..."

"Is that all?" Luca interrupted him. He was impatient to share his ideas with Lentz before tackling the issue of his mother and Kora and meeting with them. There was so much to do. On top of that, Keirinia was still waiting for him, and this peacock was standing here flooding him with his foolish offers.

"Yes, but..." The reyk cast an unfriendly glance at Lentz, nervously licked his lips and finished his thought. "My ruler will be very pleased!"

"Are you sure? Then I'll see you in my office in an hour with all your 'news.' But no talk of enchanting monsters. Bring the ringmaster with you."

Leaving Lee Vensiro to his thoughts, the emperor and the healer continued on their way. Nobody else made any attempt to approach them.

"Tell me," Ma Ju Ro said, glancing at Lentz. "Why did he do that?"

"Your interests were extremely clear before, sire. On the one hand, long life and good health; our service provides that for you. The other hand is entirely occupied with that for which I was responsible. Entertainment. You always thirsted for one thing — dispelling your boredom. Mature women and young girls, opiates and alcohol, tasty food and exotic dishes, shows, bards, songbirds and singers, magicians and other such charlatans, gladiator combat and orgies..." Lentz took a breath. "Every courtier competed for your attention and favor. And it could only be won by satisfying your primary pleasure. Some find beautiful women, organizing a whole observation network across the entire Empire, others deal with the delivery of..."

"Enough, Lentz, I understand. And this Vensiro, as it happens, decided to offer me three different options?"

"I'm sure he won't be the only one. What is the purpose of your inviting him to you in an hour?"

The emperor emitted a sinister chuckle.

"He needs my attention. And he'll get it. Just

not in the way he's trying to. Incidentally... How will this affect you?"

"There are whispers, my lord. Words of my suddenly increased influence. The courtiers agonize over how to behave with me. They can't figure out whether this is a temporary phase or whether you've really begun to listen to me."

"Are you certain of your people? Do you have a guard?"

"I haven't had time to think about that, sire. Events have developed very quickly."

"We're both going to have to think, Lentz. By the end of the day, I want to know who I can rely on."

They reached the doors leading to the imperial chambers. Two armed guards clanked out salutes in their armor, greeting their emperor.

"How are things?" Ma Ju Ro asked. "Nobody has come out?"

"Nobody, your imperial majesty!"

The emperor walked into the pompous lounge first. Lentz followed him in, and saw a woman he'd mentally buried, a woman in perfect health and full of energy. His gaze moved to the emperor in understanding and he silently mouthed the word: *Unbelievable!*

After a short explanation and upon hearing that Kora was in the palace, the woman decided to go to her at once and stay by her side. Ma Ju Ro nodded, and Lentz shouted for Koerlig to escort Prisca.

Once alone, the two men went out onto the terrace. Both were starving, and a few minutes later they cleared a table full of fruit and snacks.

"Alright. What about Yadugara?" Ma Ju Ro asked after draining a pitcher of sparkling spring water, the pride of the southern barons. "Was he upset?"

"I'll say! At first he protested, believing that I was trying to steal the donor for myself. I had to call in the guards. That worked, but angered him even more. He shouted, spluttered and threatened to complain to the guild. He screamed at me that at tomorrow's award ceremony, he would declare his departure from the guild and tell everyone of the emperor's tyranny."

"Award ceremony?"

"Yes, sire. You will be there."

"Excellent," Ma Ju Ro said. "A good occasion to declare my new order..."

Lentz listened to the emperor talk of free medicine for all his subjects, and, to put it mildly, was shocked.

"That's utopian thinking!" he said outright. "It's completely impossible. Absolutely. Nobody from the guild will agree to this! You would discredit the profession by making healing available to every beggar!"

The guild can continue to earn through paid healing," the emperor tried to calm down his subject. "Your department will be providing free healing for all the Empire's subjects, Lentz."

"How?"

"How many graduates of the medical faculty do you have?"

"In total? Or every year?" Lentz snorted. "I get the idea. Fifty each year. Three quarters of them aren't in the guild and scratch along with whatever pay they can earn. Another part of them are forced to give up ten years of their life in 'apprenticeship' with the healers, for bread and board, before they can get a license to practice if they're lucky."

"We'll set aside one of the buildings confiscated from the conspirators as a clinic. Gather your best graduates that haven't yet become practicing healers. Ensure that the state provides for them all and gives them worthy recompense. Put aside an extra reward for those that are particularly successful. Find a good manager to delegate the day-to-day operations to..."

"Koerlig," Lentz interrupted him and blushed. "Forgive me, your majesty!"

"For work issues and alone it is acceptable," the emperor said. "Let's dispense with the formalities. Alright, Koerlig then. As for the expenses, consult with Naut. He's doing nothing useful in his cage, he might as well calculate the budget.

"The budget? That's our key concern, my lord! The idea of community clinics is not new, although never for free. My teacher suggested creating something like them, so that all healers of different specialities could be in one place, instead of trying to achieve the impossible by healing everyone in the world. But nobody was interested! Especially the healers' guild!"

"We'll avoid the guild entirely," Ma Ju Ro shook his head. "They'll chase the rich, the aristocrats. We'll handle the health of the common people. We'll start with the capital, cut our teeth, then we'll open imperial clinics in the other cities."

"It all sounds very attractive, my lord..." Lentz chewed his lips. "But where will we get the money? The treasury is empty and has no chance to fill..."

It didn't escape the emperor that Lentz had said "we." The man was involved, inspired, and that was good. Before the day ended, he'd need to address the issue of his security. He'd already put the challenge to his metamorphosis, and he had a ready solution. He just had to save up some Wheel energy.

"All the money of the Empire is a constant value," Ma Ju Ro said, smiling in childish wonderment. Lentz couldn't help but smile in response. "It just swaps pockets. And we only have to direct it into the right ones."

CHAPTER 28

STICK AND CARROT

THE CASTLE LIVENED UP even more from the spreading rumors, and the fact that Lentz had had such a suspiciously long meeting with the emperor in the imperial chambers. A curious crowd of courtiers gathered outside the emperor's chambers, and the guards could barely hold them back until reinforcements arrived.

The captain of the palace guard, urgently called away from his incredibly entertaining questioning of the emperor's courtesans, had to personally visit the emperor and ask what to do. Ma Ju Ro was carried away with talking to Lentz about his health reforms, as he called them, and reacted with extreme efficiency.

"Send gawpers away, anyone with business can wait in line. When you're done, come back with Koerlig, Hector."

"It will be done, my ruler!" Hector hit his chest

in salute, grinning. "Chase away those lazy bums? With pleasure!"

Luca had just turned back to continue his exciting conversation of imperial medicine and to recommend new methods of treating incurable diseases that he'd managed to dig out of Esk's legacy, but he heard the clank of metal again.

"Forgive me, your imperial highness," Hector said, embarrassed. "But who is Koerlig?"

"Lentz?" Ma Ju Ro glanced at the healer.

He laconically explained to the captain that they were talking about the new chief of the first imperial community clinic, but for now his secretary.

"That rogue with the weaselly face?" the captain asked in surprise. He scratched the back of his head and walked to the door, muttering. "Strange are your ways, Sacred Mother! May you always bless us..."

As soon as the captain left, the doors of the imperial bedchamber opened and Keirinia appeared, and in such a salacious outfit that Lentz blushed and averted his eyes. Luca ordered himself not to stare, although he wanted to stare so badly that it was intolerable. Fortunately, the girl quickly realized this wasn't the time and didn't act up. She just threw a glance at the empty tray of fruit and asked whether the men wanted to eat something heartier. The men did, and the first courtesan got to work. A fed man was a generous man. She knew that firsthand.

Then a guard by the name of Urtso appeared. He got straight to the point and reported that Reyk Lee Vensiro was insisting to see the emperor (with a group of young women and some 'vagrants' in tow), and said he had an 'appointment.'

"They can wait," Ma Ju Ro waved him away, and those three words, uttered by Urtso outside, caused a fresh wave of excited whispering.

Soon Luca had enough Wheel energy to do what he intended to ensure Lentz's safety. It didn't give the healer complete protection, but it allowed him to relatively easily withstand any deadly wound or poison. All that remained was to see how it would work in action.

"Accepted," the emperor said in response to another of Lentz's suggestions. He stretched out a hand to him. Lentz responded with a handshake. "We'll stop there for now, we've already planned for years ahead. I expect a detailed step-by-step plan of action from you."

He grasped the healer by the forearm, as was customary in the Empire when making deals, and at that very moment, it seemed, his metamorphosis skill leveled up. Although the emperor couldn't say whether it had happened some time before. He was able to inject toxin-neutralizing agents into Kora, after all. In any case, he only paid attention to the Wheel's new message in that moment.

Metamorphosis: +1.
Ability level three reached!

BLOOD OF FATE

Ability to control body at initial level: molecular generation with properties given by request.

Gained ability to use programmed nano-agents with set replication cycles and functionality, and transfer them to other biological objects. Unlocked ranged control over objects infiltrated with nano-agents as long as they remain in view.

The number of objects connected at a time depends on the carrier's influence level and available Wheel energy.

"Is everything alright, ruler?" Lentz asked in concern, seeing Ma Ju Ro frozen and staring into space.

"Yes," Ma Ju Ro sighed.

It took time to comprehend his new skills and to get a grasp on basic nano and biomedical technologies, the foundations of molecular physics and the systems of units for naming and designating decimal fractions.

The emperor sat back in a chair, holding his head. This singular gold mine of knowledge from Esk'Onegut's legacy made him feel like he'd jumped into a well of icy water. His breath caught, his working memory of his current place and time and even recent events and thoughts was temporarily wiped, and all to explain to the young traveler the meaning of the word 'nano.'

Finally, all his knowledge had been restructured and organized in the shelves of his mind and was ready for use. There were truly incredible implications behind that short description of his new skills from metamorphosis level three.

The metamorphic agents injected into the healer through his skin, programmed to replicate and intervene against any potential injury to the healer, could save him even from strangulation, bypassing the lungs to oxygenate the blood. Only a beheading or a dissection would send the medic to the Sacred Mother. Or to Two-horns, depending on his luck at the Threshold.

Thinking for a moment, Ma Ju Ro stood up, leaned against the terrace railing and froze, enchanted by what he saw. Lentz kept sitting quietly, observing his ruler sidelong and fearing to remind him of his presence even with the sound of his breath.

Luca looked at the sun for a while as it made its way down to the horizon, studied the glittering ocean and appreciated the fact that he was observing a truly beautiful sight for the first time in his life — the sunset. It took his breath away. The giant ball of fire slowly dropped down into the sea, and the emperor would have stood and watched until the sun melted completely into the waves, giving off a barely visible light from the depths... But he had too much to do. And it was all important!

He had to provide for his mother and Kora, and in a way that didn't cause them any problems whether he remained the emperor or not. And how was he to behave with them? What would he say about Luca's fate? How would he explain? And if he told his family the truth, would they believe him?

The financial and taxation reforms required to fill up the treasury quickly would require deeper thought than a flash of an idea from Esk's legacy. In the experience of Esk's previous life, the pinnacle of robbing the people was a tax on air. That was exactly what led to the untimely demise of *that* emperor.

The webs of conspiracy all around were a subject for the creation of a separate strategy, but they were merely a consequence of dissatisfaction with his rule, and that was something that couldn't be fixed in a day.

Reinforcing the army, improving the state's communication policies, dispensing with unnecessary courtiers and surrounding himself with people whose loyalty was worth earning, winning over the northern barons in the looming battle against Rezsinius's troops...

Intelligence was extremely important, but, as he'd managed to learn from Lentz, Commander Hustig of the imperial army was far from loyal. His intelligence couldn't be trusted.

On top of it all, tomorrow was Yadugara's award ceremony at the healers' guild. He had to think of what to do with that cretin.

And most importantly of all, Fourth Advisor Cross. The only link connecting him with those whom his black-skinned khhar cell-mate Terant had called racants. He had only scraps of knowledge about the wider, inaccessible world, partly from

Terant and partly from the memory of his body's former owner.

But before getting started with all that, he had to make sure of something. The emperor decided to test one of his new abilities as soon as he could.

Ma Ju Ro turned sharply toward the healer, put a hand on his shoulder and barely grazed his bare neck with a finger. Lentz flinched.

"This very morning, you were planning to kill me. Now you're on my side," the emperor said softly. "Tell me, Lentz, what are your true motives? Do you fear me?"

"No, my lord," the healer shook his head.

Looking into the man's eyes, Luca chuckled in satisfaction. They were filling with blood. Lentz, feeling himself unwell, tried to blink, then took off his glasses, grabbed at his eyes and moaned. The emperor canceled his last command, deciding to stick to more merciful methods in future.

Lentz cowered, his face streaming with tears. He shook slightly and didn't know what to expect next from his ruler. He put his glasses back on nervously.

"It seems you've forgotten that I'm more than just a man now, Lentz. Lie to me again and you'll go blind. You can lie to others as much as you want, if it helps our cause, but never dare lie to me! Do I make myself clear?"

Lentz nodded so hard that his glasses fell off again. Luca grabbed them as they fell and offered them back to the only man he could trust. A little demonstration not only of his strength, but also his abilities.

"As for the rest, be calm, my friend and ally. Together, we will achieve our plans and bring back to the Empire not only its former glory, but the well-being of its citizens. And while ever you are loyal to me, you are under my protection. I have placed divine protection on you. You will survive a blade in the neck, or a dagger to the heart. Poisons will have no effect on you..."

"Thank you, my lord!" Lentz fell to his knees and bowed his head. "Forgive me for lying to you! I couldn't say that I fear you, I saw your mercy for me and did not want to offend you! But truly, should a loyal subject not fear the ire of his ruler?"

"Stand up. Fear is nothing to be ashamed of, for you are a living person," Luca said, surprised at his language and wondering how such lofty thoughts came to him. It happened so naturally that he just took it as a given. "But there is no reason to fear. I am not building the new Empire on fear, but on trust. I have one request for you, Lentz. Stay just as loyal as ever to science and medicine. I value you for that, not for the fake loyalty that Hector shows, or for servility. Would my great ancestor Ma Ju Ro the First have promoted his allies for that?"

"I understand, my lord. Would you allow me to test something?"

Luca nodded. Lentz grabbed a fruit knife from the table and stabbed himself in the palm. He screamed, pulled out the knife and then watched in awe as the blood congealed and the wound knitted itself closed. His eyes widened in amazement as he wiped away the bloodstain.

"Stunning! You truly do possess the power of the Sacred Mother, your imperial majesty!"

Just as Lentz was exclaiming his surprise, a whole delegation uncertainly drifted into the imperial chambers. Keirinia with the old man Nem, heading up a chain of servants with dishes full of treats, and Captain Kolot Hector, who for some reason was dragging Koerlig behind him by the ear.

"What happened, Hector?" Lentz spread his hands. "Why are you holding him like that?"

"He tried to run away, the scoundrel."

"Why, Koerlig?" the healer said in even greater befuddlement.

"This damn..." The secretary nodded toward the captain, who gave him a cuff round the back of the head. He squealed and corrected himself. "Captain Hector and his people have already brought in half the palace for questioning. None have come back! I thought that I... that they..."

"I can explain everything, my lord!" The captain fell to one knee.

"I don't doubt it, Hector." Ma Ju Ro took a deep breath through his nose and smiled. "You are all invited to dine with me. Captain, Koerlig, Keirinia... Let us discuss matters as we eat. And invite in Reyk Lee Vensiro with his 'news.' While the table is being set, give me some time alone. I have things to think about!

The old man Nem rushed out for the reyk. The others exchanged surprised glances and began to sit down at the table. Keirinia closer to the emperor's seat, with Lentz and Hector at the other side. As for Koerlig, he remained where he stood, trying to figure out if he'd misheard when the emperor had invited him personally to the table.

Luca went out onto the terrace, closed the door behind him and watched for a long time as the sun sank into the ocean. *Why in Two-horns name not?* he asked himself. *Maybe I'll be lucky.*

The universe itself considered that he was doing everything right. He glanced at the numbers in the top right corner of his view and they expanded into a line.

Tsoui points: +1. Current balance: 24.

Enough for two spins of the Wheel. But today he would spin it just once.

CHAPTER 29

RED SECTOR

THE OCEAN'S SURFACE sparkled with short blinding flashes from the reflected sun, and Luca screwed up his eyes. The longest day of his life was coming to an end, but for him — the emperor — it was all only just beginning. In the next hour or two, he needed to make sure he could rely on these people in the future, and that meant he needed to convince them. And not in the same way he had Lentz, by the carrot and stick. Demonstrating his abilities publicly would surely lead to uprising and rebellion. For them, his abilities would only serve to prove that their ruler had turned into a mutant.

And such people were feared and hated in the Empire. His royal carrots wouldn't help him then, nor the deadly stick. Rumor would abound, and by morning the palace would be taken by a roiling crowd of peasants, with the aristocrats cheering them on from a safe distance, and not necessarily only those his rebellious cousin Rezsinius had bought.

But for now, while he had a few moments to breathe, Luca activated a spin of the Wheel.

Luca'Onegut, life one.
Reminiscent. Successor to Esk'Onegut.
Influence level: 0.
Tsoui points: 24.

Activated Wheel Spin: 10 Tsoui points will be deducted.
Use?

Luca thought for a moment, and then decisively pressed 'Yes.' He needed to be more powerful, and up to now the Wheel had given him abilities without which he wouldn't survive, as if it understood his need. He would have died in a puddle to Karim Kovachar's good aim, or in Yadugara's cellar. First the healer would have drained him, then the chinils would have eaten him to the bone. It was as if the Wheel saw the future and knew with what to reward him.

He kept his eyes closed, but could still see it. Everything disappeared, the darkening sky, the ocean waves, and he saw only the Wheel. It was slightly larger than last time, and it was picking up speed. The segments merged into a speckled disc around the size of the emperor's dining table.

Slowing, it split at first into barely discernible fragments, then into fully separate ones. When it finally slowed to its last turn, Luca saw a series of white sections, then three prize sections in a row; blue, gold and... He decided not to watch, covering his eyes with his hands, but that did nothing.

Slowly, like a drop of sweat rolling down the emperor's forehead, the Wheel turned beyond the active blue zone that would give him mastery in some skill. It almost stopped on the gold section. A superpower! Luca was no risk-taker. He'd had no time to develop that skill, be it good or bad to have, in his time as a cripple. The spectral voices of the two senior personalities, Esk'Onegut and the true Ma Ju Ro the Fourth, were another matter. They watched in ecstasy... and groaned from that particular contrasting disappointment of a jackpot slipping through one's fingers.

The Wheel had stopped on red.

Wheel spin completed.
Spin result: Red Sector.
Reward:
Luca'Onegut receives the ailment (applied to current body and world of existence) UESM.

UESM? Ailment? Luca felt himself from head to toe, jumped on up and down on both legs, then felt his face. Nothing appeared to have changed, but nonetheless his heart was trying to thump its way out of his chest. The word 'reward' felt particularly mocking.

Uncontrolled Excessive Sexual Magnetism (UESM)

Classification: virus.
Threat level: deadly in certain conditions.
Contagious level: not infectious.

A rare viral illness. Created by scientists on a number of humanoid worlds as an aphrodisiac that arouses interest, sympathy and sexual attraction in members of the opposite sex. No antidote to the virus has been invented.

The base colony in the host's body releases a viral agent into the atmosphere, which infiltrates the bodies of all encountered members of the opposite sex, and if mating is possible, transfers the code of an individually configured pheromone to the database. The colony generates a targeted carrier virus, which produces an irreversible pheromone in a very short time, infecting the individual.

The carrier's life is always short. All members of the opposite sex (or sexes in the case of intelligent life requiring more than one sexual partner) that encounter the carrier immediately focus all their attention only on the carrier. Possessing (multiple instances of sexual contact) them becomes their sole and most important goal of those affected, the meaning of their life cycle.

UESM does not harm the carrier by itself, but socializing always leads to an early death due to exhaustion and physical injury incompatible with life.

Overly aroused members of the opposite sex have at times been known to literally tear the carrier to...

"My lord!" Lentz's voice rang out loud behind the emperor's back. Ma Ju Ro shivered, but the healer didn't see it, too busy staring at the floor in embarrassment. "Forgive me for disturbing you. Hector is drooling, but has so far restrained himself from starting dinner without you. Also, Reyk Lee Vensiro has arrived with his companions. Should I keep them out for now?"

"Give me a couple of minutes, Lentz," Luca replied dully, fearing to turn around. It was still unclear how the ailment he had 'won' would work and be how it might show in his appearance. It would help to get a clear picture of it soon... "They can wait. As you too can... wait."

Lentz closed the doors. The emperor carefully glanced back. The healer had definitely gone inside. Leaning against the railing, Ma Ju Ro immersed himself in thought, staring at the fine burning line of the setting sun.

Sexual magnetism. So he would be irresistible, or rather the desired partner of every woman he met? On the one hand, it sounded nice, but on the other... he was a coveted prize for any single woman in the Empire as it was. Perhaps even for any married one. But did he want that for himself? He imagined Aunt Mo, Yadugara's cook, suddenly burning with passion for him and throwing herself at him with obvious intent, and it made him sick. What could he do? Banish all women from the palace and surround himself with an impenetrable wall of guards? Or...

Detected infection by UESM virus...
Detected unsanctioned alteration in metabolism...
Detected cellular influence...
Activating countermeasure...

His heart stopped as he awaited the verdict of his metamorphosis. The power of the Wheel fought another power, but still of the same Wheel, and the text logs flashing before his eyes stilled. His hair stood on end, his limbs froze, he lost consciousness, but awoke again before he fell, seeing only the world flashing, and the stars disappearing from the night sky within a heartbeat.

The text logs were replaced by new ones, but those froze as well as the emperor read them.

Countermeasure impossible!
Recalculating data...
More non-organic energy reserves required.
Estimated time to accumulation of required Wheel energy with current tasks taken into account: 21 hours.

Hmm... He could last twenty four hours. But he definitely shouldn't meet with his mom or Kora until late the next night.

"Your imperial majesty!" Reyk Lee Vensiro gave a short bow. "You have had the grace to allow my humble companions the great honor of beholding you in person. Allow me to introduce them: he is highly active, energetic and, without a doubt, utterly loyal to the Empire and your majesty, the widely respected ringmaster of the circus, famed from the northern Wastelands to the torrid southern deserts of Two-horns, Kratomir Djobja... Bodja...

"Radomirco..." a short man next to the reyk whispered quietly. He had a bald head scattered with tufty patches of growth. Ma Ju Ro heard him and a barely perceptible smile formed on his face. "We're Dobzhani."

"...Kratomir Bodjobdzhani!" Vensiro blurted out and smiled charmingly, baring his large horse-like teeth, one of which appeared to be missing.

Lentz leaned toward the emperor's ear and quietly explained.

"He hired some cheap whores and got carried away with them, threw a lot of money about. He woke up in the morning with no whores, money, or clothes, just half a bottle of booze on the pillow. Nice of them to leave it, really. The reyk drowned his sorrows in the rest of the bottle, then wandered drunkenly into the slums and fell into a ditch.

"He lost his tooth in the ditch?" Ma Ju Ro asked with genuine childish curiosity.

"Not at all, your majesty," Hector interjected, picking at his ear with a finger. While awaiting the emperor's return, he'd had plenty to drink and had gotten a lot more open, and Luca made no effort to discourage him. "My lieutenant knocked his tooth out. They got into a fight in a pub over a beautiful girl."

"That was another tooth, we've already reinserted that one," Lentz corrected him.

"Could be..." the campaign said, stroking his chin. "That's not the point. Lettekah sincerely offered this overdressed peacock redress, but he refused."

"Why did he refuse?"

"I remember this story. It was last week, yes?" the chief imperial medic asked.

"That's right," Hector agreed.

"So why did he refuse?" Ma Ju Ro asked again.

"The girl turned out to have a surprise," Lentz explained. "And in all senses of the word. She was married to some shopkeeper..."

"Damn him too," the captain noted. "Both of them got far too carried away, and when they found out, they were already drinking together the next day. They were seen together at dawn, embracing on the stoop of a brothel..."

The protagonist of this gossip, realizing that the emperor wasn't listening to him, had fallen silent and was submissively awaiting permission to continue. The stupefied circus ringmaster shifted nervously next to him, along with three girls in a row, all dark of complexion, strong and fit, with narrow waists and impressive curves. Luca watched them as he listened to the captain's tales, unable to tear his eyes away. One of the girls, a blue-eyed brunette, sensed this and smiled at him shyly.

Keirinia on the emperor's right coughed delicately and touched his elbow. She was behaving normally. Luca had managed to use his remaining Wheel energy to 'convince' his metamorphosis to at least block the pheromone generation for a short time, even if it couldn't heal him. Luca tore his gaze away from the girl and looked at the captain.

... so he stretched out his right hand, put his left hand on the bend..."

"Hector!" Lentz interrupted him. "His imperial..."

"Apologies," the captain of the palace guard mumbled, leaning over his dish and sinking his teeth into a lamb shank.

"Reyk Vensiro, please, continue," Ma Ju Ro asked his guest.

"Ahem," the reyk began. "As I already said, Maestro Kratomir has brought to the capital, may its walls stand eternally, the most incredible circus of monsters the Empire has ever seen! At your first call, at your merest nod, my ruler, the artists of the circus will perform for you!"

"I don't understand," the captain grunted. "Are they here too, then?"

"Y-yes... your majesty..." the short Dobzhani

said after a nudge from the reyk, turning a deep shade of red and barely standing on his wobbly legs. The last ringmaster that had performed in the palace had ended up buried alive in the intermission. His artists had sung an obscene song and the previous empire had quite unfortunately thought that it referred to him. "At the reyk's command, my entire troupe has come with me to the palace."

"Why didn't you lead with that?!" the captain barked, cracking his bare lamb shank on the table, dropping the bone on the floor and wiping his hands.

Furrowing his brows, Luca stealthily and gently touched his arm, injecting several alcohol-neutralizing agents. The captain's liver obviously needed some help, and Hector needed sobering up before he went too far, after which he would have only one path — to the chopping block.

"Thank you, Radomirco," the emperor nodded beatifically. "I'm sure we'll find time to admire your performance a little later. As for you, reyk, please, continue. Introduce me to your wonderful companions."

"With the greatest of pleasures, my ruler!" Lee Vensiro moved the short man back and then dared to step forward closer to the table with his 'three beautiful flowers of the South.' "Their barbarian names are too complex and baffling for your elegant ear, so I have abbreviated them: this one, with the hair down to her a... ahem, down to the bottom of her back, is Taya. Her parents — wild, but honorable hillfolk — brought their daughter up to strictly respect the Sacred Mother and your majesty. Step forward."

Taya proudly raised her chin and swayed her hips as she stepped forward, looking Ma Ju Ro up and down playfully. Apparently, life after the girl left her father's home wasn't so strict.

"Master..." she said in singsong tones. "Serving you is the only thing I strive for."

The captain span his index finger in the air. Taya understood him and gracefully stood on her tiptoes, span several times with her arms raised. *Like a swan*, thought Luca, who had never seen a swan. *Perfection itself.*

Taya, as if sensing her ruler's interest, span faster. Her ginger hair hit a jug and knocked it off, making old Nem rush to pick up the pieces. The hillfolk daughter's emerald eyes widened in fear. She covered her mouth and stepped back.

"It's fine, Taya," Ma Ju Ro soothed her. "Our cellars are full of wine, but hair like that takes years to grow..."

Keirinia wrinkled her nose. New or not, it seemed to her that the emperor was still his same old horny self. Although more polite and... kinder. She felt a stab of jealousy, but not like before, when she'd competed for his attention with his other favorites. This felt different.

"Maya, my ruler," the reyk declared, pressing his fingers into another girl's thick ashen hair and revealing a sharp-tipped ear. "A beautiful and charming daughter of the proud forest people. This little mutation gives her a special charm."

Tall at a head higher than the emperor, Maya bent down in a bow.

"My ruler! I was born to fulfil your desires!"

Smiling widely, the girl raised her leg vertically, held it close to her body and froze in the pose, demonstrating her flexibility, coordination and stunning elasticity. Then she stood on her hands. Her short skirt fell, her legs parted and froze parallel to the floor, baring her sultry cheeks. Spellbinding views opened up before those sitting at the table.

Luca, who had been waiting impatiently for the reyk to introduce his blue-eyed brunette, froze with his jaw dropped. Koerlig at the far end of the table stretched out his thin neck and stared, immortalizing the eloquent sight in his memory. Keirinia drank her wine and stayed silent.

"Two-horns take me..." Captain Kolot Hector said in stunned tones, as a man who had likely seen a great deal in this world.

"How is that anatomically possible?" Lentz marveled. "Is the structure of the..."

Luca didn't hear the rest. He just heard the blood rushing to his ears, his heart beating up a storm. Two lines of text appeared before his clouded eyes.

Attention! Non-organic energy reserves exhausted!

WORLD 99 BOOK ONE

UESM virus can no longer be blocked!

Luca slowly turned his head to the left. The first courtesan Keirinia watched him with a frightening hunger gleaming in her eyes. She licked her lips like a predator.

CHAPTER 30

GREAT ANCESTOR SPIRIT

KOLOT HECTOR, the captain of the palace guard, enjoyed every second of his evening. It was approaching midnight, and only a day before he would never have imagined that he would see that witching hour in the imperial chambers. He'd never had the chance to attend events like this by the emperor's side. That was the prerogative of his advisors, lovers, hordes of brown-noses and hangers-on from the nobility, and of course the pernicious Crane, the imperial secretary.

The latest of the reyk's introductions by the name of Maya amazed even him, an experienced connoisseur of carnality and the female form. Her trick astounded the captain! How was it possible? Now she was standing on her feet again, but Ma Ju Ro wasn't looking at her. It wasn't clear whether her acrobatics had worked on the emperor. All the captain could say with confidence was that the South was home to people who lived without fear or shame before the Sacred Mother! Where Kolot Hector was from, such shamelessness would earn a branding for the entire family...

"Ruler," Keirinia whispered in the emperor's ear hotly, leaning over the table. "I'm on fire for you! Let's leave all these people alone and dive into an abyss of pleasure..."

Hector heard each word from the first courtesan, being so fortunately seated between her and the emperor. And although Lentz didn't so much as twitch an eyebrow, the captain frowned. The clock had struck midnight, and the old Ma Ju Ro the Fourth had returned. Any moment now he'd start doing it right on the table without a care for who could see. The animal! He was the same lascivious creature as always! Such a pity. It had truly seemed as if the emperor had changed after the transfusion procedure.

Ma Ju Ro stood up sharply from the table and whispered something to Lentz sitting nearby. Hector didn't hear exactly what.

"Hector, everyone out!" Lentz shouted predictably. "His majesty is tired and wishes to be alone!

What a surprise. Hector rose grudgingly from the table and chuckled. The blood rushing to that pig's loins had sent everything back to normal. And no wonder! That clown Vensiro had brought some incredible ladies with immeasurable charm, but Two-horns take them, the meeting was supposed to be for business! And what a performance from that flirt Keirinia! That 'fire' of hers could have waited. Everyone was having such a good time! Maybe even the circus monsters might have performed! Well, captain, time to go back to reality.

"This audience is ended, ladies and gentlemen! Please make your way to the exit!" He spread his hands and gently pushed the southern girls away, along with everyone else. Maya hesitated a moment, keeping her inviting gaze fixed on the emperor, and the captain had to push harder. "Move along! Quickly, quickly!"

The girls left the imperial chambers under furious glances from Reyk Lee Vensiro, who had decided that one of them had done something wrong and angered his majesty. Which was clearly not the case, but the captain didn't bother to convince the peacock aristocrat. Instead, he pushed him and the Dobzhani ringmaster toward the door, grabbing a jug of wine from a servant's tray as he passed.

"Hector, we're not done yet!" the emperor shouted to him. "Come back once you've escorted our guests out."

Ah yes, of course. The captain grudgingly set the jug on the table. His imperial, Two-horns-cursed majesty must need some help. Someone to hold him up. He knew all about what happened in the orgies of high society, but he'd never had to professionally involve himself in one. Sacred Mother, this was all he needed! He shut the doors behind the visitors and then heard the healer's voice.

"Koerlig, help me carry Lady Keirinia! She's sick! Kolot, you help too! She isn't as light as you might think!"

"Careful!" Ma Ju Ro ordered. "Take her to my chambers."

"What's wrong with her?" Hector asked Lentz.

"She feinted... No visible cause..." The healer shrugged, casting a glance at the emperor.

"It seems that Keirinia drank too much, got tired and fell asleep," the emperor said softly. "Everything is fine."

The first courtesan lay unconscious, sprawled back in her chair. The captain carefully grabbed her by the legs and found that she really did weigh a respectable amount. No wonder, with that ass! While the old man Nem and his servants cleared the table, Hector, Lentz and his wily secretary very carefully carried out the emperor's order.

"I wouldn't stare like that if I were you, friend," Hector advised Koerlig.

"I'm not... It's just..." the secretary mumbled and averted his gaze.

Keirinia's skirt had ridden up, baring her mighty and appetizing thighs, and it wasn't easy even for the captain to resist his rising animal urges. In the meantime, the emperor stepped out onto the terrace. Hector saw him wipe sweat from his brow and lean against the balcony railings for support.

BLOOD OF FATE

They took his favorite to the bedroom and put her on the bed. Lentz adjusted the girl's bunched-up skirt in a fatherly manner and tucked her in under the covers. Nights were cold in the palace. Noticing the captain's searching gaze, the healer blushed and left the bedroom first.

They went back to the dining table and sat in silence, waiting for Ma Ju Ro. The servants laid the table with desserts in silence, along with fruit and fresh jugs of wine, then they left the chambers. Old man Nem hovered a while, peeked out onto the terrace, heard an order from his ruler and left as well.

Koerlig thoughtfully munched away at a sweet and juicy lamai fruit, staring into the distance. Judging by his red ears, the boy was still immersed in fantasies of those three girls. And perhaps even of Keirinia herself. She was an exciting lady, why hide from it? Yet she put her efforts into arousing a hundred-year-old man.

"I want a smoke," Hector broke the silence. "What does he want from us?"

"He wants us to help him," Lentz answered, offering him a pouch of tobacco.

"With what, Jurgeas? And why is this conman here?" he nodded toward Koerlig as he rolled a cigar.

Tobacco was a luxury that only the aristocracy could afford. Hector sometimes managed to get his hands on goods confiscated from merchants, which was how he'd picked up his addiction. He lit his cigar from a candle and puffed away in satisfaction, blowing out aromatic smoke.

"What can we help him with? What sort of emperor is he if he needs help?"

Lentz stayed silent for some time, then scratched his nose and spoke.

"Want a drink, Kolot?" Lentz waited for the captain's nod, then poured him some wine. "'Jurgeas', wow. It's been a while since anyone called me by my first name. I doubt anyone else in the palace knows it."

"It's my job," the captain explained, "To know all the courtiers. So what's our ruler doing? Why as he brought us here?"

"He'll explain it himself, Kolot. And Koerlig is now his trusted man. Like us. You and me."

"Who? Me?" The captain let out a hollow chuckle. "A trusted man? Does Herdinia know?"

"The Crane?" Lentz asked. "I doubt it very much. I doubt very much that her word will have any weight at all for the emperor now."

"What makes you think that?" the captain asked skeptically. "You know the Crane, she'll wrap him around her finger. Especially now that idiot Naut has had the misfortune of making an ill-fated assassination attempt and is languishing in a cell. Or did you whisper something about her to the emperor? Was she with you conspirators? But then why isn't she in chains?"

"No, she had no part in the conspiracy," Lentz grimaced. "Why would she? Whatever the advisors might think, true power in the Empire belongs...

belonged, that is, to her. The emperor didn't trust anyone more than that old hag.

"She's only thirty nine," the captain noted. He glanced at the terrace beyond the glass. The emperor was still just standing there. From inside it looked as if he was thinking about something, which was amazing in itself. "So what about the Crane?"

"The emperor changed after the last transfusion, Kolot," Lentz answered quietly. "You may not believe it now, but you will."

"How?"

"It is as if the spirit of his great ancestor Ma Ju Ro the First has settled within him. He has started thinking of the country and its people..."

"What?" Hector choked on his wine. He'd expected anything, all the way to news that the emperor's member had fallen off and Ma Ju Ro was no longer interested in the palace's ladies, but not this revelation. "You're talking crap, Jurgeas!"

"No, Captain Hector, he isn't!" Koerlig interjected and blushed. Withering under Kolot's mighty gaze, he fell silent.

"Speak!" the captain ordered.

"Forgive me..." Koerlig uttered. "I can't tell you everything, but I can confirm Master Lentz's words. The emperor..."

He couldn't finish the thought before said emperor came back in from the terrace. He walked to the table with a spring in his step, slapping each man on the shoulder, striking them all dumb yet again. He even apologized for his long absence.

"Let us continue..." he said, taking his seat. "Or rather, let us begin. But first, Hector, tell me what you think of all this.

"My lord?"

"You sit at this table for the first time?"

"Yes, sire."

"Do you have any thoughts on that count, commander? And in general, what do you think of me and the situation in the country?"

Hector gulped. Commander? A rank promotion meant transferring to another military structure. The palace guard had never been under the command of anyone above captain, and the functions of the service were mostly ceremonial. The army defended the palace in the case of rebellion, while the palace guard specialized in minor issues; breaking up conflicts at court, quieting down drunken guests, emptying people's pockets of silverware on the way out... They protected the emperor, of course, but without zeal. Naut hadn't paid them enough for more. As for the inquisitors, they knew their place. The servants, cooks, courtiers... They had no real power, neither open nor clandestine. They were not feared.

Not knowing how to hide his embarrassment, Kolot drank his wine, put his glass down, adjusted the tablecloth, swatted at imaginary motes of dust on his trousers and raised his eyes.

"Speak openly, Hector," Ma Ju Ro warned him. "Hide anything and I will know it. And then we won't be talking like this again. Lentz added a certain potion to the wine. Your ears will go red if you speak a lie.

Hector automatically grabbed at his ears and looked at the healer. Lentz nodded barely perceptibly, confirming the emperor's words. *I should have left with Vensiro!* the captain thought. *And when and to whom did Koerlig tell a lie? His ears are redder than I've ever seen them!* He gulped down more wine.

"Speak," the emperor ordered. "Whatever you say, there will be no consequences. The important thing is not to dissemble."

"Well, why not?" Hector sighed, relaxing slightly. "When will I get another chance? You asked for it! You, your majesty, are in an untenable position! What is there to talk about if the only people you can now trust in all the Empire are myself, a healer that wanted to poison you this morning, and this pimple-faced weasel Koerlig, who you didn't know existed yesterday? And now this crook is — ha-ha! — is to lead an imperial clinic! Ha-ha-ha!" He continued laughing uncontrollably for a while. "You'll promise anything just to get the support of even a pathetic conniver such as this!"

Nobody else at the table shared in his mirth. Hector stopped. The emperor and Lentz waited coolly for the fiery speech to continue. Koerlig's ears were even redder, and his cheeks were starting to burn as well. The boy must be thinking lies. Angry at Koerlig for some unknown reason, Kolot continued with even greater ferocity.

"Rezsinius approaches from the south, with veterans and an army from the southern barons. In the North, the barons are choking on hordes of mutants. The capital is ruled by thieves and General Hustig. Even in your own palace, Herdinia the Crane has more power than you! You sleep with Keirinia, but do you at least know who she really serves? By fulfilling the whims of your favorite, you ignorantly play right into the Crane's hands! I wouldn't be surprised if she was already making a deal with your cousin!"

"All the worse for her if she is," Ma Ju Ro shrugged. "Continue."

"What do you know about the ration warehouses, my lord? That's right!" Hector nodded in satisfaction when he got no answer. "Nothing at all. Our people starve! Warehouses have been burned, Rezsinius's forces are blockading merchant ships from the sea. We haven't had any deliveries from the south for two months now! The farmers are hiding their harvests, they don't have enough to feed themselves! In your name, Hustig has squeezed them so hard that they're dying from hunger, and then he sent their grain to the capital markets with a ten-fold price increase! And, I swear on the Sacred Mother, the Empire has never seen a ruler worse than you! If another attempt were made on your life today, I wouldn't lift a finger to prevent it!" The captain fell silent, realizing that he'd just said all that to the emperor himself.

"I see, Hector," Ma Ju Ro said, as cool as

before. "Drink some wine, refresh your throat and continue."

Hector grabbed a jug and latched onto it. He might never get the chance to drink wine again. Never mind wine, he'd be grateful enough to see the sunrise! Gods, what an idiot he was! Two-horns must be laughing at him, must have forced his tongue to flap!

Gulping down wine, Hector calculated the consequences. What if he were to take out his sword and drive it into the emperor's heart? How would Lentz and his hound Koerlig react? They were no match for him, of course, and he could gut them too if he had to! Then he'd have to drag Naut out of jail and confer with him on how to get the best price out of Rezsinius...

The doors to the imperial chambers burst open, and strangers ran into the room, clanking in black plate armor. Helmets hid their faces. Three, six... Before he'd even had time to think about it, Hector had jumped across the table, unsheathing his sword in flight, and stood before the intruders.

"Not a step further. Who are you? In the name of the emperor, leave this room at once!

"At ease, captain," a huge man in full armor and a helmet said as he stepped forward from the ranks . His voice sounded muted, but familiar. "Calm yourself, Hector! Your boys are enjoying life in the capital's brothel and are most happy. I advise you to leave these chambers, forget what you have seen here and join them. All expenses paid, captain!"

"I swore loyalty to his majesty, General Hustig..." Hector's voice sounded strained. He turned and saw that the emperor was still sitting there. Either frozen in horror or shitting himself in fear.

"As did I. And?" Hustig shrugged and took off his helmet. "That emperor is no more. All I see is a fat pig! Or is this drunken bravado of yours from dining with him at the same table? Did you feel chosen, eh, captain? Allow me to disappoint you. You are not chosen. A harlot sat in your seat yesterday. This is a place for his whores, captain! Stand aside. He is not worth this. I will forget that you said anything..."

From behind came a grunting and a rustling. Ma Ju Ro rose heavily from the table and walked toward Hector. Hustig leered in amusement.

"Would you look at that. He can still move on his own!"

Laughter came from beneath the helmets. Hector looked at the object of their humor and his eyes widened; Ma Ju Ro was smiling too.

"You must be clairvoyant, Kolot. Another attempt on my life indeed. But you were wrong about one thing," he said, placing a hand on his shoulder. "You did lift a finger. It seems you value your oath and the Empire more than you think."

"Look, boys, a talking pig!" Hustig said in mock surprise and laughed. "Wow! Hah-hah-hah!"

His laughter echoed through the imperial

chambers, but received no support. Hector looked behind his back, not believing his wide eyes, and screamed.

Hustig slowly turned his head. In an instant, his scream joined Hector's, only his was louder and more desperate. The captain knew by experience that such shrill screams come only from wild, primordial terror.

CHAPTER 31

GENERAL HUSTIG'S CONFESSION

IT HAPPENED INSTANTLY, and clearly not because the emperor intended it so. As soon as he saw the strangers bursting into his chambers, his heart started thumping in his chest, spreading adrenaline through his veins. With great effort, Luca maintained the appearance of calm, and only his heaving chest gave him away to Lentz completely. That said, the healer himself was sitting in terror, afraid to move a muscle.

Not knowing what to do or how to wriggle out of the situation, he stood behind the captain, now newly minted commander, and started thinking feverishly. His first concern was his mom and sister, his second for his trusted men Lentz and Hector. But the captain's action in standing up in his defense against General Hustig gave him certainty;

he wouldn't let his people get hurt!

He put a hand on Hector's shoulder.

"You must be clairvoyant, Kolot. Another attempt on my life indeed. But you were wrong about one thing. You did lift a finger. It seems you value your oath and the Empire more than you think."

"Look, boys, a talking pig!" Hustig laughed. "Wow!"

The general's chin was smaller than the emperor's third, but to hear such an insult from Hustig, who himself had never suffered from excessive leanness? That disrespectful insult was the last straw. In the last few days, Luca had been stoned to death, beaten by guards and Senior Apprentice Penant, peeled by Yadugara's slaves, poisoned by Lentz and Keirinia, he'd had his life sucked out, he'd been eaten by chinils, and, as can sometimes happen, this boy, who had been famed for his limitless patience since childhood, lost control of himself. When he heard the general's laughter, the furious Luca exploded; he got mad, and with unstoppable ferocity he wished for everyone that threatened him and his family to die, with no thought of the consequences.

At that moment, the concept of that 'everyone' was embodied in a few entirely tangible figures in black armor. Luca imagined them being torn to pieces... Metamorphosis assessed the task and gave him an elegant solution, lighting up his direction of movement.

From there, the emperor acted on instinct. Suddenly thrusting his left arm ahead, he released a tentacle from his index finger, so fine that it could have been compared with the tether that bound the khhar Terant in the jail. The fine string jumped to behind the soldiers, curved around them from behind and tied itself into a big loop behind Hustig's back. Luca jerked his hand, felt a sharp pain at the tip of his finger as if a hot needle had pierced his nail, and the string fell off an instant later. His Wheel energy reserves had been depleted, they hadn't had long to recover.

At first nothing happened, the soldiers just twitched. The five warriors didn't make a single sound.

Then their swords and shields fell from their hands. Some them with the hands themselves, some without. The farthest one lost his whole arm at the shoulder.

Then blood started to seep out, highlighting the finest cuts.

Then their torsos began to slowly slip off, and their blood sprayed out in fountains. At that very moment, Hector screamed. Hustig joined him a second later.

Ma Ju Ro himself stared dumbfounded through foggy eyes at what his hands had wrought, or rather a single finger strengthened by metamorphosis. Then his legs gave way and he fell onto the wooden floor, feeling weakness overtake him. Lentz rushed to his side, and the emperor watched with a faraway gaze as Hector easily disarmed the stupefied general.

"What was that, sire?" Lentz asked in a whisper. "Was it... your divine nature?"

Too weak to answer, Ma Ju Ro simply nodded. Metamorphosis reported the successful transformation of carbon into a monomolecular thread and the exhaustion of non-organic energy reserves, which meant that it couldn't absorb the spent material. The knowledge of what 'monomolecular' meant floated up from Esk's legacy, and then he saw a threatening red warning floating in the air.

Tsoui points: −5. Current balance: 9.

Minus five points for five corpses? While the murder of the real Emperor Ma Ju Ro, even if it was in self-defense, had earned Luca twenty one points. He had to think about that, but later. And the same for supporting the families of the dead.

"I need to gather my men, at least those I'm certain of," Hector said. "My ruler, what would you have me do with the traitor?"

General Hustig, by now lying on his stomach with his hands tied behind his back, was trying to say something. Fruitlessly, since Hector had stuffed a woman's stocking into his mouth that he'd found who knows where. Ma Ju Ro liked the captain's nerves, but it was obvious that he had many questions he'd be asking later on, once the situation was resolved.

The emperor rose on his own, without the healer's help.

"Give me a minute," he said. "Then we'll start to act."

He needed a minute just to think of what to do. He needed to get Hustig to talk. The method he'd used to ensure Lentz's honesty wouldn't work in this case. But metamorphosis suggested another option that the emperor didn't hesitate to use. Now all he had to do was wait a little to raise the required tiny fraction of Wheel energy he needed to synthesize the substance and external agents.

While Ma Ju Ro paced his chambers, Lentz and Hector exchanged glances. The captain narrowed his eyes, pointed out the corpses to the healer, then shook his head questioningly — how? Lentz blinked, which could be taken as knowledge of the answer, and showed his thumb. Hector frowned in confusion.

The pantomime didn't escape Luca's attention, but before he explained anything, he wanted to know exactly what his subjects had seen. Did they notice the thread and its origin? Because if not, then it would be easier to explain it away with divine intervention. Call it the wrath of the Sacred Mother.

"Take his gag out, Hector, and sit him down," he said, stopping by the prostrate general.

The captain did as he was told. Ma Ju Ro took hold of the traitor's chin, lifted his head, injected him with a substance to loosen his tongue, then searched the betrayer's eyes for an answer to his questions. He didn't find it, and Hustig coughed, darkened and bent over sharply. He threw up. Waiting for his convulsions to end, Ma Ju Ro placed a chair opposite him and sat astride it, with his hands on the chair back.

"Water," Hustig gasped, staring at the others with bloodshot eyes filled with hatred.

The emperor nodded, and Lentz gave the general a jug of wine. He drank it down greedily to the last drop, then wiped his mouth with his hand and fixed the emperor with an insolent glare.

"I don't know what the hell is going on here, but this changes nothing. You can bargain for your life, 'piglet,'" he said, the last in word in falsetto tones, "and I might let you go. I'll let you and your minions escape the palace." Hustig moved his heavy gaze to the captain. "It's unfortunate that you've chosen to take a side in this, Hector. You've made the biggest mistake of your life."

"The facts so far say otherwise," the captain laughed. He was about to stay something else, but a glance from the emperor stopped him.

"Have you captured the palace, general?" Ma Ju Ro asked in such a relaxed tone that even Hector believed that the ruler didn't care either way. As if even if it had been taken, it would be clear of traitors within the hour, although it wasn't yet clear how. "Who is the organizer of this coup? Who gives you your orders? Rezsinius?

"What?! That Two-horns-cursed jackal? He's no better than you, pig!" Hustig shouted, thrusting out his lip. "The minute that bastard turns up in the capital, I'll string him up on a scaffold! There's no organizer! Nobody would dare order me around! I am my own ruler! The army obeys me, I'm practically a father to all its officers!"

"So you've decided to usurp my power?"

"I don't want the throne!" Hustig grumbled. "We'll overturn you, defend the capital against your cousin and then I'll step down!"

Lentz decided to speak up. "Are you going to give up the warehouses you've filled with enough stolen provisions to last a century, too?"

"I didn't steal them for myself," Hustig snapped. "The treasury is empty. Who will maintain the army?! If you don't feed soldiers, they go and rob civilians! Is that what you want?"

"Who are you planning to hand over power to if not Rezsinius?" Ma Ju Ro asked.

"Nobody in particular. We'll assemble a council of the worthiest citizens and let them rule this cesspit you call the Capital. Your heroic ancestor didn't have much of an imagination. An empire called the Empire and a capital city called the Capital!" Hustig coughed, experiencing the side effects of the substance, and threw up again. This time Ma Ju Ro himself offered him more wine. The general caught his breath and continued. "Power? I spit on power! I'll be in my vineyards in the east, raising my grandchildren and breeding horses. I've had enough of all this dirt!"

"And how is it that his imperial majesty didn't fit into your plans, Hustig?" Lentz asked, narrowing his eyes.

"To hell with His Fatass Travesty!" the general shouted, and Luca realized that his body — Ma Ju Ro's body — was twice as young as the grey-haired general. "If I didn't think he'd try something, I'd have sent him to the winter palace with his whole camp of sycophants, stuffed a wagon full of his whores and even given them all a stipend! His father and I grew up together, after all... Ah, those were the days! We may have kept an iron grip on the people, but they were happy! We used to burn the mutants to ashes before they hid in the caves! The southern barons prayed to the emperor for bringing to heel the Coastal Brotherhood — those filthy pirates! — and clearing the coastal trade routes to the islands! And the cult of the Sleepers? They feared to set foot out of their hideaways! Not like now, now they roam the country in the open and recruit idiots! Not to mention the Capital. All these thieving thugs and criminals flourished only under your rule... useless weasel!"

Finally done, Hustig fell silent. The general's mustache drooped, but his gaze still burned with an inextinguishable flame, save that his hatred and derision were losing ground to regret that his plan hadn't worked. He turned his head to look at where his soldiers' body parts lay, and bared his teeth.

"How?" he asked. "What did you do to my

men?"

"The thing is, general, I'm not quite the emperor that you knew," Ma Ju Ro sighed, coming to a decision. "One could even say that I am not him at all, with regard to my goals and desires..."

"The Sacred Mother appeared before the emperor and gave him a modicum of her holy power!" Lentz interjected, squeezing the emperor's shoulder. "The unbeliever will behold what will become of those that stand against the will of the emperor!"

"That changes nothing," Hustig spat, scowling. "You asked whether the palace has been taken? No. I wanted to do all this quietly. Not a single of Hector's guards has been hurt. Your worthless soldiers' training is worth nothing, captain! But if you think you can just get rid of me and go back to how things were, you are sorely mistaken! I have people in the loop! If I don't show up at the arranged location, then the palace will be taken. And no Sacred Bitch will help you! The circus ringmaster was in here before me. Are these his tricks? I don't care! If we have to, we'll burn down the entire palace along with all the rats that live in it! So get up off your fat ass and untie me, Ma Ju! I promise that if you do, I won't bury you alive or tie you to a stake in the square for the mob to tear you apart. I'll send you to the winter palace. Like I promised, with all your hangers-on and all your whores. I don't need them here, I'd send them all to Two-horns' mother if he had one!"

"I like it!" the emperor exclaimed. He thought for a moment, digging in the original Ma Ju Ro's memory for the general's name. "Hector, untie Miklos! Let's discuss this rationally, general. I think we can find common ground. Just one thing..." He smiled a boyish grin. "Miklos, buddy, while you're still the commander of my army and I'm still your emperor, could you respect the chain of command?"

CHAPTER 32

WHO IS HERDINIA CROSS?

THE CONFERENCE dragged on until the morning. Thanks to his metamorphosis, the emperor needed no sleep, which allowed him to first negotiate with the rebellious General Hustig, and then to build comprehensive and effective plans with him and the others; Lentz, Hector and Koerlig, who had wormed his way in to resume his secretarial duties and record the discussions on paper.

They took many decisions. Ma Ju Ro spent a long time listening to complaints, of which there were many. In the end, it turned out that all the complaints could be combined into a few large groups. To tackle them, the emperor invited the others to suggest options. That was where the hitches began. Nobody had any ready solutions.

284

BLOOD OF FATE

General Hustig saw their main task as maintaining the integrity of the Empire, and he built plans to reinforce the army and their defensive bastions, and to upgrade their weapons, which would be difficult due to the lack of any reserves in the treasury. His solution to the epidemic of poverty and unemployment was, in his opinion, simple: recruit everyone into the army, crush Rezsinius and the southern barons, then feed the country using the southern lands and their rich supplies.

Hustig found no answer to the question of what would happen when the war ended and the army needed something to do. He just mumbled that maybe they wouldn't have to disband any cohorts after the war if most of them were lying dead on the battlefield, to which the emperor asked a reasonable question: what kind of general was he if he didn't want to keep his army alive? After that, he reined himself in and started to listen more than speak.

Incidentally, it didn't take long to convince him that the emperor wasn't the same fat sex-mad waster that he had been. All it took was the knowledge that the emperor's favorites were no longer favorites, and the three new 'flowers of the South' in Reyk Lee Vensiro's entourage had been sent homeward. Luca could have skipped a second demonstration, but it cost him no effort. With one touch, he fixed Hustig's back, which had been bothering him for years and sometimes made it difficult for him to stand straight.

For Hector, the most important problem requiring immediate action was the issue of the increasing hunger in the capital and surrounding areas. The cost of food was sky high, the workshops were letting workers go, which increased unemployment, which in turn led to higher crime. More and more honest craftsmen fell into the care of bandit gangs, and the citizens accepted their power far more willingly than that of the government.

Nothing interested the city watch except filling their own pockets, and in that sense, the bandits were at least more honest. They never took anyone's last coin. However, as Hector noted bitterly, it was a good bet that the guards had long been in the full employ of the criminal bosses.

"So what worries you more, Kolot, hunger or crime?" Ma Ju Ro asked him.

"Hunger, your majesty, first and foremost. Even if we eliminated all the criminals in a single instant, it wouldn't change a thing. Others would come to replace them, and the violence, pillage and thievery would continue. For now, the gangs at least maintain an image of order and protect the merchants and tradespeople that pay them."

"The prices would be lower if you didn't cripple the capital market with taxes," Hustig grumbled. "And as for the corrupt watchmen, that's the domain of Sommers, and he answers only to Naut..."

The spreading poverty worried Lentz. It forced citizens to eat what they could find, up to and including garbage, which was causing infectious disease to run rife.

"We'll have an epidemic on our hands before long, sire," he said in summary. "We could lose most of the population in a very short time, and then Rezsinius won't even need an army to take the throne."

Of course, there were plenty of other problems too. Mutant raids in the northern lands, unrest among the reyks and aristocrats, looted and deserted imperial mines worked by whoever found them, the impoverishment of the Empire's intellectual elite from the government's complete lack of interest in science and the lack of funding that came with it.

A terrible storm had smashed all the fishing boats to kindling along the entire coast from the north of the Empire to the south, which was another problem contributing to the shortage of food. The nearest forests, which had been harvested for wood since time immemorial, were over a thousand miles to the south, and deliveries were impossible — the river along which the forests grew had almost dried up. The southern barons had been digging unauthorized channels without authorization to irrigate agricultural land, draining the river.

But these problems were put on the back burner. Until things were running well in the Capital, it was pointless to think about solving other problems. As Hector so artfully put it, it was like building marble cesspits in the corner of the garden while your ceiling is caving in in your house.

"Tell me about your provision supplies, Hustig." emperor Ma Ju Ro commanded of his former conspirator-general, considering that all present were basically conspirators, but none of them had tried to kill him with impure motives.

"It'll last the army a couple of years," the general growled. "I'm not giving it up."

"You'll have to," the emperor shook his head. "Not all of it, but to relieve the stress until we solve the hunger problem. I still don't understand, how can we go hungry when we're on the coast? Just stick a hand in and you'll pull out something edible, fish, crabs, mussels, shrimp, seaweed..."

"Without boats?" Hector chuckled skeptically. "Ruler, I tried to live off the sea in my youth, it's not that easy. And more importantly, the edge of the world is out there..."

"The edge of the world?" Luca asked.

In childhood, he'd heard stories from his mother that the Empire was on an island surrounded by water. The water was tears shed by the Sacred Mother, and the island itself was none other than the shell of the Defender Turtle, she who kept Two-horns from stealing away people and animals into the abyss. The water didn't fall into the abyss because it was inside a colossal invisible cup made by a Creator who had long since abandoned his creation. But now he knew they were fairy tales. Terant had told him that the Great Earth existed beyond there somewhere.

"I don't think I need to explain to you that you can't sail too far from the coast. The world ends a few miles from the shore, and the ocean waters don't descend into the abyss only thanks to the invisible walls of the cup."

"If they are invisible, then how do you know it's a cup?" Luca asked.

"I was there," Hustig asserted. "There's an invisible and impenetrable veil there. It is hard and indestructible. Ships break against it, birds that fly into it fall stone-dead in the water, and even fish can't get beyond it. My people have dived down, but the wall drops down far deeper than man can dive. Whether it's a cup or something else, I can't understand it. Only those spongers at the university know anything about it, but the fact that the edge of the world encircles the Empire is proven without a doubt.

Luca decided not to share what he knew of the existence of the greater world. Once people such as the khhar Terant got involved, he'd have to deal with it then.

They sat until daybreak, but as soon as the first rays of the sun came, they each rushed out to carry out their own part of the plan they'd developed.

Luca himself stayed on the terrace to use his traveler's legacy and come up with something new. He came up with a way to deal with infectious illness (by deciding to immediately tell Lentz everything he'd managed to get from the legacy about penicillin mushrooms and their effects on infections).

Then Keirinia woke up.

By that time, he'd saved up enough Wheel energy to block his pheromone production, but she still dragged the emperor to the bed. His masculine nature reacted to the alluring curves and cambers of her body as it should.

From the many dozens of Esk'Onegut's lives, there was a fixed axiom emblazoned across his mind: refusing a woman sex was the same as mortally offending her. Therefore he had to lie next to her so as not to offend her with a refusal, and for the first time in his life, Luca gave himself away to that intoxicating act that some call lovemaking. He felt no love for Keirinia, but his full lips made him believe in it. Which made it all the more upsetting when he finished it all before anything serious had started.

"It's fine," Keirinia whispered hotly, licking her lips. "You'll be ready again in a few minutes..."

Her head dropped down again, but Luca was not judged to become a real man on that day. As soon as he started to feel a rush of blood, and the girl spread her inviting open gate before him as she lay on her stomach, a strange noise started from behind the door, and an unfamiliar voice kept repeating his name. Considering the circumstances, this had to be dealt with as quickly as possible. And many plans required his attention.

Luca had to use all his willpower to not start

something that he wouldn't want to stop. He had to send the annoyed and protesting Keirinia to sleep, but even as slumber overtook her she still wanted to meld with him, placing her head on his chest, embracing him with her arms and legs.

And so began his second day in the emperor's body. Luca climbed out from under Keirinia's heavy thighs, jumped up from the bed and went in search of something to quench his thirst. His throat was dry, and his ability warned him that he was getting dehydrated and cried out for water. He found nothing in the bedroom except some dregs of wine at the bottom of a jug by the bed. He headed for the door.

His chambers were already livening up. The servants dismissed yesterday by first advisor Naut had returned to their duties, cleaning up the aftermath of the night's council. They moved soundlessly like shadows, bringing order in their wake, and their commander was a thin lady, dressed severely and with a perfectly even haircut.

Her slightly tremulous voice broke off mid-sentence as soon as she saw the emperor emerge from his bedchamber. She faltered in surprise, her face tightened, but she quickly got a grip on herself.

"Wow, look who's up so early! Good morning! Did you have a bad dream? A nightmare? Should I call Lentz? You could sleep more, you said yourself that the first half of the day is the most boring part, and that's why you never get up before midday..."

Luca got flustered. What was her name? The

Crane? Herdinia? She matched the description, but he felt uncertain. The careless tone with which she spoke to him told him that there had been a certain kind of relationship between her and his body's true owner that left no room for formality.

Luca decided to answer with more ceremony.

"No, don't call Lentz, I feel fine. Order a light breakfast brought, I invite you to dine with me."

"Dine with you..? Why so formal all of a sudden?" the lady said in surprise and frowned. "And for what purpose, if I may ask, do you want to dine with me? Or has your night cuckoo Keirinia been crowing at you again? I'm afraid I must say that she can't rely on any more benefits for her family! I find it quite shocking that she's decided to abuse her, if I may, *special* position at the palace to free the Vizenschnatz family from taxes! I know all about such special positions, and all of them involve spread legs!

Ma Ju Ro studied the angry Herdinia attentively, his gaze pausing below her skirt, on her long tanned legs and finely defined calves. Then he looked at her long crooked nose, which along with her legs made her look like the bird she'd been named after in the palace. He moved closer to her. A discrepancy caught his interest. According to the tales he'd heard, the woman was around forty years old, but she looked no older than twenty five.

He touched her chin, lifted it, gave into his curiosity and looked into her dark blue, purple-tinged eyes.

BLOOD OF FATE

DNA sample received and saved to database.

Biological age of subject: 39 years.

Name: Herdinia (taken from carrier's working memory).

It was entirely possible that the lady had used her influence to undergo a transfusion and preserve her youth. He'd have to ask Lentz.

"Ma Ju, are you sure you're alright?" She kept her eyes on him and made no attempt to move back. "You look different than usual. Did you at least sleep?"

"Who are you?" Ma Ju Ro asked directly. "And why do you speak to me as if I am not your emperor?"

"I see... You're definitely not yourself!" Herdinia exclaimed, then barked a sharp command to the servants. "Everyone out!"

She walked over to the door and locked it from the inside. Then she glanced into the emperor's bedroom to check that Keirinia was asleep, returned to him and started hissing at him angrily.

"So that cretin Naut managed to share his Tassurian 'spices' with you before his failed attempt on your life after all, eh? Two-horns take him. How many times have I warned you about him?! That idiot is in league with your cousin, and you never wanted to believe it! You just got high as usual! No, it wasn't Naut? If not him, then who? Ah, it must have been that sneak Reyk Vensiro? I won't let him and his filthy 'spices' cross the palace threshold ever again! That disgusting creep!"

"Calm yourself, woman!" the emperor roared. "And answer my questions! Who are you?"

"I see," she sighed tiredly. "Amnesia. The consequences of unrestrained drunkenness and narcotic abuse. Fine, it's easier to answer than wait for you to sober up. I am Herdinia. Your idiot courtiers call me the Heron behind my back, but in person they never tire of sucking up to me and groveling, knowing that only I can solve whatever problems they have. You might promise them something, but the promise will remain mere words until I get to grips with it. While I, if you'll forgive my candor, ignore your directions entirely, since they do no good whatsoever to the Empire."

"What about my advisors? Do they obey you as well?"

"Your advisors, and not counting that fool Naut, there are three more of them — Rizmayer, Lodyger and Cross — answer only for their own specific responsibilities and have no influence on the others. Apart from, of course..."

"Hustig..."

"Hustig? Have you gone mad?" Herdinia laughed. "Hustig the brave knight has gotten all too carried away playing at soldiers and wants nothing to do with anything else. As for your countless whores and endless bedroom antics, whatever they ask you for, you order me to handle it. Do you know why, Maj? Because you don't trust anyone as much as you trust me, your secretary Herdinia Cross."

"And why do I do that?" the emperor asked.

"Because that's what my husband Anthony Cross ordered you to do."

"Cross? The fourth advisor?"

"Call him what you like, but our family, in case you've forgotten, is assigned by order of the genetically perfect queen Taira and in the name of the Holy Mother to manage life on the Syahr island, which you call the Empire, you drug-addled moron! Now go back to your room, climb back onto your libidinous Keirinia and let me work!" The Crane shoved Ma Ju Ro in the chest, pushing him away. "Rizmayer, Lodyger and Anthony will be here soon, and we need to choose who will be your first advisor in Naut's place, and solve a bunch of other problems before the country irrevocably descends into hell!"

The emperor stood still. He realized now that the situation was far more complex than he'd thought during the night. And then he did the first thing that came to his mind — told his metamorphosis to stop blocking the uncontrolled excessive sexual magnetism virus.

CHAPTER 33

WHO ARE YOU, YOU SON OF A BITCH?

"H ERDINIA..." Ma Ju Ro began, then hesitated as he waited for the virus to work.

The puzzle was coming together. Part of it from the khhar Terant's tales of the Empire as the world's discarded apple core or worse, with the majority of the population living on huge continents many times the size of all of Syahr. Part of it from the memory of the real Ma Ju Ro the Fourth, which included huge black warriors with weaponry to which nothing in the Empire could even hold a candle, and a tribute that the country paid to the Cross family who controlled this land of genetic refuse.

This final link connected it all — Herdinia Cross, the grey cardinal of the Empire, and her husband Anthony, whose role in the government Luca was yet to learn. The woman stood, leaning forward quizzically, waiting for him to continue.

"Well? What was it you wanted to say?"

"Could I at least have breakfast?" Ma Ju Ro coolly asked his almighty secretary.

"It will be brought to you. That's it, begone!"

"There's something else... I'd like to be present at your council. I hope you don't mind?"

"Me?" Herdinia said in surprise. "I thought you didn't want to take part in boring matters like that. Fine, I don't..." But then her pupils expanded, her cheeks flushed and her breath quickened. She looked at the emperor with fresh eyes, and sincere interest shone through her gaze. "Forgive me, I must leave."

She quickly ran away and hid in the lavatory. The sexual magnetism had worked its magic, but Herdinia Cross had enviable restraint.

Ma Ju Ro had time to order breakfast and even eat his fill before the woman returned. Her previously perfect hair was messy, her makeup was smudged, but she'd regained her composure. She sat at the table next to him, sent away the servants, poured herself a grain brew — a traditional and very expensive uplifting morning beverage, — but didn't drink it. Instead, delicately sticking out her little finger, she placed the cup on the edge of the table and spoke.

"Maj..." Herdinia said in embarrassment. "Forgive me."

"For what?" he asked.

"For what I said before... and just for everything. My ruler, I have realized how wrong I was. Allow me to make up for it!"

"How?"

Without answering, she put her hand on his leg, ran it along his thigh and tried to reach somewhere else, but Luca hurriedly crossed his legs and pushed her arm away. It seemed the pheromones had already done their job. He mentally willed that the pheromone production be stopped again, but it didn't help.

Herdinia kept looking at him with eyes full of passion. Her chest heaved as her breathing quickened, but the woman maintained her self-control in everything else.

"So what about my involvement in your meeting, my dear Herdinia?" Luca smiled warmly and extended a hand. "This one and all those to come? I have a range of ideas for reforming our system of government, and I'd like to keep you on as a secretary, with your no doubt priceless skills, knowledge and qualifications.

"Well... Maj.... Your imperial majesty," she began, obviously having trouble talking to him so respectfully. "Your assessment of my skills is most gratifying, and I will be very glad if what you say is truly the case, and not merely a dream. How did I not see you for who you are sooner..."

She made another attempt to reach into his trousers, but Luca intercepted it, gently holding the woman back by the wrist. *Don't underestimate the power of compliments!* Esk's legacy insisted, and he gave in.

"Herdinia, you're an amazing woman! I'm sure that together, we can bring the Empire to true magnificence! And when that happens, if you are still interested in me and your husband is not opposed... I will give you what you so strongly desire. I will allow you to make it up to me. You have my word as emperor!"

It seemed to Luca that of everything he'd said, all she'd heard were the words of her husband.

"Anthony? Of course he'll be against it! Unfortunately, I'll need the blessing of the Sacred Mother Taira to get a divorce, but I don't have to do that to..." She licked her lips and winked invitingly. It was such a contrast with her appearance that Ma Ju Ro barely held back a smile that could have ruined everything. "Do you understand me, sire?

The emperor nodded slightly in favor, and it occurred to him that he had yet to see how the UESM virus would work without further replenishment.

Subsequent events started careering out of control, carrying Luca away like a crazed horse at the sight of a mutant werewolf. Just has he'd solved the problem of Herdinia, the Imperial Council session began. At Ma Ju Ro's suggestion, it had been expanded to seven people and now included Lentz, Hector and Hustig. The current advisors all voted in unison against a 'pointless expansion of the state' and a reduction in their own spheres of influence, to which the emperor reacted by suggesting that they leave the conference and willingly retire from office. He promised not to stop them.

All were amazed, particularly Fourth Advisor Anthony Cross, when Herdinia supported the emperor instead of obeying her husband as she always had. But the entire morning was one of shocked surprise, from the fact that Ma Ju Ro the Fourth came to the council at all, which caused a furor, to the sharply altered relationship between him and Herdinia, who had started saying "your imperial majesty" and "ruler" so often that even her husband accepted the new rules of the game, deciding to deal with all this later when alone with his spouse.

All the advisors judged Naut loudly and harshly for heading up the attempt on the emperor's life, but they were again amazed when Ma Ju Ro called on them not to rush to hasty demands to hang the traitor, but to give him another chance, although of course not in such a responsible position as before.

"Naut's knowledge could still come in handy to us, respected advisors," he summed up. "Do you agree, Mr. Rizmayer?"

Rizmayer, the counsellor for culture and

public relations, didn't realize at first that the emperor had addressed him personally. At the time, he was deeply engrossed in whispering something to Lodyger about a certain actress in the imperial theater who had given him an unforgettable night, but then he realized that the hall had fallen silent and everyone was looking at him. Confused, the advisor looked around in search of clues, then said, to nobody in particular:

"Perhaps."

"'Perhaps' what, Mr. Rizmayer?" Ma Ju Ro frowned.

"Your majesty... Forgive me, I did not understand the question," the second advisor finally said, surrendering to the emperor's amused smile. "Have we decided not to cancel the upcoming gladiator games? Or were we talking about the premiere of my new play in the imperial theater? Yes, of course, the ticket sales are still far below what might be called sizeable..."

"I asked you whether you agree with me."

"Agree with..? Forgive me, my emperor! I was incautious enough to be distracted while telling Mr. Lodyger of some new gifts to the stage..."

"Tell me, Rizmayer..." Ma Ju Ro stood up and leaned toward his second advisor. "Do you recognize the importance and critical necessity of the tasks that your post and the Empire lay before you?"

"Without a doubt, my emperor! But these are difficult times, and the people have stopped appreciating high culture. You see," Rizmayer took courage as he saw that the emperor wasn't interrupting him, "the people are frightened, your majesty! The entire capital! They are afraid of what your cousin will bring with his army of fearsome veterans and the troops of the southern barons! They are barbarians! Vandals! Boors! There are rumors that Rezsinius has personally promised each soldier three days of looting in the capital! The citizens are whispering, and the mood in the city is entirely pessimistic! There's nothing I can do about it!"

"Nothing?" Ma Ju Ro asked, walking around the table and approaching Rizmayer.

"There is absolutely nothing that can be done!" the second advisor stated with certainty. "Nothing! Alas, the situation in the government is such that..."

"Very well," the emperor interrupted the advisor's stream of consciousness with a satisfied nod and went back to his seat. Once seated, he turned to Herdinia next to him. "Remove Second Advisor Kris Rizmayer from his post. I suggest considering Reyk Lee Vensiro as a candidate for his replacement. I will give the new advisor his tasks personally."

"Understood, sire," Herdinia said, noting it down. "When would you like the reyk to take up his new responsibilities?"

"Immediately, Lady Cross, immediately. But first, let's deal with the other candidates..."

Once done with Rizmayer, who left the

imperial chambers on shaky legs, the emperor ordered that all the new members of the Council be summoned immediately.

In record time, all four newly-minted counsellors took their seats at the table, behind which a range of unexpected decisions were taken before lunchtime. Lodyger, now in the minority, didn't object to any of the questions. Cross, obviously bored and constantly distracting himself with some glass disk covered in colorful pictures, relied entirely on his wife's opinion as far as Ma Ju Ro could tell. And his wife couldn't tear her lovesick eyes from the emperor.

Funny, Luca thought. *The pheromones have long since stopped working, but Herdinia still has feelings. The important thing now is not to accidentally humiliate her. Hell hath no fury...* It wasn't clear whether those were his thoughts, Esk's, or maybe even the original Ma Ju Ro's, but Luca didn't worry about it. In the last few days, he'd gotten used to changes in his thinking. It might have seemed that his mind was still that of the youth he'd been, but he knew now that it was all different. It was comparable to how a person wizened by experience thinks of himself as a youth; it was him, but also someone else. Without the baggage of knowledge that only years of experience can bring. The difference was that Luca had many years of experience lived by others — Esk and Ma Ju Ro — and they'd been imprinted on his consciousness almost instantly...

In the end they negotiated (or rather, Ma Ju Ro suggested and the others agreed) the following. Herdinia took the chair of First Advisor Naut, while still keeping her post of secretary.

Lentz took responsibility over science, medicine and public health, but considered it necessary to note that as soon as current issues were resolved and the rebellious Rezsinius took up residence in the dungeon, science would require a separate office. Lentz even had someone in mind who might be a good fit for the role, if he wasn't in prison for having the gall to ask the emperor for money for certain fantastical projects.

The excited Reyk Lee Vensiro, who over mere minutes had ascended from an impoverished and ridiculed aristocrat at court to the emperor's second advisor, was unable to say a single word for some time, but then got into his stride and suggested a whole range of competent ideas based on problems already solved.

"Bread and entertainment! That's what the simple folk want most of all. And they are our chief bulwark in the looming war against Rezsinius! First and foremost, I suggest we initiate a range of charitable events in the name of his majesty: work with the temple of the Sacred Mother to hand food out to all the poor and needy, and also fill the street stalls and markets with food at cheap prices.

General Hustig, now the fifth advisor, chuckled at those words. The reyk looked at him in confusion and continued.

"In addition, we should declare the opening of a free hospital for all the disadvantaged. By my calculations, we'll have to double the number of town criers, and I suggest we employ the most respected and authoritative residents of the slums for this. Right now, the criers only operate in the districts and squares close to the palace. Most citizens get their news third-hard, and in a thoroughly distorted form..."

Then Vensiro ridiculed the pride of the former second advisor Rizmayer, the imperial theater, saying that it was absolutely impossible to watch, may the emperor forgive him, such crap while sober and sound of mind was. It was boring, condescending and, why sugarcoat it... mediocre. The actresses were mostly young maidens who were certainly very talented in the bedroom, but somewhat lacking in the sphere of artistic performance. As for the theater's plays themselves, Rizmayer himself wrote them, a man far from the common people. It was no wonder that his shows were unpopular.

"And how much do we pay for Mr. Rizmayer's shows?" Luca asked, turning to Herdinia.

The secretary answered, and all except her husband gasped. General Hustig swore profusely and colorfully spoke of the grave in which he would bury the imperial theater, all its actors and Mr. Rizmayer personally.

"Apart from that," Vensiro renewed his speech, "we need to allow street entertainment again. If I may be so bold as to remind you, by your order last year, my ruler, due to satirical scenes and parodies, street performances were banned all across the capital, along with other forms of folk fun and entertainment: magicians, musicians, bards, tale-tellers, illusionists, acrobats...”

“Enough, Mr. Vensiro,” Ma Ju Ro interrupted him. “I understand the idea. Agreed.”

“The activities of artists and sculptors have also been banned...”

“No longer. As of today,” the emperor ordered, and Herdinia made more notes.

“Fortunately, I have nurtured relationships with a range of creative individuals, and I am sure that all of them will return to the capital or emerge from the underground soon. Rest assured, I will guide them in which subjects they may use for their art...” Vensiro rubbed his hands, but checked himself when he saw Herdinia’s strict gaze, and continued without such open displays of emotion.

In addition, the reyk, who knew the court nobility like the back of his hand, had the responsibility (with the support of Herdinia and Hector) of writing up complete lists of all the courtiers and those close to the palace, writing a separate dossier on each and deciding whether their presence is necessary.

“The palace is no place for idleness!” Ma Ju Ro slammed his fist on the table for effect. “The fates of the Empire are decided here!”

Hustig chuckled with delight and Hector’s

eyes widened.

The general, with the aid of Naut and Herdinia, was to review the military budget and begin taking on new recruits. Unemployment was helpfully high in the capital and the surrounding areas, which meant plenty of potential soldiers.

Kolot Hector was to lead a united power structure: the city watch, the militia, the tax collectors and a newly created special forces unit. The aim of this unit would be explained later, in private, when Ma Ju Ro gave him the task (again with the help of Naut and Herdinia) to strike the least trustworthy rich people and aristocrats from the lists, along with those accused of corruption.

All these plans required resources. The treasury was empty and Luca planned to donate his own funds to the government.

When the council was ended and all its participants released, Lentz stayed behind to tell him of the fate of Terant, the dark-skinned khhar with whom Luca had sat in the city jail.

"He escaped after he was sentenced to fight in the Arena. He was last seen on the way to the Wastelands.

The advisor also told him that the boy Luca's sister had regained consciousness and was demanding a meeting with the emperor. The girl accused his majesty of murdering her brother, and it had taken a great effort to keep her isolated with her mother. Luca ordered them brought to him.

Hector replaced Lentz. The former captain,

now commander, privately reported that all the emperor's favorites — former and current — had been checked, over a hundred of them, and he'd found no signs of conspiracy with Rezsinius, in spite of his highly efficient interrogation methods. No, nobody had been hurt. The inquisitors had enough psychological tricks. They'd stayed up all night, but managed to question them all in a very short time. Ma Ju Ro ordered that the girls be released, but also that they be prevented from accessing the palace as a precaution.

No sooner had the door closed behind Hector than it opened again. Luca turned, ready to welcome his mother and Kora, but it wasn't them. The man who came in closed the door carefully, sat down at ease and studied the emperor's face closely for a while.

"Well, this is all very curious," Fourth Advisor Cross laughed. "You've even managed to pull the wool over my wife's eyes, and she, if I may be so bold as to inform you, is a very mistrustful woman and never believes in coincidence. I admit, you had me as well, but this here," he waved that glass disk that he'd been staring at, with the colorful pictures, "this device cannot be tricked. Who are you, you son of a bitch, and what did you do with Ma Ju Ro?"

CHAPTER 34

THE FOURTH ADVISOR

ANTHONY CASSIUS CROSS first came to Syahr a year before he came of age. The trip had been short, and not particularly memorable. The young Anthony had fallen in love for the first time in his life that summer, and for the entire three days as he accompanied his father, who had been declared the next Overseer on Syahr at a family council, he'd made it clear how much he was suffering and missing the object of his passions. His dear uncle Lucius Cassius Cross, who had served as Overseer for thirty years before his father, was tired of it and ready to retire.

Anthony didn't bother to pay much attention to this part island, part inadequate continent that normal people had abandoned, but when his father invited him, he didn't dare refuse. His father would have accepted his refusal, but he wouldn't be happy about it.

The boy spent the full three days in the family shuttle, which hovered high above the island, limiting him to a bird's-eye view of the capital of these genetic outcasts. He did, however, agree to a night-time tour of the emperor's palace. A three-storey stone hovel, pompous and crude, with crumbling vulgar gilt. A palace? Hah, hah, hah. The young Anthony had been disappointed. Their winter family residence alone was three times the size of this so-called 'imperial palace.' And the color gold was considered something crudely common and tasteless. In his family, as in all the racant families, the noble color was black — the untainted virgin-black color of a switched-off screen. White belonged to the Ra'Ta'Cant royal family as a symbol of perfection. All the other colors were the in the domain of the inferior.

The next year after his introduction to Syahr, Anthony's first love, a beautiful girl called Elizabeth, broke his heart and left him for a man who was the grand-nephew of a twice-removed cousin of Queen Taira herself, a connection perhaps tenuous, but apparently still valuable. To rid himself of all that reminded him of her, he flew out to the island to see his father.

He spent the entire summer, right up to August, within the walls of that palace, quenching his thirst for the female form in endless feasts and the orgies that followed them. Although the father of today's emperor was a fine ruler indeed, he didn't deny himself the earthly pleasures. Back then, the young Anthony was discovering all the charm and shame of what his father called 'leching with all one's might.' If it weren't for his enhanced immune system protecting him from all known illnesses, the man would have died young. Ki Ra Nun the First, father of Ma Ju Ro the Fourth, had no such immunity, and therefore his soul went to Two-horns earlier than might have been expected. Unsurprisingly, the reason for this untimely demise was a venereal illness that this backward society was unable to cure. He'd caught it from a courtesan, a migratory southern beauty who had begun her career, as it later emerged, at sixteen as a dock whore.

And so Anthony witnessed a new emperor ascend to the Imperial Throne — the nineteen-year-old youth Maj. As the eldest of the brothers, he had been brought up as heir to the throne — with strict and harsh limitations. The antics that were allowed to his younger brothers and sisters — of which there were many, it should be said, since Ki Ra Nun never abandoned his bastards, instead bringing them up alongside his lawful children — were never accepted in the heir's behavior. His strict teachers, one of whom had been Hustig, back then still a captain, spent all day and night drilling all the knowledge required of a ruler and strategist into the boy's young head.

After his father died, young Maj changed. Not right away, but every day he tired to push against the limits of the allowed, test the boundaries of the acceptable. By the time normal young men were just beginning to look at girls, and to wake up in the night from wet dreams and their first emissions, Ma Ju Ro the Fourth could have been considered a connoisseur, almost a professional in all the sins known to the world, both the everyday variety and the extremely exotic.

None of his former tutors could influence him. In the end, his mother followed after her husband, and Anthony was absolutely certain — he'd checked it himself, — that the emperor had sent her there. Not himself, not by his own hand, of course, but it was done at his order. Then the remaining offspring of Ki Ra Nun the First and his close relatives fell one after another, from various unfortunate incidents which, however, won no awards for variety. Anyone that had any possible claim to the throne.

Only one managed to escape this fate. A distant relative had taken away Rezsinius, Ma Ju Ro's cousin, just in time and hidden him in the South. There were rumors that Rezsinius had gone to become a sailor on a pirate ship in his teens, and then appeared again in public years later under his true name as a grown man. Anthony had even gone to the trouble of flying to the South to check Rezsinius's DNA. The new pretender to the throne was authentic, not an imposter.

But in that first full-fledged summer on Syahr, Anthony was only just beginning his acquaintance with this reservation of inferior savages, and poured all his energies into discovering all the charms of adult life. Immediately after this experientially rich vacation, he went to study for a year at the Academy, where he and a thousand other students were moulded into the future rulers of the planet. Then he went for another year to the Selection, a process held among those who wished to occupy even a slightly important post in society, no matter how minor. He'd made no great achievements there, but then nor had his uncle or father. He'd made it out alive and his injuries weren't too bad, which was the main thing. His wounds had of course been healed, but his Selection results impressed nobody, which is why his family assigned him the same role as his father; when the senior Cross went into retirement, his son would take his place. And so it went.

It's worth mentioning that in the vast Cross family, the Cassius branch was far from the most influential. It could even be said that it was the most unsuccessful, considering that for three generations now, the Cassius Crosses had been unable to attain even the top one hundred at the Selection...

For all these years after replacing his father on Syahr, Anthony had been openly bored. His spouse, Herdinia, who had belonged to the Servilius family as a maiden, was from a racant caste, but just like Anthony, not a particularly influential one. The Servilius family dealt in absolute trash: they held auctions for items of artistic value and considered themselves experts in the field, but could never hold their own against a couple of other competing families. This meant that year on year, they desperately tried to maintain their position at least through marriages such as this one. The Crosses had decided that the slight superiority of the Servilius genes — by a mere millionth of a percent, but nonetheless, — could make an important contribution to the future of the family. This meant that he had entered into his marriage with Herdinia purely based on the calculations of both sides.

Herdinia found things to busy herself with at the imperial palace. For the first few years, she tried to find other distractions, thinking up ideas for a future business, not losing hope that she and her husband would one day return to the big wide world, to normal life. She flew out to family councils constantly to discuss projects, but they turned down her budgetary requests every time. Despairing, she decided to find herself elsewhere and started needled her husband into giving her a role at the palace. Anthony at first laughed at his wife, but then, on the verge of madness from her constant whining, he gave in. He called Ma Ju Ro to see him and declared that from now on, his secretary would take care of all his business.

"What sort of beast is that?" the emperor asked in surprise.

"A person who will do all your work for you," Anthony said carelessly. "So that you can concentrate on more pleasant matters."

BLOOD OF FATE

Ma Ju Ro took that explanation far too literally and began to completely neglect all matters of state. Seeing this, his advisors and barons began to split the country up into still juicy pieces, maintaining the appearance of loyalty not so much now to the emperor, but to Herdinia.

However, these covert games and revolution attempts entertained Anthony. He took no side, not even that of the man whom he was supposed to advise, and watched events as he might a reality show, even if it was in such a barbaric setting. And what a show it was!

Things were moving on steadily, and the looming war promised fun times. True, concerns of safety meant that he'd had to cancel a visit from his teenage son. There was always the chance that he might end up in danger; who knew what these barbarians might think to do? His and Herdinia's son was their only child. They had too little favor with the Sacred Mother to birth a second. Anthony, not daring to hope for a successful Selection, had decided to prepare his son for the role of Overseer, just like his own father had done for him.

And now, this morning, something had changed. The shifts in Ma Ju Ro's behavior were so significant that even the constantly bored Cross noticed it. Not understanding what was happening — Herdinia was behaving very strangely too in indulging the emperor, — he'd used a gadget that was originally developed as a means of communication, but over time had taken on a mass of other functions. Genetic analysis had become so commonplace in their society, where genes decided whether or not you had rights, that it was built into all electronic devices, even watches. But Anthony had decided to save that test for later. The first thing he did was analyze the emperor's voice.

The data amazed him and he'd spent the remainder of the council session with his eyes fixed on Ma Ju Ro, and later he'd tried to get an explanation from his wife. Herdinia had wrinkled her nose and stated that yes, the emperor was unusual, but there was nothing strange about that. The way she said it, the emperor was bored of entertainment and now burned with the desire to personally bring order to the country, which was most laudable and beneficial to Herdinia herself, who was used to the palace and didn't want that Rezsinius boy to take over.

Anthony didn't answer, and silently returned to the emperor to test his DNA.

As he looked at Fourth Advisor Cross, it occurred to Luca that he was looking at the most perfect man in his life. Even Esk's legacy agreed: this male member of Homo Sapiens seemed an ideal specimen. Genetically perfect for this form of intelligent life. He was six and a half feet tall, athletic, although within the limits of necessity, without excessive muscle mass, with a handsome face and a finely outlined chin, with perfectly smooth skin without defects. The man of thirty years wore a wide smile, showing off a row of perfect teeth.

"Who are you, you son of a bitch, and what did you do with Ma Ju Ro?" There was no anger in those words, but an amused perplexity could clearly be heard.

"Advisor Cross?" Luca made as if he was immersed in thought. "Did you ask me something?"

Without answering, Cross extended a hand. Luca shook it, puzzled. He took the opportunity to take a DNA sample and discovered that the senior Cross was already over fifty, but the advisor, as it turned out, did the same thing. Without releasing the emperor's hand, he placed a glass disc against his forearm, held it there a couple of seconds, then quickly pulled away and stepped back.

Turning away, he kept his gaze fixed on the disc for some time, then chuckled in stunned surprise and dropped down onto a chair.

"Alright..." The advisor looked up at the ceiling and chose his words carefully. "I don't know who you are, and I don't know what's going on, and that bothers me. I don't like strangeness and uncertainty. And all this is highly anomalous."

"What exactly, Anthony?"

"As I already said, my device does not make mistakes. During the council session, it stated in no uncertain terms that the structure of your speech, your sentences, even the intonation you use — none of it has even the slightest relation to the Emperor Ma Ju Ro the Fourth whom I have known since birth. And even if I paid no attention to all that, I couldn't fail to notice the changes in your behavior. Yesterday I heard rumors from the palace, but I have to admit, I lent them no weight. Who knows what that idiot might be smoking now, I thought! But today... today I personally saw something so outside the bounds of normality that I suspected something was wrong. I observed you and tried to figure out what it was until I decided to analyze your speech and perform a simple comparison with source data on your usual behavior."

Cross rose and walked to the broad windows overlooking the imperial park. He started patting his pockets, found what he was looking for and lit a cigarette. Luca watched him patiently. The man hadn't yet stated his verdict, so the emperor didn't quite know how to deal with the shrewd advisor. Deprive him of his life? Would that draw a counterstrike from those who Terant called racants? The richest and most influential families of the Great World, the most genetically superior, not as perfect as the royal family of the Ra'Ta'Cants, but very close to it. No, it was best to wait and see where his advisor took this.

In the meantime, Cross finished holding his theatrical pause, returned to the table and, taking a drag from his cigarette with pleasure, continued.

"Let me explain something to you, Ma Ju Ro. Everything living on this planet has its own unique code. I doubt you understand this, but try. We call it DNA. Your code is absolutely identical to the one saved in my database as belonging to the true emperor. This means I can conclude that the body is the same. And no technology yet exists to transfer consciousness, in spite of all our efforts. That means that you really are the true emperor. But!" Cross raised his index finger. "At the same time, you're someone else. I could have written it off as the influence of psychotropic substances, narcotics, alcohol... But you're clean! Nothing clouds your blood. It's as clean as a babe's. And that makes me nervous, Maj!"

No wonder, Luca thought. *Metamorphosis neutralizes everything, it doesn't even let me get tipsy.* Cross fell silent again, but this time it wasn't an artificial pause. He was waiting for an explanation.

"I had a transfusion, Anthony," the emperor answered simply. "Something went wrong during the procedure. It's as if my brain has been cleansed of fat and my mind is unclouded. I don't know if you're aware, but there was another assassination attempt yesterday on top of Naut's. Something changed in me after that. The scales that have been growing over my eyes for decades, the filth accumulating in my mind... It has all fallen away."

"There we go again! Talking like you never have before!" Cross exclaimed, hitting his palm with his fist. "But go on, continue. You're on fire, Maj!"

"I want to live, Anthony," Ma Ju Ro said,

ignoring his advisor's words. "But to do that, I need to bring order to the country and become the man my father wanted me to become — a wise and visionary ruler. I understand your surprise, but this is how it is. And I very much hope that you will help me."

"I see," Cross drawled. "Well, I accept your explanation, but if you're relying on my help and support, you fat old savage, you can think again. I don't care who's in power here. There'll always be a fourth advisor, and the Cross family will ever rule over this land. I have spoken."

With those words, he rose in silence and left the room without so much as a good-bye.

CHAPTER 35

KORA AND PRISCA DEZISIMU

WHEN HE RETURNED from the council hall to his own chambers, Luca found chaos and pandemonium. Keirinia had woken up, and was walking around in a short gown with a cup of grain brew in her hands, lazily bickering with Herdinia. Once she saw the emperor, she immediately threw her arms around his neck. He freed himself from her passionate embrace with difficulty and again noted how easily he drove his first favorite to extreme arousal. Luca glanced quickly at Herdinia.

The new first advisor gave no sign that the scene before her upset her. It seemed passion had not conquered her mind, and she'd decided to keep her affair with the emperor secret, if there was one at all.

Herdinia nonetheless remained true to herself, and apart from simultaneously managing to give curt orders to a couple of underlings and to find out why Koerlig had brought his majesty two street tramps, she still had time to send some venomous remarks the way of the first favorite.

The street tramps, cowering in the corner of the room and not daring to sit down, turned out to be Luca's mother and sister, and his heart began to beat faster, which metamorphosis immediately reported, asking whether the carrier wanted to slow his heart beats. Waving it away, Luca worriedly looked at his sister's face, trying to find signs of a transfusion. He exhaled in relief when he saw that his sister's age was still the same — she was the same fifteen-year-old. Fine — almost sixteen.

"Sire, the Dezisimu family is here as per your order," Koerlig reported gallantly as he stood to attention. Hector's influence was clear in his tones. "Should I leave them here, sir?"

It seemed as if the future leader of the first imperial clinic kept his gaze locked on him, but Luca noticed that the boy somehow managed to mischievously glance from side to side occasionally. There was definitely something cunning in him, Hector was right.

"We'll talk on the terrace," the emperor said. "Thank you, Koerlig, you may go."

"Forgive me, ruler," Herdinia interjected, "but I need to discuss a number of questions with you regarding the free clinic. Lee Vensiro was overzealous in his duties, and his criers are going to declare the opening of the clinic as early as this morning. Koerlig, come!"

"I've missed you, your majesty," Keirinia said in playful tones.

From somewhere behind the door came the grumbling of General Hustig as he rebuked the guards, and Luca realized that the revolving door of business would never let him out once he got in, and again he'd have to put off meeting his family. So he gave Herdinia strict instructions that he be left in peace, then went over to his mother and sister, noticing that Kora was struggling to keep her mouth shut, and her demeanor in general was far from friendly. It seemed she was planning to scream as loud as she could, but her mother convinced her not to and held her back for now.

To avoid exacerbating the situation, Ma Ju Ro gently pushed aside Keirinia as she clung to him like a limpet, asking her to go run some errands. He walked to his mother, took her by the hand and led her out to the terrace, the only place in the palace where he was sure they wouldn't be overheard. The balcony hung over an uninhabited rocky shore, and the sound of the surf covered all conversations.

"Tell me what you've done with Luca!" Kora shouted as loud as she could as soon as they got outside and the doors closed behind them. "Where's my brother?!"

"Kora, daughter... This is the emperor himself! His majesty Ma Ju Ro the Fourth!" her mother mumbled in shame, trying to embrace her daughter, who instead pulled away and rushed toward Ma Ju Ro and started hitting him in the chest.

There was still plenty of fat left to absorb her strikes — he didn't feel any pain. The girl started crying.

"Tell me, where is Luca? Please..."

Answering nothing, the emperor embraced his sister and stroked her back until she calmed down. Prisca stood nearby all this time, not daring to intervene and crying silently.

"How do you feel?" Luca asked her quietly over Kora's shoulder.

"Much better," his mother answered gratefully. "I haven't felt this good for a long time, to say it true. And Kora is feeling better too, after those inhumane experiments from that wicked healer!"

Luca sat his sister down in a seat, sat opposite her and leaned forward.

"Tell me, what did he do to you? Did he lock you in that cellar with the chinils? Did he beat you? Senior Apprentice Pen didn't do anything to you, did he? Kora!" he took her by the hand. "It's all... It's all over, my dear..."

The girl drew back sharply and tried to stand up, but Luca stopped her.

"What did you call me? And how do you know all that? Did you order him to do it?"

"Listen to me, Kora. Calmly, without interrupting. Can you do that?"

The girl thought for a moment and then

nodded.

"Why are you so kind to her, ruler?" his mother whispered, hearing his warm and trustworthy tone.

"You'll understand, Prisca," Luca answered and moved his gaze to his sister. "Will you listen? Let me try to explain."

"I will," Kora nodded. Her gaze brightened. "Go on... that is, if you want to, your majesty."

"Alright. But first ask me a few questions that only your brother can possibly know the answer to."

"Why?" the girl said in surprise.

"I'll explain later. Ask them."

His mother moved a little closer as she listened to their conversation. Kora frowned and wrinkled her nose, thinking of what to ask. Finally she thought of something.

"What did I ask him for at our last meeting?"

"You asked him to convince Yadugara to help your sick mother," Luca answered without thinking.

"Hah! The healer himself could have told you that!" Kora exclaimed. "Or that ugly fat Aunt Mo! What song did my brother like to sing when he was going outside?

"Kora!" her mother reddened. "How would his majesty know that?"

"He asked me to ask him! Come on, your majesty, tell me, what was the song called?" It seemed his sister had gotten into the spirit of the game, and she looked at the emperor victoriously.

"Please pay her no mind, your majesty, my

daughter is just talking garbage, how would you know a song thought up by...”

“By Luca himself, called Running Boy? About a boy who couldn’t walk and who learned how anyway, and ran and never stopped again, afraid that if he did, he’d forget how. He skipped along, smiling a big smi-i-ile...” Ma Ju Ro sang quietly. “And the wind itself couldn’t keep u-u-u-up...”

Their eyes filled with tears Kora swallowed a lump in her throat and opened her mouth, staring dumbfounded at the singing emperor. He finished the verse, gently stroked Kora’s head and spoke quickly and passionately.

“He came up with that song when he was twelve. On that day, while mom was delayed with her customers, you took him to the market without permission, Kora. And the innkeeper Nemania’s son Karim Kovachar and his friends Fat Pete, Natus and Jamal, they all pushed his wheelchair over in the mud. You washed his clothes while your brother sat blushing in nothing but his underwear as all the people walked by. Then you went to watch an acrobatics show together. That was when Luca came up with those words. And he heard the melody at that very same show. When you were eight, you took your brother to the sea. The wheelchair got stuck in the beach sands, but you pulled it to the water, dragging it through the sand. Then you both nearly drowned...” Luca felt himself barely holding back tears too. “Ask a third question, Kora.”

She shook her head.

"I just don't understand," his mother broke the silence. "How do you know all this, your majesty?"

"I also know that your son stood up for you against Nemania, who suggested you pay for his misdeeds with your body, and that's how your son ended up in prison."

"How?" his mother whispered. "He told you?"

"Don't you get it yet, mom?" Kora cried.

"Get what?"

His sister didn't answer. She jumped up from the seat, took Ma Ju Ro's face in her hands and looked into his eyes for a long time, trying to find at least something that reminded her of her brother, but she found nothing.

"Kora..." Luca said. "Did you know what Yadugara wanted from you? He was trying to take away years of your life. They call it a 'transfusion procedure'..."

"I know!" the girl interrupted him sharply. "He was whispering about that with that disgusting Penant boy! That chump pretended to be nice at first, then groped me! He came in the night, but I kicked him in the balls so hard that he whined like a beaten dog! True, I got a bad beatdown after..."

"Did they manage to transfuse from you?"

"They'd only just started when that man from the palace got there. He brought watchmen with him, and Yadugara had to let me go."

After her words, Luca realized that the decision to transform into the emperor had saved his mother and his sister's lives. If he'd hesitated and just tried to run..." He felt as if a huge weight had dropped from his shoulders.

"How did you end up with him?" Luca asked.

"Reyna took me there, that's his lover. She wrapped me round her finger! She pretended to be a friend, said she'd bring me to you, and when I was in the house, the guard ran in. He accused me of sneaking into private property, said I was a thief!" Kora frowned. "Well yeah, sure I might'a taken a couple of apples before and... it doesn't matter, I didn't steal anything this time!"

"And then Yadugara just bought you at the trial for a few gold?"

"For a hundred. There were lots of potential customers, to tell the truth..."

"I remember how happy I was when I saw you at my trial. And then they took you both away, and that horrible 'healer' Yadugara bought me just like he bought you..." Luca faltered a moment, realizing what he'd said. "Abyss!"

"I knew it!" Kora shouted and threw her arms around his shoulders. "Mom, mom! This *is* Luca!"

His mother opened her mouth, covered it with her hand, fell down to her knees and wailed.

"Forgive her, my emperor! The girl has only just recovered, she isn't herself!"

Kora, her breath hot on his ear, whispered:

"But how, how, Luca? What happened? Why are you like this? How?!"

"Shh... Careful, sister! Quiet! If anyone finds

out, they'll cut off my head! Listen carefully! I was taken to the palace so that my life could be transfused to the real emperor. Something went wrong during the procedure, and when I woke up, I was already in this body. Don't interrupt me, Kora! Listen, listen... I'm going to get mother settled her and I'm going to help you. The important thing is that you know that I'm me!"

"I want to be close to you!"

"How?"

"Just make it happen, you can do anything, you're the emperor!"

And Luca's eyes lit up. An idea came to his head for allowing Kora to stay in the palace. He looked at his sister and was satisfied with what he saw. Kore had turned into a truly beautiful young woman!

"Want to be a courtesan?" he grinned.

Of course, his mother was entirely against it. This proud gladiator's wife didn't want to hear a word about Kora becoming the emperor's lover. In spite of all assurances that it would just be a story to explain Kora's presence at court, she stubbornly refused. But Kora could be stubborn as well, and eventually she convinced her mother. It helped that her daughter had sown a seed of doubt: however impossible it seemed, what if her son really was the emperor? Or rather, her son wasn't exactly the emperor, but through some miracle Luca's spirit had settled in this fat man with his blurry eyes. May the Sacred Mother have mercy on her for such seditious thoughts!

But the mother gave no voice to those concerns, and the son was left only to imagine whether she really suspected it or whether he just wanted to believe that she did.

In the end, she didn't dare to refuse the emperor himself, and in a daze she accepted gifts as gratitude for sacrificing her son — or so said the official account. The boy had given his life to heal the emperor. As for what he'd needed healing for, Lentz hurriedly came up with some deadly and noble options.

In honor of her son, Prisca was given a small vacant cottage in a well-to-do district. It was confiscated from Naut the day before. She also got an imperial pension that meant she never had to work again. But the woman answered that she couldn't sit without anything to do, and if any work could be found in the palace for her, anything that might put her close to her daughter, she would be very happy. Fortunately, she said that in private, and the emperor promised to think about it — as soon as he got Kora settled in.

By the evening, his mother and sister were taken to their new home. The effects of the virus on Herdinia showed no sign of abating, and in the wish to please the object of her desire, she personally organized provision for the mother and daughter. She ordered an assistant to open an account in Prisca Dezisimu's name at the bank and deposit a thousand gold pieces. The treasury was almost empty, but a thousand gold was still pocket change for an empire.

Kora quickly returned. Luca spoke with Keirinia in private and handed his sister over to her care. Keirinia's eyes flashed and she tried to make a jealous scene, but Ma Ju Ro had already learned to find the right words when talking to women close to him. He swore that he would never lie with the girl under any circumstances, even when she came of age and became an astounding beauty. Keirinia accepted his explanations and Luca took her to meet his sister. She'd already been given a few private rooms by the imperial chambers, taken from those left empty after Hector's special operation to check and remove crowds of courtesans and lovers, former and present, although the present ones were now former as well. All except Keirinia.

"Well, well..." his courtesan said in surprise. "What ditch did they pull you out of, you charming creation?"

Kora was about to spit venom in response, but Ma Ju Ro intervened.

"Keirinia, my dear, the girl has only just been freed from slavery. She is the sister of the boy to whom I owe my life. Why don't you look after her?"

"Me? Look after her?"

"You're the only one I can trust with her...

although, actually..." the emperor made as if he was recalling the names of other courtesans.

"Of course, sire!" his favorite gleamed. "I'm sure Kora and I will get along great!"

Kora learned to find common ground with anyone from an early age. She understood the rules of the game and pretended to be a child awed with Keirinia's beauty, a child whose chief interest to this day had been dolls.

"Dolls? How boring, my girl!" Keirinia exclaimed. "I know a few things more fun! Dresses! Makeup! Jewelry! Perfume!"

"Dresses?" Kora frowned. "Now that sounds boring to me!"

"You just don't know how to wear them! I'll show you..."

"Then why don't you help Kora with her wardrobe?" Luca interrupted her. "Her rooms also need furnishing. Can you handle that?"

"With the greatest of pleasures, my ruler!" Keirinia said. "Don't expect us back before midnight!"

The two girls, one short and one tall, set off for the merchant stalls at once. At Ma Ju Ro's order, Hector assigned a couple of his underlings to them — to avoid, as the emperor put it, excesses.

After a hurried shared dinner, Herdinia managed to steal a passionate kiss after all, taking advantage of a few minutes of solitude in Keirinia's absence, then she reminded the emperor that he was expected at the award ceremony at the healer's guild.

Several servants spent two hours (it could have been twice that, but Ma Ju Ro hurried them) getting the emperor ready: washing, trimming, shaving, combing, packing away his unruly mane, and then, for a long time, dressing him in his dress coat. All these procedures so exhausted Luca that he went to the ceremony in a wrathful mood. The healers had occupied a special position throughout the imperial dynasty, and they held their yearly ceremonies not in the guild building, but in a special hall of the palace with the head of state present.

The hall was in another wing and seated up to a hundred. Ma Ju Ro walked steadily, maintaining his dignity. He thought of how to deal with that bloodsucker and take vengeance against him in a way that would seem logical and give rise to no questions.

Shrouded in his parade clothes, Yadugara proudly pontificated amid a group of senior healers. He'd definitely gotten younger — partly thanks to Luca himself, and partly... No, not Kora. Senior Apprentice Penant stood nearby, leaning against a wall with his head drooping. If Luca hadn't known him personally, he would have sworn he was an old man.

And then Luca Dezisimu, also known as Emperor Ma Ju Ro the Fourth, had an idea.

CHAPTER 36

LOST YEARS

ENIOR APPRENTICE PENANT, once a homeless boy, then sold for one gold mark into five years of forced service and subsequent apprenticeship with the healer Nestor Yadugara, couldn't stand pompous ceremonies and large gatherings of people. To put it plainly, they made him nauseous. Turned him inside out in the most literal definition.

Even in the days when he was earning a living off petty theft at the city market, and a crowd of immigrant village louts provided a great service to Pen in his petty endeavours, the boy had to push himself to do it. From birth, one of the gods had blessed him with a stunning sense of smell. And Pen was sure it was Two-horns. The talent became his curse.

He could pick apart smells down to the slightest gradations, and each said more about a person than the source of the stench knew. By scent Penant could determine what a man ate at dinner that night and what he drank in the morning, which illnesses he suffered and what type of life he led. Out from under the camouflaging scent of flowery perfumes, he could always pick out those special notes peculiar to a woman who had been writhing beneath a man very recently. If there was anyone to match it to, then Pen could say who exactly she'd been beneath. And even, may the Sacred Mother forgive him, which bodily orifices had been involved.

They say that man is such a beast that he can get used to anything. But it all depends. You can learn to withstand something specific. The night soil men didn't notice the stink of the 'soil,' and leatherworkers got used to hides reeking in chicken manure. But any mass gathering meant thousands upon thousands of different scents, unique for each person and split into dozens of constituents. That was something nobody could get used to.

Right now, amid his colleagues, Penant smelled nothing. His until now impeccable sense of smell couldn't pick anything out. And the reason was that he had turned into an old man overnight.

This long-planned award ceremony by the guild of healers was outside their regular schedule. Usually the gathering voted yearly for the best member, based on the contributions of each to the development of medicine and guild business, and based on their services at large. And if none of the suggested candidates got over half the votes, nobody got the award.

The same happened this year, when the votes were divided between Yadugara (one of those judged on services at large) and a fat and rosy-cheeked short man called Demmens, who had discovered and begun to use a certain synthesized medicine that allowed even an ancient old man to recall that long-forgotten sensation of Penus Erectus.

The potion became a sensation in aristocratic circles, but Demmens didn't get enough guild votes. He'd decided to invoke the ten-year right of know-how, allowing him not to reveal the secret of how the substance was synthesized.

In the end, both got roughly half the votes and an ordinary conference was held instead of an award ceremony.

Then Nestor Yadugara made a discovery. He'd actually made it long ago, but he'd revealed it to his colleagues only that year, roughly a month before that slave boy Luca Dezisimu had come into Penant's life. Penant himself only learned of this when Yadugara's colleagues took Luca off to the palace, although he'd been involved in all the transfusion procedures and he'd noticed no changes as such. Perhaps his master had discovered it before Penant came to him.

Yadugara had managed to increase the conversion rate. For a long time, losses in the transfusion procedure made up nearly fifty percent of the available life force. The source lost a decade while the recipient only got five years, in the best case six. The master changed the technique for connecting the tethers, added something into the pre-transfusion injection and managed to reduce those losses to fifteen percent. That was even more sensational than Demmens's medicine for Penis Erectus, and it caused a furor among his colleagues. Considering how rare it was to find suitable donors, every year of life clawed back was a true deliverance for the ageing masters of the guild.

When the discovery was confirmed in practice, Yadugara was immediately advanced as an indisputable nominee for the title of best healer of the year. For the sake of formality, Demmens was nominated again as a second candidate, but this time the vote was unambiguous — almost all the guild members stood for Pen's mentor.

Then that Dezisimu girl had appeared in the house, Reyna brought her in. She was given up to the watch as a thief, and then bought up for a hundred gold pieces. But it was worth it — preliminary analyses showed that Kora was a suitable donor.

Just when everything was ready for the transfusion, she suddenly ran away, tearing a silver candlestick off the wall as she went. That thoroughly dampened his master's mood, and Pen himself was annoyed too — he'd hoped to get something out of the girl himself.

Fortunately, the maiden decided to sell her loot and Bakhr's people, a gang that survived off buying and selling stolen goods, took her to

Yadugara's house.

"I hear this is yours, Nestor," the authoritative teeth grinned, his gold tooth gleaming. He held a girl at the end of a taut leash. "If that's true, then I can return her for a reward."

In his joy, Yadugara gave him two hundred gold pieces and told him that Bakhr's people could now count on a big discount for treating any wounds and injuries of a cutting and piercing nature, as it were.

After showing the crime boss out, the master personally beat Kora and locked her in the cellar. Pen went to her to bring her food and try to convince her to perform Actus Sexuales, but left unsatisfied — he'd gotten nothing but a painful kick to the balls and a black eye.

After waiting for the chinils to work their misery, Yadugara ordered Reyna and Morena to wash and clothe the girl. Pen was ordered to handle the procedure, and Yadugara himself rushed to prepare the required medicines. He couldn't keep readily available due to the volatility of their active components.

And yet again, they were interrupted. At first the imperial medic Lentz came and stated that the emperor wanted the girl. Yadugara, driven to a furious rage by the arrogance of those palatial parasites, said that this time he wouldn't lift a finger without official papers, and anyway, the girl belonged to him by law! Lentz could come back the day after tomorrow and take what was left.

Lentz dryly said good-bye, promising to return very soon. And return he did, but no longer alone. A squad of watchmen loomed threateningly behind him, and the guard Daler lay twisted on the floor, groaning in pain and holding his broken nose. His broken rib was a clear illustration that Lentz was entirely serious in his intentions. The girl was in a coma and close to her last breath. Lentz and his men carefully put her on a stretcher and took her to the palace.

That evening, they drowned their sorrows. Once south of a few glasses of wine, Yadugara started getting emotional, as it seemed to Pen. He promised to help his senior apprentice get his healer's license as soon as possible, although in exchange he asked for a little of his life force, just three or four years, no more.

"You've grown up, Pen, my boy, and you're ready for your own practice. I've taught you all my secrets. And once you become a practicing healer, you'll return to yourself all the years you've given to me! I only have a few left, and if you could show your gratitude..."

The master moved in for a hug. Reyna had been pouring wine for half the night and looked at Pen so sorrowfully that the young man wanted to immediately calm both her and his master down. After all, his master had done him a great honor by sharing his table and such fine Tuaf wine. On top of everything else, Master Yadugara was being so nice to him, and polite, and respectful...

"Of course, master!" Pen said. "I am willing!"

"Then let's not put it off!" Yadugara exclaimed. "We'll finish by morning, and by the evening you'll be a full-fledged healer with your very own license!"

Pen could barely open his eyes after he woke from the procedure. That wasn't uncommon, but impenetrable darkness disturbed him. Had something gone wrong, had the transfusion ended before dawn?

His master was nowhere to be seen, Pen was in the procedure room alone, and there was nobody to dispel his doubts. Somehow, he slid off the cot and fell to the floor. His legs refused to hold him up. He looked at his hands in the moonlight and didn't recognize them. His fingers were thin, fragile and knobbly, trembling and covered in liver spots. His legs were no better, and as he felt his hair he cried out. It had thinned out so much that he immediately felt the skin of his scalp beneath.

"Awake?" Reyna said in unfriendly tones. "Master ordered me to feed you and take you to your room.

The procedure room filled with light. The girl moved the lamp closer to Pen and looked closely at him.

"Drink..." The senior apprentice didn't recognize his own voice. After clearing his throat, he rasped: "Reyna, what time is it?"

The girl screwed up her face. "You big dummy. The time? It's past midnight. Let's get to the kitchen. I woke up Mo so she can give you something to warm you up."

"Past midnight..? How?" The dumbfounded Pen felt himself losing consciousness from weakness. How could the transfusion have been so short? Or on the contrary, too... He realized the gravity of what had happened. He shouted as loud as his old voice would allow him. "Where's the master?!"

"Keep it down," Reyna yawned. "Master is already sleeping and asked to be left in peace. Talk to him in the morning, if it's so important to you..."

IN the morning, Yadugara casually stated that unfortunately he'd allowed himself to pass out, and the transfusion had gone on a little too long.

"A little?!" Pen choked on his grain brew. "Forty years too long, you mean? I demand that you return my years to me at once!"

"My boy..." Yadugara faltered. It was hard now to call this old man a boy, of all things. "Listen, Pen! Conversion means losses. Even if it were possible, we've already lost ten years. If we return the time to you now, we'll lose more unlived years, you understand? In any case, I have fulfilled my promise — you are now a full-fledged healer. The license is already in my study, you ingrate!

Yadugara grumbled on for a while about how he'd been at the guild office at the crack of dawn, preparing all the documents for his shameless student and getting nothing in return but displeasure in place of gratitude.

"You've had enough from me! I picked you up

as a homeless thief whose fate was the mines, brought you up in my own house, taught you all I know, gave you a roof over your head, food, options... And this is how you repay me? We're done, Penant, you may go! Gather your things and get out of here," the master finished. "If you find a donor, let me know and I'll help you perform the procedure properly. Oh, Two-horns! Mo, Reyna, wipe those tears off his face!"

Pen's face was already covered in tears as he cried over his lost years. While Aunt Mo wiped away the soup he'd spilled on the table, Reyna used a kitchen cloth to clean the old man's face in disgust. The abundance of stinking odors made Pen throw up all over Aunt Mo.

"Two-horns take you!" the woman swore. "You son of a flea-bitten mutant-raped sheep! Chinils, may the Sacred Mother forgive me!"

Under a stream of profanity from the people who were apparently the closest to him in the world, Penant threw up even more.

"Enough!" Reyna shouted, throwing the rag to the floor. "I'm not cleaning up his blubbering any more!"

Penant looked at her from under his furrowed brows and gasped. Nobody would have thought the girl over the age of sixteen. That bastard had given her a transfusion too? From him?

Yadugara approached Pen and carefully slapped him on the shoulder, trying not to get anything on his hands.

"You'll get your years back, why so glum?"

Why so glum!? Was he joking? He was seventy years old now, if not more! He was a doddering and worthless old man, and his shaking hands wouldn't let him hold so much as a spoon, let alone a surgical instrument! His life was over!"

"Give me back at least five years," Pen mumbled. He'd lost a few teeth in the morning. "I won't be able to practice, I have tremors..."

"Have your brains completely dried out?" Yadugara asked, looking at the old man thoughtfully. "I'm not a donor. The transfusion won't work."

They spent some time in silence. The master distantly drank his grain brew, Reyna smiled at something, Aunt Mo clattered around as she washed up, and Pen's will was so crushed that he could think of nothing. Practice? Where? Pen didn't even realize that he'd asked the questions aloud.

"Are you sure you need to practice?" Yadugara bowed his head, making as if he was thinking. "Pen, my friend... Why don't you just stay and live out your final years? Maybe we could find you a donor in time and make you young again..."

"What the hell do we need him for, master?" Reyna hissed. "Drink out what he has left and throw the rest to the chinils!"

"Oh, there's an idea!" Nestor said and laughed as he saw Penant's terrified face. "We're joking, simpleton. Gather your things."

"Where do I go?" Pen asked vaguely.

"You will get a hundred gold pieces as a reward for your years of service. Reyna will give them to you. It will last you a while, then you're on your own. You have a license. Start by earning a living as a healer among the peasants. By the way, I advise you to use any excuse to analyze everyone you meet! Who knows, you might get lucky and find a donor. If so, bring them to me..."

On that very day, Penant found lodgings at the market inn The Happy Bear and Anchor. The innkeeper had been his main fence for stolen goods back when he'd worked the market. The man didn't acknowledge him, of course.

It wasn't hard to make the choice — Pen didn't plan to stay there long. He suddenly accepted that all his life's plans had been swept away by his bastard teacher, who had kept him around all this time as a mere back-up plan, just a skin of young and fresh blood that he could use to refresh himself when he needed it.

His mind reeled from dozens of ideas: from complaining to the healer's guild to revealing what had happened to the public, from poisoning Yadugara to reporting everything he knew of the healer's secret transfusions to the palace inquisitors, but he formed no specific plans until he recalled the master's upcoming award.

He spent the previous night sleepless, tossing and turning and thinking of how he would go to the palace — and thanks to his healer's license, that was now a possibility — and demand to speak.

Right before the declaration of the winner, Chief Imperial Medic Lentz would ask if anyone present had any objections. And then Pen would stand up and speak of how his master had treated him... But when he thought of what would happen next, he got scared and shivered.

After thinking it over, Pen discarded that idea. He wanted to live life to the full for at least the few years remaining to him. The idea of publicly exposing his former tutor wouldn't get him anything — they were all like that. More than likely, they would quietly and subtly deprive him of his healer's license, kick him out of the guild and... Who would care about the corpse of a poor old man found in a ditch? There'd be no investigation, not with the Empire in its current state. No, it was best to keep a low profile and try to find a donor for now. Pen also consoled himself with a thought he'd once read somewhere, that vengeance is a dish best served cold.

Waking up bright and early, he felt emboldened and rested even though he'd dozed just a couple of hours. For the first time in his adult life, he was fully and entirely dependent on himself. Pen ate breakfast greedily, gaining strength and thinking of what to do.

Feeling another loose tooth with his tongue, he frowned and decided to order false teeth from the tooth craftsman, but before that he went to the workshops and paid for a sign reading 'Penant the Healer. Healing for Ailments and Maladies,' agreeing in advance with the innkeeper to lease a room with a separate entrance. The innkeeper loved the idea of the establishment having its own healer.

He even brought the healer his first patient, a brother suffering with gout, and Pen managed to ease his pain. So he went to Yadugara's award ceremony with every right to call himself a healer.

They looked for him in a list of invitees for a long time at the entrance and failed to find him. But once they confirmed that he was a guild member, they let him in anyway. Pen ground his teeth as he saw how well and young his former master looked, and he barely held back from declaring him a thief. A thief that stole Pen's life.

Deep in thought, he didn't notice a heavy hand descend on his shoulder. Gasping in fright, thinking he was about to be thrown out, Pen raised his head and saw the frowning face of a palace guard.

"Senior Apprentice Penant?"

"Yes. I mean, no, I'm a healer now. I'm a guild member! Here's my license...

"It doesn't matter. Come with me, his imperial majesty Ma Ju Ro the fourth wishes to speak with you."

CHAPTER 37

YADUGARA'S AWARD

FILLED WITH ANXIETY over the upcoming ceremony, Lentz panicked when he learned that the emperor had left to speak to someone. But Luca felt it was important to learn the details before he personally placed around the bloodsucking healer's neck the gold medal "For Services to the Empire," which came with the title of best guild member. The emperors had always valued them and separated them into a privileged caste, without which the ruler's life would have been far shorter.

Luca barely recognized Senior Apprentice Penant in the crooked and wrinkled old man, half-blind and squinting, staring at the emperor's face through watery eyes. If it weren't for the verdict of the DNA analysis from his metamorphosis, he'd still be in doubt. The transfusion procedure hadn't just taken decades of life from the boy. Luca didn't know how exactly it was possible to so age a man in so short a time, even pulling teeth without damage? He saw several missing in Penant's mouth. There was something in all this that belonged to evil and dark magic, of which, however, there was no proof in this world.

Nonetheless, mages practiced in the Empire; plains shamans, Desert Seers, black warlocks from the pirate isles, and many others, but even the uneducated among the populace looked at them with skepticism, in spite of the fact that the people burned a warlock or spellcaster at the stake occasionally, just in case.

Penant was taken to a small room intended for household purposes. There wasn't even enough space to sit down. The emperor awaited him, standing motionless by the wall, alone, without a guard.

"Hello, Pen," Ma Ju Ro said once the guard had left them alone.

"Your majesty... You know me?"

"Yes, and far better than you think."

"But how?"

"I'm the emperor, remember. It is my business to know my subjects. We don't have much time, let's dispense with the formalities. I'm sure that until very recently, you were far younger, and I know that your ageing and the flourishing appearance of the respected Yadugara are the consequences of one and the same event, something you call transfusion."

Pen nodded, dumbfounded.

"Then answer one question for me, Penant. What did Nestor Yadugara promise you for you to give up your life for him?"

"He... he..." The old man swallowed a lump in his throat, twisted his lips. "He tricked me. He said he'd take two or three years, but he... he..."

"I understand," Ma Ju Ro said gently. "Let's talk after the ceremony."

The emperor left. Penant followed after him, wondering what awaited him now. Nothing good, he was sure of that. It was entirely possible that he would be wrung out and drained of the remainder of his life for the sake of this fat know-it-all emperor. That must be it. Yadugara had given Pen away like a gift.

In the meantime, Ma Ju Ro stopped at the massive doors to the hall, engraved with a gilded monogram. There was a high chance that his first public appearance would show that he was no emperor at all.

The guests who weren't guild members were waiting for the official part in the anteroom, a ceremonial waiting area outside the entryway to the hall, which was reserved for huge events. They noticed right away that the emperor had come in with just three imperial guards, a never-before-seen occurrence. Usually he was surrounded by two dozen, or even more when he went out into the city.

The guard remained at the entrance, and the emperor marched briskly through the full hall to the dais. The walls were decorated with a red material and flowers, and not just any flowers, but ones widely used in medicine, although this escaped Luca's attention. He was collected and focused.

An orchestra began to play when the emperor appeared, and scattered applause rose up and died in the audience. Casting a glance around the hall, Ma Ju Ro counted at least a hundred people and it occurred to him that in its greed for wealth, the guild had completely forgotten that not only the aristocrats and their families live in the capital, but so did a million common people. Alas, the guild was too small to pay attention to them no matter how much it might want to. Conveniently, it also refused to increase in size.

The guild leader Veronimus and the advisor Lentz sat upon a specially installed high dais. They rose to greet the emperor. Ma Ju Ro took his seat between them, recalling Lentz's words about the ceremony program. A welcoming speech from Veronimus, the declaration of the winner by Lentz, and the awarding of Yadugara by the emperor. The official part ended there, and the head of state would leave the event while the healers stayed behind to talk amongst themselves; to exchange gossip and rumors, and just to have a good time eating their fill of the palace kitchens. It seemed the invited guests, performers and dancers would be let into the hall by then, but that didn't interest Luca.

"His Imperial Majesty Ma Ju Ro, the Fourth of His Name, Overlord of the Entire World, chosen by the Sacred Mother to defend all her people and the living world, bound by blood to the founder of the Empire, Ma Ju Ro the First, Sire and Vanquisher!" the master of ceremonies announced loudly.

A whistle came from somewhere in the hall. The emperor found the brave heckler with his eyes, and he reddened and ducked behind the back of the one sitting in front of him.

"I didn't know that the guild practices the whistle as a new method of healing," Ma Ju Ro noted.

Although he was speaking to Veronimus standing next to him, everyone in the hall heard it — the acoustics were excellent. Laughter broke out.

"Your majesty, he did not whistle for that purpose," a richly dressed man from the first row said laughingly. The emperor nodded to him, and the man rose and introduced himself. "Grade-five Healer Raimondo, your majesty."

"Go on, Raimondo."

"We've all heard of the free clinic that's opening. They say it was your idea. If I may ask, what are you trying to achieve in that? All labor must be paid for!"

"The labor will be paid!" Ma Ju Ro answered. "From the imperial treasury. Any other questions?"

"Where is the money coming from?" someone shouted from the back rows.

"From the same place as all the money in the treasury. From taxes paid by citizens. And if any of you wishes to stick your nose in and count my money, I am ready to answer in kind. A more important question: would you like specially appointed tax collectors to start counting your real incomes and comparing them with those you indicate in your reports? Good idea, Raimondo, I like it!"

None of it was going to plan. Luca himself didn't want to say too much, and Lentz had demanded that he not allow himself to be provoked, but it went the other way. Luca remembered well how it took him several hours to claw his mother back from the abyss of Two-horns even with all his abilities, while these bloodsuckers were more concerned with how to heal any rich person for as long as possible — he'd overheard Yadugara's conversations. And transfusion? When he thought of that, Luca frowned and clenched his fists, throwing a foreboding across the gathering of healers. None dared to answer him. All lowered their eyes before the firestorm burning in the emperor's gaze.

The blushing Veronimus suppressed a smile, and waved fastidiously at Raimondo to get him to sit down and shut up, then turned to emperor.

"Your imperial majesty, you have a wonderful sense of humor! Please forgive our colleague Raimondo, he is overly... ahem, excited by the occasion of your visit. I suggest we don't stand on ceremony, since we're distracting you from your day, and your time is so precious...

Luca twisted his shoulder, throwing off

Veronimus's plump hand. He quieted the alarmed Lentz with a quick nod and stood up.

"I am pleased to greet the worthy healers of the Empire within the walls of my," he emphasised that word, "palace! Very soon we will move on to that which you have gathered for, but I want to take advantage of this rare opportunity to tell to you all about something important. Perhaps the most important thing in the history of the Empire!"

The healers had, in their time, seen the emperor sleepy, exuberant, lecherous. A couple of years ago they'd seen an angry and annoyed emperor, when he slammed his fist down on the stand and demanded a donor from them at once. But this — a calm, confident and steady emperor wanting to talk about 'something important' — this had never been seen. All present leaned forward in curiosity, and some even raised themselves up.

"The greatest riches of the Empire are not its lands, but its people. People, master healers! In your race for profit, you have forgotten this. You have forgotten that, as students of the university's famous medical faculty, founded by my honored ancestor Phlamma the First, you gave an oath. An oath to do all in your power to save the lives of others!"

"We do so!" Raimondo shouted, deciding that if everyone else would be quiet, then he would be the voice of the healers' community.

"You do so..." Luca repeatedly dryly. "As much as you might want to, you are unable to provide healing to all those that suffer! There are too few of you, and you carefully keep your numbers low so that you don't get too many competitors, the abyss forbid that might happen. Someone who might take a slice of your pie. Dozens of graduating healers each year remain unemployed. Those that you take into voluntary slavery as so-called apprentices are glad of it, and yet you take from them what you wish? You have split all the rich families of the country up amongst yourselves, but you forgot that the clothes you wear, the bread you eat, was created by the hands of common people. Tell me, Lentz, how many newborns were there in the capital last year?"

"Twenty seven thousand, not counting unregistered births," Lentz answered without missing a beat. "Of them, around eight thousand were stillborn. Less than six thousand lived to be a year old.

"And how people many died last year?"

"Nobody has the precise figures, your majesty. But by our humble estimations, over fifty thousand people."

"The Empire is dying. From hunger and sickness. We aren't fighting anyone, the Capital hasn't known war for several centuries. But our citizens are dying! It is within my power to eliminate hunger. It is within my power to give free healing to all regardless of whether the guild is planning to help me do it or planning to get in my way. And I will do so!" he spoke the last words with such depth and volume that they bounced off the walls.

BLOOD OF FATE

Ma Ju Ro sat back down, in complete silence. There was no applause, no exclamations — all were stunned by the emperor's words and decisiveness.

Veronimus recovered first, coughed and unsteadily rattled off his planned welcome speech. Lentz said something, but Luca didn't listen. His thoughts were elsewhere.

The award ceremony for Nestor Yadugara passed as a routine affair, and then the emperor quickly left the event without saying farewell.

Nobody noticed an unknown guild member, a hunched and grey-haired old man, follow the emperor out. A few minutes later, he was standing in the imperial chambers, escorted there by a guard, not knowing what to expect from the meeting, mentally replaying the moments of his short and not entirely joyous life, full of beatings and daydreams. He never did have the time to know the joys of sharing a bed with a woman.

The emperor gestured for him to sit, but the old man continued to stand. And he stood the entire time while Ma Ju Ro stared at him in silence.

The emperor sought a way to help Penant and was trying to figure out how to implement his plan. He didn't have enough knowledge, nor enough information about the transfusion procedure.

Then it hit him. The logs!

At Luca's command, his metamorphosis highlighted the notes from the reverse transfusion procedure recorded a couple of weeks ago. The result was a kind of recipe for the synthesis of various substances and catalysts that, when used in the correct order, would finally provide the required reaction, switching around the recipient and the donor in the transfusion procedure.

At the carrier's command, metamorphosis produced a range of programmable agents. Each of them was no larger than a molecule, and all were set to activate under certain circumstances.

When the agents were concentrated in his right hand, Ma Ju Ro took hold of the old man's shoulder and injected them. Penant noticed nothing.

"Do you wish to return your youth and take vengeance against your former master?" Luca asked.

"More than anything in the world, your majesty!" The old man lifted his head and a furious fire burned in his eyes. "Will you punish him?"

"You will punish him yourself for his treachery."

"But how?" Penant whispered. "I am old and weak..."

"It's simple enough. And you'll punish him the same way he did you. Thanks to some recent research by the imperial medics, we were able to isolate a certain active substance from that unfortunate boy's blood. You recall Luca?"

"Dezisimu? Yes, sire!" The old man's face cleared up. He recalled and understood. "You mean the thing that prevented my tutor from transfusing all the boy's strength?"

"Exactly. Find some way to get Yadugara to

tap into you again. Tell him that you see no point in living on, that you've decided to give your final years to your master, the only person close to you. As soon as he begins the transfusion, the procedure will reverse, and he will be the one giving up his years. The important thing is to make sure that nobody else is there."

"Reyna kept an eye on it all last time."

"She might interrupt the procedure..."

"That's my concern now," Penant interrupted him with confidence in his voice. "Forgive me, your majesty. I'll say that I don't want to die in front of Reyna. I'll make it a condition..."

The emperor touched his cheek and quietly asked:

"You won't lose courage?"

"No," Penant said decisively. "I'd rather die with a hope of justice than eke out the last of my days in this decaying, dying body."

The old man reached into his mouth and pulled out a tooth. He put it in his pocket, looked at Ma Ju Ro, and a smile gleamed in his eyes.

"If..." Luca hesitated. "When you do this, once it's done, go to Lentz, or better, to the chief of the new clinic, Koerlig. He'll have a job for you."

"I will," Penant declared. "But... why? Why have you decided to help me? And why... You could have just given the order, and..."

"Yes. You're right. I could have given an order and his body would be headless right now. I could have sent an assassin to do it quietly. I could have had him locked up for his illegal transfusions. I could have even ordered him to be dragged in here, and let Lentz perform the reverse procedure. But, if you understand my meaning here, Penant; in my view, justice shouldn't look like that."

"I understand," the old man whispered.

CHAPTER 38

THREAT FROM WITHIN

THE WEEKS FLEW BY one after the other, then one morning (just as hectic as any other) Emperor Ma Ju Ro the Fourth suddenly realized that precisely three months had passed since the day he first woke up in his new body on that stretcher.

In that time, Luca had finally reached influence level two through certain decisions and deeds, and he'd saved up thirty two Tsoui points, but he didn't dare spend them after wasting another ten on spinning the Wheel with no result. He'd gotten an empty white sector.

Influence level: +1.
Influence level two reached!
Luca'Onegut, you are living a life worthy of Tsoui! Your deeds have a positive influence on universal harmony and the balance of life!

Your reward:
+0.2% chance of landing on a blue sector.
+0.1% chance of landing on a gold sector.
-0.1% chance of landing on a red sector.
-0.2% chance of landing on a white sector.

Luca was far happier about gaining a level in his sole talent, which he had to use constantly to protect himself from assassination attempts, reveal lies in complex negotiations, help to heal wounds and much more.

Metamorphosis: +1.
Ability level four reached!
You can control your body at an improved level: unlocked a basic combat form that allows you to perform a short-term transformation of your own body parts, altering their materials, shape and properties.

In combat mode, your metabolism speed is boosted by one thousand two hundred percent, which causes a time slow effect for the carrier. Combat mode duration: 3 seconds.

Now, if he wanted to, he could even fight in the Arena against the Empire's strongest gladiators, and he'd probably win. Field experiments with the basic combat form showed that neither a finely sharpened sword, nor a heavy axe, nor the head of an arrow shot from a compound bow from fifteen feet could harm him. The mode didn't last long and it burned through Wheel energy at an outrageous pace, but even without it, he had enough internal improvements to easily withstand even the fiercest attacks. However, to look at him, it seemed as though the emperor was injured; his skin and first layer of fat would break, and he would bleed. If Luca tempered the enthusiasm of his metamorphosis and its instant and rapid regeneration, then the wounds kept bleeding and looked terrible.

Everything that Luca could only have dreamed of as a cripple boy from a the slums of the Capital was becoming a reality. Now he could walk, and he had a body as good as anyone else's. His family wanted for nothing, and his mother was completely well again. She gained strength and had gotten back almost all her former beauty, that for which Luca's father, the gladiator Severus, had fallen in love with her.

Kora was making herself at home in the palace, laughing at the whispers behind her back. Each wandering rumor was finer than the last, but they all led to bewilderment — what did the emperor see in the girl? Even if you ignored her common background, the ladies of the palace couldn't understand the grip Kora had on his majesty, and they invented the most whimsical explanations for this change in their ruler's tastes. It only took a month for the new fashion trends at court to take hold throughout the capital: careless makeup, or even none at all, and thinness, which was especially difficult for those ladies that had spent the last few years carefully nurturing their curves.

Luca's sister actively helped Keirinia to support the needy. Ma Ju Ro had made charity fashionable — the nobility and rich families of the capital were making large donations at charitable balls organized by Lee Vensiro. Clothing, food baskets and medicine went to specific families in need — which was what the girls were doing.

The first free clinic was opened in the huge mansion of former advisor Naut. It opened slowly due to hidden resistance from the healers' guild and the rumors they spread about 'barely trained quacks,' but it was open. The numbers of people seeking treatment exceeded the capabilities of the doctors working there, as the healers had begun to call the clinic's physicians in protest. This meant that after only three days, Hector gave the emperor a report on the attempts of particularly zealous patients to buy themselves a place. In spite of the decent salary generously set by Lentz, there were doctors who couldn't resist simple 'gifts,' which meant that the clinic's manager Koerlig had to stand before the emperor and blush. The bribe-takers were fired, and no more cases occurred — the people there appreciated their position and the chance they'd been given.

Lentz managed to study the mushrooms that Ma Ju Ro spoke of, and he was able to determine how they suppress the life forces of even the smallest organisms that caused infectious disease. At the ruler's suggestion, Lentz called the newly discovered compound an 'antibiotic,' but couldn't resist adding his own name to it as well. The discovery was announced at a specially organized assembly of the guild, but the 'Lentz antibiotic' was offered to private healers only as a finished product, in special ampules for injection, which provided another source of income for the treasury.

Luca's mother ended up getting a job at the imperial clinic, and without any help from her son. Her education, knowledge of the common people and her skill of talking to them allowed her to work at the reception desk. Naturally, she became a person of high regard among her former neighbors in the slums. "Our Prisca!" they said with pride.

Reyk Lee Vensiro undertook his responsibilities with gusto. In a very short time, all the creative types that had hitherto been hiding underground went out into the city streets and filled the taverns, delighting the public and intertwining into their performances — directly or otherwise — the magnanimous Ma Ju Ro. Or Ma Ju Ro the Magnanimous, in contrast to Ma Ju Ro the Sour. The Imperial Theater changed its repertoire entirely, casting off Rizmayer's boring and protracted plays and replacing them with lively comedies and melodramas that the common folk could understand.

Of course, not everyone was happy about these innovations. Throughout these months, there were several attempts to poison the emperor, and attempts to bribe his guards. One bribe was even successful, and the assassin who stole into the imperial chambers would certainly have been successful if Ma Ju Ro had been an ordinary man. They also tried to give the emperor 'poisoned apples,' as General Hustig put it — beautiful girls willing to do anything, all with a special surprise... Luca himself had lost count of the times he was a hair's breadth from death.

But thanks to his metamorphosis, he not only successfully avoided it, he also found the conspirators by using a special substance that they called truth serum. Although most of the assassination attempts came from the South, displeased aristocrats at court caused their fair share.

The guilty parties with their noble, but now besmirched names were sent to the chopping block, and their property and capital added to the treasury. Ma Ju Ro hesitated in this at first, but the cruelty of the punishment worked — the assassination attempts stopped, and some families began to understand the new rules of the game and threw their full support behind the emperor. Those still dissatisfied sold their property and went to join Rezsinius.

As for Herdinia, in spite of the fact that Luca had long since healed her of the sexual magnetism virus and there were no more pheromones to attract her, she didn't lose her ardor for the emperor. It remained a mystery whether it was a side effect of the virus or whether Cross's wife truly had fallen in love with him in the end. There was no chance to test it on the other victims, those three girls that Lee Vensiro had brought to him. They'd been sent home by the emperor's order.

Herdinia embraced the idea of returning the Empire to its former glory with a passion, instantly put a stop to that which prevented this goal. Somehow realizing that the emperor, in spite of the enthusiasm and zeal with which he had returned to ruling the country, was having a hard time dealing with various issues, she readily responded to his silent request for help. No, she didn't continue to make decisions as before, without his involvement. On the contrary, now Ma Ju Ro took the decisions personally, but the first advisor finally performed the role the position demanded — to advise, highlighting all the pitfalls and making consequences clear.

Herdinia took on the forgiven, but disgraced Naut and took responsibility for directing all their financial streams and planning. The old budgets were mercilessly cut, and new ones were built with a few to spending as effectively as possible, with a focus on helping the country and its people, not just their representatives.

One of the industries financed by the imperial treasury was science. The Empire hadn't explored many sciences so far, and all of them were chosen on the principle of short-term advantage. New alloys for armor and weapons and rumors of the upcoming rearmament of the army enlivened the market. Each field created new jobs, and that meant that dissatisfaction in the society was steadily dropping.

The treasury financed the construction of tens of thousands of fishing boats, and the city was flooded with seafood. The townspeople could now complain of a lack of choice, but no longer of hunger. In addition, the emperor took a range of measures to restore the agricultural sector, giving tax breaks to land owners that hired farmers to work their lands.

The most serious problems had been solved, but the threat from the South hadn't passed. On the contrary, it was only stronger. And it struck from an unexpected direction.

"Rezsinius's troops will be at the city walls in two, best case three months," Hustig said. "We have to bring the battle to them first. Otherwise the city will be under siege."

"And bare our flank?" Hector frowned. "I don't have enough people for a full defense of Rezsinius lands from the sea. He'll take the city bare-handed!"

"We can't split our forces," the emperor interjected into his advisors' squabble.

He'd said that several times already. They'd been arguing for a solid hour, and Ma Ju Ro was starting to get sick of it. The government clearly didn't have enough military power, and if Rezsinius were braver, he would have captured the capital long ago.

Thirty thousand new recruits to strengthen the regular army brought the Empire's strength to roughly equal with that of Rezsinius, but only on paper. In reality, the rebel had tried and tested troops; the cavalry and knights of the southern barons, island mercenaries who had held saber and sword since childhood, and most importantly, legions of veterans that had fought through the capture of the North and the cleansing of the Wastelands. Fifty thousand fire-forged warriors, most of which would still stand beneath Ma Ju Ro's banners had his body's former owner not cut the military budget. The veterans had been sent into retirement, and without any severance pay. It was no wonder the offended legions headed to the South as soon as rumor spread that Rezsinius was recruiting.

"Are you still arguing?"

The men turned around at Herdinia's voice, who had gotten bored and gone out for fresh air.

"Does the respected Herdinia have any ideas?" the general asked defensively.

"I am certain she does." Even sitting at the table, Lee Vensiro managed to give a short bow. He had infinite respect for Herdinia and put her in second place in his own hierarchy, immediately after the emperor. "My lady First Advisor sees the bigger picture, unlike us foolish brutes."

Hector looked at him and frowned. He

couldn't bear the obsequious and flamboyant reyk.

"I have no ready solution for you. I just have common sense. We can't split up the troops we have, everyone knows this, and his majesty has been telling you the same. We all know that there will be only one battle, and if it were up to me, I would meet the enemy at the city walls."

"That would be a curious sight," Fourth Advisor Cross said, yawning. "I've sat here long enough. If your majesty allows it, I have some important matters to attend to."

Ma Ju Ro nodded, not looking at Herdinia's husband. Anthony was still entirely useless. He just rattled off venomous comments and foretold the coming change in power, but veiled his words so that none present but the emperor and his wife knew what he was talking about.

Anthony loudly pushed his chair back, stood up and left.

"Strike me down, but I don't even know what he does for this country!" the general murmured. "Your majesty?"

"Cross's tasks are not subject to discussion," Ma Ju Ro answered. "And they do not matter here. Let's continue. Herdinia suggests that we fight the enemy here. Any objections?"

"It'll be a siege..." Hustig said, apparently deep in thought. He stared at Herdinia heavily. "My dear first advisor! It's bad enough that you suggest that we let the enemy approach the city, so that he can pin us to the sea and cut off all our lines of retreat.

On top of that, you suggest that we hide in holes like rats! And the holes aren't even that safe! Rezsinius has men in the city. Yes, they're hidden, but if the southerners arrive at the capital's walls, we'll need to be prepared for a strike from within. Saboteurs, traitors of all kinds, or just bitter people that decide to betray the city to get favor from the new future ruler..."

"There's something else," Lodyger interjected, speaking for the first time at this council session. He coughed, looked to one side and spoke monotonously. "Speeches are not my strong suit. But there's something else. The manufacturers and workshops are already complaining that their operations are being sabotaged. The fire yesterday in the leatherworking district was the work of Ignatius the Furious..."

"He's the leader of the capital's criminal gangs," Hector explained to the emperor.

"Master Hector is correct, that he is," Lodyger confirmed. "His people are scaring the craftsmen, threatening to burn down their houses, rape their wives and daughters. Some lowlifes are throwing pig heads and dead rats through the windows of known shopworkers. And they're demanding the same from all of them — to cease work, or worse, sabotage production, vandalize the workshops. A few fishermen had their boats and their entire catch stolen this morning. The day before yesterday, an ore delivery was hijacked..."

"Why are they doing this?" the emperor asked.

"It's obvious why!" General Hustig slammed his fist on the table. "They're in cahoots with Rezsinius!"

"Now I see why some doctors are already refusing to go work at the clinic. They come up with nonsense excuses: one fell ill to inexplicable bouts of weakness, another's grandmother died and he has to go to the funeral, a third went to a wedding in a village two hundred miles away, and weddings there last two whole weeks..."

"So the enemy is attacking on all fronts even while Rezsinius's army is still two thousand miles away? Kolot, does the city watch have its head buried in the sand? Who leads it?" Ma Ju Ro frowned.

"Shoyrek. Or he did. He's retired, claims he's sick. His health has taken a turn, he says, he can't help the country anymore. I let him go without a second thought, but..."

"We need to catch and hang all the bandits! Ruler, give me three days and I will cleanse the city of this filth!" Hustig spat.

"How do you plan to do that? Just going to grab everyone and ask them if they're a bandit?"

"Why would I do that?" the general asked in surprise.

"You're used to fighting on the battlefield, where everything is clear: here are yours, and there are the others, the enemy. But all the city's people are citizens of the Empire. They don't have it written on their foreheads that they're bandits!" Hector said.

"In the light of day, they look like ordinary vagrants." They arm themselves at night, they fear nothing and no-one, on the contrary, they have everyone so scared that nobody will dare poke their nose out of their doors after sundown."

"And your so-called soldiers..." Hustig muttered, smirking, "do they too fear to stick their noses out?"

"We've had pressy... preced... ents, ugh, we've had bad stuff happen," he admitted unwillingly through clenched teeth. "And my guys got scared. Hell, they're still being threatened. One captain had 'Die!' written on his wall in blood, but the man has balls. First he found the youths that wrote it, got the name of their ringleader out of them, the one that gave them the order. He pointed them to some thug and the captain and his boys paid the bastard a visit. Right in their lair!"

"Well done him!" Hustig couldn't help but cry. "That's the way to deal with those bastards!"

"Don't jump to conclusions, general. The criminal escaped on a cart, no arrests were made. And in the morning, the captain and his family were found chopped to pieces. The walls were covered in blood to the ceiling. The chief investigator lost his breakfast as soon as he saw it!"

"What kind of weaklings do you have working for you?" Hustig shouted. "You're making a chinil's nest out of a molehill! Find those pieces of shit and send them to the scaffold! Do you have no martial men?"

"All my men are martial!" Hector shouted. "But they go home at night, to their families! To sleep, like normal people! I can't put a guard on every house!"

In the complete silence after this spat between the general and commander, someone cleared their throat loudly. After coughing a while, the pale Lodyger wiped his brow with a handkerchief and spoke up.

"You mentioned chinils. Some villains threw a few of them at me and my wife in the night. Right into the bed. The guards weren't snoozing, but they somehow got in anyway. They left a note..." He stuck his hand into his pocket and pulled out a carefully folded paper. He unfolded it and read it: "'Next time it'll be your daughters' heads, Lodyger! Don't support Ma Ju Ro...' Forgive me, but it says..."

"Read it, advisor, don't worry," the emperor encouraged him with a nod.

"'... Ma Ju Ro the Fat, his days are numbered. Death to the tyrant! Glory to Rezsinius, the true emperor!'"

"You didn't have to shout the last words so fanatically, Lodyger," Herdinia said dryly. "Who is this Ignatius character? Do we have no way at all to control him?"

"I sent some people, and everyone who asked any questions concerning Ignatius the Furious went missing," Hector said darkly. "I knew someone in their group known as Weasel, but he went missing too. We know that some time ago, he contacted all the leaders of the other bandit gangs. He invited them to a so-called Circle of Honor. To refuse this would be the first sign of weakness and cowardice for them. Nobody would follow such a leader, and so all agreed. We don't know what happened there, but the next day, the criminal underworld in the capital changed. The only thing we know for sure is that all the gangs now have one leader — Ignatius the Furious."

"Is it the same Ignatius who was once a gladiator, and then opened his own gladiator school?" Luca asked, his breath catching.

"Entirely possible," Herdinia nodded. "The school closed when it became clear that the people had no money and they preferred to spend what they did have on food rather than on study. Ignatius himself disappeared, but now it all matches up."

"Vensiro..." Luca said thoughtfully.

"Yes, sire?"

"I want all your criers and bards to loudly announce it in the capital: Ma Ju Ro the Fourth invites Ignatius the Furious to a Circle of Honor!"

CHAPTER 39

IGNATIUS THE FURIOUS AND HIS PEOPLE

"THERE'S SOMETHING ELSE," Ma Ju Ro said, holding back Lentz as he went to leave. "How is Penant doing?"

Half a month ago, the emperor had heard rumors that Yadugara was dead. Nobody knew the details, but word was that something went wrong during a transfusion procedure.

"Alive and well," the advisor on science and health shrugged his shoulders. "After Yadugara's untimely demise, it became known that he was performing illegal transfusion procedures without consent from his patients. We knew that before, sire, but his lover, one Reyna Deratto, shared details that confirmed the senior apprentice's allegations.

Reyna was a slave, but his servants were paid, so the only one who served Yadugara for free was Penant. The healer had no family, so the boy was named his heir, especially after it turned out that he'd shared his life force with his master. The court decided to give all the property of the deceased to Penant, including his manor."

"Anything else?"

"Yes. As you asked, Koerlig took the man on at the clinic. He had no chance of going into private practice, but he has knowledge. He'll be useful," Lentz concluded dryly.

Just as the door closed behind the one advisor, another appeared. Hector brought someone in.

"This is Weasel," he introduced his companion to the emperor. "He has a message from Ignatius." He turned to the messenger and tried to give him a clap round the head, but the target dodged. "Idiot! Who comes to an address with the emperor armed? "We took six throwing knives from you already. But you have two daggers and a knife in your boot-tops!"

"Dangerous streets out there, Mr. Kolot!" Weasel said in sincere indignation. "Crazy people'll take the clothes off your back in the middle of the day, and the less said about the night the better! Your city watch can't even catch a mouse!"

Hector shot a wrathful glance at his guest, but said nothing. The boy may be making fun of him, himself a member of the criminal underworld, but what he said was indisputable: the capital was in a time of chaos. And although some problems had been solved in recent months, the state was losing in the fight against crime. Not only that, but Ma Ju Ro had it on good authority that more and more former watchmen under Hector's employ were switching to the enemy camp, joining those they were meant to fight against.

"Forgive me, your majesty." The weasel clenched his fist over his heart and bowed his head. "Do excuse me."

"You're funny," Ma Ju Ro smiled. "Rare is the man who will dare to argue with my advisors, particularly the fearsome Kolot Hector."

"He's like a son to me..." Hector said, embarrassed. "As I said, emperor, I've watched over this boy since his father died before his time... Apparently I haven't been doing such a good job!"

"It's my life," the boy noted reasonably.

The emperor nodded, satisfied with the explanation, and extended a hand. The young man was surprised, but readily shook it. He looked around twenty five years old, but metamorphosis determined his age more exactly — nineteen. The boy's eyes had aged, with a visible network of wrinkles at the corners. His gaze was hard and piercing.

He had a beard and gold earrings. For his age, young messenger of Ignatius the Furious stood confidently. Especially considering where he was and who he was with. The young man sported a fitted leather jacket, with a fur collar and lots of silver buttons, a silk shirt and velvet purple trousers tucked into high boots made of soft patent leather. The toe caps were crested with metal cleats. For street fights, Luca guessed.

"Pleased to meet you, Weasel," the emperor said. "What did Ignatius ask you to pass on?"

"Your majesty," the young man bowed his head. And considering that the ceremony could now be dispensed with, he smiled broadly. "The boss said your criers are wasting their breath. This ain't how you do things..." He shied a little under Hector's gaze and clarified. "This ain't how we do things. It's like, uh... You have to understand, your majesty, we're simple people. The emperor is one thing, we're another. We don't obey your laws. Which is why we suffer when your hounds get hold of someone, and they get sent to the slammer, the mines, the block. But we get that. Costs of doing a hard business, and the only, as it were, point of shared interest..."

"Don't overdo it, Kane!" Hector interrupted the man, frowning. "What are you babbling about?"

"What's wrong, uncle Hector? I was told to say it, so I'm sayin' it. Ignatius said we make our own rules and the laws of the Empire don't apply to us. And if his majesty wants to play our game, then he'd better learn our rules better. I'm right in thinkin' your majesty is challenging the boss?"

"Absolutely," Ma Ju Ro laughed amicably.

"Well there you go!" the man said triumphantly. "You can't catch him, so you've decided to use tricks like that to get around him. But you can't just go and challenge the chief with us. Not until you prove your rights in the Circle with the captains, with the other bosses, the deputies. All the more if you're a nobody."

"A nobody?" the emperor said.

Hector clouted Weasel around the back of the head and the young man snapped.

"What the hell, uncle Hector? I'm passing on the boss's words! And in our circles, his majesty really is a nobody. You gotta earn your reputation from nothing, whether you're the High Priest of the Sacred Mother, Two-horns himself or the emperor. That's what he said."

"And?" Hector and Ma Ju Ro asked at once.

"And what? Your majesty, if he really wants to fight Ignatius and the others, has to make a challenge personally. Not like this. This is like a circus with lame horses. That's what the boss said."

"Personally? Has this Ignatius of yours gone completely mad?" Hector asked in amazement.

"He's right, Kolot," the emperor chuckled. He turned back to Weasel. "Listen, young man, I would like to make a personal challenge, but your boss is hiding like a rat in a hole. How do I challenge him if I don't know where to find him?"

"He's no rat," the messenger replied, frowning. "And if you wanna meet him, I'll take you to him. At night. Alone! We don't got no trust for you clowns. You find out where our bosses do business, you'll send your hounds after 'em. Nah, Ignatius wasn't born yesterday. He knows which side to grab a tit from."

"What does that mean?" Hector asked, frowning.

"What?"

"About the tit. Do you mean to say that his imperial majesty has large breasts? What are you implying, you little rat? Your father is spinning in his grave right now!"

"That ain't what I meant..." the young man shied back. "I mean Ignatius has reason to believe that his majesty's challenge is nothing more than a ruse to catch Ignatius, and if he refuses, to hurt his... his street cred! His reputation, I'm sayin'".

"Are these his words or are you sharing your own thoughts right now?" Ma Ju Ro asked. "About reputation and my treacherous plans?"

"My own," Weasel admitted.

"Then let me tell you; you are wrong. I see no sense in catching Ignatius, because another Ignatius will rise to replace him. Not the Furious, but the Cruel or the Kind, that's not the point. Nothing will change. Your brotherhood will still impede me and my people from building a worthy state and preparing for war. You are sabotaging construction works, intimidating craftsmen, threatening my advisors. I slept for a long time, Weasel, and gave away control of this land into the hands of dishonorable thieves, but now I have awoken. I know that rats, cockroaches and chinils cannot be completely wiped out, but I don't want them to feel at home in the city my ancestors founded. To feel like masters!" Ma Ju Ro's eyes burned with rage as he looked at Ignatius's messenger, who unwillingly took a step back under that gaze. "Set me up a meeting with that boss of yours, the chief rat!"

"Your majesty!" Hector couldn't help himself. "Don't even think about it!"

"I will go alone," Ma Ju Ro said, bringing his emotions back under control. "If your boss refuses, then I swear, every man in the Empire will hear of his cowardice!"

"I'll come back for ya at midnight, your majesty," Weasel said impassively. "He won't refuse."

Apart from Hector, the only person that learned of the emperor's upcoming adventure was Herdinia. But in contrast to Luca's fears, she didn't try to change his mind. On the contrary, she looked at him with pride, kissed him on the cheek and wished him luck.

At midnight, after putting Keirinia into a sleep, he stole through the window of Hector's office to the carriage waiting for him on the coastal side of the palace. It was empty apart from Weasel, who held the reins. The emperor and his advisor climbed inside and the carriage lurched forward, taking them to the palace gates.

"Emperor, if you would allow me..."

"No, Hector," Ma Ju Ro said firmly. "I don't want to put you at risk."

"Good luck, sire!" Hector saluted, his fist at his chest. "May the Sacred Mother give you strength!"

They left Kolot by the gates and Weasel urged the horses on to the meeting with the leaders of the criminal underworld. They were moving quickly, but the trip still turned out to be long. All across the city, past the elite districts, through Merchant Square, Hunter's Row and the stalls of the city's craftsmen; through the slums where Weasel had to use both whip and word as a weapon, shouting out the fearsome names of well-known bandits and scaring off the local rabble and street urchins who decided to take interest in the contents of the carriage and its passengers' pockets.

Against Hector's urgings, the emperor was dressed plainly. Common trousers, a shirt and a thick leather cloak with a hood. He didn't even take along the dagger that Kolot had stubbornly pressed on him.

Weasel didn't say a single word to the emperor the whole way. Ma Ju Ro kept quiet as well, busy with checking and rechecking the enhancements of his metamorphosis and modeling in his mind all the possible dangerous outcomes.

Bones, skin, vein walls — all had been reinforced. Even outside of his combat form, every vital organ was protected by a layer of fat and chrome steel, armored with titanium found by a miracle in Lentz's surgical tools. Nobody could pierce the emperor's skin with any kind of bladed weapon. The strength of the Sacred Mother kept Ma Ju Ro safe, or so thought his retinue Lentz, Hector and Hustig, but in reality, his strength wasn't mystical, it was entirely real. Except that it was from another world.

Ma Ju Ro had gotten thinner. He was still considered fat, and he had plenty of excess weight, but his metamorphosis had processed around forty pounds of his most harmful visceral fat. It was nothing when compared with the two hundred-odd that remained, but his progress was bearing fruit. It was even getting easier for the emperor to walk.

There was a reason that the first things his metamorphosis improved were his knees and his spine, to improve his posture and not damage his joints and ligaments as they carried his huge weight. The increased muscle mass allowed him to keep his back straight in any situation, and Keirinia was the first to notice his strengthened arms, when in the bedroom the emperor began to easily lift the girl up and hold her for as long as he wanted.

Yes, he had become a real man. The night after Yadugara's award ceremony, when Keirinia and Kora returned from the markets to show off their purchases, he felt incredibly tired. Kora, realizing that something was going on between her brother and her new friend, spoke delicately.

"Your majesty, may I be excused to go and rest? My first day in the palace was so full of new experiences! I'm very tired!"

"Of course, Kora, go, rest," Ma Ju Ro allowed.

Once alone with Keirinia, he felt his breath catch with desire for her. His courtesan, who had for some reason washed off all her makeup, looked so innocent and pure that the devilish gleam in her eye made his decision for him. He took her by the hand and led her to the bedroom without a word. Then the entire world had disappeared, leaving him nothing but a beautiful, limber and hot woman's body. Keirinia knew all about sex, and she guessed Luca's passing wishes in mere moments, proving beyond all doubt that she'd been the real Ma Ju Ro's favorite for more than just her looks.

As the dawn came unnoticed, feeling a song in his soul, he realized that he had discovered an activity so fine and magical that life was worth living solely for it. Since then, with all his ability to possess any woman of the Empire, he had lain only with one. Keirinia.

It was paradoxical, but at the same time he felt entirely certain that although he felt very fond and gentle feelings toward his courtesan, he did not love her, and merely gratefully accepted...

"We're here, y'majesty."

Ma Ju Ro shook himself from his thoughts and realized that they'd stopped on the coast, next to a cliff jutting out like a predatory sabertooth fang from the mountain range beyond the city. A vague shadow with a torch in hand stood by the entrance to a cave. It took a step forward and the light lit up an old face disfigured by a terrible scar. The sea breeze occasionally tousled sparse grey hair.

"My name is Law," the old man introduced himself in a hoarse voice. "First let me warn you, we have many places like this. It will not be used after this meeting, so even if you plan to return with the watch, forget it."

Law took Ma Ju Ro deep into the cave to a narrow pass blocked by stones. He whistled. A nightingale trill echoed out in response, then the groan of a winding winch and the scrape of a wheel. The stones — or the scenery that looked like stones — rose along with a previously unseen platform about three feet into the air, then stopped.

"You'll have to crawl through, your majesty," Weasel explained embarrassedly. He leaned down and shouted through the gap, "Hey, back there! Lift it up a little more! Our honored guest is a little on the fat side!"

"Tell him to take a shit!" someone shouted from the other side, braying in laughter.

Luca imagined crawling under the stones and that joker dropping the whole mess on him. That would be that, the end of Ma Ju Ro the fourth, all hail the new emperor Rezsinius! A little alarmed by that possibility, he put the situation to his metamorphosis and got an unsatisfying answer.

Modeling of situation "10-Ton Pressure"

completed.

Analyzing...
Modeling countermeasure...
Recommended transformation...
Not enough materials to morph carrier's body!
Requires...

There were a lot of requirements. Metals, time to transform the body, Wheel energy. There was no issue with the latter, but as for where he could find a hundred pounds of titanium, not to mention wolfram and iridium, Luca had no idea. He doubted that metal like that could be found anywhere in this society, at least on Syahr.

"So will his fatness crawl through, or has he already pissed himself?" Law asked.

Not justifying the old man with a response, Ma Ju Ro abruptly dived into the gap and moved his limbs as fast as he could, pulling himself through on his elbows, tearing his clothes and scratching his back and his neck. Three seconds later, he climbed to his feet next to the dazed joker and impassively brushed himself off. The joker stood with saber in hand and a blank stare.

"Hey, Ramzets, what's happening?"

"Our visitor..." The joker swallowed. "Is on this side. We taking him to the Circle?"

"Dumbass," the old man swore mildly.

A minute later, he and Weasel had also crawled through the gap. The old man pierced Ramzets — a bedraggled vagrant with goggle-eyes and a drooping lower lip — with a disgusted gaze and silently wandered deeper into the cave. Ma Ju Ro and Weasel followed after him.

They walked for almost a whole hour through endless dark tunnels, turning in unexpected places, and Luca could have sworn he was being led in circles and had walked past the same spot more than once.

Finally they reached a large cave lit by torches hanging on the walls. A large puddle glimmered in its center, reflecting the playful torchlight, and bandits sat around it on smoothed boulders and stones.

A mottled crowd of people among which Ma Ju Ro noticed both wild-looking girls and brightly over-painted ladies. But most of those present were men, and of the most aggressive breed — those for whom the lives of others meant precisely nothing, those who made a living off evil. Luca hadn't seen such a wide variety of people even on the porch of the Temple of the Sacred Mother, and all kinds of different people visited there. Bearded, tattooed, foppish, in rags... Elegant youths with patterns shaved into their beards, rakishly dressed in the latest fashion, rubbing shoulders with bare-chested giants with murderous eyes... But however varied they seemed, every last one emanated threat. If Luca had classified the degree of threat, he would have given it one of the highest possible ratings of danger.

The old man Law led Ma Ju Ro to the center

of the cave, pointing out a place in the puddle. It went up to his knees. In the meantime, Weasel had disappeared somewhere, dissolving into the mass of people.

The crowd stirred when the emperor appeared. Some laughed derisively, some whistled so loudly that the echo from the walls overwhelmed the ears.

A massive figure separated from a group sitting in a far corner. The conversations steadily quietened.

The figure came into full view and Luca realized that this was Ignatius the Furious himself. He had a short haircut in the manner of gladiators, with monstrously huge arms and a powerful torso visible under his silk shirt with rolled up sleeves. Expensive bracelets decorated his wrists, and a gold chain encircled his bullish neck. The leader of the Empire's criminal underworld moved as lightly and quietly as a Jamalayan tiger, and a broad smile was frozen on his face.

"Why's everyone so quiet? Brothers! Sisters!" Ignatius spread his hands, summoning the crowd. "Let us welcome Emperor Ma Ju Ro the Fourth, who isn't as lowly a coward as we thought!"

The crowd roared, whooped and laughed, throwing all kinds of garbage at the outsider. An apple core hit him in the cheek, a weighty stone struck his shoulder. If Luca had counted on even a shred of respect — he was still the emperor, after all! — then that illusion was shattered. He wasn't welcome here.

"Greetings, Ma Ju Ro!" Ignatius roared. Everyone fell silent, waiting for the show to continue. "Those street screamers of yours have been sayin' you want to challenge me. That so? Cat caught your tongue?"

"Yes, Ignatius, I hereby challenge you. Personally, as you can see."

The people whispered, someone shouted something and everyone laughed. Ignatius waited for the people to calm down, then grabbed Luca by the collar and tried — and failed — to lift him up. His tone turned malevolent.

"And what in Two-horns' name makes you think that just anyone can challenge me, pig? Who the hell are ya? What makes you think you've earned this? Huh?"

He shouted those final words right into Luca's face. Only then did the emperor realize that Ignatius was mad with fury, feral. The eyes of Ignatius the Furious were bloodshot and piercing.

"Because, murderer, I am the emperor!" Ma Ju Ro shouted. He grabbed Ignatius by the collar himself and tried to lift him, but the shirt didn't hold and ripped. "This is my city! My land! My country!"

"You're stark-raving mad!" Ignatius said in amazement. "You idiot, your brains have finally filled with fat! I don't know what the hell's gotten into your head, but now I know one thing for sure; we don't need a ruler like you! How many years did you drink the people's blood? Huh? Here's my answer: suck off everyone here..."

"And lick!" a lady of ill repute in the crowd hollered.

"... and then we'll think about whether to let you call anyone from the thieves' brotherhood to the Circle!"

"Then we'd better start calling you Ignatius the Weak, coward!" Ma Ju Ro shouted.

Ignatius bared his teeth and patted the emperor on the cheek.

"You're going to regret this, wretch. I swear, by morning the entire city will see your empty head with your dismembered cock in your mouth in Merchant Square!"

He cast a glance over the quiet audience and shouted:

"I call the captains to the Circle!" He turned back to the emperor and spoke quietly. "You, you disgusting pig, if you want to fight me, you'll have to go through all my captains first!"

Four men stepped into the puddle. They bared their teeth and stood next to Ignatius.

"Allow me to introduce them, piggy! One of these faces will be the last one you see in your meaningless life, maggot! My captains: Rokkan, Khudoyar, Kerkion and Otolik! If you can handle them, then you'll have the honor of dying at my hands! Which will you challenge first?

The cave fell silent as the grave. The captains kept their eyes fixed on the emperor, an amused smirk on the face of each.

"It doesn't matter who goes first. I'll kill them all!" Ma Ju Ro answered.

An amazed whisper spread through the bandit lair. Ma Ju Ro walked around the circle, gazing at the onlookers, and shouted:

"I am Ma Ju Ro, the Fourth of His Name, Overlord of the Entire World, chosen by the Sacred Mother to defend all her people and the living world, bound by blood to the founder of the Empire Ma Ju Ro the First, Sire and Vanquisher! And I challenge all four of you. Who among you is brave enough to go first?"

CHAPTER 40

CIRCLE OF CAPTAINS

A FTER A SHORT PERIOD of hesitation, the loudmouthed crowd erupted in laughter. It roared, and the overwhelming din echoing off the vaulting cave had it all: cries from shameless women, abuse from bloodthirsty men, piercing laughter, insane catcalls, unbridled snickering and scornful bleating. A cacophonous music of mayhem and excess.

The biggest comedians clapped their hands, shouted "encore" and encouraged "his imperial hogness" to keep up the good work. The horde showed no signs of quieting, but it didn't bother Ma Ju Ro in the slightest, and he was impossible to embarrass — he had the legacy of a traveler of dozens of worlds in his mind! On top of that, some time ago he had been developing a sonorous, well-defined voice, and Ma Ju Ro knew how to use it.

"Looks like your captains are shitting their

pants, Ignatius!" he shouted, cutting through the noise of the crowd. "No?"

The people quietened, awaiting the spectacle's continuation.

"I guess I'll take the challenge," a swarthy and wiry man with a short pointed beard said after the noise calmed down.

"No! I'll take this sack of shit on first!" another said as he stepped forward, a beefy tattooed man with behemoth shoulders and a thick neck. "I'll turn 'im inside-out!"

"Simmer down, Kerkion," Ignatius placed a calming hand on the big man's shoulder. "Rokkan accepted the challenge first, so he goes first. Now everyone out of the circle! And keep quiet!" he shouted, addressing the last to the crowd. "Rokkan the Black has accepted Ma Ju Ro's challenge!"

Mere heartbeats later, the puddle that symbolized the Circle was empty save for the two combatants. The captain walked right up to Ma Ju Ro.

"To make it clear: I don't give a damn about Ignatius, the brotherhood or this whole shitty city," Rokkan whispered barely audibly, slowly enunciating his words. "But the problem is you, emperor. You won't leave here alive, even if you defeat all the captains and Ignatius to boot. But me, to tell the truth, I was brought up to respect the lawful ruler of the Empire, so I ain't planning on appeasing these bastards' wishes. I'll save you, emperor. Don't resist. I'll skewer you just in the right place, so I don't hit any vital organs. Play dead and I'll drag your body out of here. Once you've recovered and everyone's gone, I'll take you to the palace!"

Hector had given the emperor a report on Rokkan the Black. It mentioned that the man controls the wharf and all the shoreline industries, including the pearl divers, and that he had close connections with the pirates of the South Islands.

"Enough whispering!" Ignatius shouted. "Fight!"

Ma Ju Ro pushed Rokkan back so hard that the man lost his balance and nearly fell.

"Play dead yourself!" he replied, and approached the enemy without lifting his feet above the water.

"Your choice, y'majesty," Rokkan slowly stepped back, shrugged, took out his duelling sword. He made a few swings, cutting the air. "What are you waiting for? Where's your weapon? Draw your iron! You plannin' to fight barehanded?"

"My iron is with me," Ma Ju Ro answered. "And if I need more, I'll take yours."

He continued to walk with such confidence that Rokkan backed off, but he still recognized that he was holding a sword against an unarmed man, and he made a thrust, piercing the emperor's fat stomach with the blade. Blood sprayed from the wound and fell into the water in bright red flecks. An elated roar spread throughout the cave.

"His blood's red! Just like ours! Give it to 'im!

Bleed that pig dry, Rokkan! Cut him to ribbons! Tear out his heart!"

The crowd was wild and feral as it celebrated the coming victory over their hateful idiot emperor. Only the captain knew that was something was wrong. It was as if Rokkan's sword was stuck in the emperor's body.

Ma Ju Ro grabbed it by its faceted blade, pulled it out of his body and then jerked it toward him, pulling in Rokkan. The man gasped, stumbled — and the emperor rushed him, still holding the sword, and head-butted him in the face. The bandit's nose shattered as Ma Ju Ro's metal-reinforced skull struck it. Rokkan reeled, blood flowed down his chin. The emperor pulled on the sword again, swung his right fist around in a wide circle and hit his enemy in the throat. Croaking and gasping for breath, the bandit fell, and the emperor pulled the sword from his grasp. Just as he was about to drive it into Rokkan's throat, the man's wail cut through the silent and shocked cave.

"Mercy! I surrender! Have mercy, your majesty! I accept defeat and give you my right to challenge Ignatius!"

Ma Ju Ro nodded, lowered the blade. Rokkan nimbly crawled away, covering himself in thick mud. Off to one side, Ignatius swore.

"Coward!" Pathetic dog! Kerkion! You're up! Cut out this pig's guts!"

The big tattooed man leapt through the crowd into the Circle, splashing the onlookers with dirty water. The other captains rose from their stones and followed, stopping in the front row. Ma Ju Ro heard the mud squelching under their feet.

Suddenly, he saw in those criminal faces not just a barrier to his ruling of the Empire, not just an annoying wrench in the gears of progress, but entirely explicit creatures of evil, the leader of which had killed his father, the like of which had robbed his mother, taking advantage of her helplessness while she was sick.

"You challenge me?" Kerkion spat, walking toward the emperor. "You? Me?"

The musclehead's empty eyes showed no feelings. Ma Ju Ro recalled the dossier that Hector had provided on this man: *A merciless reaper. Strikes fear into all with his supposed invulnerability. Takes everything he wants. Has no close ones, but needs no-one. Even Ignatius is wary of him, seeing in him a likely rival.*

"I'm the one who challenges you, y'hear me, you piece of pig shit?!" Kerkion sounded off, tossing his knife from hand to hand, throwing it up and spinning it. "Come 'ere, I'm gonna wrap yer guts around my fist! Or maybe I should spit in yer face first?"

"Go ahead!" Luca spat, baring his teeth and throwing away the sword. "I'll tear you apart barehanded!"

Kerkion stopped and really did start hawking, getting ready to spit. He looked into Ma Ju Ro's eyes as he walked toward him, and lost track of his arms. That was a mistake. Without slowing his pace, the emperor threw a lightning-fast punch with a fist strengthened with short steel spines. He barely swung his fist, only slightly bent his knees. He struck his foe right on his twisted mouth. The thug's lips split like squashed corpse maggots.

Ma Ju Ro hit him again in the same spot, this time pulling his arm back a little and feeling his fury pour out behind the strength and inertia of the strike. Just as his fist collided with the killer's skull, he lengthened the spines and they pierced the enemy's bone with a crunch, half a dozen inches in, willing them to form more spines at their tips similar to fishing hooks. The force pushed back Kerkion's head, leaving shards of shattered jaw on the spines along with crushed brain, flesh and torn skin. A scarlet mist hung in the air.

The bandit turned on one foot in the mud, spat blood and fell backwards into the puddle. His face sank beneath the water, releasing black bubbles into the torchlight, and his huge body twitched in its final agony. In the thick sepulchral silence of the cave, its twitching slowed and finally stilled.

Luca heard an amazed whisper and frightened exclamations all around him. He stopped and slowly turned. The spines in his fist had already retracted, the crowd hadn't seen them. He started licking Kerkion's blood off his fist.

"Well?!" he said, his voice shaking in fury. "Come on! Who's next?"

Ignatius urged on the other two captains, pushing them into the Circle. Otolik, the chief of the capital's thieves and pickpockets, with no qualms about controlling the local brothels, and Khudoyar, the leader of roaming bands that lived off robberies in the capital's outskirts and beyond. *Every boy from the slums dreams of getting into Khudoyar's gang*, Hector had said.

Both captains were silent and hesitated to step forward.

"Otolik! Go!" Ignatius shouted. "Show him the school of your dirty street fights!"

Otolik gulped. "I think I'll give up my right to challenge without fighting," Otolik said. Panic flashed in his eyes. "I'm an honest thief, I don't want to get my hands dirty! Ma Ju Ro! My right to challenge Ignatius is yours!"

"Disgusting coward," Ignatius spat. "You always were a coward, pickpocket! Can't do nothin' but shank people in the kidneys in back alleys! Filthy stinking rat!"

Otolik rose his head in anger, but said nothing. He backed off, left the Circle and disappeared into the crowd of onlookers.

"Khudoyar!" the chief of the criminal underworld cried to his final captain. "At least you won't piss on the honor of the free brigades!"

"Damn right I won't!" Khudoyar shouted back impassively. "I used to think our emperor was a shit-filled worm, but now I see he's a glorious descendent of his great ancestor!"

The bandit took a step forward, bowed his head and dropped down to one knee.

"Ma Ju Ro the Magnanimous, you are my emperor!" he said simply. "With a pure heart, I give you my right to duel Ignatius. You may challenge him if you wish!"

"What the hell are you sayin', captain?" Ignatius roared. "How's he your emperor? The true, the real emperor is Rezsinius! You're betting on a lame horse, idiot!"

"Rezsinius is a traitor," Khudoyar declared, still as calm as before. "I don't intend to follow your orders any more, Ignatius, not until you prove you have the right. The emperor could have set up a raid, sent his hounds to bring him your head. Instead he came himself, without a guard, unarmed! He offered you an honest challenge, and you can no longer refuse!

Ignatius was more furious than ever. His face darkened. Roaring, he jumped into the Circle and sent the cowardly captain out of it with two precise strikes. Paying no attention to the frozen Ma Ju Ro, he walked around him, staring in frenzy at those present, and shouted, spitting in fury:

"Who else thinks this pig is worthy of challenging me in the Circle?" Huh? I'm asking you a question, you crowd of inbreds! Look at your chiefs. You piss-soaked cowards chose your captains and chiefs yourselves! Look at them!" Ignatius spat on Kerkion's lifeless body. "None of them is worthy of leadership! From now on, you take all your orders from me alone! Until someone among you appears who deserves more!"

While Ignatius was catching his breath, Weasel's mocking voice rang out from the crowd.

"Your majesty! Now's just the time to challenge Ignatius the Furious! You earned the right!"

Quiet whisperings grew into reverberating cries in support of the emperor, although in a somewhat vulgar and familiar style.

"He's worthy! Challenge him, Ma Ju Ro!"

"The Magnanimous against the Furious! Ha-ha-ha, it's happening!"

"Y'majesty!" the crooked old man Law said, crawling into the first row of spectators. "Go on! Challenge 'Natius!"

Luca looked at his system logs. His lifesigns were all normal, the wound on his stomach had already closed, and he'd suffered no consequences from his two duels. He could kill the man who murdered his father Severus Dezisimu right now, and this rampaging and corrupt horde would have supported him. And if not, then all the better for the Empire!"

He could have killed most of those present in moments, giving them no chance to escape. But the wisdom of Esk'Onegut's legacy told him that such a deed, though certainly useful for the country, would drop his Tsoui points so low that he could forget about having a positive balance again for his next several lives.

And that it would be far more useful to fight Ignatius elsewhere. Not in this bedraggled hole. Ready for anything, Ma Ju Ro raised his hand for silence, and was obeyed. The people quietened and even the Furious froze in expectation, furrowing his brows.

"Ignatius!" the emperor's voice echoed endlessly off the cavern walls. "I summon you to the Circle for the right to lead these people! Tomorrow night! At a place you know well... the Arena!"

Ma Ju Ro fell silent, and the crowd exploded. They never expected such a show! The damn emperor himself against Ignatius the Furious! In the Arena! Before the entire capital!

When the elation subsided, hysterical laughter sounded out in the total silence and turned into an even more insane chuckle.

"You bitch! These are Two-horns' tricks! Sacred Mother, ha-ha-ha, I've learned my lesson!" Ignatius fell to one knee and pounded the water with his fist. "Three years ago I had my last duel there! And in front of you, Ma Ju Ro!" I swore then that I would never set foot on the sands of the Arena again! But now it seems I have no other choice. Is that so, good people?"

"Fight! Fight!" the public chanted.

"I accept your challenge, Ma Ju Ro," Ignatius said, growing calmer. "Tomorrow at dusk, before the people's very eyes, I will rip your thick head from your shoulders!"

CHAPTER 41

NEW BOSS

THE DAY WAS BRIGHT and warm, so unbearably beautiful and sonorous that Weasel felt something magical and inspiring spreading through his chest. It didn't burn his insides like a glass of strong brandy thrown back on an empty stomach; it was gentle, friendly, whispering of a better future and impending change.

And even in this damp cave with its smoke-fouled walls, amid the stench of unwashed bodies, amid the smell of musk that spoke to the arousal and suppressed fear among the crowd, Weasel's sense of inspiration and excitement never left him.

The hoarse voice of Brosco, one of Ignatius's hounds, snapped him out of his lyrical mood.

"The boss said everyone has to be ready. We're movin' out soon."

Orkh, the head of a small gang, grumbled. "What're we gonna do, split up through the stands like cockroaches?"

Brosco was in front of him in a second, grabbing the man's throat in his huge hand and pinned him against the wall.

"Ignatius's orders are not subject to discussion!" he hissed. "And neither are mine! Got a problem with that, Orkh?"

"Let me go, Brosco..." Orkh wheezed. "I'm just sayin', ain't it safer if ours stick together?"

He raised his hands in peace and Brosco let him go. Orkh coughed.

"Together?" the hound asked venomously. "You plannin' on fightin' bare-handed? Or with that little penknife you tied to your ankle?"

"I still don't get it..." Zaram announced thoughtfully, a cowardly but perfectly psychopathic thief and robber. "Why do we gotta show up there at all, Brosco? We know Ignatius is gonna tear the emperor apart, then that'll be that. What's next?"

"Next ain't for you to think about!" Brosco snapped. "Each group will get orders from its commander!"

Weasel knew what those orders would be. Immediately after his victory in the Arena, the boss planned to take control of the city and hand it over to Rezsinius. The conspiracy would lift up all the captains and chiefs to high-society positions, and Ignatius himself would become an imperial advisor, and would rule the city watch alongside his hounds. The mere thought made Weasel feel sick. He had no doubt that Ignatius would bring order, but he knew too well what kind of 'order' it would be.

The hounds had formed a chain of power in Ignatius's underground empire, and each of them was once a strong gladiator in their day. Ignatius continued to suspect that this challenge was nothing more than a treacherous trap, and he worked out a plan of action just in case. If the watch blocked the exits from the Arena, then practically the entire criminal world, all its most prominent figures, would be locked in and completely helpless, since you couldn't get in with weapons. Not to mention the smaller fish, the 'fodder-boys' that stole sacks from farmers at the market, the 'fishermen' who cut baggage from coaches, the attic-dwelling pigeoners, the crowd cutpurses, pickpockets and brothel thieves. The last category worked alongside prostitutes, stealing from their clientele as they sweated and panted, and Weasel felt nothing toward them but disgust and disdain.

But that was the trouble; those types would slip away without much difficulty, since nobody knew their faces. The leaders were another matter, the captains and chieftains and foremen like Weasel himself, or that 'hound' Brosco. Uncle Kolot, more widely known as Imperial Advisor Hector, had a dossier on every one of them. And Kane, who was known by the nickname Weasel even in his youth for his agility, shrewdness and wild fury in street fights, valued the fact that Hector never demanded that the son of his dead friend give up all he knew. They both knew that Kane wouldn't live long if he did. He wouldn't have said anything anyway, and if the former captain of the palace guard had nosed around, he'd have lost the trust of his ward.

Thieves, robbers and murderers will always be there, no matter the ruler, Hector had said. *Such is human nature. But I want every criminal in the empire to know that they're making a choice and taking a risk, to know that punishment will catch up to them sooner or later.*

Weasel was entirely in agreement with him. Weak authorities corrupted not only those who ate from the palace trough, but the common folk too. Why would a laborer slog his guts out for a whole week from sunup to sundown for a couple of silver coins when he could take a couple of well-built friends out into the streets at night and steal just as much from another laborer? The law in the Empire was strict, but its enforcement had been pitiful since Ma Ju Ro the Fourth took the throne.

Anarchy had taken hold, not right away, but steadily over years as people began to realize that they could get away with whatever crimes they wished. It turned out that there wasn't even much risk. Even if you got caught red-handed, you could always come to an agreement with the watch, or you ended up in jail, then with the judge. All the market traders to a man began, at first carefully, and then with ever greater courage, to cheat their scales and short-change their customers. The shopkeepers sold rotting fruit under fresh, the owners of drinking establishments watered down their fortified wine and beer. It was as if Two-horns had emerged from the depths and brought in his own laws. It quickly became unsafe in the capital even in the daytime.

The merchants and traders learned to assemble huge caravans, banding together to hire no less than a hundred guards. Even the common folk no longer dared to travel the Empire alone.

Then Ignatius appeared, irate over the failure of his gladiator school. Along with a few friends, former gladiators like him, he put together a gang.

After the witching hour, after dealing with the guards, they crept into the houses of rich men and threatened them, forced them with a waking nightmare to tell them where their valuables were hidden. They got drunk on their first successes, and the bandits went even further. Instead of just making threats, they realized them; they raped daughters and wives, cut throats and struck fear into the whole city, leaving behind their mark written in blood — an eight-sided shield with an eight-sided star at its center.

The spoils were generously wasted at the capital's most expensive establishments, and legends formed around the band's revelries. Ignatius got full of himself. He started handing out gold left and right, giving him the reputation of a noble thief, a defender of the poor. But there was more imagination in it than truth. Weasel knew that first-hand. He himself had witnessed Ignatius ordering a round for a whole inn. Then he refused to pay the tab.

"What about my money?" the innkeeper had asked him, catching up the bandits at the threshold.

Ignatius said nothing, pinning the sweat-soaked innkeeper with a heavy gaze, then asked:

"Who's that gorgeous piece behind the bar? Your daughter?"

The innkeeper gulped and fiddled with the edge of his apron. He nodded.

"Her name?"

"Ariadne..." the innkeeper muttered.

"Keep an eye on Ariadne, innkeep," Ignatius said coldly. "Do you understand me?"

Ariadne's father nodded so much that his cap fell off, but his understanding didn't save him or his daughter. For a few nights in a row, the bandits took advantage of the man's hospitality, and then, in a drunken frenzy, raped the girl before her father's eyes. In righteous anger, the innkeep took up a fire poker and got a dagger in the ribs for it. In the end, the inn was burned to the ground.

The fury of Ignatius and his gang engulfed the entire criminal underworld. The captains summoned the hell-raiser to give them an answer. In front of the assembled gang leaders, Ignatius defeated each, one after another. And by their own laws, he took control of the criminal underworld. Weasel, who was then already gaining a reputation as a lucky, brave and fearless thief, saw it all with his own eyes.

Ma Ju Ro's nighttime duels might impress

some, but not Ignatius and his hounds. The defeated captains let their arrogance get the better of them. They'd forgotten that the emperor had been forced to train in the martial arts since childhood: boxing, fencing, battle. He may have gotten fat, he may be out of shape, but he hadn't lost his ten years of daily training. And Ma Ju Ro had proved it.

Now a battle awaited the pampered emperor, and not a battle for life, but to the death with Ignatius himself, the winner of the Games and the ultimate champion of the Arena. He had no chance at all, and that thought annoyed Weasel somehow. He liked Ma Ju Ro; he didn't boast of his lineage, he was easy to talk to, and he had no fear of entering the viper's nest alone.

A couple of days before, when Kane heard the endless praise for Ma Ju Ro the Magnanimous that spread throughout the city from the singers and artists fed by Reyk Lee Vensiro, he just sneered derisively. But he had to admit, after he woke up that morning, or if he was honest about it — that day, he thought about it and his thoughts surprised him. As he'd idly played with the small breasts of a lady of the evening he'd hired in Big Bo's inn the night before while she slept, he realized in shock that he admired Ma Ju Ro! And Uncle Hector had completely changed his opinion of the emperor... Whether his promotion to advisor played a role in this or not, Kolot's tone when he spoke of Ma Ju Ro in their rare meetings had switched to one of approval.

"It's time!" Brosco declared. "Let's split up into pairs. We'll approach the Arena by different entrances and different streets, as we discussed."

"Ain't it too early?" Zaram asked.

"Early? The fight is in four hours, the streets are already full of people — everyone is going to the Arena! You think everyone is gonna get in, dumbass? Come on, let's go!"

There were many groups like the one Weasel was in, and they were scattered all throughout the capital. One of the hounds reinforced each of them. It was all drawn up the day before, as soon as the emperor was escorted out of the cave The old man Law took him right to the palace, then came back excited and struck everyone dumb.

"'e invited me to the palace! Said it was late, dangerous at night and that, said I could sup and sleep in the palace! Sacred Mother, holy cripes! Me! In the palace!"

"You didn't say yes, I guess," someone's laughing voice said.

"'Course not," the old man said, offended. "Here I am standin' 'ere, in front o' ya!"

"Idiot!" the same man answered.

Narrowing their eyes, the people left the cave in pairs and wandered down different paths to eventually meld into the human stream and enter the city. Weasel's partner was Ramo, a slow fodder thief who recently made his way to the capital from some ramshackle village.

"So they sayin' true that you and Hector are

close like?" he asked.

"We were," Kane condescended to answer. "He and my pa went to war together. But now, ya know how it is... Different paths."

"Yeah, I get it," Ramo agreed. "He's a Jamalayan tiger, we're ferrets. And the wolf ain't no sheep-friend! You're like a fifth wheel to a dog for 'im now!"

Having released this snippet of his own folk wisdom on the world, Ramo's mental reserves were exhausted and he was silent for most of the journey to the city gates, save for wheezing and snorting, until another question finally occurred to him.

"What's gonna happen, eh?"

"Ignatius and the emperor gonna fight," Weasel muttered, wiping sweat from his brow. "That's what."

"Naw, I know that," Ramo said, stretching out his syllables. "But I'm sayin', all this ain't no accident. When we ever seen the emperor fightin' in person like, just for fun, for us dirty common folk? He gone crazy or what? Listen, listen..." Ramo suddenly got worked up, stopped and grabbed Weasel by the arm. "Listen, what if he's gone west?"

"Uh, what do you mean..?"

"Y'know, gone west. His mind's gone. Got a screw loose. Eh? What d'ya reckon? And 'Natius agreed for some reason... Damn, this ain't no accident! Must be Two-horns putting the Sour up to this!"

The Sour was the people's title for the

emperor. Weasel realized that Ramo had been absent from the previous night's performance, but he had no plans to explain matters to the village boy. They melded into the crowd.

Like a swarm of hornets, the crowd buzzed in the streets. Weasel felt himself part of the stream, found himself enmeshed in this tar-thick mass, surrendering to the flow of the walkers around him. Among them he saw dirty and ragged beggars from the outskirts and suburbs, clean-shaven tattooed craftsmen from the workshops... And some madman in a torn black cloak bearing the symbol of Two-horns hung from a street lamp and shouted of the coming end of the world and the awakening of the Sleeping Gods in comparison to whom Two-horns himself was nothing more than a peon.

The crowd soon stopped. The people continued to pile in from behind. Weasel and Ramo had to deal out some punches to some of the less patient types. *We ain't gettin' in by nightfall if this goes on*, Weasel thought.

"What's goin' on there?" he shouted. "Why we stopped?"

"The palace guys're comin'!" someone shouted from up ahead. "They closed the street!"

At that moment, someone threw a cobblestone at the prophet of Two-horns. He fell, caught his cloak on the lantern and hung there, helplessly waving his arms and legs. The crowd roared and writhed with laughter.

Eventually they started moving again.

BLOOD OF FATE

Frenzied and impatient with youth, Weasel surged forward, elbowing away and knocking down the snail-paced people ahead of him. Ramo hurled out abuse, kicking and clouting people left and right. It helped, but not much.

Nonetheless, soon they managed to squeeze into a familiar alleyway where they had a little more freedom. Their pace quickened; they knew these twisted alleyways by heart. Soon they merged again with the procession, this time at its head as it moved into the arena.

It was oval-shaped, and you could get inside through one of many arches all around its edge, apart from one — the Imperial Arch of Unity, built by the first emperor Ma Ju Ro, the founder of the dynasty. That was where the stand for the best people of the Empire stood, divided from the other stands by deep pits with sharpened stakes at the bottom. There were soft benches there for the imperial family, the advisors, the numerous courtiers and courtesans, the upper aristocracy, the reyks and the barons staying in the capital.

Uncle Hector must be there already, Weasel thought, walking past the Arch of Unity. According to Ignatius's plan, their group was to station itself in the narrow stand above the Gates of Death, where the disfigured bodies of the deadly wounded and slaughtered gladiators were carted out.

"Hands to yourself! Now!" he commanded Ramo, noticing the village boy's hand stretching toward a spectator's pocket.

"Huh, why..?" he began to argue, but withdrew his hand.

Not realizing how lucky he'd gotten, the nearly-robbed self-important merchant clapped his chubby palm on the backside of a matron in front of him. She gave a shrill laugh, turned and shot the merchant a promising and playful smile.

Sitting down, Weasel started looking around in boredom, searching for familiar faces. Shket and his crew were sitting a few rows down. He was the underage leader of a street gang. A little further along, hiding his face in his hood, blind Uritim was banging his cane around; one of the senior members of the Beggar's Guild. The western stand of the nobility was still almost empty, but steadily filling up.

"Oh-ho!" Ramo said, clapping and rubbing his hands together. "Grub! Hey! Come 'ere!" he shouted at a marketwoman with a basket.

She nodded with a smile and elbowed her way to the men. A breathtaking smell emanated from the basket. Weasel's stomach began to rumble; he hadn't eaten since yesterday.

"What ya got there?" Ramo asked, inhaling the aroma.

"Fried fish for two coppers, crabcakes or baked cassava for a copper."

"Crab, eh? If it turns out to be rat, you know where I'll shove those cakes?"

"My cakes are good!" the tradeswoman frowned, an older woman with a face covered in bright makeup. "Me husband catches the critters, I cook 'em! Ya don't like it, go sup with Two-horns!"

"Woah there," Ramo chuckled.

"Gimme one of each," Weasel said. "Anythin' to drink?"

"Mash beer."

"Pour me some of that piss," Ramo said happily. "This is the life!"

While they ate and drank, the Arena filled up with people. The advisors had arrived, along with courtiers, reyks and their dolled-up wives and lovers. Only the emperor's seat remained empty. Weasel saw that giggly girl by the name of Kora in the seat next to the emperor's, the one he'd met in the palace; word had it she was Ma Ju Ro's new favorite. They'd exchanged a few words then, and something about her made his heart beat faster.

Suddenly everyone fell silent. A familiar figure walked out confidently from the gates opposite the Gates of Death. The emperor!

The excited whispers and cries abated in vague expectation. All the eyes in the Arena were fixed on him. Ma Ju Ro stopped in the center and slowly looked around as if trying to look into every face. Clapping broke the dead and strained silence, at first weak and scattered, then stronger, echoing throughout the Arena.

The emperor raised his arm and the applause cut off instantly. Weasel even felt as if he'd gone deaf.

"Brothers and sisters!" Ma Ju Ro said, his

booming voice echoing throughout the Arena. "Today you have gathered here to see me fight Ignatius, former gladiator, champion of the Arena and leader of the criminal world..."

"You hear that?" Ramo grinned like a cat and elbowed Weasel. "We're the emperor's brothers!"

"We will fight..." the emperor continued.

"And you'll die!" someone from the stands interrupted him. Weasel's gaze sought and found the heckler. One of Ignatius's hounds.

"Perhaps I will," the emperor replied coolly. "In any case, this will be a fight for the Empire. Ignatius is in league with my cousin Rezsinius, and if he is victorious, then you will have a new ruler."

"Better him than you!" the same man shouted.

"No, not better!" Ma Ju Ro raised his voice, although it seemed it couldn't get any louder. "Because I am more than an emperor. I am more than a man! And now I will declare it openly to all! The Sacred Mother came to me and showed me the way! With her aid, the Empire will be great again! With her blessing, I will make our citizens' lives better! Free medicine! Free education for talented children! Peaceful and safe roads and cities..!"

Weasel thought Ma Ju Ro was overdoing it. An unremitting fool could see that all his words were empty, and the emperor was saying them to fool an already fooled people even further. He only half-listened to the rest of the emperor's rousing speech, surprised somewhat that the majority of the spectators were listening to the emperor's promises with fascination.

But the last words the emperor said suddenly stirred something not only in the stands, but in Weasel himself.

"Rezsinius wants to break up the country! I want to unite it! Now, before my fight with Ignatius, I will prove that the Sacred Mother is on my side. Any cripple or sick person may descend to me now from the stands, and I will heal them!"

The emperor fell silent. In the resulting silence, the stunned audience suddenly heard a voice:

"Hey, y'majesty! I'm Finn, I ain't walked since I was born! Everyone knows me, I ain't no sham! Want me to come down, eh?" The shouter laughed mockingly.

"Go on, Finn! Call the Sour's bluff!" the people laughed. "We know ya!"

Everyone knew Finn. The leader of the Beggar's Guild, whom every citizen met at least once in their life, was something of a respected figure and would have been able to live in the upper crust of the capital in a fine manor if it weren't for his strict ideas about what a beggar could and couldn't have. If you call yourself poor, you have to be it. He donated his money for the good of cripples like him.

"Of course, Finn!" the emperor managed to shout above the noise of the stands. "Come down!"

The cripple crawled agilely on his powerful arms toward the stairs leading to one of the few metal doors to the Arena's fighting ground. It was surrounded by a twenty-foot tall fence and a pit.

Accompanied by the crowd's sarcastic commentary, Finn crawled across the bridge over the ditch onto the Arena's sands, then to Ma Ju Ro, leaving a trail behind him from his dragging legs. He sat down and stared at the emperor. He turned back to the crowd and shouted:

"His majesty is real! Just like... in the paintings!"

The crowd laughed, then fell silent in expectation of a rare spectacle. Weasel even rose up slightly to get a better view.

The emperor placed his hands on Finn's shoulders and froze, staring into space. The cripple went limp, but the emperor held him up. A minute, two, three... Weasel could hear Ramo breathing, his eyes wide like a child's, his mouth agape in expectation of a miracle. Finally, the emperor jumped back and the beggar started to fall, but at the last moment he caught himself with his hand and froze.

A voice from the stands impatiently cried out. "What's 'appening, Finn?"

Finn was listening closely to the emperor's voice as he spoke quietly. Then he nodded. Then his foot moved. Then the other one. After that, he lifted his legs and tried to stand. He nearly fell, but Ma Ju Ro held him up again. Then something even more surprising happened! The former cripple embraced the emperor, dropped his head onto his shoulder and burst into tears! In the growing noise, as the emperor held him, he raised his head and lifted his arm.

"A miracle!" he shouted at the top of his voice. "In the name of the Sacred Mother, a true miracle! People! I feel my legs! I can walk!"

All hell broke loose! The crowd came alive. The people went ballistic, crazed, shouting that they too were sick and in need of healing. Some tried to break through onto the sands, but the guards slammed the doors shut. A stampede formed...

"Make way for the blind!" Uritimu shouted, waving his cane.

True, he was going the wrong way and had nobody to direct him.

A large woman broke into the fore, carving a path with her prodigious bosom. "I'm barren! Heal me, your majesty!"

I'm deaf in one ear!" Ramo added to the general clamor, but Weasel held him back.

The emperor's sonorous voice boomed out over the Arena. "People of the Empire! Silence! Return to your seats at once!"

That brought the people to their senses. The afflicted unwillingly returned to their places, reining in their thirst for a miracle cure. Finn returned to the stands. A crowd immediately surrounded him and drowned him in questions. His legs were still weak, but he could stand with support.

"As of tomorrow! At the free imperial clinic! We will be accepting patients!" Ma Ju Ro said, brokenly as the thoughts came to him. "I will handle the incurable and the terminal myself! And now — that for which you have come!"

After this miracle, the arrival of Ignatius received a more than cold reception. It occurred to Weasel that at least the cripples would now be fans of the emperor.

The former gladiator, clad in armor with the purple cloak of a champion on top, raised his hand to greet the onlookers. The stands hummed, and Weasel didn't know if it was from the healing of Finn or the accusation that Ignatius was in league with Rezsinius.

"Greetings, respected people of the capital!" Ignatius roared and drew his sword. "Thank you for coming to support me in this duel with the usurper!"

Some of the assembly buzzed, some started to chant the boss's name, but the majority watched the events on the Arena's sands silently. The emperor crossed his arms on his chest and waited for Ignatius to enter the circle. The boss was in no hurry. He drank in the almost forgotten attention of many thousands of eyes.

The gong sounded. Ignatius walked into the circle and spat. The gong sounded again and Ignatius stood in his battle stance. Only then did Weasel realize that Ma Ju Ro was standing unarmed, just like the previous night. He wasn't even wearing armor, unless the Sacred Mother had endowed her chosen one with invisible defenses.

BLOOD OF FATE

Kane was no longer sure of anything.

The gong sounded a third time to signal the start of the fight, and the ringing echo resounded through the stands. The enemies moved toward each other. Ignatius crouched, his round shield extended before him, his sword held over his head. Ma Ju Ro walked with the heavy pace of a fat slob. The sight was so unusual that some people laughed hysterically.

Once he was less than twenty paces from his foe, Ignatius rushed forward, bellowing a dreadful battle cry. Running to the emperor, Ignatius dealt a crushing blow. Ma Ju Ro blocked it with his hand, but against all expectations, he didn't lose it; on the contrary, he grabbed the sword and pulled it from the former gladiator's grasp. With fingers extended, he thrust his hand beneath the shield, piercing Ignatius right through.

The onlookers' breath caught, and all heard the bubble of blood spitting from the mouth of Ignatius the Furious. The emperor pulled out his hand and raised it high, squeezing the heart of his enemy. Ignatius fell to the sand, convulsed and stilled.

In the sepulchral silence that followed, Weasel heard Ramo's voice.

"Holy Mother. What now..?"

Weasel closed his mouth, gulped and answered.

"We got a new boss now, Ramo. We got a new boss."

CHAPTER 42

AMBASSADOR
OF THE NORTH

THE COUNCIL HALL had had a dark reputation since the palace was built. After the triumphant arrival of the first emperor's family, an advisor's head was found underneath the set table.

A month later, during a meeting, a second advisor whose name history has forgotten fought with a third by the name of Panchen, and once all intellectual arguments were exhausted, he resorted to a physical one. This turned out to be a dagger which he inserted into Panchen's eye. The emperor quartered the unnamed killer, but kept the knife as a reminder of the danger of allowing weapons within the council walls.

It didn't help much. The advisors of the second emperor, Kiloug the Defender, were poisoned to a man, including the fourth advisor, of the Cross family. They said it was the work of Kiloug's spouse, offended by a lack of respect toward her (it seems the statesmen didn't let her take part in the council sessions).

Over time, cases like these became rarer, but they never quite stopped. Remembering this, the superstitious Hector and Hustig even suggested that Ma Ju Ro find a new place for his council. The emperor just laughed. But now he felt uncomfortable. He'd had no fear of facing Ignatius, the undefeated champion of the Arena, bare-handed, but alone with this predator with his perfect snow-white teeth, he felt a shiver run down his spine.

"The transport will arrive at one o'clock," Cross said, yawning. "The contribution must be delivered in full. I repeat, in full."

"And I repeat, with the current state of affairs I cannot do that," Ma Ju Ro answered quietly, but then unwillingly raised his voice as he continued. "We've only just solved the starvation problem, there's a civil war around the corner, and you're demanding ore, precious gems, fruit, vegetables, fur and more in the same quantities as in peace time! The south hasn't been making deliveries for an age! Give us a reprieve!"

"The agreement makes no provision for reprieves. If you are unable to meet the terms of the agreement, then we will consider swapping you with an emperor who can."

"Rezsinius..."

"Yes. I dare say the pretender to the throne will cut the Empire in half, but he will make the deliveries in time as well. That's exactly the kind of leader we need for Syahr. You've been up to some very strange business, Ma Ju Ro!"

"Strange?" the emperor said, amazed. "Taking care of my people is a strange business? You really think that, Anthony?"

"Your job is to deliver us materials!" Cross cut him off. "That is the emperor's main task! Your predecessors understood this well, which meant they died their own deaths. I would happily demonstrate our power to refresh your memory, but I don't think that will be necessary. You have two weeks, Ma Ju Ro. If you fail to deliver the contribution, you are done. And thank the Sacred Mother that we don't take everything from you."

Ma Ju Ro barely held back from answering as he wanted to. He knew too little of the true strength of the racants, and all his attempts to find out more from Herdinia resulted in a categorical 'no.' In spite of all her attraction, if not love, for the new Ma Ju Ro, the woman refused to say a word about anything concerning the wider world.

"You mean to say that giving over half of what the country produces every three months is something to be grateful for? You prevent us from rising from our knees, you keep us in the dark ages!"

"Wow, Ma Ju Ro!" Cross exclaimed. "The dark

ages... What do you know about them? The dark ages of the human race have nothing to do with you people. You genetic outcasts began your history only when you were resettled here! You've only just reached the dark ages! Say thank you for the fact that you still exist! Hell, we give you support... You don't have to go far to see that! Where do you think your healers get their medical instruments? Who do you think you have to thank for the benefits of civilization?"

The benefits... The emperor laughed bitterly. Those cheap trinkets that Cross's man traded in... single-use gilded lighters that the reyks bought for ludicrous sums, cigarettes that cooled the mouth and changed the tastes, music boxes and other garbage. The emperor had checked the glittering 'diamonds', 'rubies' and 'emeralds' that the beauties of the court wore. His metamorphosis told him they were mere glass. The cost of a bottle of 'divine fragrance' reached a thousand gold pieces. The 'rejuvenating' cosmetic ointments for wrinkles cost several thousand. Luca had no doubt that all this was the cheapest trash from the wider world. Thanks to Esk's legacy and his previous life, he guessed the structure of that society and how things were arranged there. But judging by the marker placed on Cross, the advisor didn't see himself as a hypocrite. He really thought he was bringing 'benefits.'

In representing the interests of his family, Anthony Cross filled his own pockets by accepting payment in pure gold. The emperor decided to use that.

"I am grateful," Ma Ju Ro answered after a short silence. "Your contribution to the Empire is priceless. Advisor, I do not refuse to pay a contribution. That is the ancient right of the Cross family. I ask merely for a delay while I solve the issue of Rezsinius. Believe me, I can also be... useful. I was lost, but this conversation with you has opened my eyes."

The emperor tried to show pleading in his eyes. Cross nodded.

"Continue."

"A hundred thousand gold to you personally, Anthony. Delay the next delivery by a month."

Cross smiled contentedly, but then his face took on its usual expression — dispassionate and haughty. He waited, clearly enjoying the sight of the emperor out of his depth. Luca bit his lip, slouched and obsequiously flattered the mighty advisor with his gaze. This was what Cross had been seeking, and he'd got it.

"So be it, Ma Ju Ro. You have a delay of one month. Don't even think about asking me for another. The family won't accept it. You have forty five days to defend the throne and gather the tribute. You may go."

Luca showered the advisor with thanks and tried to kiss his aristocratic hand, but he pulled away in disgust. Thanking him again, the emperor hurried to leave the cursed council hall. Cross shouted to him.

"Maj, wait!"

"Yes, Anthony?"

"I don't understand; why did you fight against Ignatius? He came to the Arena. You could have taken him without any risk! Along with all those criminals who came to support him!"

"As you said, we're in the dark ages. There's only one way to win the respect of the people here."

"But... how? I was in the stands. I saw it all! Are you truly so good at duels? Or was it some kind of trick?"

The blood of a warrior flows in my veins, Master Cross. Don't forget that my great ancestor united the country and took power into his hands."

"Genes I understand," Cross muttered, thinking aloud. "But..."

"I also had many years of daily training with the best tutors, since the moment I learned to walk. Good day to you, Anthony!"

Ma Ju Ro left. Cross pulled a device out of his pocket and began to watch the duel over and over again. Something was wrong.

Grabbing hold of the sword? he asked mentally. *With a dull sword and thick gauntlets, sure. Piercing the breastbone barehanded? I've heard of that skill as well. But all that, done by the obese, alcoholic, drug-addicted and lazy Maj, and against the champion of the Arena no less? Something is definitely wrong...*

WORLD ⋫⋫ BOOK ONE

The North of the Empire was divided into nine baronies. Historically, there were fifteen northern barons, and each was reputed to be an enemy of the first Ma Ju Ro. The decades had since redrawn the map: some failed to produce an heir, and their territory was absorbed by a neighbor; some combined into one family, by force or by will. Others merely lost wars.

There had been over ten wars in just the last quarter of a century. And almost all the barons fought against each other. Alliances formed and fell. Allies treacherously stabbed each other in the back. Yesterday's enemies became friends, hostages were taken. Borders, villages and sparse fertile lands became things to be bartered.

The barons united only when facing a shared threat.

So it was when Emperor Jakhamad the First, who the people called the Insane, wished to take triple the taxes that the barons could afford to pay, and sent a huge army to the North to take them. Fortunately, almost half of the troops were born there. As soon as they got to the battlefield, the soldiers deserted en masse for the enemy camp. The rebellious barons threatened to secede, and so Jakhamad had to come to an agreement. Instead of triple taxes, he reluctantly agreed to give the northern barons ten years of complete freedom from any taxes at all.

So it was when the hordes of mutants gathered strength and united into the Cursed Host, sacked the land and moved on the Capital. Only through combined strength had they been repelled and the lands won back.

So it was relatively recently, when the father of the current emperor helped the North crush a new Cursed Host, not as bloodthirsty as the first, but even more terrible — the modern mutants had organized into something of a society and even founded their own capital of the Wastelands, the so-called Shelter that grew from a small village through a network of caves.

In that war, Reyes, now the ambassador of the northern barons in the capital, was a general of the united forces of the North. They met with the army of Emperor Kiranon the First, father of Ma Ju Ro the Fourth, and combined forces to drive the mutants back to the Wastelands. Since the memorable war with Jakhamad the Insane, the lessons of history had kept the northern barons from thoughts of secession. The mutants reproduced much faster than the Empire's citizens, and the North constantly needed the emperor's help.

The South had it easier. The island pirates who raided and looted merchant ships were no great threat, and the narrow strait between the South and the central part of Syahr allowed any land army to be easily beaten back. At sea, the South ruled unchallenged.

But without the Empire, that part of the country would decay. The South lived off farming and fishing. Even the wood and ship timber was delivered from the center, not to mention metal and finished products. The Empire needed the South, and vice versa. This suited all involved, and unlike the northerners, the southern barons had made no attempts to secede.

Now, on the contrary, the situation was that the South under Rezsinius's leadership was the main threat to the Empire's security. Ma Ju Ro put all his hopes for successful resistance in the North. He invited the ambassador of the North, Reyes, to negotiate in the palace, and he was in agreement.

"The North shall support the emperor," he said. "I have no doubt of that, your majesty."

"Thank you, Reyes," Ma Ju Ro answered. "When can the northern barons assemble their troops and send them to the capital?"

"There is some difficulty here," Reyes admitted. "Long ago, they all decided that we should not intervene in the intra-family affairs of the emperor. Three months ago, Gudmund..."

"Baron Gudmund Gudmundson, the Voice of the North," Lentz whispered to the emperor.

"... Gudmund convinced the others that Rezsinius's claim to the throne is no threat to the country," Reyes continued. "He said it doesn't matter to us who gets to be emperor. The north has paid and does pay taxes to the emperor regardless of who it is."

BLOOD OF FATE

General Hustig chewed his lips and coughed, drawing attention.

"Tell me, Reyes, how does that match your words that the North will help us?" he asked directly, as military men far from politics were wont to do.

"Please let me finish, general," Reyes answered. "Three months ago, the North chose a position of non-intervention. However!" the emissary raised his index finger. "All this time, I have been sending reports of the situation in the capital, and this has caught Gudmund's interest. You will agree that what is happening in the city, and in particular his majesty's decisions and deeds, are exceedingly curious. I have described these positive shifts in the ruling of the country in all my reports."

Reyes paused to refresh his throat with some tart Tuaf wine. Impatience showed on the faces of all present, from the emperor himself and Herdinia to the military advisors Hector and Hustig. Ultimately, the fate of Ma Ju Ro, his close ones and the entire country was being decided. Everything depended on whether the northern barons would support the emperor.

"Gudmund assembled the others. Each of the nine barons was so impressed with what has happened here that they sent their own people to the capital to confirm the truth of my stories. And they haven't even heard yet of the emperor's astounding victory over Ignatius, the chief of the criminal underworld!"

"Master Ambassador, please, get to the point!" Lentz pleaded. "What have the barons decided?"

"I am getting to it," the ambassador answered impassively, but Ma Ju Ro saw pleasure in his eyes. "The barons wish to meet the emperor personally, and then they'll decide."

"When can we expect their visit to the capital?" Herdinia asked curtly, preparing to write it down.

Reyes didn't answer. Hiding his smile in his mustache, he took to studying his glass attentively.

"Not this time," the emperor said in his place. "They won't come. The northern barons want me to ask them personally. By going to see them personally. Is that right, Reyes?"

"His majesty is very wise," the ambassador answered neutrally. "Such an act by the emperor would melt the cold hearts of the rulers of the North."

"Send a runner to the barons, tell them I'll come tomorrow," Ma Ju Ro said. "Herdinia, you do the same, but in my name..."

"Tomorrow? But, my lord! I won't have enough time to prepare escort troops!" the general exclaimed. "You can't..."

Everyone started talking at once, demanded that the trip be delayed, or that they be taken along for the negotiations. The ambassador was clearly enjoying the chaos he'd caused.

"Quiet!"

The emperor's enhanced vocal chords cut

through the noise. The wine glasses shook from his roar. A portrait of one of Ma Ju Ro's ancestors fell from the wall. The gathering fell silent, and the ambassador finally lost his cool and froze with his jaw dropped.

"We will decide all this at council," the emperor declared before addressing the ambassador. "Thank you, Ambassador Reyes."

The man rose and took a half bow. After the door closed behind him, all turned to Ma Ju Ro.

"I need a dossier on each of the barons, along with a full history of our relationships with the North," he began to give orders. "Herdinia will plan the trip. I have to go to the clinic, for I fear your incurable patients will not live to see my return otherwise, Lentz."

"Your majesty, two thousand guards…" Hustig began, but the emperor interrupted him.

"Nonsense, general! Hector, select a dozen of your guards for an escort. I'm going alone. This is a friendly visit."

CHAPTER 43

THE NINE

ROKKAN THE BLACK, one of Ignatius's former captains, had met the emperor face to face some time ago. The meeting in one of the secret hollows of the catacombs was incredibly interesting and curious for the former pirate, now right hand of the capital's criminal underworld. At least, so the emperor could judge from Rokkan's initially dumbfounded and stunned, then inspired expression.

The victory over Ignatius made the unthinkable possible. By all the laws of the criminal community, Ma Ju Ro had become their chief. But what did it mean when the emperor personally ruled murderers and thieves? Since no law-abiding citizen of the Empire could understand that, the decision was thus: Rokkan, as the most authoritative of the remaining chiefs, would lead the criminal world, at the same time unofficially obeying Ma Ju Ro. Weasel became the middleman between the leaders; nobody else was better suited to the role. True, Kane himself had to give up on his past life and become subordinate to Hector to do this, for which Hector was infinitely pleased.

At that meeting, Ma Ju Ro asked Rokkan to set him up a meeting with the most respected of the pirate captains. The Coastal Brotherhood had an agreement with Rezsinius, according to one of Lee Vensiro's men from the South, but Ma Ju Ro decided to try anyway. Even if he didn't succeed in his plan, then perhaps he'd at least manage to sow a seed of doubt in the pirates' heads.

"It won't work," Rokkan said, sucking his teeth. He paused, but the emperor expected an explanation, and the bandit continued. "With all due respect, your majesty, they won't agree to it. I can guess what you want from them, but I can't imagine that you can suggest it to them. They'll be fine without it; the barons leave them alone, Rezsinius has promised them a full pardon as soon as he comes to power, along with a million gold. And that's not counting the amnesty for all those in the Empire's prisons."

"Who specifically did my cousin come to an agreement with?" the emperor asked.

Ma Ju Ro decided to compare his information with what Rokkan knew. Lee Vensiro's reports were always worth checking thrice, since the cultural advisor's inclination to exaggerate often overcame his common sense.

"With the Nine," Rokkan shrugged. "The nine captains with their forty ships."

The fact that the Nine had forty ships always at their disposal was a legend unto itself. The magic of numbers: the captains in the Nine changed, as did the ships, but the number remained unchanged.

"What about the others?"

"The independent captains have half as many ships, the crews aren't as strong, the rigging is poorer, and in any case... They won't go up against their own, against the Coastal Brotherhood. And the Nine are basically the Coastal Brotherhood on their own.

"What is the Nine supposed to do?"

"Generally speaking, their task is to transport supplies, provisions, siege engines, and to provide fire support for Rezsinius's army during the siege of the capital."

"I see..."

Ma Ju Ro thought for a moment. He could beat his cousin's offer, but how was he supposed to communicate that? The emperor made a decision.

"Rokkan, I'm going to find something to offer the Brotherhood," he said. "Can you convince them to meet me? Just a meeting, I'm not asking for more."

"Also unlikely, your majesty," Rokkan shook his head. "The pirates are a hard people, they'll suspect a trap."

"You know me. There won't be a trap."

"I do, your majesty. But Rezsinius has a hold

on their minds. And... well, why skirt around it, the recent years of your rule have given you a very bad reputation even among those that pay little attention to it."

"I value your council, Rokkan," Ma Ju Ro said. "But I'm still asking you to try. How about this... Go to see them yourself. Go by sea, it won't take long. Tell them that the emperor offers the following..."

Two weeks later, a pirate ship bearing a black flag dropped anchor just outside the port bay, so as not to alarm the citizens. The rumors of the Coastal Brotherhood were so frightening and contradictory that the very appearance of such a ship within sight could have caused trouble in the capital.

The city continued to live its life, day by day finding more meaning in it. More order, less chaos. That's roughly how any citizen would have characterized the changes of recent months. The pirates' visit from the South Islands would have changed that, so Ma Ju Ro was pleased to see that the vessel was out of sight.

The emperor's vision had been become very sharp: on the Arena's sands, he'd easily been able to pick out the face of anyone in the stands, and right now he could see the ship. It also helped that the highest point above sea level was the terrace in his palace chambers. That was where he was after he'd met with the ambassador of the North and then spent four hours in the imperial clinic before returning to the palace. Going out for a breath of fresh air, he saw on the horizon a pirate ship with its sails furled.

That was quick, Ma Ju Ro thought. He'd hoped that they would agree to meet and would come, but he hadn't expected it to be so soon. It was a good thing that he could solve this problem before he left to see the northern barons.

Soon, Rokkan came to the palace. He was dressed as a real aristocrat specially for the occasion. Even so, the guards knew what to do, and he came to the emperor escorted by Hector and his people.

Rokkan bowed and nodded ever so slightly. The emperor made a practiced motion with his brow and his chambers emptied of all those who didn't need to be there. Even Hector left at his nod, and Ma Ju Ro and his guest went out onto the terrace.

He hospitably offered some Tuaf wine, and Rokkan didn't refuse. Drinking his glass to the bottom and enjoying the taste, the bandit got down to business.

"Your majesty, the Nine await you at dawn."

"All nine captains came?" the emperor said in surprise.

"Nobody wanted to come at first. Then Blackbeard came to me and said he wanted to hear you out. Gimp and Flea noticed that, started talking about it. They don't trust each other, they suspect betrayal, but at the same time their greed drives them. Rumor spread through the Coastal Brotherhood that you're ready to offer heaps of gold." Rokkan grinned. "A few incautiously thrown words in a tavern and the crews began to demand that their captains hear you out. So yes, all the Nine have come. They have a condition; you must come alone."

"Completely alone?" Ma Ju Ro said, surprised. "I'm supposed to row myself to them on my own?"

"The Coastal Brotherhood's people will await you in Frog Bay. They'll take you to the ship. Unfortunately, they don't wish to see me, they fear a leak..." He hesitated. "Anyway, they consider me your man now, your majesty. A traitor of a sort."

Rokkan wasn't prevaricating, he was telling the truth. The emperor had injected him with substances that would have sent blood to the captain's face if he tried to lie about anything.

"I'll do it," Ma Ju Ro nodded.

The rest of the day flew by as he gave his final orders to his advisors before his departure. Lodyger reported on the progress of construction and production, Hector and Hustig argued, Herdinia mediated between them, Lentz bragged of the clinic's success and the sharply decreased rate of deadly cases from infectious disease. Lee Vensiro expressively recited new poems in honor of the Empire, and Cross dropped his venomous comments. All was as usual.

The sun was beginning to sink into the foamy waters of the ocean when the emperor, dressed as simply as possible, walked his beaten path through the window in Hector's office to the carriage awaiting him. He sat behind the driver and clapped him on the shoulder.

"Rokkan's friends are already here, Kane. Head to Frog Bay."

Without answering, Weasel sharply whipped the horses into motion. Ma Ju Ro judged by his silence that the man was unhappy. The reason was the emperor's refusal to take him with him to the North.

For some unknown reason, the young bandit had gotten seriously attached to the emperor, considering it his duty to protect him and help him as much as he could. It was no wonder that he organized such secret trips to the city, knowing it as he did better than anyone else.

Moreover, being close to the emperor meant being close to Kora. That was all the explanation necessary. There was a reason that Weasel was testing the waters; with roundabout, as he thought, but simplistic questions, he was trying to find out the emperor's relationship with his new young favorite. When he realized through directly questioning Ma Ju Ro that the latter had no intentions toward her, he exulted and didn't hide his joy.

And a few days ago, when he saw Kane talking to Kora, Luca spoke to his sister and learned that she had feelings for the boy too. Although not strong enough to refuse the trip to the North, the homeland of their father. The senior Dezisimu had often told the children of the wonderful forests there, of the full and boundless rivers and tall trees stretching their long masts into the calm blue skies. So once she heard that her brother was headed there, Kora nagged him until Luca reluctantly agreed to take her with him.

"What did Rokkan say?" Kane asked, breaking the silence.

He drove the horses along lively streets, the people moving out of the way when they recognized him. In his short career, the thief and bandit Weasel had earned enough of a reputation among the street vagrants that they knew him by sight.

"Nothing, apart from the fact that the Coastal Brotherhood is ready to hear my offer."

"So we're headed into the frying pan again," the guy muttered. "I get it, the Sacred Mother's blessing and all that, but you need a safety net. In our business, nobody goes into anything without a good partner. Those that go it alone end up in a bad way. Usually either hanging from a scaffold or with a dagger in their neck."

"You think that's a threat to me?" Ma Ju Ro asked cheerfully.

"Not at all, sire. But you should keep me close! I'll watch your back..."

"No. I have to be alone, that's their condition."

Weasel scowled and whipped the horses in silence for a time, toward the northern gates leading to Frog Bay.

"And the North?" he broke the silence. "Why don't you want to take me with you?"

Kane's reply derailed Ma Ju Ro's train of thought as he went through his plan with the pirates for the thousandth time. He answered with annoyance.

"If I promise to take you with me, will you shut up?"

"Consider my tongue swallowed!" Weasel laughed.

They arrived in the dusk. Their path then led along rocks and through undergrowth. They could go no further in the carriage. Ma Ju Ro climbed out.

"Wait here," the emperor ordered.

By habit, he touched the surface of the cliff, picked up some stones and pebbles to resupply his store of required elements for his combat form. That had become a regular practice since the day his metamorphosis reached level four.

Climbing down from a hillock to a narrow stretch of sand, he saw three silhouettes standing out against the cliffs.

"Name yourself," a hoarse male voice said.

"Emperor Ma Ju Ro."

One of the figures ran up to the hillock and froze, looking around. *A girl*, Luca realized.

"He's alone," the stranger said.

"Get into the boat, emperor," that same hoarse voice ordered.

Ma Ju Ro walked into the water up to his knees, following behind one of the pirates. In the meantime, the others pulled a boat out of the bushes.

BLOOD OF FATE

The sun had already disappeared completely behind the horizon. Only a reddish blaze showed where it had been an hour ago. Holding his gaze on it, Ma Ju Ro missed the moment when someone hit him in the back of the head with something heavy and hard. Screaming from the sudden pain, the emperor fell down, but the sailors picked him up and dragged him to the boat, swearing. There they bound his hands and feet, and thrust a stinking rag into his mouth. He played his part and decided to wait and figure out what the pirates wanted.

"Damn, he's heavy!" the hoarse one said. "Why'd ya knock him out, Wasp? Could'a let him climb in himself and hit him then..."

"Stop whining, Donno," the girl shot back. "I decided this was better. It would have been harder to sneak up on him in the boat."

So that's it, is it? Luca thought. *Alright, I'll get onto the ship and then figure out how things stand.* He sent himself into apparent unconsciousness; slowed his pulse and breath, weakened his muscles. Then he listened to the conversation.

It was clear that these three all belonged to different captains and had no trust between them. They fell silent after exchanging a few words, nimbly matching each other's pace on the oars. An hour and changed passed without his kidnappers exchanging a word.

If Luca thought that stunning him was just a way to get him onto the ship and that there would still be a conversation there, he was mistaken. Ma

Ju Ro was lifted aboard, and from the words accompanying a detailed examination, he realized that nobody here planned to talk.

"He ain't as fat as I thought," someone noted. "Heavy, sure, near five hundred pounds even!"

"Big-boned, for sure," someone answered sarcastically.

He was undressed, and they saw his golden tattooed bracelets. They were inscribed by the high priest of the Sacred Mother as a special sign of the emperor, and couldn't be faked. The runic pattern shined in the darkness and shimmered in sunlight.

The pirates delighted once they confirmed his identity. Someone couldn't resist spitting in his face, another kicked him in the stomach, and the crew's laughter turned into jubilant shouting.

"What a haul! After this we'll deliver the throne to Rezsinius on a platter!" said a repugnant, mocking voice.

"Five million gold! Damn, I can't believe it was that easy, Flea!" someone else shouted in a deep rumbling voice.

"Shove an anchor up my arse if it ain't so, Beard!" Flea agreed. "It was a great idea to talk to Rezsinius!"

"Two-horns, this emperor is even dumber than I thought! He just went and turned up on his own without any guards! Abyss, if I'd known that, I'd have come here on my own too!" Beard howled.

The pirates burst into laughter again.

"Cut the shit, boys! We'll celebrate later!" Flea

interrupted the merrymaking and started giving commands. "We're setting sail! Weigh anchor! Tie that pig up good and put him in the brig! We'll be counting our gold in a couple of days, boys!

Everyone leapt into action. Some shouted "Gold!", others started babbling about buying a house in the capital. Beard suggested that they celebrate anyway, and the other captains agreed with him.

"Let's whet our whistles!" they cried. "To the Coastal Brotherhood! To Rezsinius! To the death of Ma Ju Ro!"

The emperor spat out the partially swallowed rag and started dealing with his bonds. The ropes fell from his hands and feet.

"I don't think so!" the emperor boomed, cutting through their cries.

The four pirates that had been planning to drag him to the hold jumped back, stunned by the shout. The merriment ceased, and Blackbeard froze, pouring rum onto his feet without realizing it.

Ma Ju Ro rose, shook himself, stretched, forced blood into his numb limbs, then turned to the Nine. They were watching with mouths agape. Nobody reached for a blade, nobody got scared. Yes, what was happening was odd, but the emperor was alone on a ship filled to the brim with pirates armed to the teeth. He was far from the shore and his guards.

"Do I understand correctly that you do not wish to listen to my proposal?" Ma Ju Ro asked the most richly and ornately dressed group. "Yes, you, Nine, I don't know which of you is which, but I don't even plan to ask your names! I'll find out later when the ones that are left make their choice."

"What crap is he talkin'?" Flea asked Blackbeard with faux concern. "We got a talkin' pig aboard!"

The strained atmosphere caused by this strangely brave prisoner relaxed. The pirates shouted over each other to shower the emperor in epithets very distant from 'your majesty.' Some ganged up on the three that bound him, accusing them of bungling the job and not knowing how to tie a decent knot.

Ma Ju Ro raised his hand. The gaiety ended. In the resulting silence, all heard the loud and confident voice of the emperor.

"I wanted to offer you far more than Rezsinius promised you. As is the case with the autonomous subjects of the Empire, I planned to give you — officially! — all the Southern Isles, including Diamondtooth Isle! You could have become barons, and your descendants would be aristocrats! You would have had more than just gold — you'd have had land! You could have lived a fine and peaceful life, ruling over your own domain! But you have chosen otherwise..." Ma Ju Ro paused, and whispers spread among the pirates.

"How 'bout you tell these tales to Rezsinius? Maybe he'll be merciful!" Flea shouted. "We are the Coastal Brotherhood! We don't want peace. You can't trick us with your empty promises!"

"Must have shit hisself!" Blackbeard shouted, causing a burst of laughter. "And now he's talkin' shit! Sure as the sea, by morning he'll be promising half the Empire and his wife to boot, bury me with the fish!"

"He's married..?" one of the captains asked in surprise. "I heard he prefers men..."

"If not, he'll find some other way to pay us! Ha-ha!"

Luca waited for the laughter to fade. Under the folds of his cloak, his hands had already moved into battle form. His clothes hid that a durable metal net was now beginning to cover his body, stretching across it, piercing his skin, weaving into monomolecular strands like the kind he used to suppress General Hustig's rebellion...

"I will ask you for the last time," Ma Ju Ro hissed, barely restraining the adrenaline rushing through his veins. "Are you with me, or against me? Choose!"

"Go to hell..." Flea muttered, reaching for his sword.

Whatever else he wanted to say remained a mystery. None understood why the leader of the Nine suddenly fell silent, grabbed his throat and croaked, gurgling blood. At the same moment, the heads of the other captains fell off as if by magic.

Someone in the crew realized that the emperor was the cause. "Kill the bastard!" a sailor shouted, and men attacked Ma Ju Ro from all sides with sabers and daggers shining in the moonlight...

Toward midnight, Kane heard a rustling in the bushes. The emperor climbed out of them, soaked wet through. He silently sat in the carriage and spoke in a strained voice.

"Let's go."

"What happened with the Nine?" Weasel asked.

"The Nine are no more," Ma Ju Ro replied dryly.

He'd sent his balance of Tsoui points into the minus this night.

CHAPTER 44

THE OFFER OF
ANTHONY CROSS

THE CROSS FAMILY inhabited a part of the palace closed to all, even to the emperor. They tried not to stand out outside of that area, so as to fit in with the courtiers, but in their home, nobody could prevent them from living to the full and enjoying the benefits of civilization.

A huge video panel stretched across one wall, showing not only the various parts of the Cross family's lands, meaning the Empire, but also the television channels from the wider world. And there, comfortably sat in a massage chair, the youthful and handsome man by the name of Anthony Cross read the news from his communicator and drank real aromatic coffee.

His wife Herdinia was getting ready for, as she put it, a business trip. She was putting her makeup on at the dressing table. Few in the Empire realized it, but intentionally or not, this woman dictated the fashions of makeup and eyeshadow. For her part, she carefully followed the trends of the greater world.

Her things were already packed, her traveling clothes ready, and all she had to do now was make some finishing touches befitting to the status of first advisor to the emperor.

Suddenly, her hand with its brush froze in the air. Herdinia stopped and looked at her husband. Feeling her gaze, he sighed, put his communicator aside and raised his eyes.

"No, Herdi," he said firmly.

"But why not, Tony? Ma Ju Ro is doing fine! Under him the economy is booming, which means our profits will be up! I believe in him!"

"I have no shadow of a doubt in that," Anthony chuckled. "Otherwise I'd have no idea why you'd want to traipse after him into the wild north. Do you really have nothing better to do?"

"This is giving me something to do!" Herdinia answered sharply. "While you... forgive me, my dear, while you sit here and languish in idleness!"

"I'm just betting on another horse," Anthony answered softly. He didn't like to argue with his wife, preferring to pick his battles. "Rezsinius is younger, more ambitious..."

"Don't tell me you've already been speaking to him!" The woman jumped up from her chair and stood before her husband. "Anthony! Answer me!

Cross impassively lifted his cup from the table and drank his coffee, smiling ever so slightly. The emerging situation had amused him, but everything had its limits. It seemed his wife had begun to take her role in the Empire and the family hierarchy too seriously. It was time to put her in her place.

"Herdi, I haven't just spoken to him, I've also explained to him what is what in this world. You don't think you're the only one with the right to help their candidate?"

"You told him about Syahr's place in the world?" Herdinia gasped. "You cretin, Anthony! What an idiot you are!"

"I don't think so," Cross shrugged. "He'd have found out anyway. Better sooner than later. At least he'll have fewer illusions. Anyway, even now that he knows he's striving for power over a genetic garbage heap, he isn't about to give up. On the contrary, the ability to strive for something more has inspired him!"

"Maj will kill him, don't even doubt it!"

"We'll see," Anthony muttered, immersing himself in his communicator.

He knew that at times like this, it was best not to clash too much with his wife. Once she cooled down, he'd be able to talk to her. She'd definitely calm down in her two weeks of absence, and a trip at sea would do her good. The only path to the North on land led through the radioactive Wastelands teeming with mutants, so the imperial delegation would have to first travel by sea along the coast, then land at the foot of the mountains and then travel the rest of the way on the awful local roads where the fertile lands of the North began.

By Anthony's calculations, it would take a week to get there, they'd be there two to three days, then a week to get back. Half a month of freedom!

Cross already had his eye on a few nice examples from among the emperor's favorites. Importantly — his former favorites. And still more importantly — those that knew the value of such trinkets as good perfume or a diamond ring, and thus of keeping their mouths shut. It didn't matter that the diamonds were synthetic. None on Syahr knew the difference.

Immersed in lascivious thoughts, he absently noticed Herdinia leaving without saying good bye.

"So long, dear," he said automatically.

Cross watched through a security camera as the imperial retinue left the palace. Time for him to get to work as well. If Herdi thought he was languishing in idleness, she was mistaken. He didn't like to lose, so he'd decided everything in advance.

Decided, but hesitated. However, the conversation with his spouse was the last straw; in the same five minutes, she'd called him feeble-minded and accused him of indolence. Anthony would see what she would say when it turned out her husband was right. And he'd order the new emperor to not let Herdinia within a mile of state affairs!

Anthony walked into a part of the building

hidden behind a thick steel door, a kind of huge metal egg concealed within the cliff. One of his ancestors had built the hermetically sealed bunker after a Cross was assassinated in a council session.

To enter the bunker, he had to go through a multi-level confirmation system. He used a voice command to start the identification process, then the system checked his biometrics: fingerprints, facial recognition, DNA analysis. The system concluded that he was alone, calm and not under duress.

The bunker contained combat stealth suits, exo-skeletons, plasma weaponry, molecular blades and a medical capsule. There was also a server that contained complete information on the Overseer's activities and synchronized it to the cloud, communication systems, and huge supplies of provisions and drinking water in case something went wrong and the place had to be defended. Not every newly minted emperor had taken the true state of affairs calmly after their first conversation with their fourth advisor.

Anthony sent a request to the head of the entire Cross family — Tiranius — to speak on an encrypted channel. Syahr had become theirs by order of the shining queen Taira Ra'Ta'Cant, but competing racant families wouldn't miss a chance to get hold of any intel they could. And the worsening situation with deliveries from the island wasn't something Anthony could be proud of.

The answer came at once — although it was

midnight on the other side of the world, Tiranius confirmed the communication session. Within three seconds, they were connected.

"Speak, Tony!" Tiranius ordered, wasting no time on ceremony.

"I need confirmation, First One," Anthony said right away. "Our analysts have reviewed the reports and given their verdict — my suggestion has been accepted as rational. I ask for your personal confirmation."

"It isn't all so clear-cut, Tony," the leader of the Cross family shook his head. "It was rational half a year ago, but now, by my data, the situation is stabilizing and the current ruler is handling it. Or rather, will handle it, once he defeats the competitor."

"Does that mean 'no'?"

"It means do what you think is necessary. You're there, you know best. The responsibility is yours!"

"Understood, uncle."

The connection cut out before Anthony could even say good bye. The head of the Cross family was a very busy man, and Syahr wasn't even the family's most profitable industry. Well, so be it.

He'd have to fly to the North. If he hurried, he could get back by nightfall. Anthony glanced over the armory and stopped at a compact single-use stasis field generator, which looked like a cone-shaped blue crystal. It would be a bad idea to give the northern wildlings anything deadly, but this thing would just break down into dust after use.

As he disembarked onto the shore, Luca stopped for a moment, closed his eyes and took a few deep breaths. His father was right. The air was fresher in the north of the Empire. It smelled of pine needles and sea salt, and these were the only scents in the cold, crystal-clear air.

His people were unloading the baggage and saddling the horses while he stood immobile, surrounded by his people, breathing freely. He wanted peace; for the country, for himself, for his mother and sister. There was one final step left — to get the northerners on his side and meet Rezsinius in battle. He planned to keep things bloodless if he could successfully sneak into his cousin's camp and send him into a long sleep.

In the end, Kora, Weasel and Herdinia went with him, not counting thirty of Hector's guards and the crew of sailors.

The first advisor had managed to convince Ma Ju Ro to take her along after all. The reason wasn't just the rational argument that her feminine smile and knowledge of all the industries in the Empire would be essential in the negotiations. It was also his departure from Keirinia.

With each passing day of their relationship, Luca realized that no matter how sweet and seductive his courtesan was, he was bored of her. Without the sex, there'd be nothing left. In turn, long conversations with his former secretary turned first advisor Herdinia Cross led to Luca starting to see her with a fresh perspective. He saw her sharp mind, her sense of humor, the unique color of her beautiful blue, purple-tinged eyes. Not to mention her perfect figure in light of the knowledge of who she really was. A racant. A person with perfect genes.

And even in the age difference didn't bother the emperor. Biological years were a thing of the past for him under the weight of millennia of heritage from Esk'Onegut and the decades of life Ma Ju Ro's body had lived.

Moreover, Herdinia actually loved him, unlike Keirinia. Her love may have been initiated by the sexual magnetism virus, but that effect had long since disappeared, giving way to real feelings. The one thing holding Luca back was that Herdinia was taken. He was happy to spend time with her, but he didn't even allow himself the thought that anything more would happen. Most of all, he didn't want to cause her problems.

So when Keirinia dropped her eyes and asked the emperor to allow her to marry a certain successful and handsome reyk, Ma Ju Ro gave his approval.

At the same time, he relieved Kora of the status of courtesan, although that happened after they set off. His sister came to him with Kane and asked his blessing for their relationship. Weasel was so frightened of the conversation that as soon as the emperor opened his mouth, he closed his eyes in horror, then lost control and tried for a long time to embrace his ruler's immense body...

Under Weasel's direction, the horses were harnessed into teams, the packs unloaded and the group set off for the lands of the northern barons, surrounded by mounted guards. The ship's crew stayed at anchor to await the emperor's return.

Their path took them through a twelve-mile stretch of no man's land. It wasn't the Wastelands, nor the fertile land of the northerners. It was stony, lifeless soil with rocks jutting out here and there. The guard captain Tarson was worried about this leg of the journey, and for good reason; it turned out to be dangerous.

First they were shot at in a narrow gorge. Three guards were lightly injured, but the group managed to fight back. The wild band of mutants barely managed to run from Hector's plate-clad warriors, leaving four dead behind them. That was the first time Luca saw the mutants. Monstrously misshapen creatures in whom it was impossible to see signs of humanity. One of the dead had six legs and four arms, and some sort of rot oozed from the body. The scythe-like nails on its fingers and toes were longer than a grown man's hand.

"We're lucky these were ordinary mutants. Probably first-generation, or exiles," Captain Tarson said. He was from the North himself, which was why

Hector had sent him to lead the emperor's guard. "The supers don't come here, they're happy enough at Shelter."

"Supers?" Ma Ju Ro asked.

"Supermutants, your majesty," Tarson clarified. "The high shamans of the Wastelands continually make selections. The most powerful and smartest are bred, those who pass the challenges become supers, and from them the leaders are chosen.

Selection, Luca thought. *Once I'm done with Rezsinius and the South, I'll need to deal with the Wastelands. Maybe we can live in peace with the mutants?*

The Wastelands occupied the entire central section of the Empire, sending its venomous tentacles into the clean lands: the capital West, the fertile North and the desert, but rich and hot South. The West of the Empire was overgrown with impenetrable ancient forests, and not only did it teem with deadly beasts, it was also covered in a mist of poisonous acid fumes.

Man couldn't live there, but the lands were raided for wood and the special fruits of the Tassurian trees which were later boiled down to make drugs. But even the mutants didn't live in the center of the Wastelands. Two-horns' curse at the Core was so strong that even the dwellers of the Wastelands rotted alive there, throwing up their innards.

"Well, at least that's how it was when I was a

boy," the captain said. "My father told me tales, he was a guard on the Wastelands border in his day..."

Everyone listened to Tarson with interest. The wounded were bandaged, they'd almost passed through the dangerous leg of the journey, so now they merely enjoyed an unusual journey. But it was too soon to relax.

The arrows turned out to be poisoned. By the evening, the three wounded fell into a fever, spitting up brown liquid with the contents of their stomach. Then, one after another died in convulsions.

Ma Ju Ro rushed to help, but failed. It took more time to find and create an antidote than the victims had left to live. The problem was his negative Tsoui balance. After Luca's bloodbath on the pirate ship, the Wheel had penalized him heavily.

Tsoui points: -41. Current balance: −18.

Negative Tsoui balance!
Punishment for traveler Luca'Onegut until zero or positive Tsoui point balance is achieved:
—   Wheel Energy regeneration slowed by 1000%
—   Metamorphosis talent effectiveness reduced

Swearing, Luca still prepared an antidote just in case, and saved it in his internal reservoir.

The antidote came in handy very soon.

Rushing to leave these apparently lifeless, but as it turned out entirely inhabited lands by nightfall, they galloped into a suspiciously quiet narrow pass between two cliffs jutting out like fangs.

"Stop!" Weasel shouted, the first to notice something was wrong.

The leading guard suddenly fell chest-deep into the ground, and a second sank after him into the unnatural earth. The others managed to rein in their horses.

Both the trapped guards howled in anguish. After determining the edge of the anomaly, the captain threw a long rope to his people, and managed to pull both out of the pit. By then, nothing was left of their equipment; their clothes were turned to rags and their plate armor hissed with a vile yellow smoke. Blood streamed from innumerable minor wounds. Both the guards were seriously burned up to their chest, their skin peeling off in crimson strips.

The emperor healed them, but not fully, merely neutralizing the same poison that had been on the mutants' arrows, stopping the burning and injecting them with nano-substances to regenerate their tissues. By habit and for the look of the thing, he continually muttered praise to the Sacred Mother as he healed them.

He managed to amaze everyone except Herdinia, judging by her skeptical glance. She had seen the so-called Sacred Mother, Queen Taira Ra'Ta'Cant, that morning on the television. She was sure that no prayer in her name could heal such wounds unless the patient was in a medical capsule.

"Is this how you healed mom?" Kora whispered.

Luca nodded and sent her sister to the guards for protection. He himself went with Tarson and Kane to look at the obstacle.

The basin was just ten feet wide. The cliffs prevented them from going around it. Carefully investigating a drop of the liquid from the armor of one of the victims, Luca realized what it was. The pass between the cliffs was covered by a perfectly rectangular reservoir indistinguishable from the surrounding ground. It wasn't filled with water, but acid.

It was home to snake-like creatures with an extremely venomous bite. They were what had chewed up the guards.

Tarson muttered that if they returned to the sea, then they could find another path, but right now they were only three hours from the closest lands of the barons.

"Put the wounded in the carts and send them back to the ship with six guards. Tell everyone else to mount up. We're going to jump over the acid pit and reach the castle walls by dusk."

After a short argument, it was done. Tarson and Kane put the girls on their horses, mounted behind them. *It's a good thing I've lost some weight*, Luca thought as he looked at the deadly acid puddle beneath his jumping horse.

They reached the castle of Baron Rasmus after dusk, in the darkness. An escort met them and they were accompanied along the rest of their path by people with torches, shouting cries of welcome to the emperor.

The baron had been informed of his coming the day before, and had made preparations. Ma Ju Ro was welcomed with festive lights, wreaths, the piercing melodies of northern songs, and tables creaking under the weight of delicacies.

The other barons were expected to arrive by lunchtime the following day, and until then there was a little time to relax from the long journey. After giving the baron his due for his hospitality and talking to him and his family, Ma Ju Ro pleaded tiredness and went to rest in the chambers given to him by the castle's lord.

After midnight, he heard a quiet knock on the door. It was Herdinia.

This time they didn't hold back, and gave in to their passion with an ardor known only to those truly in love and together for the first time.

CHAPTER 45

NORTHERN HOSPITALITY

L UCA FELT a ringing emptiness in his thoughts and a thorough exhaustion in his body as he tried to fall asleep. Somewhere at the edge of consciousness was the unread line of a notification: metamorphosis noted two thousand energy units burned in this short night, as if Luca had run ten miles.

His ability quickly neutralized the biochemical effect that man called fatigue, letting him boil over with energy all night. As he took Herdinia, the emperor was so full of energy that the entire castle no doubt heard his lover's cries.

Turned on by this passion from the ever unavailable and cold Herdinia, Ma Ju Ro achieved the impossible and broke both his own record and hers. There weren't enough fingers on both hands to count how many times they reached the peak — the flawless Herdinia couldn't be sated, and that only aroused Luca even more. They didn't even talk in their short breaks, instead just lying together and stroking each other.

This had never happened with Keirinia, this fierce blaze of desire, passion and... enough about that. After Keirinia, he'd always gone back to his business or gone to sleep.

With Herdinia, everything was different. Alone with his lover, Luca lost his head and saw only her. That was probably why he failed to notice the notifications not only about the energy he'd burned, but also about the neutralization of a sleep-inducing substance not only in him, but in his close ones protected by his nano-agents.

However strong his superability was, he still needed sleep. In sleep, his Wheel energy would regenerate faster and his mind would clear, and... he couldn't embarrass his courtiers any longer. Sooner or later rumor would spread, and they wouldn't take long to turn into whispers that the emperor was some blood-drinker of the night. The rumor mill was a terrible thing.

It wasn't long until dawn. The castle would soon come alive, and Baron Rasmus would likely want to speak to him in private before the other rulers of the North arrived.

Sleep didn't come. Hera's head comfortably rested on his shoulder. She'd asked him to call her that. Her thick blonde hair tickled his chest as it rose and fell rhythmically.

The mirror ceiling above the bed reflected the lovers. Luca grimaced in annoyance as he compared himself to Herdinia. He couldn't see a single blemish on her body. Velvety skin with a light tan, long eyelashes, slightly plump lips, perfectly even teeth visible in her half-open mouth.

And then him — with his balding head, tiny piggy eyes, short crooked legs, huge paunch and a chin merging into his neck in thick layers of fat. His broad chest, powerful shoulders and strong arms were the only parts of his body that could be praised. Without a doubt, he had to fix it. But what next? Would he live his entire life in this body, ruling the Empire? Or would he wait for his changeling ability cooldown to end and get his own body back? Did he even want to remain the emperor? Right now he had to, especially until the issue of Rezsinius was solved, but what next?

His thoughts returned to Hera. Maybe he should grow out the hair in his bald patches? He suddenly had an insurmountable urge to be handsomer. For her.

In the quiet of the pre-dawn hour, he heard the unmistakable sound of steps creeping up to the door. Ma Ju Ro froze, expecting a cry from the guards at their post, but instead he heard a dull rustling, then quiet again.

Carefully, trying not to wake up Hera, he freed himself and rose from the bed. Slowly walking barefoot on the carpet, he approached the door. It was locked from inside, but could be unlocked from either side.

He heard a key turning in the lock. The emperor froze in place. The chambers were small, and the only place to hide was behind a small table at the foot of the bed. And that would only fit a child. There was no place that Ma Ju Ro could hide his huge frame.

Another rustle from beyond the door, and someone whispering. Then there was a noise in the corridor, a clatter and shouts. A girl's agonizing cry rang out from a distant room. Kora!

Luca rushed toward the door, switching into battle form as he moved, and at that very moment the door burst open. People in cloaks burst into the bedroom, and Ma Ju Ro suddenly realized what was happening when he saw that their leader was Daven, Baron Rasmus's son introduced to him the day before.

"Kill him!" the young man shouted.

The four cloaked figures rushed the emperor with daggers. Two of them tried to grab him by the arms, but flew away as he hit them with his morphed elbows. The emperor's metamorphosis was slowed, and the blades he grew weren't long enough to kill the traitors.

The spines he grew from his fingers were even worse. Ma Ju Ro struck with them side to side, without a doubt that the hits were deadly, then he jumped at the baron's son — not to kill, just to wound, but so that he wouldn't think of doing anything else. He needed to hurry and help Kora and Kane.

Daven kept his coldblooded composure. He dodged the emperor's punch and struck back. The blade should have pierced through Ma Ju Ro's leg, but that failed and it went in only an inch before it hit something hard. *A bone?* the baron's son just had time to think in shock when a stunning strike from Ma Ju Ro's fist hit him in the cheekbone. Breaking the bone, the spines tore off half of Daven's face and the traitor lost consciousness from the shock of the pain.

Luca absorbed the end of the dagger lodged in his leg and fell down; one of the remaining guards tried to crack his skull, and the other knocked him off his feet. Lying on the floor, the emperor staunchly took the hits, realizing with surprise that all four were still alive. They were trying to kill him, but his internal armor was holding up.

"Maj!" Herdinia shouted, waking up.

Instantly getting a grasp of what was happening, she grabbed a half-full jug of local wine from the table and smashed it down on the head of the nearest traitor. Roaring indistinctly, he fell on Luca, who by that time had managed to extend a short hardening monomolecular thread from his hands and was running it through the legs of the attackers. Two collapsed as they lost their limbs. The thread lost its structure and disappeared into dust, but the emperor now had the advantage. He smashed the chest of the one Herdinia stunned and tried to get up.

The legless men screamed continually. The last bearded guard standing on his own two feet backed off, then jerked his head as he felt movement — a naked and furious Herdinia slipped past him. Ma Ju Ro picked up a dagger, extended his arms toward the guard and moved toward him.

"Get dressed, Hera," the emperor said, keeping his eyes on the traitor.

She ignored him. Instead, she searched the stunned guard, pulled out a knife and cut his throat without a second thought. Then she moved toward the groaning Daven and did the same in the blink of an eye. Rising up, she bared her teeth like a tigress.

"You can die quick if you tell us who's behind this! Rasmus himself, or the entire North?"

"Help! Here!" the bearded man shouted, breaking through the screams of the legless.

He backed off to one of them, his eyes darting from side to side, seeking a path of retreat. Less than a minute had passed since the men burst in, but Kora's scream had already died out, and there was no time to lose. Luca jumped at the guard with a wild roar, taking the dagger to the chest and stabbing his own into the man's temple. His head fell to the side, his corpse went limp and began to fall, blood flowed through the beard.

"I'm going to save them! Wait here! Hide!" Ma Ju Ro shouted to Herdinia and flew out of the room.

Running into the dark corridor weakly lit by stifled torches, the emperor's gaze darted back and forth. Wherever he looked, he saw the corpses of imperial guards and the baron's watchmen.

Some figures flickered in the distance along the corridor to the right, and the emperor rushed over there. Through the open doorways in the corridor he saw his own guards, killed in their beds as they slept.

As he ran to Kora's room, he realized he was too late. Kane's body lay by the threshold, blood bubbling from uncounted wounds. Three dead men lay nearby, and another writhed in agony — Weasel's life had been costly. If it had cost his life at all. Luca was sure that the agents in his bloodstream were already regenerating the damaged organs. He'd need to work on Kane himself to make sure of it, but right now his sister's fate was more important.

The emperor walked into the room. The baron himself was there, laughing and watching as his men bound Kora. The girl had had no time to get dressed, and Rasmus was greedily drinking her almost-grown young body in with his eyes.

Luca clenched his fists, took a deep breath and reactivated his battle form. It didn't last very long even without the Wheel's penalties, but he should have enough for ten seconds. Feeling an itch where the barbed spines and deadly blades grew through his skin, he jumped on the enemies silently.

The baron's troops had no time to think. One after another, flooding the room with wild screams, they fell down, trying in vain to close the terrible wounds inflicted by the emperor. Ten seconds later, his battle form ended; metamorphosis retracted and reabsorbed his weapons of death while Ma Ju Ro untied his sister.

He'd killed them all except the baron, who had taken a blow to the face from the emperor's reinforced forehead and was now writhing with a broken nose.

"Are you alright, Kora?"

The emperor hugged his sister and checked her condition. She was fine; a couple of bruises, a scratch, adrenaline.

"Luca..." Kora whispered. "Where's Kane?"

"Wait here..." he muttered.

He returned to Weasel's body and dragged it into the room. There was no pulse. Holding his hand on the man's neck, Ma Ju Ro realized that all the nano-agents in Weasel's body had been used up. With a powerful pulse, he injected regenerators into his body and tried to start his heart.

"Luca!" Kora howled in a voice not her own.

He turned and saw that Rasmus had come round and was piercing him with his gaze.

"Where is Daven?" the baron asked. "Where is my son? What have you done to him, Ma Ju Ro?"

"He is beyond help. He attacked me and paid for it. As you will pay, and your..."

The baron reached into his pocket, took something out and aimed it at Ma Ju Ro. Before he knew what was happening, the emperor was thrown to the floor and couldn't feel his body. To his surprise, his ability wouldn't even respond. It was if only Luca'Onegut's mind remained, suspended in time and space.

An image reflected in his eyes; the baron stretching an arm toward him, Kora's mouth opening in a scream. The scene didn't disappear, didn't change. It was all frozen as if someone had stopped time. The same thought kept spinning in his head, each time perceived as if new. What was in his hand?

At dawn, in Baron Rasmus's castle yard, the emperor's lifeless corpse lay right in the dirt and horse shit, and all had gathered to see it.

The wind howled down from the mountains, making the grass rock on the rare patches of untrampled ground. It rustled in the bushes and fluttered in the baron's flag on the central turret. Stormclouds gathered in the heights, illuminated by the dawn, and those assembled who weren't staring at Ma Ju Ro raised their heads in wonderment at the beauty of the sky.

The sun flashed between gaps in the clouds, lighting up the castle and flooding the walls with a thick, blood-red, fiery light, pulling from the shadows piles of dead men with glassy eyes staring into the abyss.

The bodies of dead guards, first unshod and undressed, were loaded into carts to be taken to the Wastelands. The creatures there would leave nothing but bones of them by nightfall.

Ma Ju Ro's people lay next to his massive body, their hands and feet bound; some girl who was apparently a courtesan was chewing the rag in her mouth and striving to crawl to another person who had survived the night's terrors, a young man, his chest just barely rising and falling. The third — the emperor's first advisor, called Herdinia — gazed at the crowd like a savage with her surviving eye. They took out her other when they tied her up — the bitch resisted too much.

Rasmus blinked, wiped away his tears. That palace snake was the one that killed her son, cut his throat. The emperor's slut! The only eyewitness left alive lost both legs and a bucket of blood, but when they took Herdinia, he managed to say a few words: "Daven... She..." The baron didn't know where he was now, the man had been sent to the healer, though it was as much use as putting a poultice on a wooden leg. He wouldn't survive.

They'd lost far more people than they expected, but everything went just as the ghost said it would. That night, Rasmus had been standing on the balcony of his castle tower, smoking a pipe and admiring the sickle moon, when he heard a voice nearby.

"Ma Ju Ro has already left for your lands, baron.

BLOOD OF FATE

Gasping, Rasmus looked around and saw a figure in the thick shadows. The edges of the uninvited guest blurred like scorched air above the ground. At first, the baron didn't even bother thinking of how the man had gotten onto a balcony the height of nine men while the door was locked.

"Who are you?" the baron asked calmly, maintaining his composure. His trembling voice gave away his fear.

"A friend," the figure answered gently. "I don't have much time, so listen carefully..."

The ghostly shadow, realizing that Rasmus feared him, gave an explanation that was hard to believe — that the very spirit of the first Emperor Ma Ju Ro had come to him to call on a son of the Empire to serve his land. It defied the imagination, but it was easier to believe in the spirit of the first emperor than in anything else. For example, that Two-horns himself had come to him as a ghost.

"The emperor is traveling to the North. He will promise you everything you ask for as long as it puts you against the southerners. This will break the Empire in two and start a civil war. Brother against brother, son against father — I did not wish this for my people," the ghost's level voice shook. "Ma Ju Ro has rejected his ancestors' creeds. Kill the defiler and take him to Rezsinius. The reward will be generous..."

Ultimately, the ghost gave him a strange crystal and told him to use it by aiming its peak at the emperor's body.

"The body will decay before you reach the southerners' camp. Rezsinius might not believe that the corpse belongs to Ma Ju Ro. The crystal will keep the body in stasis."

Not knowing what to answer, the baron stood long, never quite knowing when exactly the ghost that was just standing next to him disappeared. The words burned into his soul, and when he received a message that the emperor was traveling to the North, he made his decision.

"Your grace..." the guard captain gently tapped him on the shoulder. "What should we do with the prisoners?"

The baron sighed. No imperial spirit, no squabble for the throne could possibly have been worth the life of his son. They were supposed to be sleeping! His confidence in that is what made him send his son for the emperor — there was no risk, and letting his beloved offspring kill the tyrant by his own hand would have made the boy a hero. So he'd thought. So he'd been mistaken.

But he couldn't get his son back now, and this plot had to be brought to an end.

"Cage the girl. If the boy doesn't die, then send him to the mines. Quarter the bitch that killed Daven. Do the same with that bastard Ma Ju Ro."

"What will we bring to Rezsinius? The head?"

"The head..?"

The baron thought for a moment. The ghost's crystal used in his time of desperation had collapsed into dust after he'd killed Ma Ju Ro. There was no point in taking the whole body. Not only would its huge weight slow the baron and his people on their way to Rezsinius, but it would probably also rot. He came to a decision.

"We'll bring only the arms and the head."

"What if the head rots?"

"Then we'll still have the arms."

"The imperial symbol?" the captain asked with understanding. "The golden runic pattern tattooed on his arms?"

"Yes. That should be enough proof. Whatever remains of him and his bitch, take it to the Wastelands. Let the beasts eat them! I don't want so much as a memory of them to remain in this world."

They managed to cut the tyrant's arms off at the shoulders, but the legs only at the knees. They failed to cut off the head. No axe or saw could break his skin. The baron's people whispered that the emperor truly was protected by the Sacred Mother. Only Rasmus himself knew the truth — that it was the action of the mysterious colorless crystal.

Those to be put to death were sent to the Wastelands. Nothing remained of the woman's body. Even her bones were gnawed and boiled down.

It didn't work out that way with the man's corpse. Tooth and nail both broke against the hardened flesh.

A huge desert dragon grabbed the body and carried it into its lair, almost at the very Core. There he tried endlessly to chew up his prey, but only dulled his teeth. Disappointed, the reptile got rid of its useful cargo and went in search of new prey.

There it ran into an even larger predator, and never returned.

The husk of the former emperor's body frozen in its stasis field lay in the center of the Wastelands for a month.

Once the effect ended, the body left stasis.

His mind played the same picture over and over: his sister screaming, the baron standing there, his face soaked in blood, stretching out his hand, something flashing. Some sort of crystal.

The next instant, Luca was suddenly in a scorched place, under a blinding sun, trying to open his eyes, but unable. They'd dried out.

An instant later, signals traveled along his nerve endings, reached his awakening brain, and he screamed. An intolerable pain shot through his entire body. His time with metamorphosis had made him unused to pain. In spite of that, not a sound came out of his parched throat but a hoarse wheeze. He tried to stand up, and then the real pain hit him, overtook his threshold. His survival instinct kicked in and he lost consciousness.

BLOOD OF FATE

It was impossible to say when he came round again. Maybe an hour had passed, maybe days, but he finally managed to unglue his eyes and raise his bone-dry, uncooperative eyelids. He saw that the heat had softened a little, and the sky, so recently yellow, was now a deep blue. The circle of the sun was reddening and dropping lower, but a suppressing, pulsating heat still bathed the desert.

Unable to withstand the unceasing nagging pain all across his body, especially in his limbs, he groaned noiselessly again. He had sand in his eyes and couldn't even raise his arm to wipe them. He lowered his eyelids. Faded letters appeared through the bloody darkness. His clouded mind told him that it was the logs of what had happened.

Detected memory access failure.
Detected looped time segment: 0.1 seconds.
Analyzing...

Detected memory access failure.
Detected looped time segment: 0.1 seconds.
Analyzing...

Detected memory access failure.
Detected looped time segment: 0.1 seconds.
Analyzing...

475

The same lines repeated each other again and again, for pages and pages, and the letters blended together like raindrops on glass. Green raindrops on glass in the night.

The wild pain stayed with him. Worse, it gained strength. Luca opened his eyes a second before losing consciousness again and realized that he had no limbs. Just two stumps at his knees. Blood poured from his wounds in thick streams, and his ability was silent.

He woke up next from a piercing cold. A boundless sky stretched out above him, scattered with myriad stars. His teeth chattering, Luca began to shift his body, trying to dig deeper into the warm and sharp sand.

Some scaled creature around the size of a dog, with an unblinking gaze, growled loudly as it tried to chew on a bone sticking out of his ribcage. He panicked in horror and immediately gave an order.

Red threads leaped out of the stumps of his legs to the beast, stuck to the carrion-eater's face. It shrieked and tried to jump back, but instead the threads went to its legs. The reptile struggled with its legs, trying to pull away, but only got itself stuck worse, and its limbs began to absorb into its former victim's body. The hunter became the hunted.

Refusing to watch the sickening absorption of the reptile, Ma Ju Ro delved into the logs.

Much had happened since he lost consciousness. The traveler interface finished reloading just as the time loop cycle suddenly broke. Detecting its body's numerous wounds, it stopped the blood loss — moreover, it even managed to collect what had leaked out and return it to the body. Of course, that meant it had to fully reprocess the clotted blood.

The biggest problem was dehydration. The ability managed to partially fix this thanks to the absorbed reptile, but the human body was too fragile and inefficient to maintain life in the conditions of this environment.

The new environment was extremely aggressive; harsh radiation, a burning sun, predatory carnivores, no water. There were also his amputated limbs and Wheel penalties. His cells were dying, and the ability couldn't keep up; radiation sickness, the curse of Two-horns, was picking up its pace. Organ after organ failed, and if it weren't for the body's huge fat stores, burned at a rapid pace to restore his tissues, even metamorphosis would have failed.

Keeping the traveler alive was difficult and resource-intensive. Did he want to stay here for long weeks while metamorphosis used all the available reserves to restore his body? Would it not be easier to merely depart this life and start a new one?

Luca refused to be reborn. While there was still a hope that Kora was alive, he had to fight. He worried for Herdinia, regretting that she had killed Daven. The baron wouldn't forgive her for killing his son.

He kept trying to figure out what had happened in the castle, breaking off only to catch and absorb any mutant vultures that came along.

Metamorphosis had studied this form of life and adopted its most successful mutations as weapons. With the traveler's consent — and Luca was willing to consent to anything to get a chance of seeing his loved ones again — it activated the transformation process, accepting the carrier's wish to maintain, at least on the outside, a human shape.

There wasn't enough organic material, but there was plenty of iridium. The emperor was lying on veins of the stuff. The ability suggested taking it as a base and using it in the skeleton, and Luca accepted it.

The new form allowed him not to limit himself to organic matter, and to use silicon-based nerve fibers. An alarm bell rang in his head, his vision darkened. Luca couldn't even read what his ability suggested as material for muscle mass and a skin imitation, so he blindly gave his confirmation.

A fountain of sand exploding beneath him pulled him out of another dull revery. Thrown up to the height of a man, Luca felt himself turning. After a short fall, he saw that he was flying in a monstrous jaw, surrounded by uncountable rows of fangs. He couldn't see anything except this wide-open maw brimming with steaming, stinking drool — the monster's body was hidden beneath the sand.

Crumpling, he activated his battle form in

panic and prepared to tear the beast apart from within, even at the cost of his own barely burning excuse for a life. And he did it.

Metamorphosis neutralized the acid drool and thrust a hundred symbiotic threads into the creature, taking control of the nervous system of this conveniently appearing beast. The sandy half-worm, half-bug creature chittered and died.

Little was left of it by the next morning. It had all been used up for transformation. On top of that, the monster had given up plenty of information. The ability had analyzed it and created weapons not only from the bug's telescopic chitinous tungsten limbs that could extend thirty feet, but even from its corrosive saliva. The contents were optimized and the formula added to the combat arsenal. The ability's highest priority was its traveler's survival, and the changing environment required total transformation.

His metamorphosis was running at full steam, and gave Luca no choice. It began to regrow new limbs. Powerful, functional, invulnerable limbs. It kept using iridium and its compounds as a base material.

The process could take more than a week. The ability put Luca into active defense mode in case anything damaged the body, and sent him into a deep sleep.

A few weeks later, a dozen deep raiders approached the spot, something catching their eye. The band of mutants consisted of a chief, a tracker, a digger and warriors. The key selection criteria for its members was that each could easily withstand the Core's heat and Two-horns' curse.

A small barrel-shaped creature walked at the front — the tracker.

"Heh!" he emitted a gargling guttural noise in joy. "I told yas! I got an arrow inside, and it always points to fresh manflesh! I smelt it in the Core from the edge of the Wastelands!"

A human head jutted out from a sandy elevation. The chief, a tall and powerful mutant, approached the discovery. Crouching, it passed a hand over the sand, revealing the buried neck.

"'Sfresh, Gecko!" the barrel-shaped one yowled.

"Shut it, Zee," Gecko muttered lazily. He pressed his hand to the neck, felt the jugular vein and listened. "He still breathin'! Hey, you!" he shouted to the digger frozen nearby. "Dig him out! How the hell did he get here?"

"He ain't ours," Zee said with authority. "I'm seein' this mug for the first time. So thin, all skin 'n' bones!"

The tracker parted the layers in its stomach and stuck out a long snake's tongue from it, touching the tip to the body.

"Enough lickin', snoop!" the chief snapped. "This meat ain't for you! He's alive!"

The tongue withdrew with a sniffle.

"Quit it, Gecko, stop, why you talkin' like that? Nobody'll know! Huh?"

"I know," Gecko said, jabbing his finger at his chest. Then he pointed to the others. "They know. Forget it. The orders are clear. We take all newcomers alive to Shelter. The shamans'll figure out what to do with him, got it? What if he's a super? Or a chosen one? Huh? You thought of that, dumbass?"

Zee sighed and sat down on the sand. He took some dried cockroach meat from a sack, threw it into his gut and did what he was ready to do it any condition: chew. A second piece followed the first, and in the meantime the others got to work; they dug out their find, tied it up with a thick rope at the arms and legs and loaded it onto a stretcher.

"Where to?" Zee asked. "We finishin' our round?"

"Not with this cargo," Gecko shook both his heads. "Don't know what's up with him, but he's as heavy as three supers."

"So?" the tracker asked with hope in his voice. "Maybe we can just eat him?"

"Eat your socks, greedy!" Gecko snapped in annoyance. "We're taking him to Shelter!"

The tracker sighed deeply. The road ahead was long.

Carrier body transformation completed.
Do you wish to familiarize yourself with the full list of changes made?

Metamorphosis: +1.
Ability level five reached!
Ability to control own body at master level...

Luca'Onegut, an interdimensional universal traveler in his first life, woke up.

END OF FIRST BOOK

Want to be the first to know about our latest LitRPG, sci fi and fantasy titles from your favorite authors?

Subscribe to our *New Releases* newsletter:

http://eepurl.com/b7niIL

Thank you for reading *Blood of Fate!*
If you like what you've read, check out other LitRPG novels
published by Magic Dome Books:

Level Up LitRPG series by Dan Sugralinov:
Re-Start
Hero
The Final Trial
Level Up: The Knockout (with Max Lagno)
Level Up. The Knockout: Update (with Max Lagno)

Disgardium LitRPG series by Dan Sugralinov:
Class-A Threat
Apostle of the Sleeping Gods
The Destroying Plague

World 99 LitRPG Series by Dan Sugralinov:
Blood of Fate

Adam Online LitRPG Leries by Max Lagno:
Absolute Zero
City of Freedom

Reality Benders LitRPG series by Michael Atamanov:
Countdown
External Threat
Game Changer
Web of Worlds
A Jump into the Unknown

**The Dark Herbalist LitRPG series
by Michael Atamanov:**
Video Game Plotline Tester
Stay on the Wing
A Trap for the Potentate
Finding a Body

Perimeter Defense LitRPG series by Michael Atamanov:
Sector Eight
Beyond Death
New Contract
A Game with No Rules

Point Apocalypse *(a near-future action thriller)*
by Alex Bobl

Captive of the Shadows *(The Fairy Code Book #1)*
by Kaitlyn Weiss

The Game Master **series by A. Bobl and A. Levitsky:**
The Lag

You're in Game!
(LitRPG Stories from Bestselling Authors)

You're in Game-2!
(More LitRPG stories set in your favorite worlds)

***Moskau* by G. Zotov**
(a dystopian thriller)

***El Diablo* by G.Zotov**
(a supernatural thriller)

In order to have new books of the series translated faster, we need your help and support! Please consider leaving a review or spread the word by recommending *Blood of Fate* to your friends and posting the link on social media. The more people buy the book, the sooner we'll be able to make new translations available.

Thank you!

Till next time!